Being

Book I

KEDI DANIELS

kediduvide

BEING

For little Kedi

Contents

Prologue

MIL GUNDE WAS looking down at someone. Or something. He brushed his forefinger against his peppered designer stubble. His eyes were intense and focused, already lost in what he was about to say.

What he had to say.

He ground his teeth while shifting his weight to his better side. There was a beat of stale silence before his voice hit the air as if his lips were moving.

"*You're not good...*"

He paused a moment as that truth sat between him and his eager audience, wishing he could see the look on the creature's face.

"*Since our initial meeting I've felt this...I've known good, in all its forms and you've not even managed to fall short. It feels to me as if your morals are muddled, and no matter how long you endure what you try to imitate, I don't believe you'll ever be a person. You're just not right...*"

A stiffness planted itself between the disks in the shadow's back as Mil's words took shelter in the hidden thing's temple.

"*You've been indifferent with this life — something you didn't ask for but also never bothered to earn — allowing what you've acquired a taste for to devour you from the inside out.*"

He stopped to prolong the effect he'd created, studying the dangling black strands of hair momentarily trembling as if a chill had swept between them in a fury.

"*But not after this moment.*" Mil straightened up as the words invigorated the nerves in his spine. "*Something has come for us. Something new and pure, and right. You will be humbled and I pray transformed into this semblance of a human being. Something your Creator can marvel at again...Wouldn't you like that?*"

They were in a small, dark outhouse just lit by a camp light. A few yard and power tools were faintly seen on a wall behind Mil, and in front of him was the bowed figure. His face shrouded, he remained in a servile position.

"*I would,*" the figure thought, the words filled with a depth that nothing on Earth could reach.

Mil turned around in his folding chair and began scribbling in a notebook as if he'd been doing that before he got interrupted.

"*Ah. I almost forgot. You know your brother is coming.*"

The figure stopped himself from lifting his head.

"*I understand that you and he think on a plane that is far above my comprehension. But his presence is vital, so I'll manage to reach that plane by whatever means.*" He glanced back at him, picking up his pen as if to think. "*...Well, I'm not sure if I should even ask this of you.*"

That stiffness fought to loosen but had lost.

"*Ask of me,*" the figure pleaded, ravenous.

Mil attempted a smile and pivoted in his chair to face the being.

"*Look at me.*"

He lifted his head, his countenance barely veiled, divine and ageless. With an eternity glistening in his eyes, he longed hopeful as he fixed on his master. His pupils dilated, smoldering, awaiting his next order.

"*Thiere...*"

Chapter I

KSHH! KLSSH!!

Iela shattered a couple of plates and glasses as she teetered onto her creaky dining room table. She clutched her burnt almond knees wide open, like she was in stirrups, bracing herself. Her jeans cut around the meaty part of her calves, she had on no underwear and her shirt clung to her with sweat.

"Get a fuckin' towel. Hurry up!" she barked at a middle-aged Roxa, who was about ready to slap the mess out of her.

The aged woman's biting scowl took over the bottom half of her face as she hustled to a basket of folded laundry to get a towel.

"I know what the hell to do. You lie down and breathe until you can't no more."

Iela's breaths stuttered as Roxa pulled her jeans down some more.

"I can't believe this shit," she muttered. "Been tryin' since I was as old as you and ain't never. Now, here you go again..."

"Shut the fu—" she gasped as her eyes darted toward a black duffle bag near the front door. "Where's my bottle? Get my bottle."

"Not till I see the head—"

"Get it—"

"No! Now, shut up and push!"

Iela's eyes watered as she bit her tongue and her head fell back from exhaustion. Roxa tried to hide her satisfaction, but she'd never mastered concealing her truths and didn't plan on learning anytime soon. Iela was the most hardheaded person she'd ever met, her extenuating circumstances only making it worse.

"We shoulda went to the hospital. Or at least a church—Keep pushin'." The woman steadied Iela's knees as she matched her breathing.

"Fuckin' church," Iela griped. Just the thought made one of her elbows buckle and she had to catch herself.

"Almost."

Iela was biting her face off at this point. Her canines pierced the skin just under her bottom lip and she held her breath.

She gave one last inhale.

One last push.

"Ahhg!"

Roxa swiped the towel and was at the receiving end to bundle the child, but something was strange.

It was silent and still.

It didn't cry and move the way a new life should when entering an unfamiliar world. And that wasn't even the strangest part.

The child was glowing.

The skin over the area where her heart was sheltered had a light emanating underneath as if due to some form of toxic radiation.

Iela and Roxa stared in awe. The light was bright, but not so much that it hurt the eyes.

"...We gotta go."

Iela could hardly get it out, she was so shaken to the core.

"Yeah, to a hospital—"

"No."

She slipped a knife out of her pocket to cut the umbilical cord. Then, flinching and sopping wet, she tried to shimmy back into her soiled jeans but slipped off the table.

"We gotta get that sack out!" Roxa urged as she went to help her with her free hand. Iela refused and used the slimy table to get back onto her wobbly legs.

"It's not just for you!" Roxa exploded. "Look at ya. You can't take care of yourself, how you gon' take care of her?"

Iela's head dropped. She got lost in the blood in her lap and the tears began to fall. She quickly wiped her face, struggled onto one of her knees, but it gave out and she collapsed into a heap. Her cries crept into the silent room on tip-toe, knowing it wasn't invited. She wasn't someone who cried and found her own behavior a nuisance, but she couldn't stop it.

Roxa went to her and kneeled. "Lord, if you cryin'..." She waited for her to lift her head, but instead of meeting her gaze, Iela's attention went to the child. They both stared holes at the quiet thing, who was just content as can be.

Iela finally fixed on Roxa, eyes wide.

"...We need to get her safe."

Roxa's shoulders leveled, but her jaw remained locked. "Safe from what? What you done?"

Iela didn't answer at first, hypnotized by her radiating seed.

"...I don't know."

That helpless look on her face was enough to put a fire under Roxa's sneakers. She shot up and hustled to the front door to grab the duffle bag.

"No. I'll get the bags. You get the car."

"You can barely stand."

With a grunt and a grand appearance from the veins in her neck and temple, Iela got to her feet and finished pulling up her jeans. Roxa watched her jaw lock as she made it to the bags as fast as she could. She checked on the life that was breathing quietly in her arms before she headed to the bedroom to get her own packed bag out of the closet.

In less than an hour, Iela had heaved the last of their apartment in the trunk of her black car. It was her unofficial first child. When Roxa found her that's where she was sleeping. It was hers now and she held onto it like no previous owners existed.

"Give me the keys."

"I'm drivin'. Here."

Roxa held the child out to Iela but didn't miss the brief pause when she placed the bundled joy in her arms. They got in the car and sat there a moment, minds racing.

"Where we goin'?"

"Just head south. You'll know when to stop."

They met in the rear-view at the exact same moment.

"Are you sure?" Roxa asked.

Iela instinctively pulled the child closer to her chest. It looked like they didn't have a choice.

Suddenly, a sound seeped into the car, filling it with a rumbling bass.

It was humming. Out of nowhere. Not any specific tune. It just hummed. Steady and soothing. Neither Iela nor Roxa seemed to hear it as she started up the car.

The hum, the voice, was strong. It drowned out the engine and the tires, but the child's ears had perked up as she looked around in wonder. She was the only one that could hear The Voice. It was like a lullaby. The glow began to soften as if it really was being calmed.

The black car disappeared out of the apartment complex and down the street amidst the humming and into the unknown. Into another town and another life.

**

A few sparse rows of common garden flowers added color to a dark cement tower that was at the epicenter of a dead-end street.

Azaleas. Baby's Breath. Gardenias.

The house was tiered, but modest. Iela's car rested in the curve of the inner circle just nearing past where the neighbor's fence separated both properties. Iela most likely parked there on purpose. They were the only Voids on the block as far as she could tell. If there were others, they'd take a bullet before admit it.

The Voice was humming again, a familiar tune this time, but a tad different. It had grown to fit the one being comforted. What once floated, was now leaden with a sort of redundant triteness.

Swish!

A suppressed Beretta sliced through the air, hoping to silence what was now incessant white noise, but it kept going as the barrel pointed to different hours of the clock.

This was Mary and her wielder was a now seventeen-year-old Caiden Waters.

Her big, knowing eyes, soft and ingenuous, hadn't yet been touched by the sad truths of the universe. She got lost in the sound of the wind breaking in half by her own power, and as if she remembered why she was breathing, her hand faltered.

"Could you please be quiet? You're putting me to sleep."

The humming ceased before she could finish.

"It's what I do," The Voice said. "Especially when you're on edge like today."

"I know. But not now," she said softly.

There wasn't an instance in her memory where she never heard The Voice. It's always been there, doing what Iela or Roxa didn't have the ability to do. A little understanding is all Caiden wanted. Roxa was the only one that tried. Iela gave birth to her so she already figured that made up for more than what anyone else could do. Caiden didn't have enough gall to tell her mother that wasn't enough. Iela had snuffed that out before she even knew she had any to begin with.

Caiden glanced down at her watch and quickly jumped to her feet. Not a second passed before a bullet grazed her cheek and she dropped to a knee. Wide-eyed, her head jolted around. The scar burned hot as she touched her face. She felt her eyes change instantly. She was bleeding.

She stared down at her hand as if it wasn't her own blood. It wasn't supposed to be. Mary was aimed, but her target was nowhere to be found. Her eyes followed the contours of the house and dashed from the clump of the small thicket on either side of it.

Nothing.

"I hope you get her this time," The Voice said.

She remained quiet. Shaking. Sensing.

"I keep telling Roxa Mary's too good for you."

Caiden spun around at the sound of the taunting voice, but as soon as she did, another shot. She jumped out of the way and pointed the weapon in the direction where she heard her mother's voice. She went to the side of the house and hit the corner.

No Iela.

Then, the sense snuck up on her. Iela was near, but by the time she figured out where she was, it was too late. Her legs were kicked out from under her and Mary knocked out of her hand. She bolted for it, but Iela latched onto her shoulder and slammed her on her back.

She was about to connect her boot with Caiden's face, but she blocked with both arms, flying up at lightning speed.

Iela, glaring down, dropped her foot to the ground instead. Her hard eyes, permanently taught, were now staring, steely, at her daughter's knee-jerk defense.

Caiden was trembling. Her heart pounded in her ears and adrenaline was like acid in her veins. She put her arms down and saw her mother standing over her, composed. Her tresses whipped her shoulders from the slight breeze, her eyes red afire. She was a towering inferno.

Caiden managed to follow her eyes, which had moved again to her weapon. It was so far from where it was supposed to be.

"You're too lax in execution."

Caiden knew she should look at her when she was speaking, and she did if only just.

"Your guard is fine. Excellent. But Mary doesn't feel safe in your hands. Which is why she's way over there."

"I had you, but—"

"You never had me, because you didn't get me."

Caiden's breathing steadied as she internally kicked herself.

Iela's gaze had now moved to the cut on Caiden's cheek. She kneeled over her daughter and reached out. She lightly touched her face and Caiden tensed up. This show of intimacy was foreign to both of them. If Caiden couldn't look Iela in the eye before, she definitely couldn't do it now, so she tried to focus on a blade of grass, a broken twig, Mary, anything until it was all over.

"I hope when the time comes, you won't hesitate so much," she prayed.

Iela stared at her a moment more, then she finally got up, eyes averted, and headed toward the house.

"Oh, and happy birthday."

Caiden crawled to Mary with a look on her face suggesting that's something she completely forgot.

"Roxa cooked, so hurry up and get ready."

She reached Mary as Iela went inside.

"Are you all right?" The Voice asked.

She touched her cheek again, wincing.

The sound of a barking dog revived her trigger finger. She found Mary aimed at Zinc, a white bear of a thing, who'd poked his head out through the bushes.

Caiden relaxed.

He seemed to be checking on her.

She pulled herself up and went inside, but gave Zinc a few scratches on the head before closing the door behind her. Roxa was too busy setting out plates to notice her just yet. She rolled her eyes as Iela strolled in and threw her jacket on the table. Caiden instinctively braced herself.

"She's all yours."

Roxa balled up the jacket and slung it on the couch.

"Hurry up if you want time to eat." Roxa glanced at Caiden and quickly grabbed her chin. "What the hell is this?"

Caiden's eyes shot to Iela's back.

"It was an accident," Iela tossed back over her shoulder as she disappeared down the hall.

"That's all she do is have accidents. She don't know how to do nothin' else," she said to herself, but loud enough for everyone to hear.

"Roxa, I'm fine. I have to hurry up."

Caiden quickly climbed the stairs as she heard Roxa slamming nearly everything she touched in the kitchen. She got to the top of the stairs but stopped cold.

The double doors across the hall from her bedroom beckoned to her. She walked up to them and hesitantly hovered her hand close to one of the knobs.

"Is there something wrong?" The Voice said.

"No," she replied but didn't sound sure.

There was a warmth emanating from the knob and door. Just like before. Like The Voice, it was something that had always been there.

She looked down at the tattered watch on her wrist.

"The time," The Voice warned.

"I know."

She backed up and went into her room to put up Mary before heading down the hall to the bathroom to shower and brush her teeth. She soon found herself staring in the mirror. She leaned closer to get a better look at her wound. She opened a drawer and found an antibiotic ointment to dab on her cut. Her hand went to a box of bandaids but she didn't pick them up.

"Don't give 'em a reason Cai..." she told herself and closed the drawer.

Those deep russet eyes caught her in the mirror. They caressed the wet curly baby hair plastered to her forehead and followed a bead of sweat as it slid off the curve of her collarbone and down her cleavage. She opened her towel and her moist body shocked her into what she was doing. Caiden wrapped herself back up, tight, and went back to her room to get dressed.

Black jeans, thick opaque top, and boots. Iela wanted to make sure that no one even suspected that her daughter had a flame as a heart.

Her room was windowless. A bed, a desk with a lamp and chair, and a closet were all there was. Caiden swiped a Pessoa off the top of the stack of books occupying the small space between the wall and her bed.

"Do you have all that you need?" The Voice asked.

Caiden raked her hair back into a low ponytail and smiled as she opened the book.

"Yes, Roxa."

"Forgive me for making sure you're prepared for your first day. You aren't worried? You're reading Pessoa..."

She smiled faintly, remembering what she was about to do today, and propped herself up on her elbows. "You worry enough for the both of us. I did ask for this, so I'm more excited than worried."

Caiden jerked and jumped out of bed. She opened her closet and grabbed Mary out of a steel lockbox. The weapon was cold as she slid it in her back holster.

Knock. Knock.

She quickly pulled her sweatshirt down over the gun and threw herself across the bed to start reading again. "Roxa?"

The woman came inside with a floured apron on. "Every time I come in here I get a knot in my chest."

"And so do I," Caiden said as she sat on her knees. "I like how my room is."

"Cuz you don't have a choice." Roxa closed the closet door and put her book back in its place. "If you was my daughter..." She stopped and eyed Caiden.

"Roxa."

Roxa went to the girl and embraced her so tight, she heard her back crack.

"...Roxa?"

"Nope."

It was a second before Caiden felt her backside had lightened. Roxa had snatched Mary out of her holster and was checking to see if it was loaded.

"I need her," Caiden stated in near physical pain.

"I have a briefcase for your books and chicken salad for your lunch waitin' for you downstairs." Roxa eyed her like she was crazy. "You won't make it through the front door with this thing. I'm talkin' about my front door."

"What if something happens?"

That gun was both her peace and pride. She rarely went anywhere without it. When she did go somewhere that is. High school was going to be her first venture out alone and from all the cautionary tales Iela has been feeding her since she began asking to attend school, she would need all the protection she could get.

"Relax, child." Roxa sat next to her on the bed. "You have all the weapons you'll need if anything should happen."

Roxa looked her over, particularly at her top. Caiden instinctively put her hand over her heart.

"This..." Then, she suddenly panicked. "Can you tell?"

"No. And they won't be able to either."

Caiden's brow furrowed.

"What's the matter?"

"Nothing." Her eyes attempted to change to another color.

"You can't lie, so stop tryin'."

"I don't wanna be late, Roxa."

They locked eyes, but somehow, Roxa knew. She gently took Caiden's hand in her own. "Iela taught you everything you need to know. You gon' be fine. Okay? Say 'okay'."

Caiden couldn't bring herself to believe that but nodded anyway. "Okay."

"Now, get your butt to the table. I cooked."

"You always cook."

She followed Roxa out of her room, with her nose in the air, but as they got downstairs, her appetite diminished. Iela's boots were propped up on a chair, her face hidden behind a newspaper. The headline "*Brint Infects The South*" was blazoned on the front page of the business section. It was above a picture of a sultry pin-up styled woman.

Today it was business, yesterday it was real estate. Caiden had no idea why her mother was reading the paper. She didn't need to work because she was allegedly on disability. Caiden had no idea what disability her mother had, but Roxa always joked and said it was for being too hardheaded. Caiden was forever curious about the real reason, but nothing concerning Iela was ever her business, even if it had something personally to do with her.

She sat down across from Iela and began to nibble.

"What kind of a name is Brint, anyway?"

Roxa brought a tray of assorted teas to the table. Her mouth twisted when she saw how comfortable Iela was with her handcrafted oak chairs.

"Sound like a typo— And get yo' filthy boots out my chair."

There was a defiant pause before Iela's boots slid to the floor.

"I think I should start walking," Caiden cut in.

"Eat," Iela said, as she turned a page.

"You'll need extra strength for all the lyin' you gonna be doin' today."

Iela daggered the woman a look before going to Caiden again.

"Eat some more."

"Yes, ma'am."

Caiden started forcing down more food as she and Roxa watched Iela get up from the table first. The Voice began to hum softly in her head and she chewed in rhythm with it until she couldn't eat anymore. She grabbed her briefcase, a functional look-at-me sign that belonged to Roxa's dead husband, and stepped outside into the peeking sun rays. It was hard to be nervous when the weather was like this, but she was a natural.

She saw Iela leaning in her car, rummaging in the glove box.

"Are you okay?" The Voice asked.

Caiden answered as low as she could, "I don't know yet."

She was about to be on her way when Iela got out of the car. She looked like she wanted to say something, though Caiden already knew what it was. She'd been hearing it all her life.

"Remember what I've been saying." Her tone was firm and rehearsed. "You don't exist. So act like it."

"Yes, ma'am."

And Iela didn't look her way again.

She looked around at the houses as she started on her way. The beaten bricked faces were as emotive as the people that used to live in them. As far as she knew, they were the only Voids that lived on the dead-end street, maybe in the entire neighborhood. It was difficult to keep track of the Void population because anyone could become one at any time, according to her mother. The only other Void that Caiden had intimate contact with was her mother, so that made her ten-minute walk to school even more nerve-wracking.

Myerworth's steps were teeming with students, diverse, and somewhat cliqued off. They were posted up against the medium-sized brick building, at a perfectly convenient distance, so it could be known who associated with whom in a couple of glances. Even if you were in a class with the girl or boy next door, that didn't mean that you had any automatic rights to a friendly nod.

Caiden's strides started to slow and as if on cue, she quickly became self-conscious.

"Go on," The Voice pushed. "Though your pace was like the beat of a death knell, you've managed to be on time."

"How did you know—"

She sucked in her words as a boy with ombre locs slid her a weird look before crossing the street. She eventually followed after him and joined the crowd heading to the front door, until something hit her.

Hard.

A wave shot through her.

Pure energy.

It hit like a wall, damn near staggering her. She had to stop.

She *needed* to stop.

Caiden felt an urge to search the crowd and that's when she found herself being drawn to a boy. He was looking down, his face being struck with every thought that crossed his mind, so he barely lifted his head. She watched him for a moment, making sure he was indeed the cause of this lightning bolt. He got in the crowd next to an all-American type. Their hands interlocked, warm and brief, before breaking as they entered the building.

She continued to stand there as the feeling subsided the further away the boy got. There was nothing else she could do and she stood there in a daze.

"Caiden," The Voice called.

She snapped out of it and cautiously made her way inside.

To say things got worse would be an understatement. This new world engulfed her all at once.

The emotions.

They were electric, hollow, and potent. They were exactly what emotions sounded like when you felt them.

Caiden was trying her best to keep up with the bustle but was experiencing an empathic sensory overload. She had to find some refuge.

Small relief washed over her when she got to her first class. The teacher was already writing on the board. She noticed his sleeveless vest and glistening Oxfords and for some odd reason found it strange. Not exactly on a teacher, but on the man himself.

Caiden walked into class to a few curious eyes, mostly to her briefcase, and headed straight to an empty seat in the back.

"Good morning. Welcome to your last year of high school. I'm Mil Gunde," he said as if he was starting a keynote presentation. "Or Mr. or Prof. Gunde, and this is Government."

There was some light chatter as most of the students already knew each other. Caiden just kept her eyes forward.

"Let's not waste any time and get the business out of the way first."

Mil motioned with a stack of papers to someone sitting in front of Caiden. She wouldn't have paid them any mind if it weren't for their ice cream melting smile and the obviously heavy bun on top of their head, fighting a tattered ribbon, bouncing down the aisles.

It wasn't until Caiden received her sheet of paper that she noticed that the person was a boy. She tried not to stare.

"Welcome to Myerworth," he whispered, leaning slightly down for a second.

Caiden gave him a faint smile as he noticed the wound on her cheek.

"Thank you," she whispered back.

"Looks like that hurt."

Before she could stop it, her hand went straight to her cheek and her eyes shifted like a switch. She hid immediately as a reflex, but the boy had already seen it. He gave Mil a look, who acknowledged him but didn't return it.

Caiden ducked her head in her briefcase to hide her face and to get something to write with. She spotted a black box with a note on it.

It read: "*and one to grow on.*"

She opened the box. It was a brand new shiny watch. She managed to smile to herself. Roxa remained consistent with her practical gift-giving.

Then, almost abruptly, the atmosphere turned on a point.

Faint, muted screaming flooded the classroom just like the emotions. Caiden's head jutted around, but it was only calm. She was the only one that could hear it.

Mil eyed her briefly as he continued to take out another stack of papers.

"Keep it."

Caiden saw a pencil placed on the edge of her desk. Not sure of her eyes yet, she didn't lift her head to see where it came from.

"Thank you," she said, just under a whisper.

She put her new watch on and tried to look up at the girl who came to her rescue. She wasn't sure how she would react if she did see her changing eyes, but she assumed that she probably wouldn't still be smiling at her like she was doing now, so everything seemed okay.

But when their eyes met, the screaming entered the classroom again. A loud, alarming force.

"I'm Alise."

All Caiden could do was stare into her eyes.

Friendly. Human.

She wasn't even sure she heard her name.

Caiden had to look away. She dropped her head to her paper and began filling it out. Alise assumed she didn't want to risk getting in trouble and began working on her own sheet.

Caiden read over everything, which seemed basic at first until she came across an odd question: "*What kind of being?*"

She hesitated. Torn.

The pencil between her fingers became moist with sweat as it contemplated checking the left or right box.

"If you're finished, please pass your papers forward and I'll collect them," Mil said, at the board.

She quickly checked the box labeled "Void".

"Finished?"

The boy had turned around in his chair, not checking once to see if she was, but watching her face.

She didn't look up but handed him her paper. He looked it over like it was his own before he glanced at the front of the room. He got the most subtle of go-aheads from Mil. It was like an exchange didn't even take place.

The boy erased the checkbox marked "Void" on Caiden's paper and checked the "Human" box instead.

"Alise, do you mind running these down to the front office after class?" Mil asked.

"Sure, professor."

Caiden turned away from her class to look out of the window. Everything slowly began to fade into the background as she continued to focus on getting her bearings. Her eyes, a striking shade of amber, hadn't completely gone back to their dark brown yet.

Chapter II

THE SCIENCE ROOM on Myerworth's main hall was one of the most frequently empty classrooms in the entire school. Not a soul went in there unless they worked in the building. Office staff occasionally had their small meetings there, but the principal had moved them to a more secluded part of the building, not trusting that their privacy was being kept from a certain type of student.

But not on this particular afternoon. The lights were off and breathy laughs bounced off the walls from Timothy in a state of rare bliss. His eyes rolled momentarily back in his head as he grabbed a handful of the dirty blond head nestled in the soft burnt chestnut of his neck.

"Bryan..."

Timothy could barely get his name out as it got comfortably lodged in his throat.

Both boys were more relaxed from when Caiden saw them that morning. More present. And how could they not be? In that room, located on the busiest hall at their high school, was the only place where they didn't have to not exist. Apart, it was difficult, but it had to be done because that's how they were conditioned to act. Together, though easy, was not acceptable. It was inappropriate, and there was only so much the both of them could take.

Bryan pushed Timothy against a desk in the corner. Though they were about the same size physically, he could easily overpower Timothy when he was over-excited. This was the only time both of them could be this raw. A maelstrom of contradicting emotions had shadowed his expression as he ran his fingers through Bryan's hair. If his mind wasn't sure, his heart always was.

"Bry, Bry, babe. We gotta stop—"

There was a smile on his lips as he cut off Timothy with his kisses.

"Tell me to stop again."

They kissed some more, but Timothy gently took the jock's face in his hands.

"We gon' get caught."

Bryan gauged his expression and pushed pause.

"It's your mom again, right?" Bryan was tired of hearing about it and rested his head on Timothy's shoulder for a second before picking it back up. "You're not doing what she says anymore."

"Yeah, but fuck her."

"Fuck you," he said, playfully giving into the innuendo.

Bryan started to head south, but Timothy firmly touched his broad shoulders in protest.

"Bry."

"Just shut up. It's okay"

They stared at each other, intense. For that moment, Timothy was convinced that everything would be all right. Bryan was there, in front of him. Nothing else mattered. Even if it was eating him up from the inside.

Right now, it didn't matter.

Bryan started back up again, but something was still holding Timothy back. He was still not all there. A part of him was enjoying every moment, but the other part, the part that had been consistently calling his name, seemed to be growing. And he couldn't stop it.

Iela watched William, a heavy middle-aged man hunch and sprint to her car. He was average-looking, balding, and normal, but it was clear that normal was something he definitely wasn't.

"Looks like this one is very well to do," she said while her eyes scaled an impressive high rise. She was parked downtown, where before she was watching the thinning corporate lunch crowd making their way back to their stuffy cubicles.

"He is," William said, rubbing the palms of his hand on his pinstriped slacks. "With a wife and kids and everything."

She eyed him, noting his sincerity.

William's brow furrowed as he gathered his strength to speak again. "Iela..."

"You know I used to live here, right." She turned off the car and allowed her back to rest comfortably in the seat. "I don't know if I told you or not."

He quickly looked at her but didn't get a read on her face. This had happened far too often where she would slip into some instances from her past. Rarely did it ever have anything to do with nostalgia, so William braced himself.

"Years back. A lot of years. I know I don't look it," she continued. "I remember if you go down about two or three lights, there's a stop sign around there." She stared at a woman who almost tripped rushing across the walkway before the red man showed up. "It had graffiti at the top of it to where it said 'Please stop' instead of just 'Stop.' I have no idea if the words are still there...It seemed too simple to be funny, but I thought it was a little."

William readied himself, not knowing what she was getting at. Trying to read her expression was futile, especially when there was rarely one there in the first place.

"At the time..." Iela slid out a Glock 19. The action was smooth, and even William thought Iela was unaware of what she was doing at first until he saw how steady her hand was.

"Please," he begged as calmly as his heart would let him.

She positioned the gun warmly just north of his femoral artery, never losing that far off gleam in her eye. He was right in that she was remembering a golden pastime that she thought was long forgotten, but Iela also hated going there just as much as William did.

"I had this pastor right where you are now. Same look in his eye. And I saw that sign. It was blaring like it was giving me an order...At the time, I did think it was from God. I only find myself believing when it's necessary." She paused a bit, her thoughts being trampled by sudden emotion.

"...But then I started to think that it was my conscience. That I had somehow projected this manifestation of another version of myself onto this pole for everyone to see..."

She finally met William's gaze, who was on the brink of tears. Her eyes were damn near shining, too.

"Have you ever been so terrified of yourself that not even a god could stop you from saving someone's life?"

William stared into her eyes, wondering if this was the real Iela. Not the one that he'd been rendezvousing with for the last couple of years, but actually this human body with a pulsing heart. While he waited for that proof, he mustered up enough saliva to finally try and state his case.

"Please listen..." He pivoted to face her as much as he could without disturbing the ticking weapon near his genitals. "I wasn't much of a person before or after I became this...thing. We both know that."

She eyed him, waiting patiently for him to get to the point.

"But I've always prided myself on my job. I can find anyone. I have for over a decade and believe me, I found your guy...Please...He hasn't moved since we last met."

Iela considered him a moment before answering. "...Okay." She put away her gun and William could breathe again.

Now, she seemed to have drifted to another distant memory as she looked blankly through her windshield.

"You can go."

He didn't move.

"What?"

"I was actually wondering about my assurances...I can feel it getting bad. I know it is."

She watched him shaking and could feel his desperation. A minute part of her felt for him. William was the only Void that she'd ever met that she'd tolerated for this long. Initially, it was for obvious reasons. He provided a service that she needed. It soon turned into an opportunity to learn more about who she was; what they were. Why they were. There was no way she was going to cut him off.

"I assure you, the cure is real."

William didn't waste any more time after that and got out. He zipped up his jacket tight, though the sun was beaming and passersby were in summer wear. His skin was pale and his forehead moist, but he got the shivers like he'd been hanging out in a freezer just now. He gripped himself tighter as he went inside the building.

***

Mil was sitting back at his desk, staring out the window of his empty classroom. This was his usual ritual during off periods. Thinking. Or writing, if he was in the mood.

"Are you sure about this?"

He was shaken out of his reverie when he spun around in his chair and saw his star pupil giving him that signature look of a lost traveler without a map.

"Aza, you really shouldn't miss your meals. Soon you'll weigh as much as the ghost if you continue on like this."

The bun on top of his head couldn't help but shift from side to side as he closed the door behind him. That was the perfect moment to smile to himself, but he hadn't done that for some time now. His feelings about the thoughtful things that Mil said to him had changed over the years, just like the man himself.

"I'm going."

Aza watched him run his finger under his bottom lip and tried to guess how long he'd been sitting in that same position. These meetings that took place in between classes throughout the day were like clockwork and he was never prepared for what was on the other side of the door.

"I know you won't believe me, but I'm never sure about anything. Nothing's ever certain." He looked at his student, who seemed to always be looking expectant of something that was taking too long to arrive. "But I've always told myself, I'd know the Soul when I saw it. I just wasn't expecting it would walk right into my classroom."

Aza's face darkened some, but his personality wouldn't let the hope go out in his eyes completely.

"Remove that look from your face. Everything has its time."

"But you saw her today. She doesn't know anything," he said, balling his sleeves up in his palms.

"Well, I assume he's not awake yet."

He shifted on his feet and his grip tightened. "Awake?"

Mil fixed on him to make sure he was coming across without question. "We need a catalyst, Aza."

Aza took a few steps toward his teacher to make sure he heard right.

Mil pierced him this time.

"Bait the Arch."

There was a moment as Aza tried to get his head around what Mil was saying when they both felt a pull towards the classroom door. At that moment, Caiden walked by.

Aza looked back at Mil.

"Make sure not to spoil your appetite for later," he said, turning back to his desk. "No snacks is what I'm saying. I'm preparing your favorite tonight."

"Japchae?"

"Borscht," he replied, blankly.

Aza watched Mil mechanically open his notebook and begin writing. He lingered with his hand on the doorknob before he left the classroom and followed after Caiden to the cafeteria.

She walked into the room still trudging through all the sensory arousal from her peers. She was an alien there and lugging around a briefcase didn't help.

The cliques were more defined now. They were scattered about, but not a single place to sit without invading someone's personal space.

"Caiden?"

She turned around and found Alise smiling at her. She was flanked by two of her friends.

"Yeah. Hey."

"Know those sheets that we filled out this morning that asked for everything, but our blood type? I took them to the office, remember?"

Caiden nodded.

"Come on."

Aza had made his way across the room to sit where Caiden was still in his line of view. It wasn't a few minutes until a group of strangers had congregated around him. He barely knew them; maybe they were acquaintances, but this was a natural phenomena.

He casually greeted them and even participated in the conversations that popped up around him while he continued to watch Caiden with fierce curiosity.

"So you were home-schooled this entire time? That must've been boring."

Caiden had begun eating her chicken salad, which looked too gourmet to be packaged in a dollar store brown paper bag. Roxa had also thrown in a brownie, which was what she wanted to eat first, but old habits.

"I read a lot, so I didn't notice."

"Did you just move here?" Alise asked. Her thumb was moving across her phone keyboard as they were picking over food from each of their lunches.

"I've been here most of my life. On and off. But mostly off, though."

"And you suddenly decided to start public school your senior year? Your parents must hate you." Caiden flinched at the joke and bit into her brownie.

"I guess I can't be your tour guide around town, but if you need help finding a class or signing up for clubs, etc., you can ask me. I've been an office aide since I was a freshman," Alise said with a confident smile.

"Okay," she said, wiping some chicken residue out of the corner of her mouth.

Caiden was waiting for more invasive questions, but Alise was satisfied with that answer. She had done her good deed for the day, so her now free hand joined the other for a while as they all took a short break to eat. Caiden sipped her water and wrapped up the other half of her sandwich. Her eyes wandered around the room, but every time she got caught by someone, she'd immediately look away. When she looked back up, Aza was staring at her. Her head dropped to the water bottle in her lap. It was a few seconds before she lifted her head again, thinking that he'd looked away, but he hadn't. He was still staring at her. Caiden was expecting him to turn away when she didn't, but Aza wasn't budging.

"I thought you didn't know anybody here."

Caiden broke Aza's gaze and turned to Alise, who now took her place at staring across the cafeteria.

"Oh, he's a good boy."

Caiden glanced back at his table and saw that he'd turned back around to the group of students awaiting his attention. At that moment, someone accidentally bumped into the back of one of their chairs and one of the girls spilled her drink all over herself. It happened fast, but Caiden's eyes were on them instead of their victim. The guy had slapped the end of the table to catch himself before his face met with the floor.

She instantly felt his fear as their eyes met briefly when he bounced back onto his feet. He displayed all the looks of someone who was once at the top of the social food chain but had fallen hard from the false grace.

"M-my fault." Mortified, he headed for the exit as fast as he could.

Caiden watched him quickly stumble out of the cafeteria while the girl was overreacting.

"Calm down, you're so dramatic," the other friend drolled.

"God, that's just David. He's harmless," Alise said. "I thought it was one of those Voids. But most of them stopped eating with the humans before I got here."

Caiden froze.

She was one of those Voids.

But as she looked around at how composed they were now compared to a few seconds ago, they didn't seem to notice. It was then that those screams from earlier surfaced again. Louder. Harsher. Caiden felt her eyes being pulled towards Alise's and the screams intensified.

Aza had stopped as well. Now, completely ignoring the girl in his ear asking about what his hair care routine was, he sensed something as he turned in his chair to catch a glimpse of Caiden. Everything seemed to be fine, but now he couldn't take his eyes off the group of girls.

Alise finally looked at Caiden and her smile faded.

"...I'm so sorry," she said, haunted.

There was a sharp pause as silence sat amongst them. It took a second too long for Caiden to get her bearings. She wanted to disappear once they had.

"I'm sorry," she said again, grabbing her briefcase and lunch.

All of them just stared at her as the bell finally sounded. Caiden left first, lugging her briefcase as she got swallowed up by the exiting cafeteria crowd, but Alise managed to find her.

"I'll see you around," she said, forcing a smile.

Caiden gave her an apologetic look, not knowing what else to do. She pulled out her folded schedule, and began spinning on her heels in different directions looking for her next class. After memorizing the entire thing, her mind went blank after whatever that was that happened just now.

She continued to follow the crowd until someone shoved her and her briefcase and its contents went sprawling across the hall floor.

"I'm sorry," she said again to no one.

After she put everything back, with no help from the humans or the voided, she stood up and felt something in her hand. It was a note and she had no idea how it got there. She gave the hall a once over before opening it.

It simply read: "*I know what you are.*"

Caiden's breath got caught in her throat as her eyes cautiously searched around the halls. She looked at the students surrounding her as her heartbeat began to race. None of their energies stood out from the other. Everything was muddled and her mind was whirling. She felt something surging from within her. Something new and different, and not of herself.

Chapter III

CAIDEN CLUTCHED THE damp notebook paper wrung in one of her shaking hands and had her schedule covering her face as naturally as possible with the other. She knew her eyes were all over the place, but she didn't know which disaster to deal with first.

Someone knew what she was.

But that was impossible.

She didn't exist.

That surging from within began to come back, bursting to get through. She searched in vain for an area with as few people as possible, but those traveling packs of her peers that she'd encountered in the morning had migrated and occupied every hall she turned onto.

"Caiden?" she heard a voice call to her, but she had no idea if it was in her head or not, so she didn't answer and kept walking. She lifted her arm to eye level to check the time to make sure she wasn't late for her next class.

"Caiden."

She slowed down and stood in front of a wall, eyes still focused on her schedule. That voice felt like it had a body so she pretended not to hear it.

"Caiden," The Voice called.

"You okay?"

That voice sounded a little familiar. She turned a little and stood there.

"Hey," that same voice turned soft.

She cautiously lifted her head, having no clue if her eyes had gone back to neutral or not, and saw Aza looking back at her, his own eyes heavy with concern.

"...Caiden," he said, taking a step closer.

She instinctively took a step back. Why did her name sound like that coming out of his mouth, like he knew it before they'd even met?

She managed to lock eyes with him and wondered what he could possibly be thinking. Then suddenly, like a switch, the color of his eyes changed to a deep, dark violet.

"It's okay," he assured her.

Caiden stared at him like an idiot, still not able to act. Until her legs began to move on their own, anywhere far away from this awkward situation. She jetted off down the hall from which she came as if nothing happened.

No one's supposed to know.

She made it out the front door of the school and thrust herself into the warm, humid air. It took her some time before her breathing steadied, but it didn't last.

Timothy again.

She felt him near and searched the handful of students that had finished their classes for the day. Timothy was gripping the two straps of his backpack and looking off down the street. Caiden only took one step in his direction before The Voice broke her trance.

"Caiden."

She backtracked and almost fell backward as the step scuffed the heel of her boot.

"Have I ever told you how much I've hated our one-sided relationship?" The Voice asked.

"Many times..." she said under her breath. "I think he knows."

"You haven't made it one week and you're already paranoid. Have you checked the time?"

At the mention of time, she glanced her watch and inched unwillingly back inside the school.

Timothy pulled out his phone as Bryan came up behind him. They shoved each other a little in greeting, Timothy's smile devouring each cheek. Bryan attempted to grab Timothy's hand, but he didn't let him, not forgetting where they were.

"Are you comin' tonight?" Timothy asked, his voice high at the thought of seeing him in a safe space.

"I always do," Bryan said, eating the distance between them. "The question is, do you want me to stay? You've been acting suspect lately and not like somebody who sent me anonymous locker notes for two years."

That made the corners of Timothy's mouth twitch. "I need you there."

"But?" Bryan sighed and stepped back, losing his appetite.

"You can't, you know that."

Bryan slung his bag over his shoulder as it turned cold and grabbed his car keys out of his pocket. Timothy felt his hand disobeying all the strict conditioning he'd put himself through since the two met, but he massaged his arm instead.

"I'm gonna go," Bryan finally said. "It's fine if I see you tomorrow, right?"

His hand had won. Timothy grabbed Bryan's bag strap.

"Drop me off first."

***

Some deep monotonous cello strings mingled with the smoke coming from the soup pot from the living room. The burnt umber ambiance oddly clashed with the soft heather gray in the mid-sized kitchen. The record player was on a small wooden hutch on the wall parallel to the entrance. It was doing its best on what seemed to be its last leg of life. Willard had it before he'd met the twenty-something Roxa and insisted that it be used until it died completely.

Roxa naturally looked at the antique as it skipped a few notes as she was in her rightful place in front of the stove, tasting and mixing. She stopped and stuck her neck out to listen, thinking she heard something, but the music was too loud. She went into the living room to pick up the needle.

Knock. Knock.

She heavy sighed and cut down the heat on the stove. She threw off her apron and opened the front door. There were two women older than her, dressed in casual church wear. One was nestling a stack of books against her bosom and the other was bustling her way back to an ancient delivery van.

"Sister Lucy."

"Roxy," Lucy said, looking her up and down. "I didn't expect you'd be home at this hour, but I figured I'd give it a try."

"Where else would I be?"

The woman's lips parted momentarily, but nothing came out.

"It took eight years, but it's nice of you to drop by."

"I don't appreciate your tone." Lucy's back relaxed when Roxa leaned in the doorway. "You don't know how hard it was to make it down here. I'm the only friend you got left in the congregation and I don't know how long that's gonna last."

"*Sister* Lucy, what are you doin' here?"

"Please don't be like that. May I come in?"

"No."

They fixed on each other a second and Lucy held out the books to her.

"I'm here with an olive branch. For the girl." She waited as Roxa took the books and clasped her hands in front of her. "How is she?"

"The nerve you got."

"Excuse me? Don't I have the right to know how my god-daughter—"

"God..." Roxa couldn't finish from laughing so hard.

Sister Lucy's head fell in shame for a moment before she straightened her shoulders. "I didn't mean to presume. I just figured as much as we been through that you'd be the forgiving person that I thought you were and we'd be able to fix this."

Roxa folded her arms across her chest. It was the only way to stop herself from slamming the door in the old woman's face.

"I want to fix this, Roxy."

"Stop callin' me that and tell me what you want," she said, glancing down the street. "I don't know when that girl is gon' come saunterin' back in here."

The sister's eyes widened for a second. "Iela is still with you."

"Why wouldn't she be?"

"That incident with the pastor, I thought—"

"What did you think? That I'd throw her out on the street for doin' something that you have proof I would've done myself?" Roxa's eyes narrowed. "Now Sister, what kind of hypocritical shit is that?"

Lucy had flinched at the curse word but wasn't about to give up. "Yes. Well, it's God's place to know the truth, not mine—"

"You right."

"I have more books for the girl if she'd like," she said, taking a step back and checking on the van. "I know I have some time to make up for."

"Caiden will finish these soon as she touch 'em. I've no doubt word spread like wildfire after she stepped foot in that school."

"Uh, just slightly before. Our brother, Reverend Graham, is a former member, like yourself. He just got hired up there."

"Hm, that so." Roxa rolled the foot around that all her weight was on. "Thank you for the books, Sister."

"Roxa..."

She waited for a long while before the Sister could get her words together. Roxa was just reminded of how much that got on her last nerve. That sort of cautious nature made her want to grab both of the Sister's shoulders and toss her off a cliff.

"I wasn't the only one devastated when you decided to choose them over us—"

"Us? I chose my family, Sister. So it wasn't much of a choice."

"They aren't you're family, Roxy...Not yet."

Roxa's eyebrows almost brushed up against her baby hairs. "Say what you gonna say or get the hell off my doorstep."

"I'm gonna get right to the point...Sister Roxanne, it took some time, but our patience has borne fruit. We might can save them now."

"Save 'em?" She said it as if the Sister just created a new word, it was so ridiculous.

"I've seen it work myself. Just come back down to the church. I'm sure as Jesus rose you won't regret a thing."

The Sister hung on every word she said. The belief in her eyes and mannerisms were so blind and so true, it was near feverish. A tinge of pity set in with Roxa for the poor woman.

"Everyone knows there's only one cure, Lucy, and it's permanent."

"Everyone doesn't know God."

"Yeah, and that's they loss, ain't it." Roxa felt her hands itching, wanting to get back to the stove. "Good evenin', Sister."

Sister Lucy gave Roxa a terse smile before she headed back to the church van, but Roxa could still see that fire in her eye right before she closed the door.

They would be back. She just wasn't sure that the next time would be as opportune as this one. Roxa naturally looked toward the stairs out of habit before she went back to her cooking.

Upstairs in her room, Caiden was sitting at her desk, squinting at her flickering lightbulb. She heard the front door close and paused a moment before she opened her briefcase. It wasn't a house rule that she stay out of sight whenever they had an unexpected visitor, but her instinct always led her to go into defense mode when she felt an unknown presence so near to the safest place in her world.

She pulled out her syllabi from her classes to see if she could get a head start on some of the work. It didn't look so bad, but she had to remind herself that the year was just getting started. The months ahead began to worry her, wondering if she'd be able to keep up with the rest of her peers. Roxa was the only teacher she'd ever had, but her schooling wasn't as extensive as what was on these sheets of paper.

"Stop it, Cai," she sighed, leaning back in her chair.

"Yes, stop," The Voice said.

"I'll feel better in a moment."

Caiden got up and left her room. She stood outside the doors across the hall before she reached out to grab one of the doorknobs. It was just a brass knob. No warmth.

She pushed the door and almost floated through. Surrounded by piles and aisles of books, the room had shelves that seemed to have been thrifted without a thought of style. Both wooden and metal bookcases lined the walls and one lone row crossed the width of the room. Their library, initially a game room, was incredibly humble, but it was theirs. But to Caiden it felt like her own place to escape to outside her bedroom, for Iela and Roxa rarely went in there. She smiled to herself. This was her happy place and no one else's.

"Better?" The Voice asked.

She was squatting next to a wooden shelf, scanning the spines near the bottom, and didn't seem to hear the question.

"Caiden?"

"I'm still here." She pulled out a book and began flipping through its pages.

"I think you should tell Iela what happened."

That made her pause and she closed the book. "Can I get a good thirty minutes before you ruin my mood?" She headed straight toward the back of the room where she'd been compiling a stack of to-reads on a corner chair and set the book on top.

"Then, tell Roxa."

"It's enough I told you."

There was a long moment of silence before she realized The Voice was taking a while to answer.

"...Often your warm words sear as from a flame," It said.

"You know what I mean," she apologized. "You're always the first to know everything. You always have been, and I feel better knowing that I'm not by myself."

"And what will you do when telling me is no longer enough?" The Voice countered. "I'm just here as a reminder of how delusional you are."

She laughed a little, but the smile quickly faded.

Caiden hadn't really thought that far ahead. She'd never needed to before. Iela would snatch her out of school so fast if she got an inkling that Caiden was losing control of whatever this was inside of her. It was more than just an organ beating in her chest; even more than its light.

"Nothing actually happened," she said after a moment of reliving the freakish event.

A book called to her on one of the aisles and she went to peruse the spine. "...But I've never felt that before."

"How did it feel?"

"Different. Not like myself..." She pulled the book off the shelf and put it with the others. "Maybe that boy has something to do with it," she said with some confidence but wasn't sure.

Ever since she started going to school, everything began feeling even more unsure than when she was studying at home. Specifically the people. They were so young and complex, and their emotions were in a constant state of this and that. It was what she both loved and feared the most about taking in all those variable energies. Most of the time it was either an extreme high or an extreme low. No middle ground. And when you have nothing to stand on, you'd do anything to keep from falling.

Her hand slowly went to her chest, then she looked at her wrist.

"I didn't tell you that Roxa got me a new watch for my birthday."

"A birthday which you forgot," The Voice teased. "Let's not change the subject."

Caiden grabbed another book off the shelf, amused, and headed toward the door. She was completely unaware of the pair of royal blue eyes watching her leave from the other side of the bookshelf.

"I'm sleepy."

"So, you're not going to go back to your room and read until you pass out."

"I only have enough energy to read is what I meant."

She went back to her room and tucked herself into bed. She laid there, staring at her unevenly painted ceiling, her hands comforting each other.

"What do you think? You think it was my heart?"

"I'm not sure."

Caiden flipped over onto her side and reached for her book, but her hand went limp. She got up instead and turned off her lamp. Her heart's light showed through her cami as she slid back into bed. She let her hand hover over the light, letting it play between her fingers before wrapping herself up in her duvet. In a matter of minutes, she'd fallen into a deep sleep.

Chapter IV

CAIDEN HOPED HER school days would've gotten easier to get through or at least more comfortable, but they hadn't. Not even close.

Being constantly in a state of anger, sadness, or on edge was all that she got from her peers. She understood that this was normal, considering the time of life they were all in, but none of them had to feel all of that every day all at once. They didn't have to get used to it. Which was why she couldn't wait until the bell rang for her to go home. At least there, if Iela or Roxa's emotions got too much for her, she could just go to her room.

The bell rang for lunch and Caiden was about to follow the traffic when she felt that pull again. She looked around for that familiar energy, but couldn't find him yet. He was near though. At that point, the searching and the need to be with this total stranger was getting ridiculous.

Who was this guy?

She stood in the middle of the hall as it began to empty, but Timothy was nowhere in sight. Caiden caught herself as she felt something nudge her arm. She spun around.

"I'm gonna brave the free fare today. What about you?"

Aza was holding one of those vintage pail lunchboxes. It was lolita-themed and orange with a few shiny scratches on the bottom corners where the paint had come off.

"Bacon turkey wrap," he said, smiling and admiring what seemed to be a collector's item.

"Aza, right?" she said, distracted. She knew that was his name, she had no idea why she posed it as a question.

Timothy's energy was still in the vicinity, but she didn't know how long he would be there.

"That's right. Caiden."

Again with her name.

She wondered what he was trying to do to her or even if he was aware of what he was doing. Awkwardness arrived and a few clunky seconds of silence sat wedged in between them. Aza was usually more conversational than this, but he found himself losing natural word flow when he spoke to Caiden. He was more focused on not saying the wrong thing. And not saying something that would get him into trouble.

"I'm sorry," she said, which seemed to be her knee-jerk response to everything bad that happened. "About before, I mean. And now. I have to go."

He noticed her eyes wandering. "You're forgiven both times." He gently swung the lunchbox by the handle. "I'll keep this for myself if things go south."

"I'm gonna go to the restroom," she said, forever penitent, and turned down a hall.

A few stragglers were gradually finishing up in their lockers. All, but three boys. One's attention was split between his friend's raunchy jokes and his phone. The other two were intent on playing with Timothy. It seemed he knew them or he used to.

Caiden was standing by the lockers, not too far away, but she could tell Timothy looked different from the very first time she saw him. The bags under his eyes were heavier, his dark circles were more prominent, and his gait had slumped to where he looked shorter than he really was.

"Aye! It's that boy Tee-Tee. Nigga get hard hearin' his own name," one of them jeered. His expression indicated that he was enjoying every second of this teasing and it was going to get worse.

Timothy didn't have it in him to fight back. "Yeah and you can suck it," he fired, trying to escape into the boys' room.

"Ooh. He mad. Tee-Tee mad," the other boy joined in, laughing and following the leader into the restroom.

Like they were taunting her as well, Caiden began to follow them.

"Caiden?" The Voice called, sounding puzzled.

At that moment she heard shuffling.

"Bitch! Get yo' hands off me!" the first boy yelled.

And she couldn't be stopped. She bum-rushed the door of the boys' restroom and three things happened in just a matter of seconds:

A sword slicing gust of wind was heard.

The lights flickered as if the wiring was faulty.

And Caiden found herself knocking out two of the students and choke-holding the other, all without dropping her briefcase. All without thinking.

Now, they were struggling to catch their breath, trying to figure out what the hell just happened. Caiden was perhaps the most shocked of all. She was a bit astonished at how easy fighting came to her. Not the act itself, because Iela would be remiss in her duties as a mother if she hadn't taught her self-defense, but the fact that she could naturally use these learned skills like they were an innate form of preservation for herself and for others that needed her whenever a situation called for it. Like now.

Timothy needed her.

She looked down and could make him out on the floor, looking lost and bewildered at her and the three boys.

Their eyes locked. He stared at her in confusion and then he stared at his bully, who was considerably taller than Caiden, wrestling against her chokehold.

Then, the lights went out completely.

"Get out. Now."

With The Voice's words echoing in her head, Caiden released the boy and hauled ass out of there. She went straight into the girls' room and dropped her stuff.

She was alone. She could sense it.

Her mind, her eyes, her heart were running ragged.

"Why did I do that?" she said, still not able to breathe steadily.

Adrenaline and that something else, that unfamiliar and foreign something, had invaded her system again. She hurried to the mirror and got lost in her reflection's eyes. They were shooting through the rainbow as they were now beginning to water. She couldn't even blink. Not yet. Not until her eyes told her what happened. They could never lie.

"Why did you do that?" Caiden was staring at herself, waiting for an answer.

"That was far, Caiden. Too far," The Voice said.

She took deep breaths and tried to center herself. When it got as close to regular as she could get it, she picked up her briefcase and walked to the door. She lingered. Her trembling hand went to her chest where her light was pulsing underneath her sweatshirt. Then, she walked out of the door.

Caiden left the girls' room and headed straight towards the cafeteria. Aza had watched her with the boys and could see she was still in the process of calming herself.

Moments later, Timothy came out of the restroom still looking bemused. He scanned the halls for the girl that had just saved him, but like his bullies, she was nowhere to be found.

Aza waited for Timothy to leave before he went into the restroom himself. As the door closed behind him, the lights began flickering again.

***

Iela was in the library of all places, skimming through pages. She wasn't reading, just trying to keep her mind occupied, at which she wasn't doing a very good job. It was clear that she rarely frequented this particular part of the house, but it was the quietest next to the study downstairs. The only reason she wasn't in there now was that she'd just come out of Caiden's room doing her daily inspections. Nothing that required flipping over mattresses or rummaging through drawers, just to make sure she kept it how she left it. Iela knew Roxa couldn't help herself sometimes and would peek inside every now and then.

She heard one of the doors open and saw Roxa come in with an armful of books. She was briefly startled to see her.

"Your daughter is just as messy as you are."

"If you got those out of Caiden's room, you can put them back where you found them."

Roxa rolled her eyes. "You know, for somebody who's barely here, you sho' is sayin' a lot about how to run my house. What are you doin' in here, anyway, of all places?"

"I was waiting for you," Iela said with dry facetiousness.

She eyed Iela as she put the books up in their assigned homes. "What do you want with me?"

Iela's attention went to the books Roxa had and she'd forgotten about what she was initially going to say. Roxa already knew what was coming.

"Those better not be from where I think they're from." Her face had turned hard as she took one of the books out of Roxa's arms.

"They're Caiden's," Roxa defended. "You don't have to worry about the Sisters. They should know better by now."

"Do they?" she asked, knowing full well they hadn't.

They both fixed on each other. If Iela could rid the world of anything, it would be the church. Just the mention of the word or anything known to have a connection with the word cooked her blood to a boil.

"It seems they must've forgot." Roxa continued putting them up. "...Now, they talkin' about some cure..." she said, hesitantly.

She watched Iela out of her peripheral just to see if that got some reaction. Iela watched Roxa as she took her time before making eye contact again.

"You look convinced."

"I'm convinced that they convinced. You know how these southern baptists are. The Word is law, and if you don't originate in the Word, then they make it their duty to fix it to where you do." Roxa swatted the air with her hand. "Heathens. Every last one of 'em."

"So, when are you going down there?" Iela asked, knowing she would sooner or later. Being a Sister was in her DNA whether she wanted to admit it or not.

"I'm not," she said with her nose slightly up in the air.

"Not today," Iela said to herself.

Roxa remained quiet.

"Just let me know when I should drop you off because it will be the last time you see me or Caiden."

"Who the hell you threatenin'?" Roxa turned and rested her knuckles on her wide hips. "They said they have proof. If I do go down there, it'll be to see what poor, pitiful fool they got chained up in they holy water shark tanks."

Iela had been told off by Roxa numerous times, but the response she got back when she mentioned separating her from Caiden was one she never understood.

"There's no way in heaven I'd forgive them for what they did to that girl," Roxa said, now shoving the rest of the books on the shelf.

"Good," Iela said as memories of the past flooded her mind.

She left the library immediately with a glaring Roxa as a parting gift. Iela stood in the dark hall a second as her eyes wandered to her daughter's bedroom. She went up to the door about to go inside but thought better of it.

"Iela..."

She turned and saw light before anything else. Caiden was standing at the top of the stairs with her briefcase handle clutched in both hands. What her heart illuminated and from the lights that were on downstairs, Iela could see that Caiden seemed a little confused as to why she was standing in front of her door. For some reason that made Iela angrier than being caught about to trespass into her daughter's room for the second time.

"Why do you call me that?"

The question caught her off-guard and she didn't answer at first. She wasn't sure of the answer herself.

"I'm sorry."

"That's your answer for everything," she said, walking toward her.

Caiden naturally tensed up and though it was dark, she could tell her mother saw it and she slowed down.

"Roxa's got some more books for you."

Iela felt that was a good way to end this unexpected talk. Caiden moved out of her way and she headed downstairs to her study. Well, it was Roxa's study. It was Willard's before and after he died, Roxa would rarely go in there. It brought up too many memories, so Iela made it her own as soon as they were sure they'd make this place somewhat of a home.

The room was small, like a box, with a desk and a couple filing drawers. A few small lamps were set up on the only flat surfaces. Similar to her and Caiden's bedrooms, the lamp was the only source of light. The study had a window, but like Iela's bedroom, they had been boarded up.

She turned on the lights and went to sit at her desk where she unlocked a drawer.

Iela paused, not sure if she wanted to see what was inside. She transformed into a different woman, almost gentle, but her expression remained unchanged. She pulled out a small box big enough to hold letters, and when she opened it, that's exactly what was inside.

All white. Sealed elegantly with white wax, professional and classic, from an old forgotten time. But there was no return address, just her name written in sloppy cursive on the front. There were about five of them. All were opened.

She looked at them a moment, her eyes sinking from her natural deep auburn to a dark carmine as she skimmed over them, reveling in the words that she could probably recite in her sleep.

Iela calmly closed the box and locked it away again. It took some time for her to pull herself back together, but she did like a slow dimming switch. She stood up, turned off the lights, and left.

Chapter V

TIMOTHY'S ROOM WAS tight like the rest of their two-bedroom apartment. He shared it with his ten-year-old brother who'd fallen asleep on the couch watching reruns of an old classic cartoon DVD.

Two small twin beds were parallel to one another, one on either side of the room. They both didn't have much in the way of possessions, but their mother allowed his little brother a few stuffed animals and an old gaming system. Timothy only had necessities. Clothes for his back, shoes for his feet, and whatever supplies he needed for school.

If he wanted to enjoy himself he'd head over to Bryan's. Or Bryan would come over like he was now when his mother was at work. Usually, Timothy was paranoid with his brother still in the house, but he was getting restless being away from Bryan for too long.

They were in Timothy's bed, the one farthest from the door. It looked difficult for both of the boys to fit, their limbs jutting out from under the covers, but everything was working out how they wanted. They'd done this a few times before and could now read the other's movements like it was their own.

A table lamp with a low-watt light bulb caught flashes of their skin magnificently contrasting between, on top, beneath, and wrapped around each other. This was the only time they could be comfortably one, in their own shard of time where no one else was supposed to exist because no one else mattered.

Bryan gave a pleasurable moan as they both continued to fall deeper into each other, but that's when the door cracked open a sliver. They didn't notice as it opened soundly below a whisper, so they didn't see Timothy's little brother's eye peeking through the crack. Watching his brother grabbing, caressing, and kissing Bryan with so much care and tenderness rooted him to the spot. This was a side of his big brother that he rarely ever saw.

But this Timothy was new to him. There was no way he could look away.

Timothy turned over and looked up at Bryan. His head tilted back off the edge of the bed, sweaty with a smile on his face. Bryan covered his neck with more panting kisses and Timothy's muscles rippled as he pulled Bryan closer.

It was then that they emerged. Black veins popped up around and in the whites of his eyes which were now becoming the same color as his irises.

He was Fading.

It didn't last long, so Bryan didn't see that his Timothy had devolved. They just said their goodbyes with the quiet anticipation of seeing each other next time.

The following morning Timothy was awakened out of his sleep and dragged out the front door by his mother.

"Mama?"

He fell back into the guarding rail, his face gaunt and his eyes were a milky white. His mother was looking as sick as he did, but for an entirely different reason. She was crying in disgust, but most of all, she was pissed.

"I didn't raise you like that! Get the hell outta my house!" she spat.

"Mama..." he pleaded.

He'd grown extremely weak in the last twelve hours to get his words out and he was too ashamed to look anyone in the eye, especially his mother. He caught his little brother looking out at him from behind her in the doorway, wide-eyed and gripping the door jamb.

"Mama!—"

Bam!

***

Volx's serial killer glare lingered a moment in the rearview. The driver in the two-door sedan on his tail stopped a little too close to his bumper.

His eyes black, nearly gone, held an endless abyss of darkness, waiting there in what some have likened to pure emptiness whenever his eyes would meet the driver behind him. An accumulation of everything he'd ever witnessed in his life up to this moment; events and people he'd survived when he shouldn't have.

His pick-up truck stopped at a red light and he switched on his turning signal. He wasn't going anywhere, in particular, he just enjoyed driving around sometimes. No radio on, not a cold drink in the holder or the AC blowing around the collar of his neck, just the damp Southern night and the possibilities that lurked within them.

The sedan honked a few times when he saw Volx was one of those infuriating drivers that waited until the light turned green to go even though no cars were coming. Volx looked into his rear-view again to see the horn heckler, and though their eyes met quite briefly, the honking ceased immediately.

Volx tilted his head some like he got a whiff of something. His nostrils flared a little as he turned his head in the direction of the smell. It was fresh and it was new.

The light turned green and he turned the corner. He kept driving until he found himself behind a small shopping plaza. It wasn't too late to where the after-work crowd was still out and about, but this particular shopping area was nearing its closing time, so only the employees were left to go home.

Volx parked behind the building in the narrow alley. He got out and sniffed the air like a dog that suddenly caught a scent. He looked about a pile of trash bag heaps until he heard groaning.

He paused to listen again, but there was nothing. He walked closer to the bags and opened the dumpster that they were stacked in front of. Right then, Timothy looked up at him through his tired slits for eyes. He was soaked to the bone in sweat and trash residue. Volx was drawn to the small cut on his arm but fought off the temptation. From what he could see, Timothy's eyes were still white. No color in sight.

"...Please." His voice was barely audible.

Volx lifted the kid out of the dumpster effortlessly and set him on his feet. He finished the job of knocking him out, then put him in the backseat of his truck and drove away.

Fifteen minutes hadn't passed until they found themselves in the most suburban neighborhood. Volx parked in front of a small one-story house and went to the window.

Inside, ruffly curtains framed that semi-wide window next to the front door that he now peeked through. A long comfy couch with an obvious slipcover to match the drapes was tucked tight around the curved arms, and a set of armchairs faced each other from different corners of the room. Right in the middle of it all was a faux retro-styled TV facing an out of place antique coffee table, which pulled everything together.

It was cozy and quaint. Completely welcoming. Not at all reflections of the inhabitants that dwelled there.

"Aza," Mil called.

Aza came into the living room, hair down to his waist, and in pajama bottoms. He began digging in the couch, looking for something. He stopped a moment before he started to peel the slipcover off for further inspection.

"The table is set," Mil said.

At that moment, Volx decided to come through the front door with Timothy hanging off one of his shoulders like a bath towel.

"Move," he said in a deep grumble.

Aza glanced at him, momentarily disoriented, but did a double-take when he saw the body.

"Mil!"

Mil came into the living room and slowly took in the situation.

"What are we having?" Aza asked.

Volx laid Timothy on the couch.

"A Wellington— Where did you find this one?" Mil asked in a borderline accusatory tone.

"Behind the plaza, five miles from here."

Aza kneeled beside Timothy. "He's Fading."

"Please..." Timothy mumbled. Then, he lost consciousness again.

"What's this?" Aza had finally seen the bruise on Timothy's head.

"Our location can't be compromised," Volx explained.

"What happened to the black bag?" As far as Aza knew, Volx was never this careless on purpose. There were times before where he would get too riled up or he'd miscalculate his strength and the people they were helping would end up getting more hurt than they were before they were saved.

Volx didn't answer.

"Put him in Pneuma's bed until he comes to."

"Volx."

Aza caught his eye before it moved to the open wound on Timothy's arm. Volx just looked at him before he took the boy into another room.

Aza resumed his search to shake off that small shiver that flowed up his back.

"Here it is."

It was one of his many hair ties. He'd lose or misplace a few of them every week. Aza never worried about his disappearing collection though. His love-hate relationship with the numerous ribbons, bows, and string that he had in his closet was a feeling he believed would never leave him.

"He's been sniffing them out faster than usual lately," he said, throwing his mane on top of his head as fast as he could.

Mil's expression waxed grim. "He's eager. As am I.

"Yeah, any moment now..." Aza was fishing for more than that.

"Aza. Food's getting cold."

He unwillingly took the hint and went into the kitchen. Volx came back at that moment.

"And no worries," Mil said, looking up at him. "I've prepared yours extra fresh."

If possible, Volx's skin was salivating.

He followed Mil into the kitchen where Aza was already sitting at the table in their joined dining room. The style matched that of the living room, keeping the dainty and delicate motif alive in the tiles and wallpaper on the floor and backsplashes.

Aza started to fix Mil's plate while Volx got started on his. He couldn't help but throw him a small smile. No matter how big and scary Volx seemed at times, Aza was always touched when he did mundane things like that.

They said their prayers and ate in silence. It wasn't until much later when Timothy woke up that business was really about to begin.

Mil came into the living room holding a tray with a sandwich and a glass of milk. Hospitable as ever. He placed it on the coffee table in front of Timothy. His sunken eyes had gone back to normal, but it was apparent to everyone present in the room that Timothy's transformation was complete.

Mil watched the boy's eyes as they scanned the granny-infested living room.

"Please. Sit."

Timothy just stared at the man before Volx posted up in the doorway and he sat down.

It was silent as Timothy sized up both of them and tried to figure out how he got to this point in his life. He never would've imagined that who he was could turn him into the hated thing that he'd now become. That had to be the only reason. He couldn't think of anything else.

Another moment passed and Aza came through the front door with leaky Styrofoam containers in Thank You plastic bags.

"Real food."

He sat the bags down on the coffee table next to the sandwich and settled in for what seemed to be his favorite part of the job.

"Usually when I do these things. These sit-downs. I start off with who we are," Mil explained, sitting down in his favorite armchair. "I believe that establishing this rapport is important to the relationship, no matter the length."

Timothy just watched him, listening.

"My name is Mil." He gestured to the others. "This is Aza and Volx. We're just three of the seven that make the Argenta."

Mil paused to gauge Timothy's expression.

"I've been alive for quite some time. All of us have. We've borne witness to many moments. Some you may be familiar with and others, I'm sure if you heard about, you'd be more thankful to not know existed at all...But the only moment that matters is the one that brought us here."

Aza shifted on the edge of the other armchair in anticipation.

"The Call is what I've christened it," Mil continued. "I can't say it's something we accepted without resistance. There were questions, but no one or nothing to pose them to. We were walking in the dark in the beginning, but not anymore. Each of us heard this call and we answered it...To help save souls like yours."

Timothy regarded Mil, haunted.

"...What happened to me?"

"That's why we start with these chats. To get to know each other, to find out what happened."

There was a long moment before Timothy decided to play along.

"I'm Timothy," he said, eyeing Mil and the others self-consciously.

"Yes, Timothy."

Mil was patient.

"...I don't know how I got like this. I'm like sick now, right?"

"Sick?" Aza asked.

"I seen Voids do some fucked up shit and I ain't tryin' to end up like that."

"Timothy."

His gaze fixed on Mil.

"Why do you think you're like this?"

Mil knew full well, but he wanted to hear it from Timothy. He needed to. Like so many voided before him that he'd come into contact with, the one thing that they found so unbearable was admitting why they believed they'd become tainted with the label of abomination. The truth or what they had learned was the truth, was all they needed to speak, and for all of them, that task proved far too evasive.

"I know why I'm like this. How do I fix it?" Timothy challenged. He could sense what Mil was after, but something inside of him just couldn't. It just wouldn't.

"I'm afraid there isn't an antidote for beings like us," Mil said, matter-of-fact. "But this may not be the end for you. Countless Voids live well beyond their circumstances, a decent life."

Timothy began to shake his head. "You said a lot of shit, but you ain't told me nothin'. Y'all like me, right? We the same."

"We're Voids, yes, Timothy. Except we asked for it."

He threw Mil a questioning look. Then to Aza, and to Volx, who might as well have been a statue.

"Why?..."

Aza's head dropped as he couldn't bear to look at Timothy's aching expression any longer. That question had been on repeat in his mind since that day and he still couldn't find an answer that made any sense. He couldn't speak for the others, but he was still looking for his "why."

"We specialize in maintaining the voided inventory," Mil explained. "Who's a threat and who isn't. All over the world. We're few, but so are the 'blue bloods'; the outliers. Special Voids are the ones we're really after. Those that have Faded and kept going, until they've lost themselves completely."

"What do you mean? What could be worse than I already am?"

"Well, our meaning will be up to you. Some Voids that Fade tend to remain mostly human. While others, simply don't."

"Look man, I feel exactly the same. I am exactly the same." Timothy's head darted around the room to each of the Argenta for them to see that he wasn't one of those things that had invaded the topics of their evening five, seven, and nine o'clock news broadcastings. He was the same Timothy. Bryan's Timothy.

"Really?" Mil questioned.

In a flash, Timothy's eyes shifted fearfully with the flurry of self-doubt in what he'd just proclaimed.

"The dark lights all," Mil sang, gravely.

He gave a sad smile at Timothy's realization of what he had become. His expression, neither indicating that he felt pity for the boy or indifference to his entire existence. He had a face that no emotion could get attached to. All of that seemed to be with Aza, to whom most of the Argenta left the sympathizing.

Chapter VI

ROXA HAD PUT steaming pots of comfort food in the middle of the table. Hearty aromas of thick cubes of beef in heavy gravy, fluffy buttered Jasmine rice, spicy red beans with chopped bell peppers, sautéed collard greens, and moist cornbread just out of the oven filled the air with a celebratory atmosphere.

The plates and silverware had already been laid out. She gave the setup one more once over to make sure everything was how she wanted it. There wasn't any special occasion, but getting Iela to eat dinner with them was one of the hardest chores in Roxa's daily routine. She'd always say she was going out, but never say where or she'd come in late. Sometimes she wouldn't see her for days.

"Caiden!—"

"Ma'am?"

Roxa spun around, startled. "Child, don't creep...Ie—"

"I'm right here."

"I see that," she said, giving her that signature scowl.

They all sat down at the table without a word and began making their plates. Roxa's eyes were casually ping-ponging between the two. She could see Iela fixing her mouth to say something, but decided to pick up her phone instead.

"I guess I'll ask." She turned to Caiden with a warm smile. "How you been doin' at school? You adjustin' alright?"

She looked up slightly puzzled and then saw Iela, who was already staring at Roxa before she turned to her. She was waiting for Caiden's response. Her head dropped to her plate as the gears turned.

"I'm doing okay...I've got some good teachers. Most of the stuff they teach, you already taught me, though they may teach it a little differently. But I like it so far."

"I'm relieved to hear that," she said, busily going in on a tough piece of meat.

Iela, on the other hand, maintained her poker face, just exposing the merest of twitches.

"What about friends? I know you don't say much, but you got a kind face that people wanna talk to. Just make sure not to respond to the assholes," Roxa added with an edge.

Caiden didn't expect the question and it showed. She tried to lower her head as naturally as she could without making it obvious that she was trying to hide her eyes.

"What happened?" Iela threw the question at her, assuming that if something did happen, Caiden was the cause.

"Nothing...Just on the first day, I met these girls and sat with them at lunch..." she said, lifting her head a little. "They thought I was human."

"That's good, right?" Roxa asked, looking at Iela. "Ain't that good?"

She was unsure, but Iela's expression didn't look right.

"Nothing bad happened," Caiden said in the smallest voice she'd ever made.

"Nothing yet," Iela corrected, her boiling blood creeping up her neck.

"Iela..." Roxa tried to jump in.

"What part of 'you're not supposed to exist' don't you understand?"

"Oh shut the hell up. If you didn't want her to socialize, then why'd you let her go to school in the first damn place?"

Caiden looked to her mother, hoping to finally get an explanation. She'd been asking Iela to attend public school since she was eleven. Making oaths and promises that she'd take any punishment that her mother could think of if she slipped up and caused any of them to have to move again. After several years of hearing "no" or "maybe in the next city," Iela gave Caiden a "yes" on her sixteenth birthday. She was so happy that she didn't ask why, not that she'd ask such a blunt question, but now that she was going to school, her curiosity had been getting the better of her.

"I thought that after seventeen years of everything that I taught her, she would have enough sense to know that I was doing all that because of what she is." Iela searched to find the right words. "I have to keep her safe and it would help if she thought before she did something stupid like this."

Caiden's hand grappled her fork as her body went into rigor.

Those hollow screams again.

They entered the room like a raging storm, but they were a full 180 degrees from before. In sound. It was more forceful, with more depth. Sedated.

She kept her expression fixed as not to let it show that she was hearing these things. Her mother was still talking. She prayed her eyes didn't betray her now.

"...I thought she'd make it more than a month before some shit like this happened."

"They didn't seem threatening," Caiden uttered.

Iela turned on her. "How do you know?"

She didn't answer immediately. Wondering if she should say it or not. She could never lie to Iela. Caiden had been feeling that she somehow already knew and that maybe she was ignoring it, hoping that it would go away. But Caiden just knew how people felt, even without them knowing themselves. It was impossible to make disappear the essence of who she was.

"I know," she finally said, hesitant.

Iela knew exactly what she meant.

"Caiden." Roxa had turned to her, waiting to learn more about what she, as a human, couldn't understand.

"I just know..." she said, trailing off. "Like from before...With the church."

At that moment, both Roxa and Iela fixed hard on her. Caiden could feel it, but kept her eyes low and kept going.

"I knew before it started."

"Child." Roxa was horrified as she tugged on one of Caiden's hands.

"They're Redhearts. Human. What about the voided?" Iela asked, but again, she didn't need to ask a question she already knew the answer to.

Caiden didn't want to look her mother in the eye when she was going to say what she was thinking at the moment, but she managed.

"...That pastor."

Iela's jaw locked. Roxa's head shot in her direction to catch her natural response to the mention of that dark part of both of their pasts. That pastor was someone that they never mentioned. Especially Caiden, since she'd never met him.

"What about him?" Iela said, without a hint that she knew what Caiden was talking about.

Caiden didn't say anything and Iela assumed the worst.

"Get upstairs."

She obeyed, bewildered, as Roxa slumped back in her chair. She spurted out a ridiculous laugh.

"Subtle."

Iela went searching in the kitchen cabinets for a much-needed bottle and poured herself a drink.

"Caiden doesn't lie. Now, this. Whatever this is..." She downed the glass like a shot. "I gotta head out."

"Before you go runnin' away to do all that other more important stuff than your own family, why don't you first admit what's really botherin' you?"

"Besides realizing I may have made a mistake letting her go to school?" Iela ignored that initial jab.

Roxa watched her for a moment. "Why did you let her go to school?" Her eyes flipped through mental pages for a list of possible reasons and couldn't find any. "And you gave her Mary, a prized possession of yours...And, after years of treatin' her like that chunk of steel, you hand her to the world that you've been hidin' her from, now expectin' her to protect herself."

Roxa then sat up in her seat. Iela was staring off with her drink in her hand.

"You afraid, ain't ya?"

That word didn't seem to fit Iela's outward appearance at all, but on the inside was an entirely different story. The real one. The one she'd been working to rewrite ever since Caiden was born.

"Everybody's afraid of something," she said, facing her makeshift mother. "I'm not so full of my own shit that I can't admit that. But fear has nothing to do with it. Right now, I'm trying to right a wrong."

"You up to yo' neck in 'em, ain't ya, child?"

The old woman continued to watch her and was both saddened and relieved to see that expert bravado that Iela had perfected for nearly two decades was showing some signs of wear.

"My dear, anyone can see that you scared of somethin'. It might not have to do with Caiden entirely, but she's a huge part of it."

Iela poured herself another drink.

"...The truth is, you don't know what she capable of any mo' than she do herself."

***

Aza pulled up to the curb of Timothy's apartments in Mil's silver SUV. It was well after midnight and he wanted to drop Timothy off as close to his front door as possible. The neighborhood wasn't dangerous, but it also wasn't safe either. Aza had wanted to stop to get some food, but Timothy had no desire to eat or drink anything. He was still in Mil's living room, listening to the echo of "the dark lights all" in his already crowded mind. He wondered if those words were true or if he was just being toyed with because he was new to this world. The Argenta seemed to know more about him than what they actually said and he wasn't sure if that made him feel better or not.

Timothy eyed Aza typing away on his phone. They were both the same and yet his body had a weight of something else attached to it. It was in the way he spoke and smiled and even consoled. He wondered if he'd chosen this life that was thrust upon him, would he give off that same weight-of-the-world aura that Aza possessed with such nonchalance.

Timothy's attention went outside his window when Aza looked up from his phone. He was hesitant to get out when he saw he was back outside his mother's place.

"How'd you know where I live?" he asked, resembling a zombie as he got out.

"Here."

Aza handed him a card that had the Argenta's name and number on it. He took his foot off the brake and started to move.

"Don't lose that."

"Wait."

Aza braked, already knowing what Timothy was thinking.

"What I'm supposed to do? I can't go back in there. She kicked me out."

"There is a shelter you can go to," he offered. "But it's not a place for children."

Timothy looked helpless and Aza had to stop himself from giving in.

"She works graveyard, right? Try to be gone before then."

"How..." he started to say, still drowning in confusion.

"Look, just relax. If you start to feel nauseous or anything else out of the ordinary, call the number." Aza wished he could do more, not just for Timothy, but for his brother as well, but that wasn't his job. "I gotta go."

Timothy watched as the SUV got farther away until it was out of sight. He didn't know what to expect as he walked up the stairs to his front door. He forced his knuckles to knock and his brother answered.

"Hey, man," he said a little too bright.

"Hey."

His brother was acting strange. Maybe slightly ashamed from before. He didn't even look him in the eye.

It was quiet except for the low TV as he followed him inside. The place looked the same except for his brother's pillow and blanket on the couch. The dishes were piled up in the sink and he got to work on those.

"Did mama leave yet?"

"You know she did," he said, automatically.

Timothy relaxed a little and quickened his pace. He rinsed and dried the dishes, then looked around to see what else he could do. His brother did well with picking up after himself so there wasn't anything on the living room floor, besides his game console. He lingered by the table, watching his brother fold up his blanket and set it on the arm of the couch.

"What did you eat?"

"Pizza."

Timothy went into the fridge and saw the generic pizza box, slightly opened, and got a slice before sitting next to his brother on the couch. They watched cartoons in silence.

"You can change it if you want to. My show gone off."

He looked down at his brother handing him the remote and for a moment, everything felt like old times. But his brother seemed less and less of himself the more he stared at him.

"Hey. You alright? Mama whoop you or somethin'?"

The boy shook his head as he suddenly molded himself into his brother's side.

"...I said you could change it." His voice cracked under the weight of such heavy emotion.

Timothy could feel his sleeve dampening and reached over to gently place his hand on his brother's head, soothing him. His attention never left the TV, not having the heart to face him, knowing that all of this was his fault.

Timothy's eyes began to water as well and he pulled his brother in tighter. He was surely forgiven.

They stayed like that until morning. Timothy, not wanting to wake his brother after seeing how comfortable he was buried in his side. He'd turned off the television and wrapped him in his blanket.

As if feeling how late it was, Timothy came out of his sleep like someone splashed cold water on his face, but at the same time, the knob on the front door began to jiggle. His mother was home.

Timothy's body locked up and his eyes warped to another hue.

And there was something else, but everything was happening so fast he didn't notice what it was. Not until his mother walked in and flipped on the light.

It was then that she started yelling. At the summit of her lungs, unbearable screams.

Timothy jumped off the couch, forgetting his brother, not noticing that that's where his mother was focusing all of her attention. She was shaking and had lost the ability to walk as she hit the floor. Her mouth was agape and she couldn't blink if she wanted to.

He slowly followed her wide, horrified eyes to his little brother, who was now lying on the floor, in a charred heap.

Chapter VII

CAIDEN WOKE UP and her hand went to her chest immediately. Her heart faintly glowed between her fingers as she felt its thumping beneath her skin. It was a little fast, which meant she had another dream that she could only vaguely remember or she'd been doing some nightly bedtime aerobics in her sleep. She turned her head to the side and felt the subtle unevenness of the wood on her cheek. She was on the floor, so it must've been the latter.

Her eye caught the spine of one of the few tragedies she could tolerate and saw beyond it that other books were scattered open around her. She sat up and a throw fell off of her shoulders. She saw that her blankets were hanging off the side of the bed like they'd been dragged as she got up and noticed that her stack of finished books at the head of her bed was trampled as well. Though this wasn't her first time waking up on the floor, she was certain she would've never just left her books out of place like that.

Caiden checked her watch and hurried to grab some clothes out of her closet. She cut off her lamp, left to shower and get ready for school before she headed downstairs for breakfast.

Roxa was waiting for her alone. She was quieter this morning, silently fixing Caiden's plate and pouring her a cup of tea. She assumed that the fight that they had last night went on well after she was banished to her room. That was why she never wanted to say anything about her knowing, it was bound to get people into more trouble than they were already in. The truth had always been like that, which is why Caiden mostly kept her mouth shut.

She thanked Roxa for the food and bid her goodbye before she started walking to school. When she got to Mil's class, she was one of the first people in their seats.

"Morning."

Aza had given her one of his staple toothy smiles. Not too much and not too little. It was warm and welcoming like everything was going to be okay. Caiden nodded a kind hello and focused on the front of the class until Mil started teaching, but found that a little hard as Aza was staring at her again. Well, it felt like he was. She didn't want to check, remembering the last time. No one had ever looked at her like that before that didn't know her.

"What are you doing?"

"Waiting for Mr. Gunde," she replied, giving in and looking him right in the eye.

"You're in my seat."

Caiden looked around and saw her empty desk. She got up immediately.

"Oh, I'm sorry." She sat down at her desk, patting her warm cheeks.

"You're forgiven," he said, holding back a grin. "Just don't let it happen again."

She saw his smile burst through and a small one appeared on her lips as well. A cozy cloud floated around her back and arms as she watched Aza go in his backpack for a pen. He held it over his shoulder, waving it to get her attention. It took a second for Caiden to notice that he was giving it to her. She took it and felt that cloud's embrace pull her in more.

She was about to thank him when she saw Alise come in. She nearly missed the bell as Mil had already begun writing on the whiteboard. Caiden attempted to get her attention when she sat down next to her, but something was off. Alise accidentally met her gaze and ignored her.

For the first time in her life, Caiden had never felt one of her own emotions so potent as she felt now. To feel like she wasn't there. It was an act that her mother had wanted her to embody whenever she left the house or when they were state-hopping, eluding this vague enemy that might or might not have been real. This was what it was to be invisible and Caiden didn't know if her mother was ignorant of what she was asking of her or if she was just cruel, but this couldn't have been for her own protection.

Mil's classes felt like they were just there to copy what was on the board and listen to him summarize each of their textbook chapters for an hour. The bell for her next class couldn't ring fast enough.

Caiden stumbled around in her head about what had happened with Alise as she walked into the cafeteria. She spotted her two friends and stopped in her tracks. At first, she turned around to head in the opposite direction but thought she'd try to ask them about Alise instead.

"Hey," she said, her voice tiny.

They didn't even turn around. The longer she stood there waiting to be acknowledged, the more obvious their energies began to resemble Alise's. It seemed Caiden didn't exist to them anymore either.

Dejected, standing there like an idiot, she finally walked away. One of the girls glanced back at her to make sure she got the hint, but there was also a faint look of pity in her eyes.

Caiden sat down at the end of a table alone and began to eat. Thoughts of both her encounters with Alise played over and over again in her head. She wondered about the things she did and said and only the incident at lunch made the most sense. Caiden flinched as those seconds of embarrassment soared through her mind. She wondered why she'd said anything. It wasn't like Alise would've answered her, no one else heard the screams. She shook her head some more and tried to eat. Roxa must've been feeling awful. There were two brownies in her lunch bag today. She didn't feel like enjoying anything right now, so she didn't touch either one.

She sat there, watching the students enjoy and pretend to enjoy the company of their peers, while a few tables behind her, David had been watching her since she entered the cafeteria. Caiden felt a pull towards his direction and looked his way, but he was already heading out the door.

***

The death of the little human boy by his big Void brother didn't take long to hit every news outlet within a hundred-mile radius.

Timothy had found his way back to his apartments where a crowd had accumulated across the street from his building. He had on a hoodie and tried to blend in. He saw the ambulance leaving the gate, passing a couple of TV news vans that were parked farther up the curb. That same curb where Aza had dropped him off not even twelve hours before.

He felt the onset of tears. He'd been replaying that image of his brother falling to the floor and his mother burying her face in his blackened chest. Timothy felt dizzy, physically, and emotionally sick. He had to get away.

As soon as he turned around to leave, he found himself face to face with some done-up zaftig. Her makeup was minimal but packed on pretty thick and she was staring back at Timothy full of sincerity, like she'd been reading his mind.

"You look like you could use some help," she said, her voice lowered some.

"Nah, I'm good."

He started to leave again, but the lady nearly got in his ear.

"Timothy, ain't it?"

He turned on her, breaking out in a sweat.

"Keep it together," the woman said, glancing around at the crowd. "Meet me at Faber's in an hour."

Timothy was about to turn her down again, but she gave him one last enduring look before she disappeared out of the crowd. He watched her leave, not sure if he should be on his guard or not, whatever that meant. He had no idea who that lady was, but her eyes. Though she didn't flash them in front of the crowd and cameras, he could feel that they were sharing the same pain.

He found himself at the front door of the homey ma and pop deli. There were maybe three or four people there. Hands-on types that worked around the neighborhood on lawns and indoor plumbing. A flatscreen sitting lonesome on an empty dessert cart was showing a news reporter just outside Timothy's place. The chyron at the bottom of the screen read: "Another Child 'Voided' By Black Death."

Timothy gathered what little courage he had and went inside, glimpsing the beefy wide back of Faber himself through the open kitchen door. He spotted the lady instantly as she was the only woman in there. She was sitting at a table, pouring sugar in her coffee. Wary, Timothy sat down across from her.

"You should get a cup," she said, looking like she wanted to hand over her own to the poor boy.

"Who are you?"

"You really should," she offered again. No matter how much she wanted to save face, that side of her was difficult to stomp out.

"Who are you?" he repeated.

"You know I'm a Void or you wouldn't be here," the lady said. "I'm not gonna tell you who I am. I'm not even gonna tell you my name, cuz none of that matters. Just know we're the same..." She let that float in the air before she got more to the point. "I can help you."

"You don't know nothin' about me."

"I know you killed your brother."

She didn't mean to play that card so soon, but Timothy looked like he had already given up. It didn't get the reaction that she wanted. Silent tears started to fall down his face. The lady handed him a napkin, but his sleeve caught them first.

"It's gonna be fine, son..." she consoled, watching him wipe away his tears. "But you see how the media's spinning it. That's how I found you. So how long do you think it's gonna take for them to do it if your mother hasn't already given you up."

His face indicated she would in a heartbeat. She most likely already had. "...I should turn myself in."

"That's even worse," she said, anticipating his response. "Then the police'll have you and anyone above them will have their stake, too."

Timothy sunk further down into his shoulders. He knew that what she was saying was true, especially for someone like him. Not only was he out of options, but even if he somehow was to obtain any sort of get-out-of-jail-free card, he didn't deserve to use it.

Then, a light bulb burst in his head.

"Argenta."

The lady read his face after a moment, the name of those eleventh-hour saviors ringing a bell that hadn't been rung in several years. And like that, she realized that some pieces of Timothy's light bulb had made its way across the deli table.

"...Argenta," she repeated, her voice dropping several decibels.

"You know them?"

The lady's hand fidgeted with her coffee cup. "Not personally. But I've heard the name mentioned around a few Dantean circles."

"What does that mean?" he asked, as his spirits hit the floor.

He watched the lady try to settle back down and felt a chill prick his spine at the thought of his last visit to Mil's house. Seeing another person react this bad when they hadn't even met them, caused the little gratitude he did feel towards them to diminish completely.

"Me and the Argenta have a very different definition of what helping is." She paused to sip her drink. "What did they say? Or I should ask, what did they want?"

"They said somethin' about me bein' stuck like this. Sayin' I can't change who I am."

"Really?" she asked, intrigued.

Timothy looked her in the eye and he got a rush of something he never thought he'd feel again. Hope. The lady could see that she had reeled him in and now all she needed to do was hook him.

"You know what wasn't in the news was how you did it." She leaned in and Timothy, whose hands had been clasped on top of the table, slid them off so they fell between his thighs. "Timothy."

His head dropped and he balled up his hands into fists. He felt the tears coming again, but he fought them as if he was putting knuckle to jaw. "...He felt bad cuz he snitched on me. I wasn't even mad at him. I don't think I've ever been since he was born." His voice cracked and he sunk lower.

"Everything happens for a reason."

"I'm really not tryin' to hear that shit right now."

He lifted his head and glared at her, but she was too focused on Timothy the Void, not Timothy the big brother.

"I believe I was supposed to find you, Timothy. You with your hands and me with..." She trailed off and leaned in a little closer, so close that Timothy had to straighten up a bit. "Do you know what we are, Timothy?"

"They called me a blue blood," he said, eyeing her more warily than when he first sat down. The look in her eye had suddenly changed.

"No, Timothy." It was getting harder to hide her excitement with each passing second. "We are more than that. We're blessed. We're the elect."

Timothy felt his body jolt into flight mode at the spark in the lady's eye. He glanced out of the window and spotted a cop car patrolling past the deli.

"I gotta get outta here."

"Hold on," the lady said, grabbing his sleeve.

Without thinking, he touched her hand just to free himself and saw smoke rise from the contact. Timothy, eyes bulging, let her go and ran out the door. The lady cradled her shaky, seared hand in her lap as she watched him sprint out the deli, the opposite way of the cops.

***

Mil, Aza, and Volx were sitting in front of takeout at their kitchen table. They were all holding hands. Though their heads were bowed in a moment of silent prayer, Aza couldn't help but glance at the pair of bowls and spoons drying on the counter.

"Amen," they all said and began to eat.

"He called," Aza said as he got up to open the cabinet by the fridge. There was a box of cereal missing from the top shelf. He went back to his seat as his eye landed on Mil, who always looked unfazed whenever he delivered any sort of good news. "But you knew that already," Aza added. "You know everything." That part was said more to himself, but it was no use as their home seemed to always be so quiet.

Volx took care of Aza's plate and of course, he got a cute smile in return. He wasn't trying to be adorable, but the soldier had that effect on him. Aza was going to have to admit one of these days that he liked Volx more than any sane person should.

"Blasphemy," Mil finally answered, not in the slightest bit playing along. "Not everything."

Knock. Knock. Knock.

They didn't break the rhythm, except Volx, who left first. He opened the front door and Timothy was standing there, his hands still balled up. Mil came up on the side of Volx and took in his disheveled appearance.

"We were expecting you sooner," he said, motioning him inside. "And I take it my directions were clear."

"Yes, sir..."

He didn't have the courage to meet their gaze as he went and sat on the couch. It was gradually sinking in that he was a murderer. He dared not lift his head to anyone.

"...Oh, man. This don't feel right...This not right..."

"Timothy, have you come into contact with anyone else?" Aza asked.

"I don't wanna hurt nobody else," he said, heavy with despair.

"We'll put you up here," Mil said. He didn't like where Timothy's head was. He was disappearing right before their eyes.

"Then what?" He lifted his head, managing to give Mil a little eye contact. The man spoke like he held his future in the palm of his hand.

"Then...we all must do what needs to be done." Mil shot a look to Aza, whose eyes he felt on him. "Aza will help you get settled in."

He obeyed and went towards the doorway entering the hall, but Timothy didn't budge.

"...A woman came to me today...said not to trust you."

The Argenta didn't respond through any form of expression. Timothy did look at them just for their reaction, but all he got was the same show he got the last time he was there. Then, he thought about what Mil said. The Argenta had been alive for so long, he wondered how many Timothys had sat where he was sitting now and began to wonder where they were and if they had survived the "what needs to be done."

"Do you, Timothy?" Mil finally asked.

He wasn't sure. All he knew for certain was that the atmosphere between them and that lady was no doubt different, but it was also the same, which just confused him even more.

"Right now, I ain't got no choice."

He got up and followed Aza out of the room. He gave him a change of clothes and offered him a shower, but he couldn't accept. Doing anything from his old life, before he was a Void and before he killed his brother, didn't seem natural. Even eating or tying his shoes was not something he could take on without feeling some sort of guilt.

That was what humans did.

As the night waned on, Timothy's conscience had gotten the best of him. The next morning, Mil found the Argenta's calling card on the coffee table and Timothy's bed without a wrinkle in sight.

Chapter VIII

THE ARGENTA PILED into Volx's truck and went driving around looking for Timothy. For the first time in Mil's incredibly long life, he was taken by surprise. No one had ever purposely gotten away from the Argenta and he didn't know whether or not he should be bothered. The special ones also didn't take as long as Timothy did to reveal that they were special. Right off it would be clear to Mil how they would go about dealing with a Void that possessed enhanced abilities, but it had never gotten this far. It had never made them change their routine of save, evaluate, and resolve.

"How'd he leave?" Aza asked, his head shooting from Mil to Volx. "This has never happened before, right?"

They all kept their eyes peeled out on the blurred streets as they zoomed down the road.

"He has nowhere else to go."

"I'm afraid he does," Mil said, his gears turning. "Volx, the nearest police station from our house."

"Approximately six point five miles, two-point thirty-four miles from our current location." Volx gassed a u-turn before he finished his calculations.

They'd gotten to the neighborhood precinct and parked the truck a block or two away from the building.

"What makes you think he'll be here?" Aza asked, getting out and already analyzing people to see if they matched Timothy's height and description.

"There was never a third option. He has no idea what he's about to do."

Mil began to casually search the perimeter of the building, studying passersby that looked similar to Timothy, while Aza went to look inside. Volx just kept up with his nose.

After minutes had passed, Aza came out of the building with nothing to show for it and that's when they all began moving outward from the police station and toward the streets. Mil's attention was caught by a bus coming up. He watched as each person got off and noticed a hoodie. He followed it with Volx, and Aza eventually coming up behind him.

"Gait analysis is eighty-one percent," Volx stated.

"That must be him," Aza said, stopping himself from running to the stranger.

The closer the person got to the police building, the more certain that Mil was that it was Timothy.

Suddenly, the hoodie started to slow down and changed routes to go onto another street. The Argenta continued after and the hoodie picked up his pace.

"Timothy," Mil called out.

He stopped dead in place for a few seconds before he spun around and threw back his hood. Both of his hands shot up on either side of his face, tempting. Praying.

"I'm gonna turn myself in. Get back!" His eyes were darting frantically from Aza to Mil to Volx.

"You don't know what you're doing," Mil said, the epitome of calm. He'd been waiting for this since they met.

"They lookin' for me. My time been runnin' out." Timothy broke down. "...I didn't mean to kill 'em. It just happened..."

"We know that, Timothy, but they don't." Mil carefully took a step forward.

Timothy jumped back, his hands now closer to his face. "Stay away or I'm a do it! I swear!"

Aza glanced at Mil, who didn't seem the least bit concerned.

"Timothy." He took another step toward him, aware of his shaky hands. "I know what your endgame is, but it's not going to match up with theirs."

"That woman told me what y'all about— Don't!"

Volx's arm had shot out across Aza's chest, stopping him from taking another step forward.

"You'll die in there."

"Yeah? And what's gonna happen to me out here?"

He didn't respond, hoping that Mil had another plan other than trying to provoke an already agitated blue blood, but it didn't seem likely as he took another step toward Timothy.

"I told you to stop."

Right then, Timothy squeezed his eyes tight and his hands sprawled open on either side of his head. With all his might he tried to crush both sides of his skull, as he welcomed the fire to take him over.

The Argenta watched and waited with bated breath for something to happen.

But it didn't.

Confused, Timothy began backing away, gaping wide-eyed at what he thought was the source of his mysterious newfound power. But his hands were now just what he'd hoped they'd always remain. Human.

He snapped out of it and sprinted down the street.

Volx, gunning for action, looked to Mil for orders.

"Leave him," he said, watching the boy running for his life.

"Help! Somebody help! Help me!"

Timothy's head jutted up and down the empty street. He was definitely in the wrong place to be making such a spectacle. A few curtains rustled through the windows of the nice red brick homes with manicured lawns and recycling bins. And soon enough, sirens blared out in the distance.

"Jais."

Before Mil finished his own call for assistance, a cop car skidded around the corner and down the street, heading straight for them. The Argenta simply stepped aside. The cop didn't see them at all.

He got out of the car and saw Timothy, who'd stopped running after he heard the sirens. He looked around even more crazed than before.

The Argenta were gone.

"Hey. What's the problem?" The cop naturally had one hand on his gun.

"I'm sorry—"

"Okay, what happened? What's the problem—"

"I did it. I killed him..." Timothy sputtered, drowning in his confession. "I killed him..."

Before Timothy could take any more steps forward, the cop had whipped out his weapon and pointed it at him. But the boy's mind wasn't on the cop or the gun, or even on that moment. It was on his dead brother. His tears were blinding him at this point and right then, the worst thing that could've happened, did.

Timothy's eyes shifted. They changed right in front of the cop, who just happened to be a human, and in a blink—

Bang!

He watched as Timothy's breath got caught in his throat, his tears stifled as he gawked at the cop, astonished. Neither he nor the man could break the other's gaze. He almost looked betrayed. He was just trying to make it right.

Blood started pouring out of the wound above Timothy's ribs as the cop sheathed his weapon and scrambled across the pavement.

"Shit," he panicked.

Timothy dropped to his knees, clawing at the man's uniform, still staring up at him. His eyes changed again and again. It was impossible for the cop to look away and Timothy made sure he didn't.

He gently helped him onto his back and checked to see how bad the wound was, though it was quite obvious.

"Hold on. Please, hold on." He prayed that his words were coherent because all the blood was making him lose his mind. "I need somebody down here! Now! It's all over the place," he spat into his walkie talkie.

Two more cop cars careened into the neighborhood as people began coming out of their houses and peeking through their curtains. The Argenta, who'd never left, continued to watch the entire scene play out. Now, Timothy was no longer a threat. To anyone.

Another child voided by black death.

***

The bell had rung and Caiden spilled out of her classroom door with the rest of the students, but something began to feel wrong. She had found herself in an anxious atmosphere that was slowly being taken over with news of their fallen peer. Timothy's body hadn't gotten safe inside the ambulance yet and already Myerworth was talking about how the child killer was now dead himself.

Caiden felt stifled beneath all the malicious whispering and had to get out of there. She walked out of the front doors and inhaled deeply, taking in the fresh non-toxic air. David had seen her from across the street by accident and continued to watch her again.

But just as her heartbeat started to steady itself, a hollow cry wailed out against her eardrums. Except for this time, it was piercing and soft.

Caiden stood there and listened.

"You know what'll happen if you're late," The Voice said.

"Wait..."

She looked around at the crowd, but couldn't find that familiar energy. She began walking down the steps and toward the side of the building where the track was. Bryan was there, staring at his phone. He looked like he wanted to be anywhere else, but where he was. He kept walking until he clipped the corner of the rusting fence. Caiden felt her heart swelling as she began to go to him.

"Caiden," The Voice said.

But she refused to listen. The sound of her heart seemed to overpower her ability to reason. She watched as Bryan began to cry and sink to his knees. He began to beat himself in the gut with the bottom of his fist. He kept pounding and pounding.

Caiden wanted to keep her distance, but Bryan had caught her in another crying fit. He was trying to catch his breath, but not even his broad stature could keep down those aching cries. He didn't care that she was there watching him do something that not even his family had seen before. Once he saw her eyes, he began to cry even more.

"...I didn't know...Timothy," he choked. "I didn't..."

"...I'm sorry."

That's the only thing she could say and it didn't want to come out. She said it as if it was her fault. Like she was the cause of his and Timothy's misfortune and his suffering. Bryan locked eyes with Caiden as he watched in total abandonment as his pain crossed her face. Then and only then, for the first time in his life, someone knew exactly how he felt.

***

Iela sat in her car, parked a little ways down the street outside of Piccolos, the only Void-friendly bar in the city and possibly the state. This place, a refuge to not just Voided outcasts, but human ones as well — read as humans that were also Void-friendly — was a sort of reformed old film house. It was a church in the eye of the beholder and since most of those eyes could change colors, it didn't matter what the people thought of it whose eyes couldn't perform the taboo magic trick.

She looked up at the words "Welcome to the Void" on its old-time theater-sized sign and nostalgia washed over her. It had been some years since she had strutted through those doors. She hated she was back now, but this was something she had to do to protect what was hers. At least that's what she kept telling herself. Ever since Caiden started school, she felt the schism that had been present between them grow considerably with each day. It was getting out of control and there was only one person that could get it back.

Iela pulled a tiny handgun out of her glove compartment but had to stop herself. She didn't want to put on a distressed front. Her eyes followed the security guard and a few people outside smoking by the entrance. She felt the synthy blues that reverberated through the bar's bricks flow down the sidewalk and into her car's tires. Iela hurried and stepped out of her car before she lost her nerve. The fact that this man made her lose anything was already a sign that she shouldn't be there.

She kept pulling the form-fitting LBD down and scrunching up her toes in the six-inch strappy heels as she eyed the guard. He kept shoving a drunk away from the door until he gave up and stumbled on his plastered way. It had been a while since she dawned such risqué attire, but she needed as much of a confidence boost as she could get if she was going to face this brief, indelible part of her past again.

She started to make her way to the front when she noticed one of the employees throwing out the trash from the side door. Iela switched gears and walked down the side of the bar where the door was and knocked on it. The music was too loud, so she banged a couple more times and waited.

"Iela?"

A stranger had come out of the shadows as Iela turned around to see who that unfamiliar voice belonged to when—

Shwep.

Right in the gut.

Her knees buckled and she hit the ground.

"Fuck..."

She caught a glimpse of some dirty white Chucks as she tried to apply pressure over the bullet hole, but the black blood now oozing between her fingers was gradually turning red as it stained her semi-new dress and the pavement.

Her eyes turned a milky white as she bled outside the Void-welcoming bar.

***

Mil and Aza were gathered in their living room. They had barely left their spots from the time they got home after the shooting. Each of them were thinking of what they could've done differently and how Timothy was able to just walk out of their front door in the first place.

Something was wrong.

Ever since their first encounter with Caiden, things were not turning out how they were supposed to.

Aza peeked out of the window as Volx's truck lights shined through the frilly drapes. Seconds later, he came through the door.

"The woman?" Mil asked, wasting no time.

"Her scent ends at Faber's."

Mil stared off, lost in thought. "No matter. We have the Soul to contend with now."

"And his Arch," Aza added, not hiding his uneasiness. The feeling was mutual as Volx's jaw tightened at the mention of the creature. "Once he shows up, it might be impossible to get near her."

"You let me take care of that," Mil said, absentmindedly. "For now, let's turn in. It's been a very troublesome day."

Aza began ripping off his clothes and left for his room as if waiting to hear those words. Volx followed after once he saw he was no longer needed. Mil looked toward the hall, waiting to hear their doors close and there was an aching silence before he turned back around.

At his feet, a bowed figure was waiting.

"*Thiere,*" Mil thought.
"*Master... He's here.*"

***

It was already two months that Caiden had been at Myerworth and it seemed like the number of students had dropped noticeably within each month. She could tell as she rushed toward the girls' locker room for the gym. It was her last class of the day and the only one she didn't like as much because she had to take off her clothes. She hurried past the lockers and into one of the stalls before the other girls got there.

She was early, so no one was there yet. She supposed she had Timothy to thank for that. The school had been offering to counsel anyone that needed to talk after what happened. Of course, some of the students, mainly the humans, were taking it as an opportunity to skip class or just not come to school at all, so Caiden didn't know how to feel about her nearly empty gym class this period because she was also able to change without feeling self-conscious.

She opened her briefcase and pulled out her gym clothes. Just some sweat set she got from home, and she began to change like she was being timed. As soon as she pulled off her top, the lights went out.

Her heart illuminated the stall and she smothered it as fast as she could. She shoved her top back on before she froze and listened.

It was silent except for her pulse beating in her ears. She looked down out of habit and pressed down on her sweatshirt. Caiden had taken to wearing a thick undershirt as an extra precaution, not letting the sweat bother her, just as long as it provided more coverage.

Everything was quiet for a long while. She thought at least a few other girls would've shown up already.

Suddenly, the door was kicked in and she was blinded by lights that were being shoved in her face. From what she could see, they were from cell phones.

She felt someone grab her hair as a familiar screaming filled the locker room. So loud that it pierced Caiden's eardrums directly. And that's when she felt who her bully was.

"Alise," she pleaded as her feet were snatched from under her.

But the girl didn't say anything, it was just the screams from her past. She was too focused on what she needed to do. It was the only thing that was making her feel better; making her feel avenged.

Caiden couldn't make out if what she was hearing was intelligible or not, too focused on the emotions that they were encumbered with. She was dragged across the floor by one of her legs. The air was knocked out of her. A kick in the back. The face. Alise had brought her friends.

She felt her top being tugged at and she shrunk into the fetal position immediately. If nothing else, she had to protect her light.

Echoes from Alise's past raged against Caiden's ears, attacking from all sides. She curled tighter into a ball, taking what seemed like endless blows. At the same time, their hate was coming off in waves.

But so was their sadness.

Something had happened to them, something horrible, at the hands of the Voided. Caiden couldn't imagine what those terrible things were, but she understood, and that's why she took it all in. If she could do nothing for the suffering they had been put through already, she wouldn't at that moment be grouped in the same category as the Voids that caused them to suffer in the past.

She started to feel the beating intensifying, but she also felt something else. There was peace coming over her. A familiar warmth began to move her way, searching for her. Alise and her friends seemed to have felt it, too. Their kicking and punching tapered off until it eventually stopped.

Pure silence.

Then, a light slowly began to take over the locker room. Caiden lifted her head with caution, her eyes were a deep maroon and full of tears. There was nowhere to look where the light wasn't.

But she saw, almost floating, fiery, royal blue eyes. They were coming toward her, but she was too transfixed to be afraid. She nearly wanted to run towards them as all her pain disappeared at that moment.

And in a flash, everything went white.

Chapter IX

"CAIDEN?..."

Caiden's eyes gently slid open as she adjusted to her lamp light. She looked around her room, then down at her clothes. They were the same. Even her boots were still on. She sat up and realized she had been lying in bed from foot to head. It took a moment as everything that happened came rushing back. She sprung up out of bed and out the door for the bathroom.

She locked it behind her and got as close as she could to the mirror so that her breath began to fog it up. Her cut had healed like it was never there. She hesitated before lifting her top to study her sides and whatever of her back she could see while turning around in the mirror.

Nothing.

"...Cai."

"Caiden," The Voice called.

"Yeah?"

"Where did you go?"

She stood there staring at herself, trying to force back into her mind the memories she'd lost. After a minute or two, she was getting a headache.

"I'm fine."

"That wasn't the question."

"Child, you in there?"

She jumped and spun around in the mirror again to make sure her top was all the way down.

"Caiden?"

She cracked the door a little and saw Roxa staring at her with concern.

"I didn't hear you come in. You alright? You not sick or nothin' are you?"

"No, ma'am, I'm not sick," she said carefully.

Roxa eyed her a moment, but she remained natural.

"Okay...Well, come down and eat."

"Yes, ma'am."

She lingered a second before heading back downstairs and Caiden closed the door. She could tell Roxa wasn't convinced at all.

"Are you sure you're okay?" The Voice asked.

"No..."

Caiden took a shower and got changed before she met Roxa at the dining table. She saw her look down the hall before she sat in her seat.

"She's not here yet?" she asked, picking up an asparagus stalk off her plate and biting the head. Her stomach thanked her with a grumble.

"That's what it look like. Not even a call...I just wanna strangle her sometimes." She glanced at Caiden and backtracked. "But I'm sure she fine."

She exchanged a worried look with Roxa before she fully dug in.

A few seconds later, the doorbell rang.

She stiffened.

"We have a doorbell," she said, going to the door to peek out of the window. "Your heart," she whispered.

Caiden ran down the hall to a closet and grabbed a thick flannel. She rushed back so Roxa could see she was decent.

A small smile appeared on her lips before she opened the door and stood face to face with Aza.

"Uh, evening. I'm sorry for the hour, but I'm here to see Caiden?" He lifted Caiden's briefcase. "She forgot this."

"Oh, ain't you a sweetheart," she said, backing up to let him in. "You ain't have to do all that. Please come on in here."

Aza waited for Roxa and followed her inside the house.

"Your name, child?"

"Aza," he said, then grinned. "Yours?"

"Roxa is fine," she said, slightly tickled.

Caiden was standing awkwardly next to her chair, the buttons on her flannel off by one. She didn't miss the look of relief on Aza's face when their eyes met.

"Look. Aza's here."

He lifted her briefcase again. "You left this."

He held it out to her and it was a moment before she took it. They accidentally touched and she was struck with a bolt of energy. Both their eyes met in brief surprise.

"...Thank you," she said, softly.

"We was just about to dig in. You more than welcome to a plate." She'd already started scooping the dirty rice before she offered.

Caiden eyed Roxa before going back to Aza. His gaze never strayed from her since he came into the room.

"No, thank you. My dad's already got a plate waiting for me back home."

"Maybe another time, then?"

"Absolutely," he said with a warm smile.

"Thank you, again," Caiden said. For some reason, she felt she had to repeat herself.

"You're always welcome. I'll see you at school." Then, he turned to Roxa. "Good night."

"Caiden, see the boy out now."

Her tone was polite, but Caiden did sense she was being pushed.

"Yes, ma'am."

Aza followed her to the door as she slipped on some old sneakers and they headed out. Her eyes naturally went to the street, but Iela's car wasn't there.

"Nice house."

"Yeah, it's nice."

Caiden waited for him to say something else, but he seemed to be actually admiring her home. When he did look at her, it was the same look he gave her in the cafeteria on her first day.

"I'm happy you're okay."

She crossed her arms to stop herself from reacting, but that was a reaction in itself.

"Why wouldn't I be okay?"

He didn't answer, but waited for her instead. It would be better if her curiosity led the conversation.

"How'd you know where I lived?"

"Your address was on those sheets that we filled out on the first day."

"You remembered my address?"

"I remember a lot of things," he said, carefully.

She relaxed a little and her arms loosened, but she didn't let them fall, not knowing what else to do with them. When she looked back at Aza, he was still staring at her.

"...You're a Void like me."

"Sort of," he said, loosening up a bit himself. "You seem to like being a Void."

"You don't? It doesn't feel like there's much of a difference."

"Wow, morbid. I like that."

Caiden patted one of her cheeks and he smiled. He then started swinging one of his legs around until he nearly fell over. Laughed to himself. Caiden watched him as her arms completely dropped to her sides.

"What are you feeling right now?"

The question flew out of her mouth. She was so used to already having answers to that question and found it odd that she couldn't feel Aza's energy.

"I'm feeling like I don't wanna go home," he said without a thought. He pulled out his phone to check the time when he got a text message. "And it looks like I have to."

"Oh," she said, her tone falling. "...Well, thank you for bringing over my stuff. I mean, it's not really mine. It's Roxa's."

"That's three times you've thanked me."

"Sorry." She didn't know what else to say.

"How about having dinner with my family? If you're really thankful. Or sorry," he said, offering with confidence.

She didn't know what to say. It's not like she could just make decisions like this on her own without endangering herself and her family.

"Caiden," she heard The Voice call.

"I don't know if I can."

"Think about it...Because I know you felt that," he said, casually closing the distance between them.

Caiden looked up at him a moment without a word, trying again and again to get a sense of what kind of person he was. But there was nothing speaking to her; nothing reaching out that she could hold onto.

"Aza..."

Right then, she saw headlights turn down her street and was about to rush back inside, until the car pulled into the house in front of it just to back out and turn around. Her eyes slowly went back to normal as she calmed down.

"You're really sensitive, aren't you?" He'd glanced behind him as the car drove off her street.

"I don't mean to be."

He took another step forward to where he was at a comfortable distance in front of her.

"I know."

She gazed up at him again and was about to finish what she was saying before that car came along, but his phone vibrated. It was a call this time.

"'Scuse me," he said and answered it.

"Go ahead."

She was hoping he'd turn around or step off to the side or something, but he just stood in front of her and talked on the phone like the call was for the both of them.

"Yeah, I'm still here," he said, grinning down at her. "Okay... Mm-hmm." He hung up.

"That your father?"

He nodded a sad affirmative. "Um, you mind if I call you? I mean like we exchange numbers."

"Why?"

"Uh, to talk," he said, flustered. "If you want, I mean. About homework...Or anything else."

That seemed to be a stupid question, so she tried to remedy it as best she could. This would've been easier if she could read him.

"We don't have a phone in our house. Just my mother."

"Oh." His voice had dropped an octave.

"What are you doing?"

"Apparently trying too hard," he laughed to himself. "I'll see you at school."

Caiden watched him turn on his heel and head toward Mil's SUV.

"Thank you."

She said it a little too loud and he fought back another smile.

"Any time." He got in the SUV and started it up. "Good night, Caiden."

She couldn't tell if he was still sore about what she'd said, but headed toward her front door anyway. Caiden glanced down at her watch and couldn't believe how long they'd spoken. She got inside the house and thought Aza was going to leave, but he didn't. She realized he wasn't going to drive off until she closed the door.

But before she did, their eyes fixed on each other one more time and Aza suddenly flashed those deep violets again. That's when everything slowed down, just like before.

She felt something, more than what she felt when they were inside. More than she felt from any other person in her life.

Pure good.

When she came back to the dining room, Roxa was giving her one of those smiles that indicated something more was going on than what was actually going on. She took off the flannel and hung it back in the hall closet. Her heart was glowing brighter than before.

"I know that was outta his way."

"Yeah, I don't think he'll do it again." Caiden got back to her plate, hoping he wouldn't. She kept her hand over her light the entire time.

"What's the matter?"

"Nothing," she said, removing her hand. It wasn't that bright so she prayed Roxa wouldn't notice.

"Classmate?"

"Uh, yes ma'am. Government. I sit behind him." She glanced up at Roxa from her plate, wondering what she was getting at. It took a moment since the feeling wasn't that strong, but Caiden felt Roxa thought that there was something between her and Aza, though she had no idea what.

"I see," she said, pouring Caiden and herself some tea. "Well, whatever he is, that was real kind of him to bring back our stuff. Willy couldn't stand to lose things."

Caiden looked up at Roxa. She seemed like she wanted to say something else, but didn't.

"That earlier," The Voice said. "I felt it, too."

She sipped her tea feeling a little bit better at the thought of that. But there was a big difference between sharing something just in thought rather than having it coupled with the physical touch of another person only a few steps away.

Caiden had no idea what that was between her and Aza. Nothing had ever happened like that before. Even her heart knew it. The only thing she did know with certainty was that Aza knew more about her than she ever learned or will learn from her mother. And that was more than enough to say yes to dinner with him.

Chapter X

THE BAR WAS at full capacity tonight. Burnt bamboo double and quad tables were proportionately placed in front of a lapis accented stage with velvet curtains scalloped to lazy perfection. There were so many people that they lined the walls with sweating bottles in hand, waiting for a chair or two to open up. That was a consistent milestone for Nova, Piccolos' most recent house singer. She'd only been there for a few months, but her voice had brought in new patrons.

She was belting some R&B soul classic from the sixties, dressed to the nines in one of her signature maxi gowns. Her faux rhinestone jewelry shimmered as the adjustable lights hanging from the ceiling hit her at the most devastating of angles. She sat at a table with a few beer bellies playing cards while a regular held the mic for her, sometimes tipsily ad-libbing along.

Everyone was used to her kind of performance, nonchalant about the presentation, but her singing was flawless and full of emotion. She looked out at the small crowd, smirking at the sea of shifting hues. Nova folded and gently patted the head of the winner. The song was coming to an end as she headed for the stage. She was taking off her earrings and gloves as she sat down to relieve her mic stand with a ruby kiss on the cheek. That was the start of her nighttime routine.

She finished and blew kisses to the audience. They whistled and applauded as she headed to the bar to pick up a drink that was already waiting for her. The Bluetooth speakers filled the dead air with down-home blues.

"You know you always speak to me up there," the bartender said with a gushing leer. He'd set his phone back on the dock after starting up his bourbon playlist.

"Sweetie, you don't have to kiss it. I already like you."

They both smiled as she took a sip, getting invigorated as the heat climbed down her parched throat.

"Mm, wet," she approved, patting his hand.

She continued toward the back and gingerly took off her curly fro revealing a handful of chunky two-strand twists pinned down with bobby pins. Nova stopped to peek inside the ladies' room and saw two women sitting on the counter. One of them was on her knees, straddling one of the sinks.

"Mira, that ain't no two-glass. Why you tryin' so hard?"

Mira's daisy dukes and tube top were a size or two too small. She threw Nova an annoyed eye roll as she continued applying her thick eyeliner.

"I'm waiting on my check," she spat. "And get the fuck outta here. It don't matter how much clown makeup you put on your face, you still can't sit on these toilet seats."

The church mouse wrung her hands as she watched their regular back and forth.

"Heffa, you don't work here and I can sit this sexy ass wherever I want. Ain't that right, Rane?" She gave the timid girl a wink to let her know that they wouldn't be making a trip to the emergency room tonight.

"I danced here the other night— Last Friday, matter fact. You know, you was here..." she smiled licking lipstick off her teeth. "You couldn't keep your eyes off me."

"Who?"

"Tell Piccolo to stop fucking with my money. Everybody in here knows I'm the top biller in this bitch."

"Was," Nova teased and stuck out her tongue.

Mira, who'd been talking to Nova in the mirror, turned around to face her. "You gonna tell him or not? You owe me."

"Coco is a hell of a drug," she said, finger detangling her wig. "I don't owe you shit. I dropped you off one night cuz you ain't have no bus fare—"

"My car was in the shop—"

"And I saw that little flimsy hiring sign Piccolo had on the door when I tossed your ass out my car." Nova made sure Mira was looking at her. "Same night, I walked in and hit 'em with a few vibratos while he was adding me to the schedule that weekend."

They fixed on each other as the already present tension between them got thicker.

"I ain't never needed help from anybody like you, understand?"

Mira tossed her hairspray drenched waves over her shoulder like a petulant child. "Well, if I knew Piccolo was that way..."

"Mira." Rane had felt like she was herself provoked and turned to Nova, hoping she wouldn't bite the bait.

"What way is that?"

Mira kept her back to her and continued applying her makeup, though she was finished. Nova was already taller and broader than her. Her four and half-inch heels made her even more formidable.

"Are you going to ask him or not?"

"Bitch— Yeah, I'll get right on that. Rane, you off now?" Nova brushed a stray lock from around Rane's small face. "You live too far to be stayin' this late."

"I got an hour left...And, Nova, you were beautiful up there. Really."

"Girl, you better stop before I grab them cheeks," she laughed, marinating in that high praise.

Rane gave a shy smile and began redoing her ponytail in the mirror.

"She'll do it, too. Hard," Mira said, speaking from experience.

Rane couldn't tell if she was joking or not.

"Bitch, shut up." She turned to Rane again. "Have a good night, okay? Text me when you get home."

"Don't forget," Mira persisted.

"Anything for Selena," Nova sang and closed the door.

She continued to sip her drink, thinking of how Mira loathed being compared to the late bombshell of which she looked nothing alike. Nova's smirk endured as she kept walking towards the back. She got to a door at the end of the hall and opened it.

"Get in here, quick."

Startled, Nova got inside Piccolo's office and locked the door behind her. His dirty blond hair was covering his face as he was carrying a body over to his desk. His voice was steady, but she didn't know how as he was holding what looked like a corpse.

Nova watched him lay Iela's dead body on his desk. "Piccolo..." she managed to get out, not sure what the hell she just walked in on.

"Lock the door, please."

"It is. What the fuck is that?"

He pulled himself up to his desk. Nova hovered over his shoulder as he examined the wound. It was too bloody to really see anything. All Nova could think about was how it wasn't gonna ruin the dead woman's already black ensemble.

Piccolo opened one of his drawers to pull out a first aid kit and tweezers.

"Do I need to call somebody, cuz she look fuckin' dead."

He gave her an assuring smile. "It does look that way," he said, as he turned back to concentrate on the wound. He hopped out of the chair to grab a bottle of vodka from a small reserve in the corner and sterilized the bullet hole and tweezers. Then, he removed the bullet quickly and applied pressure with a towel.

Piccolo found Nova's panicked eyes again to make sure she was still holding it together.

"I'm about to call somebody."

He turned his attention back to Iela. "You won't have that option for long."

His composure was making her more anxious like dead bodies was a regular everyday thing to him. At that moment, Nova was struck with a few memories of her first month working at the bar. Piccolo had designated his office as her changing room because she still wasn't comfortable using the women's restroom yet, and there were about a handful of instances where she would walk in and she could swear someone would be leaving out the back door. She never saw anyone, but there would be clues left behind. The end of a sound she'd hear or something would be out of place on his desk, and she could've sworn she saw blood one time, way too much for a paper cut. Black blood. Nova loved her job so of course she never questioned him about it.

She continued to eye her boss as he sat patiently gazing at the woman. It was obvious he knew her. Not that Piccolo was that type of person at all. He'd probably spent more time with Nova than any other woman since she'd been working there. Actually, despite what she or Mira or any man or woman that had ever felt any attraction toward him assumed, he didn't give off anything relating to those kinds of romantic vibes at all, in any direction.

It took a moment, but Iela eventually started to stir. And like she was struck by lightning, life shot throughout her body. Her limbs locked and her eyes flipped open. Iela slowly sat up and looked around, bewildered, until they fell on Piccolo.

"...I feel empty," she said.

Iela seemed to be talking to herself as her head dropped and saw the state of her clothing. She suddenly remembered why she initially came to the bar tonight and shoved her dress down some more. Piccolo was still applying pressure to her wound and noticed how she tried to shy away from his touch.

"That's because you got a couple of pints sitting out back by the dumpsters," he said, trying to lighten the mood.

Iela could barely sit up straight but saw Nova out of her peripheral.

"Put it away."

Nova had taken out her phone but locked it when she exchanged looks with Piccolo.

"Honey, you was just dead."

"Make her go or I will." Her voice hadn't caught up with the rest of her yet and sounded like someone she didn't recognize.

"Nova."

Worried, she unlocked the door and backed out of the room.

Iela became too aware in the near quiet, the blues outside being the only thing in the room with them. She avoided Piccolo's glances moving between her eyes and her wound. His hands were still comfortably on her side and lower back, but she seemed to be the only one tensed up.

"Lock it."

"No one else comes in here, but me," he assured her.

Iela fell into his soft eyes and nearly used up her remaining strength to look away.

"You're not gonna ask what happened?"

"You're still here."

The calmness of his reply confused her as she now couldn't keep her eyes off him.

"I got it," she said, attempting to take over the towel.

"I got it."

She allowed him to keep the towel on her abdomen and began to scan the room. The bottles of vodka in the corner were the first thing she saw. All top shelf and imported. That wasn't what she was used to, but she felt her mouth suddenly parched.

"I got some water in the fridge behind my desk."

"No thanks..." she said, looking back at him. He still hadn't lifted his head, still focused on the black towel. "I came to see you tonight."

"I know." Piccolo looked up at her this time and she didn't turn away. "That's the same dress you had on the last time you came to see me."

Iela snatched the towel away from him as he grinned and leaned against the wall.

"Well, I was hoping like last time you would help me, but I see I'm not gonna get that." She winced as she gradually swung her legs over the side of the desk.

"You need to drink something." He opened the fridge under his desk by her legs.

"I don't want your damn water." Self-conscious, she tugged at the hem of her dress again.

"Iela, it's late and you just came back from the dead," he said, setting the water next to her. "That's all you're getting from me tonight."

She felt a little light-headed but kept her eyes fixed on Piccolo. It was like she was seeing him for the first time since she woke up.

"I see you haven't changed inside or out."

"Let me drive you home."

"I thought you weren't giving me anything else tonight." She slid off the desk, a little woozy, and got to her feet. "I can drive myself."

Piccolo had no choice but to back off, but kept his arms out around her just in case she lost her balance. She didn't make it a few steps before she fainted. Piccolo caught her before she hit the floor, her head nearly missing the corner of his desk.

Chapter XI

CAIDEN WOKE UP the next morning after a night full of heavy REM. It'd been a while since she truly felt well-rested, and she even managed to wake up in bed this time.

"Good morning," The Voice said.

"Hey."

Caiden could tell It wanted to see where her mind was. She got up and went to her closet to get some clothes.

"Last night."

"Yeah," she answered, not missing a beat.

The Voice didn't respond, forcing her to say something.

"You wanna know how I feel...Happy for some reason."

She cradled her clothes in her lap and sat on the foot of her bed. So much happened yesterday that, at first, she didn't know how to feel. Losing a chunk of time and getting a surprise visit from Aza was too much for her to sift through in a night's rest.

"I'm pleased to hear that you're choosing to look at the upside of your problems."

"Aza's not my problem," she said, not sounding sure of her words. "He let me read him."

"That should be caveat enough to heed," The Voice stated. "Who is he if he has to hide in the first place?"

Caiden got up to leave but stopped with her hand on the knob. "I've never seen you like this."

"My words, exactly."

She left for the bathroom to get ready for school. While she was brushing her teeth and taming her hair in the mirror, she had to check herself out again. Still, there was nothing.

She got downstairs and Roxa was waiting on her with a bigger breakfast than before. Pancakes, waffles, sausage, eggs, fruit, but still no Iela.

"Roxa, I don't think I have enough time," she said, her eyes scanning the table for a starting point.

"Oh," she glanced at a clock on the wall. "Not even a little? I was so busy, I didn't even check the time."

Caiden found a chair and began to eat.

"Well, don't force ya self," she said, a little too rough.

Roxa turned to face Caiden and saw the fork loosen between her fingers. She went to her and massaged her arm.

"I didn't mean that."

"I know," she said, eating some more. "Maybe she'll come back today."

"I hope she do. I got somethin' waitin' for her."

Caiden got up and gave Roxa a side hug. "I'll see you later."

She left the house with a small prayer for Roxa. She always got mean when she was anxious. It was Iela's modus operandi to be secretive about the things she did outside of the house, which is why her absence hadn't been on her mind that much. Maybe it was because Roxa had both of them to worry about now that she didn't study at home anymore.

Caiden got to school and her thoughts about Iela had vanished. It wasn't enough room for her mother and her classmates. Timothy was still fresh in some of their minds.

She felt herself being drawn down the hall to where David was. He was rummaging in his locker pretending to look for a textbook while trying to keep an eye on Caiden at the same time.

"Hey David," a kid yelled.

He naturally responded to his name and got a shove instead.

"Not you."

David took the hit and watched him dodge students as he jogged down the hall. It was just another day. Until he looked Caiden in the eye. He quickly shoved his head in his locker for a moment before slowly taking another peek. It took a few seconds before he noticed she was looking past him. He took a deep breath like today was going to be the day, but Aza got to her first.

"Caiden."

Her steps slowed as she casually acknowledged him. He noticed she didn't give him much eye contact.

"Hey...I can't go."

"You can't or don't want to?"

She stared at him a moment. "...No. I want to. I just can't."

"It's nothing big. Just dinner," he persisted.

"I'm sorry," she said, which was all she could say. There wasn't enough time to explain to him the power that was her mother. She turned to leave.

"Please..." he said, as he waited for her to turn back around. "Have dinner with us." Like Iela was in the back of her mind, Mil was in the back of his.

She tried to read his face, but no dice. She took a step closer.

"Aza...Who are you?"

"I just wanna help."

That pulled at her a little more. A simmering hunger appeared on her face.

"...Why do I need help?" she asked as steady as she could.

At that moment, Aza saw it. That small spark of intrigue. He took a step closer, knowing he had her then.

"Come to dinner," he repeated.

She watched him disappear around the corner and noticed that her hand had found her heart.

"What are you thinking?" The Voice asked.

"About myself," she said, just below a whisper.

David continued to watch her until she vanished into a group of sophomores. He'd felt the weight of their conversation from across the hall, and like Aza, he also felt his time slipping away.

***

Roxa had the record player on in the living room playing soft seventies. She was folding laundry, trying to keep her mind preoccupied with the task at hand. There was still no Iela. So many thoughts had crossed her mind on what could've happened to her. She'd always been into some dangerous stuff, most Roxa had to find out by prying, but she felt this time was different. Maybe because she just knew Caiden had something to do with it.

As she continued to work on the same towel she'd had balled up in her hands for the past thirty minutes, there was a knock and a ringing at the door.

She got up to answer it and saw Sister Lucy with that same woeful look on her face through one of the sidelights. Roxa opened the door and headed to the kitchen to get them something to drink. She could tell that they might be talking for a while.

"I'm sorry for stoppin' by," Lucy said, closing and locking the door behind her.

"No, Lucy, you not. But I'm not gonna hold ya upbringin' against you."

"You letting me in, so she's still not here."

Roxa set two cups and a steaming electric kettle on the table. She motioned Lucy, who had her nose inching toward her hutch, to one of the chairs in the dining room. She poured the hot water into the two cups and opened a small chest of her assorted teas.

"Maybe," Lucy said, tearing open a chamomile packet, "she up and left like she used to."

She let Lucy continue to peek and peer around, searching for someone she was never going to see. She watched, amused, as she added a little honey to her hibiscus.

"She impulsive, not stupid," Roxa said, leaning back in her chair. "The girl been locked up for seventeen years. Ain't no way she disappearin' herself without disappearin' them both."

Lucy gave her a questioning look. "Now I know why I haven't met her. She's one of those anti-everything parents, ain't she?"

"Lucy, you ain't met neither one of 'em because you a Christian," she chuckled. "Especially, Caiden..." Roxa's expression waxed grim.

Lucy set her cup down and reached out for one of Roxa's hands.

"Can't you see I'm tryin' to save her? Why else would I keep comin' back here to get tore into by you?"

Roxa took her hand back and fixed on her a moment. "What the church gon' do for Iela? That shit only work if you willin' and she lost her will when her blood turned black."

"Not her." Lucy sat up in her chair, her back straightened as she clasped her hands together. "The girl...I told you that a lot has changed. I meant it. I have proof of it."

Roxa saw that the woman had held her hands together to contain her excitement. It was the same as before but seemed to have grown now that she was finally inside the house.

"I think you need to leave, Sister." Roxa stood up and waited for Lucy to do the same.

"...It's because of her light, ain't it?"

"As far as you and the pastor are concerned — may the snake rest in peace — Caiden is just the same as any ole' other Void that you think is damned to hell. Say you understand."

The woman stood, not yet done explaining herself. "No."

"Lucy, what happened to you? By you, I mean the church. Never in all my years could I've imagined seein' somethin' that saved my life try to tear it up now."

"Tear it up?" Lucy asked, making a small fist on her chest. "...I can't stomach that. That you feel like we're ruining your life when all we trying to do is help."

"We don't need your help. We never asked." Roxa softened a bit. "Caiden is not somethin' to be fixed. She's perfect just as she is, and I can see that terrifies you."

There was a moment of silence as the two pierced each other. Lucy felt tingles in her fingers, but couldn't bring herself to give a retort. Not because she thought Roxa was right. She did find Voids a little terrifying, but in a way a puppy being surrounded by giants with minds of children would be terrified.

"I'm not giving up on you," she said, heading to the door.

"Nah, your faith too strong for that." Roxa followed behind her and waited until she got on the other side.

"Just please be careful," she said, clutching her collar. "I'll be prayin' for y'all."

"You the one meddlin' in the Lord's affairs. Save that prayer for ya self."

***

Faber's lunch crowd was thinning out when a man came in limping with a wooden cane. He was fairly young; the cane was to further support his prosthetic which was visible between his cuffed blue jeans and ankle socks. Faber glanced at the man like he was just another customer and continued ringing up an order.

"Where is he?" the man asked, coughing up a lung.

Faber just stared at him. "I sell cuts, sir. Pick something and get in line like everybody else."

The man walked closer to the counter, his cane clug-clugging the tile, and waited until Faber finished with the person he was ringing up.

"It's me," he said, getting his attention again. "Where is he?"

Faber eyed him a moment longer and finished with another customer.

"The back."

The man clonked out the front door and went around toward the back of the building. He went inside to one of the smallest offices he'd ever seen. A broom closet almost.

He flicked on the dim light and saw a shabby young man curled up on a cot in a corner. He was asleep and his arms were wrapped tight around him.

The man tapped the guy's white Chucks with his cane and he shot up, whipped out his gun.

"Relax," the man said.

"William?" The guy wasn't going to drop the gun until he got confirmation.

"Did you do it?"

"Do what? Who the hell are you?"

The man grabbed him by the collar and pulled him closer just to wake him up and come to his senses.

"Did you do it or not?"

The young man pierced him, looking into his eyes until he could see who he was really talking to.

"William..." Relief washed over him as he teared up a little.

"Yes, yes."

William gently let go of the young man. He had to use the wall for assistance, but even this weak front made the young man feel uneasy.

"Did you?"

"Yeah. I think— I think so. Yeah, I did..." He tried to hand William the gun, but he didn't take it.

"I told you to get rid of it," he said, slightly frustrated. "Barry, if they find you, I won't be able to save you."

"I forgot. Everything was happening so fast. I just ran and didn't stop." Barry's head fell as he thought about what he'd done.

"It's okay." William walked back to him and placed his hand on his shoulder. "Clean it and just toss it anywhere.

Then come back here. Faber will take care of you like the others."

Barry crawled across his cot to get a better look at William. He didn't know whether to be amazed or afraid. He reached out and held William's hand.

"...That woman...Why?— I mean if she has the cure..." Barry dropped William's hand as he sunk to his knees and his head fell to his lap. "I never killed anybody before..."

The young man's whimpers floated in the air. William had to ball up his fists to stop himself from reaching out. A boy was in front of him, a child. He'd asked a child to do his bidding. William watched his greasy, ladened head until he looked at him again, but he didn't.

"Barry, that woman is bad. I don't trust her." He lifted the young man's chin and saw his puffy brown eyes. "We're getting closer. Just hold on some more."

William turned and was about to head for the door.

"I can't..."

He looked back at the desperation in Barry's eyes, but that wasn't enough to bring on any sympathy for him. He was just like the others. New, naive, and willing to do anything to be saved. But William had been cursed longer, in much more pain. His strain had mutated and was becoming insatiable. This was William's last hope and no one, not even this kid, could keep him from getting what he was promised.

"We're close," he said, warmly cradling the back of the boy's head. "I promise."

Barry, drying his tears with the back of his hand, got back in the corner of his cot as William shut off the light and left.

Chapter XII

CAIDEN WALKED OUT of the cafeteria doors to a table in the courtyard. Ever since Alise had mentioned that most of the Voids hung out there, it had been on her mind to be around others like herself. She looked around at a few of the picnic tables and saw that there weren't a lot of them, at least during this lunch hour. She wasn't even sure if everyone out there were Voids or not. She believed she was the only one that couldn't do that little eye trick that Aza could do to where he could blend in with the humans. But Aza didn't seem like an ordinary Void.

She hurried and opened up her book, shaded under one of the older trees that were out there, and began to read. She'd read only a couple of lines before she was interrupted.

Tap, tap.

Right on the front cover of her book. She slid it down a little and saw David staring back at her. His dark brown eyes watched her curiously in silence. Caiden was calmly getting a sense from him, though she'd already had before he built up the courage to bother her.

"Uh, hi."

She stared at him as a response, waiting.

"I'm David," he said, clearing his throat. "You're Caiden, right?" he asked, awkwardly stopping to put out his hand and rubbing it on the side of his jeans instead.

"The cafeteria that day..."

"Yeah, I had a lot of shit going on upstairs. Should've been looking downstairs at my feet, see where they were going."

"But you're okay now? You aren't scared anymore?" she asked, suddenly remembering how he felt as he scurried out of the cafeteria.

David sat up, slightly stunned, but it had shown on his face as impressed.

"I wasn't until now." He leaned in and lowered his voice. "So, it's true...You can read minds."

Caiden's eyes were about to change, but she calmed after reminding herself that she didn't need to feel threatened by David at all.

"I know. I gave you that note." He anticipated a scarier reaction, like a calm warning or a death glare, but she looked more nervous than he did before he approached her. "I didn't mean to do it in that way, but I have to be careful with you."

That was the second time today she'd heard something similar pertaining to how people should respond to her. Needing help and now having to be handled with care. If Caiden wasn't motivated to find out who or what she was before, she surely was now.

"What do you mean?"

"You really don't know anything, do you?" He didn't mean to sound rude, but he felt excitement bubbling up and didn't know why. He slid her another note with an address on it. "That's Faber's. Meet me there. I'll tell you everything I know at least."

She looked up at him, gears turning, as he stood up.

"When? I have to be home as soon as school's out."

"Tomorrow. It won't take long." His head was on a swivel as he made to leave.

"Hey."

He stopped. Caiden wanted to say something else, but there was too much to say. She just studied him; reading him some more as he stood there itching to leave.

"I'll try."

Caiden fingered the note before getting back to her book, but she couldn't concentrate after that.

"Why didn't you say anything?"

"He's human."

***

Saint Peter's was a decrepit chapel that sat in one of the corners of another mid-sized town that orbited Austin, Texas. The people were surprisingly friendly and protected their own. It may sound odd from visitors passing through that likened the city to one of their bigger neighbors, but the people, who were mostly churchgoing folk, would give all the credit and maybe to some fanatics, all the glory, to Saint Peter's.

This particular day, Father Tate, one of the church's most popular priests, was now in confession with a young man who seemed to have strayed too far from the flock. A solemn pair of baby blues stared off into a dusty memory before piercing the father's side profile.

"...These feelings that you've had — that you are having — may not be natural, but they do exist for some purpose. Things out of the norm usually do."

"But I hate myself when I get this way," the young man barely managed to say, clearly wrestling with his past actions. "When I get these thoughts, I feel like I don't deserve anyone's sympathy...Like I don't deserve to be here at all."

"People like you deserve the most sympathy and here is where you'll get all of that and more," Father Tate explained. "Hope, love, a will to go on. You're alive the way you are for a reason."

The father paused to get his next words together, seeing the young man was slightly affected by that last piece of wisdom.

"...If you truly want to rid yourself of these feelings, you have to come into complete agreement with the Lord about why He put these urges in your heart. Nothing He makes is flawed without the help of His creation. We're just simple humans. And that's okay. But all that He touches, he makes pure again."

Father Tate stopped, seeming to do a little bit of wrestling of his own.

"Continue to repent...And you'll be forgiven forever. That is His will."

There was a moment of silence as Father Tate's advice hovered in the air. He'd had so many conversations like this from so many different types of people. He'd sometimes needed to seek counsel himself from the sickening accounts of what a surprising amount of people did in the dark. Especially on the really bad days like this one. Some of the things he'd heard just now quickly rose to his top ten.

"Are you sure, Father?"

The atmosphere changed with the shift in the young man's tone. What was once the voice of the meek was now the strength of the self-assured.

"So every time Father Marcus unloads one in a Montessori preschooler, all he has to do to cleanse his palate is say a couple of hail Marys?"

The father had to look at the face of this impostor. He was nearly beside himself.

"Our God is an awesome God."

The young man stood and walked out of the confessional in desperate need of a cleansing by fire as two cops cut off Father Tate. His eyes found Dontae immediately, still in disbelief at what just happened.

"Officer Kyron."

"Dontae."

A cop had spotted Dontae from the entrance and his spirits dropped. After five years on the force, he still had the gait of a rookie. His short side part and sad eyes didn't assist in his gaining any immediate respect over the years, so he had to work that much harder at his job.

"You're way out of your jurisdiction," Dontae said in greeting.

"You snatched the words right outta my mouth." Kyron wanted to be curt, but Dontae carried around with him the scent of his father's money. "You working alone or big brother just keeping his hands clean?"

"If you're going to talk shit behind his back, at least say his name," he said, leaning on a pew. "He already thinks you're useless."

"Look who's talking."

Dontae crossed his arms as a silent warning. One of his bad habits.

"What's with the face?" he said, backtracking. "I got a Catholic kiddie diddle ring to investigate— And just yesterday a shitload of Void murders come in scattered across not one, but three counties outside Harris. If my tone sounded insulting, forgive me."

"Okay. I will." Dontae could see he was up to his neck, and this was not just the boys in blue. "What are you doing way out here? I thought after what happened to that kid they weren't putting any of you guys out on loan for a while."

"You know how those things are. In a week or two people are going to forget about who that cop killed, including the reason why. Even if that why was a little black boy." That last part left a bad taste in his mouth. "But I owed a friend and thought I'd look into something for him."

"Ah. That friend," he blankly teased.

"Dontae," Kyron warned, almost pissing himself.

"That's the stress, not me. I got my own problems." He looked over his shoulder at the back of Father Tate's weighted head. "Can you blame me after all of that? Makes me question the whole human to Void algorithm."

"You better have gotten something for this."

Dontae's phone vibrated and he saw who it was.

"I got another cog," he said, backing away. "I'm leaving. Pneuma sends his regards."

"Don't say that."

"Remember, he's not a Void." He began to sprint toward the exit. "Break whatever laws that you can get away with."

"Don't say that either," Kyron yelled after him.

Dontae flew past the pews and out the door with a faint smile on his lips. He slipped into his lavish midnight blue sedan that he'd had for years and headed straight out of town. He looked down at his phone just to see the text again. It had been so long since he'd received anything from that number. He slammed hard on the gas.

A few hours later, he found himself outside of Piccolos. The place hadn't changed from the last time he was there. He wasn't legal at the time, but Piccolo would let him hang out in the back, lounge on the stage with a ginger ale when they'd close, and just be a place that he could go to when he didn't want to go back to his father's penthouse.

He shook the nostalgia off as he got out of his car. That was when they met in New York. He hadn't fully taken over the underbelly of the the Voided world. Assisting the ones at the bottom, doing any and everything that they could to survive because the humans in their life had thrown them away. That's when Dontae would show up with his father's money to do whatever he could to help. It didn't take long for his name to start getting around the country. Once the Voids knew that there was someone out there that could make their living afterlife a little less hopeless, they began to believe that things would get better. And it didn't matter that Dontae was human, though that was a hard sell at first, all they cared about was getting back their will to live in a world that wanted them dead.

He walked through the front door and Mira, who'd been trying to extract a free drink out of some guy with her perky Cs, pounced on him instantly.

"Where you been, Daddy? We thought you were gone for good."

She had wrapped herself around him, purposely pushing her chest against his arm. He knew the routine and played along.

"It's Dontae," he said and politely maneuvered out of her grip. "Is he in the back?"

"Yeah. He practically lives here now." She started to smile as she noticed he was still holding her hand.

"Thanks," he said and kissed her hand goodbye.

He floated past the bar and glimpsed Rane, who was making drinks. Her eyes widened as they both gave each other a silent hello. Dontae smiled as that was the most animated he'd seen Rane ever. He got to the back and pulled out his phone to text Piccolo. There was no getting in his office without an invitation.

Piccolo was leaning on his desk watching Iela sleep on one of his couches. She was still bandaged up when his phone vibrated. He didn't need to look at it to know who it was. He opened the door and Dontae came in.

"She's been out the whole time?" he asked in a rushed whisper. That didn't matter as the music was beating through the walls, but she was out like a light.

Piccolo slowly shook his head as he herded Dontae back out of the room. He followed him towards the front and they took a table in a corner.

"Sadly, you can't trust her even in her sleep," he said, getting Rane's attention to bring over their usual. He looked back at Dontae just to take him in. "I just wanted to give you a heads up. You didn't have to come all the way down here."

"I missed you," he said, his cheeks reddening.

Piccolo watched him drop his head in slight embarrassment and smiled at him. Rane had brought over their drinks and he put Dontae's bottle up against his temple. He flinched from the cold glass.

"I'm happy to see you haven't changed."

"I had to come back anyway," he clarified, taking his drink out of Piccolo's hand. "You haven't either. I mean physically. Is there something you wanna tell me?"

Dontae said that in kidding, but Piccolo hadn't changed at all. He suddenly wondered if that was just him gushing over the guy.

"I should be saying that to you. Why'd you all of a sudden pop back up now?"

"You probably already know."

"The Soul?"

"How do you always know?" he asked, genuinely surprised.

Piccolo shrugged and drank. Dontae knew he wasn't going to get a straight answer out of him if he got any at all. That was part of his job, knowing things that no one would think he'd know. Dontae called it an occupational hazard while Piccolo called it a perk.

"I guess my eyes shouldn't be so wide. Her mother is passed out on your couch."

"Shot."

Piccolo pulled the bullet from his pocket and handed it to Dontae.

"Nothing special," he said, examining it. "Though, I should let an expert back me up."

"He would know."

Dontae eyed him at the mention of the soldier and gave the bullet back. "Nothing special," he repeated, putting the bottle to his pinkened lips.

"That's probably why she's still alive." Piccolo propped his sneaker on the bar of his chair. "Unless you've got a death-wish, no Void is killing another Void outside a Void bar ever and going to live to tell anyone about it."

Dontae studied him, not able to place his tone.

"Maybe it was a message."

"Maybe."

Dontae locked eyes with Piccolo. "You want me to take care of this?"

Piccolo gave him a faint smile and took another sip of his drink.

"When are you gonna stop trying to thank me?"

"Till your last breath." He finished the rest of his beer, then got serious. "It's really not a problem. After all, this is my life," he said as he spun his bottle cap.

"You're right." Piccolo got up and took Dontae's empty bottle. "I think you've got somewhere to be."

Dontae looked up at him, wondering when the awe of Piccolo's vast knowledge about the goings-on in his life would go away. He stood up, embraced him in the only hugs that have ever warmed him from the inside out, and left the bar for Mil's.

Chapter XIII

ROXA SAT ALONE in the living room next to the record player, gently massaging her hands. She'd never played her records this much before, only using it when she had to ruminate over things that required more than her slaving over the stove to make a full course meal. The lamp light gently touched her face and hands, which now reached for her needle and thread. She had to keep reminding herself that this was what Iela did and the people around her would have to learn to get used to it or do something about it.

Roxa chose to wait, praying that she wouldn't have to result to calling the cops, not that it would help. It was just better sitting around and not getting a call from them instead.

"She's still not here."

She looked up and saw Caiden in her sweats, ready for bed. Roxa's eyes went to her heart glowing softly through her long sleeve tee.

"I can turn the air down."

"Oh, I'm fine. Comfortable," she said, curling her toes. She had on a pair of crew socks instead of her usual ankle.

"You worried is what you is." Roxa studied her to see if her assumption was right. "Ain't you?"

"No, ma'am." She didn't mean to be so honest, but some of Roxa's blunt tongue had rubbed off on her over the years.

"Me, too...Me, too."

Caiden inched toward her and sat at her feet. They were like that for a long moment before her eyes wandered around the room and landed on a familiar skid on the wooden floor leading away from the wall the couch was up against.

"I remember I did that moving my desk upstairs to my room. I just knew Iela was gonna lock me in there when I was finished."

"If it was me, I woulda just put a belt to you and been done with it," she said, smiling to herself. Then she rested her hand on Caiden's back. "...Sometimes I wish she'd do that instead; give you some kind of affection."

Caiden idly played with the thread and sunk further into Roxa's lap. "You give me more than enough. More than I want." She said that last part to herself but felt Roxa's hand press down a little more on her shoulder blade.

"At least she left yo' education to me," she said, patting her fluffy ponytail. "You was my favorite student."

"I was your only."

Roxa watched the top of Caiden's head as she nestled it deeper into her thigh. She was still fingering the thread and drifting away to wherever had been occupying her mind.

"Somethin' wrong with school? You even restin' at my feet, and you ain't did that since I caught you with that mutt in the laundry room."

It was a moment before Caiden pivoted to face Roxa. She could see that the girl's mind wasn't wandering at all, but was gathering strength to say what she was about to say.

"Roxa."

"Yes, child?"

"Were you serious about having Aza over?"

"Course. He always welcome here."

"But you only met him once," Caiden said, not expecting her to hand out so freely her precious hospitality. "You don't know him at all."

"The only thing that matters is how you feel about him."

"He's just somebody that I see at school."

"That's not what I meant."

Caiden looked up at Roxa, who seemed to be hinting at something that was taking her a while to understand.

"He doesn't seem like a bad person..."

"But?"

"But I don't know...I just wanna make sure."

Roxa waited for her to muster some more strength and she had to admit it was a little amusing. She'd nearly raised Caiden on her own. When Iela wasn't around, she'd be there telling her that her mother would be back soon even when she wasn't sure. Roxa didn't realize at the time that Caiden could read emotions, but she did everything in her power to keep her shielded from her mother's neglect by simply being present. So, she couldn't see how Caiden was reluctant to ask even the most benign questions, even to her, for fear of getting ignored or yelled at.

"Hurry up," she teased, giving a long tug on her ponytail.

"Well," Caiden started, relaxing some, "he wants me to have dinner with his family instead."

Roxa waited for Caiden to look at her, but she didn't.

"Tonight woulda been perfect for that."

"I don't think she'll let me. But, I don't know..." she trailed off, her mind filling up again. "I feel like I have to. I don't know how to explain."

Roxa didn't respond at first, continuing to wait for Caiden. She wanted to see her face, or rather her eyes. This was a day she knew would come. After all the arguments with Iela about Caiden being on lockdown for seventeen years and only going out alone with a chaperone — read: bodyguard — Roxa knew that Caiden would grow up and do something that everyone does and try to find some way to understand who and what she was. Iela, who had instilled in her daughter the notion that she shouldn't even be alive, let alone out about in the world with other people that were beneath her, had overestimated her abilities to beat out Caiden's innate curiosity. And that was just a building catalyst to not only know more but to know everything.

"I know you wanna understand ya self better," Roxa said, "but you have to think about the position you'll put ya self and ya mama in if somebody finds out about you. You not meant to do these ordinary things."

Caiden adjusted herself again, safely cuddling Roxa's leg. She still couldn't look at her, especially for what she was about to say next.

"...What if someone already knows?" She asked so low it seemed she decided to ask at the last minute.

It was a second before Roxa grabbed Caiden's shoulders, not sure of what she heard. She turned her, forcing a face-to-face.

"Caiden."

"I didn't do anything. They already knew." Her eyes had turned dark.

"They?"

"Iela." Caiden had gotten on her knees, looking to Roxa to make sure that this stayed between them.

"Don't worry, now. Don't worry about her." Roxa's grip moved down her arms to her hands. "I'll do that. For goodness sake, take care of ya self."

Caiden allowed Roxa's assuring energy to settle between them and was put a little at ease.

That felt like a yes to her.

***

Aza was asleep in bed. He hadn't gotten ready to turn in yet, still in his jeans and staple plain solid t-shirt. His laptop was lying open by his head on an unfinished essay for Mil's class of all classes. His door glided open without a sound as Dontae came into his room. He stood there a second to look around.

Everything seemed the same. All of Aza's ribbons, bows, and his small pile of scarves were noticeably larger, but that was it. That was the only thing really out of place. Aza didn't have much, none of them did really, having to move around a lot guaranteed that they held no attachments.

Dontae walked over to the bed and gently poked Aza's cheek. There was no reaction at first, so he did it again. Aza swiped his finger and pulled him in. Dontae fell forward and Aza naturally wrapped himself around him.

"Mil doesn't like surprises," he said, still half-asleep, but his arms were ironclad around Dontae's back.

"That's why I come through whenever I feel like it." He tried to free himself, but Aza wasn't budging. Dontae stopped struggling and looked at Aza's face. His eyes were still closed, but he could tell he'd fully woken up already. "What's wrong?"

When he didn't answer, Dontae attempted to get up, but Aza wasn't done with him yet. He decided to take a more childish approach and pulled the ribbon out of his bun. Aza's hair collapsed in a mess all over his face.

"Speak up. You're the only little brother I like and I can't have you looking this depressed when the shit hasn't even hit the fan yet."

"I'm older than you," he finally said. Aza opened his eyes and moved a huge portion of his hair out of his face.

"You love saying that."

"What took you so long?"

"Don't ask stupid questions." He adjusted himself more comfortably in the bed. Dontae knew that hugs with Aza weren't over until he said so. "I can make you talk."

"Your money's no good here," he said, tightening his grip. Then, he turned pensive. "...I've been talking to him. At school, I mean."

"Her."

"Mil wants us to address the Soul first." Aza loosened his arms a bit and began flipping Dontae's collar up and down. "...But he can't be with us all the time."

"What does it feel like?" Dontae asked, genuinely intrigued.

"I don't know. At first, I couldn't explain it," he said, thinking back. "Like I don't have control over my body maybe?"

"Really?" Dontae couldn't tell if Aza was being his normal romantic self or if he was being literal.

"Well, I do, but I don't." He couldn't find the words. He wasn't even sure if that feeling had words. Aza looked at Dontae, who seemed to be living vicariously through those conversations with Caiden by his every word. "I can't tell if that's the Soul or if that's Caiden."

"Maybe it's both."

Aza pondered that option with some confusion. He felt his arms go limp around Dontae and he sat up to continue working on his essay.

"Dinner."

They looked up at the door and saw Volx, who only came to deliver that message before leaving.

"You'll see when you meet her," Aza said, saving his document and climbing over Dontae.

"Why do I feel I already have?" Dontae asked with a gentle smile.

"Don't," Aza said, feeling slightly embarrassed after spilling out his guts. Dontae didn't tease him as much as the others did when it came to things like that, but he knew when he'd said too much when Dontae was this understanding.

Dontae got up and followed him into the kitchen. He saw the takeout in the middle of the table and wanted to turn back around. He decided to give the fridge a try, find something local instead. He'd fallen in love with the locally brewed beer and had announced to the house that he'd like it kept in stock whenever he was coming back home. This visit wasn't on the schedule, but he checked anyway and was in luck.

"The chief must be off," he said, popping open a bottle.

"He's probably out back. You know how he needs his alone time." Aza gave him a chiding look, watching him drink that beer. "You're not gonna eat?"

"Maybe. I was expecting the gourmet's menu tonight."

Volx began putting food on Dontae's plate when Mil walked in.

"Dontae." He said it like he was announcing the time.

"When the devil hears his name..." He sat down at the table, waiting for Mil to look his way, but he never did.

Mil was privy to each of the members' baiting of which they all took part in their own way, except for Volx, so he knew when to respond and when not.

"Proceed then," he said, then to Aza, "Could you get the Riesling? Sweet."

Aza went to the fridge and got the bottle. He grabbed a wine glass and filled it halfway.

"Things haven't changed much," Dontae observed.

"By your stating that you've proven your point. You've come back, so that means you have something to contribute. It's been almost a year and I'm ready to hear some promising news."

Dontae and Aza exchanged looks. Nothing had changed at all.

"Iela. She was shot outside Piccolo's last night."

Mil and Aza stopped eating.

"She's still alive. I saw her before I got here," Dontae added. "That's good, right? That's big."

"Yes. That's excellent."

But it didn't sound excellent at all. Dontae just watched him take a drink for a moment and go back to eating. Aza, on the other hand, was waiting for more details.

"How? She's alive."

"Right now, Iela is the Soul's only defense. So it's best if she keeps breathing for as long as possible. Or until Caiden is with us."

Aza noted how Mil said that all in one breath. He looked at Dontae to see if he shared the same sentiment.

"And someone did try to kill her."

Aza nodded in thought, but he filed Mil's remark in his mental folder with the other things he'd said similar in the past.

"Yes..." Mil started to say. "Volx?"

He had been in the fridge weighing two packages of raw meat in his hands. He put them back and left the room when Mil called his name, which was an order in this case.

"I thought I'd handle this," Dontae said. "If Caiden's who you think she is, then I should be doing whatever I can."

"He," Mil corrected.

Dontae stared at him stone-faced.

"You've informed us and you did wonderfully." He ate a little more and sipped his wine. "I honestly don't know why you've wasted a trip with something that could've been relayed in a simple text message."

Aza's attention darted between them both as his sleeve made its way into his palms.

"Volx?" Dontae called the soldier back.

He came to the door and naturally his attention went to Mil first before going to the one that called him.

"I'm driving," he said as he picked up his beer and left the room.

Volx looked to Mil to give him the go-ahead before he followed behind.

Mil calmly went back to his wine while he pulled out his notebook to begin taking notes.

"Any word on the invitation?"

Aza glanced at the pages, but couldn't make out the chicken scratch. Mil usually wrote in his notebook in private, but even if any of them got a peek over his shoulder, he doubted they would be able to understand it. The rest of the Argenta just chalked it up to an odd idiosyncrasy.

"Yeah. He'll be here."

Chapter XIV

MUTED HEAVY BASS from Nova's act woke Iela from her deep sleep. She adjusted her sight to the room to make sure it was the same one she'd passed out in. The thin blanket that was covering her fell as she sat up with a wince. She felt the hole in her dress had been cut wider and was bandaged. She looked up and her eye got snagged on the alcohol reserve in the corner. Her first instinct was to grab a bottle and escape out the back door, but she didn't have time to inspect the labels when Piccolo walked in. He was holding a grease-stained brown paper bag.

"Morning."

It took a while for her to answer. She was suddenly more aware of everything. Her wound. Her clothing. The music. Piccolo. Especially Piccolo.

Iela had been with a plethora of men who'd been physically blessed in her previous life, but something was striking about the man before her; something from the inside. Not like calling his mother every week or donating to charities, Piccolo had an entire universe inside of him that just kept expanding every time she was with him.

He sat the food down on a tray on his desk and she watched him go to her and kneel. She didn't know what he was doing at first until he pulled the blanket down some more to better see the bandages.

"Does it still hurt? Or did it?" he asked, making sure it didn't need to be changed.

"Not anymore."

Neither one of them said anything for a while. Piccolo was focused on checking to see if her wound was infected and Iela continued to watch him. He got up and went to get more gauze out of his desk drawer.

"Who is he?"

"I'm the wrong person to ask," he said. His answer flew out of his mouth like it was waiting at the ready.

"You've helped me before."

He finished putting on a new bandage and went to go lean on the front of his desk. Iela searched his face, trying to guess why he was shutting her down. Well, she knew of one reason but didn't think their past warranted such a strong reaction.

"If they came for me, then they'll come for her—"

"That's why it's not my place." He stood up and walked behind his desk. As long as he'd known Iela, she always had tunnel vision when it came to something that she wanted. Right now, she was trying to get two things, even if it meant harming anyone else involved. "You can't afford to be yourself. You have a child to protect...I would think you wouldn't wanna mess that up again."

"Piccolo..." That clearly hurt, but she couldn't be angry at him for telling the truth.

"I would do anything for you, but this is not one of them." He knew that was a sore spot, which is why he went there. "Eat. You've been out for nearly a day."

Iela got up and went to his desk, only now realizing she didn't have any shoes on. "I don't want your food."

"That's all I can give you right now," he said, grabbing a burger out of the paper bag.

Iela stared at him as he put it down in front of her. They fixed on each other a moment too long before she lost her nerve. It was times like these that she wished she was packing, but that thought quickly left her. She couldn't hurt him even if it was to put him out of his misery.

"...I died," she said, unable to grasp that she'd lost this round, though it wasn't much of a fight.

"I know." Piccolo's expression turned soft. "And because of who you are, it might happen again. That's why I'm asking you to put down your pride. It'll be easier for Caiden if you do."

She continued to look at him in disbelief.

"Eat. Before it gets cold," he said and left the room.

At that precise moment, just outside, Dontae pulled up in front of the bar and Volx's nostrils wrinkled before he put the truck in park. They were across the street where they could get a good view out of their side mirror of Iela's car.

"I'll wait for you inside," Dontae said as he attempted to get out. He was waiting for Volx's response but his arm shot out to stop him instead.

"His blood is young."

"Where is he?"

Volx looked at his wing mirror and saw Iela walking out from the side of the bar. Dontae followed his eyes and watched her get in her car.

"We're gonna follow her?"

"No."

Dontae waited for the rest, but it seemed Volx was finished. He started up the car and began driving, Volx only giving him monosyllabic directions. It wasn't five minutes when they pulled up to Faber's.

"This is a deli."

Volx didn't say anything and got out. Dontae followed him to the back. He took out a mini flashlight and started working on the lock immediately as Dontae's head darted around in the dark.

"What about security?"

The door was opened before he finished his question.

"'This is a deli,'" Volx echoed.

They got inside and Volx sniffed out Barry who was still balled up in the corner of the office.

Dontae was the lookout at the door as Volx came into the room like a shadow. His hand shot out for the boy and gripped the better half of his face. Barry's eyes bulged as he quickly went for the gun in his jacket, but Volx swiped it out of his hand like butter. Then, he hit him over the head with it, knocking him out cold.

***

Caiden's lamp flickered on and she calmly sat up in bed. She wasn't even sure if she'd gone to sleep. Her mind had been occupied by so many things that she was working harder than usual to get used to.

"You didn't dream," The Voice said. "Which means you didn't get a good night's rest."

"How do you know?" she asked, sliding out of bed. She went to her closet to grab some clothes when her light started flickering again.

"Be careful today."

"I'm always careful."

She took a shower and headed downstairs to Roxa setting the table. At that moment, Iela decided to come walking through the front door. Caiden stopped and hit reverse until she was back at the top stairs. She waited and listened.

"Where the hell you been?" Roxa fumed, glaring at Iela's unkempt hair and the huge hole in her dress.

"Please. I'm tired and I need a shower." She dragged her bare feet to the refrigerator and got a bottle of water, purposely not looking Roxa in the eye.

Roxa snatched her arm as she tried to head toward her room. She focused on the bandage before going to Iela's face.

"What happened to you?"

Iela had only seen Roxa with that expression once before. That look, that mixture of pity, worry, and anger, made her sick.

"What did you do?" Roxa demanded.

"...I didn't do anything."

Iela stared her down to let her know that it wasn't the time and went straight down the hall to the bathroom. She got into the shower and let the hot water get into her skin and the steam soak into her lungs, taking care of her wound as she tried washing away everything that happened to her in the past forty-eight hours. It didn't feel as bad as Piccolo was making it out to be and that was one of the things that she hated him for. He always made her fall at his feet for caring too much, like watching out for her was the only thing on his mind, especially when he knew that what was between them was laughably one-sided.

She gingerly pat-dried the area around her wound as she wrapped the towel around her. That mirror was beckoning her, but she wasn't going to look. Since she hit the double digits, she never looked in the mirror longer than she needed to.

She finally opened the door and Caiden was standing right there waiting for her. Iela could see that she was doing that thing again, and she noticed that Caiden either couldn't hide it or she had a natural look of worry on her face.

"What are you still doing here? You're gonna be late."

"I'm sorry," she said, moving out of the way. "Does it hurt bad?"

Iela only gave her a look before walking past her to her bedroom door.

"Stop saying that." She stopped and their eyes met. Iela just studied her wondering face. "There are some people out there who would die to be what you are, so you're not sorry. Nowhere near it."

At first, Caiden wasn't sure what was going on and Iela, making light of what she just said, didn't give her any time to respond.

"I'm picking you up from school today."

Before Caiden could question her, Iela closed the door.

"Hmm," The Voice said as she stood there blankly staring at the chipped off-white paint.

She went to grab her briefcase and threw a goodbye to Roxa, who had disappeared in her room, before leaving for school.

"Caiden."

"I don't think I've ever heard you say 'hmm' before," she teased.

"It is a minute of firsts, isn't it?"

"Yeah."

She suddenly felt a wave of anxiety as she continued to walk up to Myerworth's front steps, but it wasn't because of the students, which she'd gotten used to, but Iela's behavior. Never in her life did her mother praise Caiden's light. It always seemed to unnerve her. She felt it for years whenever they would spar in the yard or when they would go out to a grocery store. Iela would always be watching Caiden out of the corner of her eye, but now Iela let her go to school, so she couldn't tell where her mind was.

"Hey."

Caiden didn't turn around, still halfway in the middle of her thoughts. Then, she saw a pair of skate shoes stop in her line of view and realized she was looking down the whole time.

"Hey, again."

She looked up and saw David a little more relaxed than the last time she saw him.

"Oh. I can't meet you today."

And like that his spirits fell. "Why? Something happened?"

"Yeah. My mother," she said, saddened for them both. "She's picking me up after school."

Suddenly David brightened back up again.

"That's cool. Let's go."

Caiden watched him as he started walking away from the building.

"Go where?"

"We'll be back before the bell."

There was a moment before her feet started to move away from the school as well, but then they stopped. She looked at him again, making sure to try as hard as she could to blur out the other students in the area. It took a moment for David to see what she was doing.

"Hey, we don't have to if you're that scared."

Caiden felt the corners of her mouth twitch a little.

"See?" he said, giving her a comforting smile. "I'm funny, not a bad guy."

"Yeah." She began walking away from the school again. "What's funny is you thinking I'm scared of you."

David got in step with her as they crossed the street and she noticed his head drop before she felt that spike of anxiety. She was going to explain, but the feeling was gone as soon as it came.

"What if we get in trouble?"

As they got further away from the school and into parts of the city that she'd never ventured to alone, Caiden was now thinking of all the ways Iela was going to punish her. Her mother's punishments weren't anything trivial like being grounded or not giving her dinner. She remembered they up and left one of the many towns they'd moved to when she was eight because she'd lost her in a park one time.

"We're seniors. They expect us to do stuff like this," he said as they came up to the deli.

David opened the door and Caiden timidly went inside.

"Thank you."

"Relax."

Faber and David gave each other an acknowledging nod.

"We have reserved seating."

He led her to a booth in the back and she sat down, trying to take the place in. It was still early, just opened up, looked like, so maybe two or three people were dining in. Faber's was mostly a pickup place where people would call in the number of ounces or pounds of a particular cut that they wanted and would come in and pick it up when it was ready.

Caiden watched as a woman came in and David ducked his head into the corner of the booth.

"Get down, that's my mom," he whispered frantically.

Caiden's eyes went to him, then to the woman, and back to him again.

"But, it's not."

David peeked out from over his arms and became embarrassed.

"I was...Yeah. I'll be back."

She watched his face turn red and smiled a little to herself. Caiden thought that maybe she should've pretended for his sake, but then her eyes might've given her away. She didn't know if David would've been able to tell.

She people-watched and read every person in the place until David came back to the table with two plates with overstuffed sandwiches on them.

"Thank you..." she said, admiring the ridiculous amount of meat on the two thinly sliced pieces of toasted bread.

"It's really good." He sat down and became ravenous. "Prime."

Caiden watched him as he dug in, wondering.

"Is that why you're excited?"

He stopped and wiped his mouth.

"How do you know that?"

"Are you?"

"Yeah, I guess." He managed to swallow and averted his eyes.

Caiden began to feel foreign emotions coming from David. They were confused and exhilarated. He quickly went back to eating and changed the subject.

"You're a Void," he said, watching her expression. "But different."

She stared at him. David was about as smooth as a porcupine.

"So, it's true."

"Everyone's different. I'm not the only Void at school." Caiden pulled a slice of meat out from the sandwich and bit off a small bite. She didn't really feel comfortable with the way he was looking at her.

"I know, but you are the only one I've met that can do whatever you just did right now."

"Who told you about me?" she asked, getting on her guard.

Fear swiftly showed up at their table and Caiden held fast her gaze on him so he couldn't escape. She almost regretted asking the question when she saw how terrified he looked.

"A little birdy," he said, haunted.

There was a tingling in her chest, a gravitation in her hand as she reached out to touch his. He leaped out of the booth as he felt the heat emanating off her fingertips before skin could caress skin, and massaged his hands.

"I'm sorry."

"Nah. It's not your fault." He then proceeded to fall into her eyes. "I won't tell anyone."

Caiden fixed on him for a moment.

"I believe you."

He slid back into his seat and began eating again.

"Is that everything?" she asked, softly poking her bread.

"Why? Do you feel like I'm holding something back?"

She stared at him until he looked her in the eye.

"Yes."

He swallowed and straightened up in his seat.

"...I don't think you can lie."

"Everyone knows that," she said, slowly. "That's why our eyes change."

"No." David rested his elbows on the table and leaned in closer to her. "You don't know how, I think. Or you don't want to...from what I've seen."

She watched him avert his eyes on that last part, but he looked back up at her when she didn't say anything immediately.

"What else?" Her voice had softened.

"Eat."

"I'm not hungry."

David noticed she was focused on her sandwich again.

"That's it, I promise."

He waited for her to look at him again.

"Eat."

Caiden felt his sincerity and began taking small bites of her sandwich again. They ate in silence for a while until both of their plates were empty.

"So, are we going back to school now?" she asked, getting that confused feeling from him again.

"Yeah," he said, glancing at his phone. "We can slip back in before lunch."

"Thank you," she said, slipping out of the booth.

"For what?" He scooped the abandoned pieces of meat off her plate and plopped them into his mouth.

"You didn't lie to me."

"I couldn't," he said, smiling as he opened the door for her. "Who knows what you'd do with my body?"

When they got back to Myerworth, they went their separate ways. Caiden had to assure him that they went to the same school and that they would indeed run into each other again. David didn't notice how sensitive her abilities were until she said that and wasn't sure what that meant.

The rest of the school day was over before she knew it. Caiden came out of the front doors and found a place to stand with the other students that seemed to be waiting to be picked up. After a while, she began to notice that they were just hanging out in small groups and not waiting for a ride at all.

Aza spotted her looking around for a sign or something and he smiled to himself.

"You can just stand anywhere."

"How'd you know what I was looking for?"

"Just call her and tell her where you are."

"I don't have a phone, remember?"

"You can use mine."

He took it out and tried handing it to her. She gazed at the sleek, black device, and was tempted, but didn't give in. In Iela's book that aligned with not keeping a low profile and after seeing her that morning, she didn't want to take any chances.

"That's alright."

He put it away and waited with her.

"You weren't in class," he said after a moment.

Caiden kept quiet.

"Don't worry, I'm not a snitch." He saw her shoulders relax. "But next time you ditch, maybe I could get an invite?"

She turned to him. "Why?"

"You're not the only one that hates this place."

"I don't."

"Still," he said, fixing on her.

Caiden got that sense again that he was telling her something without really saying it. She spotted David further down the sidewalk, but he just gave her a nod and got on the school bus.

"How is she? Your mom."

Caiden completely faced him this time.

"...Aza."

He was done being passive and demanded her undivided attention.

"I know you wanna come. You wanna know everything. I saw it that day in the hall."

"She's not gonna let me go," Caiden said, not entertaining the idea despite Roxa's offer to help her.

"Caiden." Aza wanted to grab her shoulders, her arms, her hands, anything to shake some understanding into her. "This has nothing to do with her. That feeling of wanting to know more about yourself, that's your innate right and nobody else's."

She gazed up at him, her heart affected by his words, but Iela pulled up in front of them right when she was about to respond.

"I gotta go," she said without a look back.

She got in the car and Iela naturally glanced at Aza as she scanned the other students. Caiden braced herself for whatever questions she was ready to fire at her.

"Is that another human?" she asked, popping two oval-shaped white pills into her mouth.

"No, ma'am."

"I'm gonna drop you off."

"Is something wrong?" Caiden was studying her face.

"...No. Why?"

Caiden watched her until she glanced her way.

"This morning..." she started low, trailing off.

"Do you do this at school? This thing. Reading people, invading their privacy?"

"Not on purpose..." Caiden could see she was more curious than upset.

Iela went quiet for a moment, her gears working. They pulled up to their house and Caiden got out. She stood there patiently waiting.

"I'm not gonna leave until you're inside."

Caiden turned and walked to the door. She glanced back before going into the house and heard Iela drive off.

Chapter XV

DONTAE HAD BEEN staring through the kitchen window for about ten minutes now. After he and Volx left Faber's, the man had disappeared into the storage house with Barry, who was already a sniveling mess when they found him. He could only imagine what he'd become now after hours in that wooden box with the only man that Dontae had ever met that could slow down his heart rate while maintaining the ability to run a mile at will. He supposed it was unfair to call Volx a man, or any of the Argenta for that matter, but it still freaked him the hell out, so he sympathized with their hostage.

Mil and Volx were the only two that used the oversized shed. Mil would occasionally lock himself in there to meditate or write, but it puzzled Dontae at first as to why Volx would use it. If they needed answers from a particular Void that fell in the outlier category, then they would simply question them together or at least in pairs. There was never any need to further interrogate someone after they got what they wanted. According to Aza, it was hard to Hide when they were under extreme duress or the influence of certain inhibiting agents, but Volx always had to have a separate session out back.

It was eerily still with just a dim light seeping through the bottom of the door. Dontae was standing over the sink, focused on the little house. His phone buzzed and he tore his eyes away.

"Who are you talking to? We don't have any friends." Aza walked into the kitchen with his laptop, fresh out of the shower, and sat down at the table.

"Just put a gun in my mouth." Dontae saw it was a message from Piccolo. He put his phone away and continued to look out the window. "Mil's not back yet?"

"Why are you looking for him?" He flipped his hair down about to twist it up on top of his head but shook it out like a wet dog. "You're hungry, aren't you? We're not always gonna have beer waiting for you, especially since Mil doesn't want us to drink."

"Says the guy with a wine glass soldered to his manus." Dontae managed to focus his attention away from the window and joined Aza at the table. "Now I know why Jais doesn't spend the night."

A loud crack from outside made them exchange looks. Aza wiped off water drops from his computer screen with his bath towel and began typing again. Dontae wanted to spring out of his seat to see what that sound was, but his body wouldn't move. He didn't want to keep hoping at the window.

"I can fix you something," he said, closing his laptop.

"Oh." Dontae cupped Aza's delicate, manicured hand. "You're sweet, but my palate isn't accustomed to your peasant cuisine." Dontae teased with a consoling head tilt and let his hand go, but noticed that Aza held on a second too long.

"I'm making ramen."

"You poor child."

Dontae pulled out his phone again just to reread Piccolo's message. He was waiting for Aza to throw it back at him, but it didn't come. He watched him tear open a shrimp flavor pack and pour it in a pot.

"...You said he's a kid. Around our age?"

"Yeah, he looks like it." Dontae straightened up in his chair. He knew that tone. "I don't think he's gonna make it."

It was silent for a moment. Dontae sat thinking, not ever getting comfortable with the idea of staying in one place for too long, especially when things were so close to getting started.

"I admire him," Aza said, turning up the heat. "His will, I mean."

"He's being stupid. The faster he tells us something, the faster it'll all be over." His mind wandered some as he thought about the many people they'd questioned over the years since he'd been with them. "Why do they try so hard?..."

Aza gave him a back hug before going back to the stove. "You at least want some coffee? I can never really sleep when we have guests."

Dontae watched his hair floating behind him like a jet ink waterfall as he searched the cabinets for coffee mugs. "What's worrying you now? It feels like you're seconds away from leveling downtown."

"I'm fine," he said, filling the pot with water.

"Have you tried getting out there? I love the psycho like everybody else, but even Mil knows we can get answers a lot faster with you or Pneuma."

Aza visibly turned pale, but he didn't turn around. Dontae locked on his back and regretted asking the question.

"You know Pneuma has no conscience...And Volx, he doesn't seem to know anything else." He glanced back at

Dontae, whose phone was vibrating again. "Mil would scalp me if I did, anyway."

"You're not any less useful because you don't have the stomach for it," Dontae comforted in earnest. "And since when does Mil have two pets?"

Aza had to turn around then. Dontae had been counseling him about his diminishing spine whenever he got a chance, claiming it was about his calling. Aza agreed with him, but if he was at the end of a leash it wasn't because he didn't have a mind of his own. He simply didn't trust himself.

"Do you have to go?" He didn't feel like arguing and the way each of them lived, he didn't know when they'd see each other again.

"I have to do my part."

"Stop saying that."

Dontae smiled and got up out of his seat. "I'll be back. But only to kiss you goodnight. You couldn't pay me to sleep here."

As Dontae was about to leave, he caught a gleam of light out of the window. He looked and saw the shed door wide open. He turned to the kitchen door and saw Volx calmly standing there. His hands were covered in blood.

"I didn't hear the door," Aza said, startled himself.

Neither one of them had seen or heard the giant make a peep back into the house or into the kitchen.

"'I don't think he's gonna make it,'" he stoically quoted Dontae from earlier.

They both could only stare at him; Dontae getting a shiver hearing his own words being repeated back to him in such a definitive manner.

"...What'd you do with him?" he asked, though he truly didn't want to know.

Volx said nothing, turned, and left. It was only after they heard him rev up the truck and didn't hear him drive away, did they realize he wanted company.

***

Iela pulled up to Piccolos' and parked further down from the entrance than she normally did. She took out her phone and called someone, but they didn't answer. She spotted a man towards the back of the building, just standing there, looking at her through her windshield. She hung up her phone, got out, and began walking right toward him. He turned down the back and her steps slowed a little.

"William," she called.

The man turned around and they exchanged knowing looks before she continued to follow him to the back of the building. She watched him go behind a dumpster and drag out Barry. His face was bruised and blood seeped through his shirt and pants where open cuts existed beneath. He was crying and looking around, manic, at Iela and William. But especially at Iela.

She naturally pulled out her gun.

"Here is your killer," William said.

The guy's eyes bugged out, darting between the two of them.

"Why?" he asked, his vocal cords scraping against each other in agony. "What are you doing!?"

"What the fuck is going on?" Iela had her weapon aimed at William instead of the shriveling heap.

Barry suddenly realized something as he noticed William's calm demeanor and Iela's reflecting his own expression.

"William..." he said, shaking and pleading.

Their eyes met and he seemed to have lost all the feeling in his legs.

"I told you we were close," he whispered to him.

William's expression was cold and vacant. At first, Barry couldn't fathom what was happening to him, but when he did, he saw red. He elbowed William across the face and flailed his body and arms until he got loose.

"Shit," Iela spat, watching him make a run for it. She was about to shoot but dropped her weapon. She started after him in pursuit but stopped when she saw that there was nowhere for any of them to go, yet she couldn't hear him anymore. The sound of his footsteps seemed to have dropped out like he was picked off into thin air.

She pulled out her phone and turned on the light, pointing it all around. It was just a brick wall. There was no way that kid could've gotten away from her.

Then, Iela's face suddenly deflated as she slowly backed away toward William. He'd already put two and two together when she got back to him.

"...He's gone," she said, barely.

"We can't come back here again."

"Why'd you come here in the first damn place?" She shoved her gun up against the curve of his saggy jaw.

"We don't have time for this," he trilled.

Iela thrusted William to the side and—

Schwep.

Got him perfectly in the thigh. She'd been wanting to do that ever since they met up in her car that day. She swiftly made it across the street, glancing back as he hit the ground like a ton of bricks. The last thing she saw before she drove away was the darkness where Barry disappeared, thinking chillingly how that could've been her.

At that moment, Piccolo opened the back door and tossed out a bag of trash. He saw William bleeding out from his leg.

"Hey, are you alright?" He ran to him. "What happened?"

"I'm fine," he managed to say, though harsher than he wanted. The bullet burning through skin and muscle seemed to be taking its time to get to the point. He hurried as fast as he could crawl to the dumpster for some leverage.

"Hold on."

Piccolo ran back inside to get his phone, but when he came back out, William was gone.

He canceled his nine-one-one and went out to the street to check if he was limping around out there, but he only saw cars. As he turned to head back, there was a truck heading his way. It was speeding a little, but gracefully parked by the curb.

Volx, Aza, and Dontae got out.

"What's this?" Piccolo asked, eyeing Dontae and his company.

Volx didn't waste any time going to the blood drops that had been left behind from William. The others watched him as he stood up and sniffed toward the streets. He then turned around and his nose flared toward that brick wall.

"Jais."

Dontae took a step closer, but couldn't see anyone.

Suddenly, there was sobbing and Barry appeared coming out of the dark. He had a hand gripping the back of his neck as he was shoved further into the light shining from the open door. His stubbled, curly-haired captor had no intention of letting him go.

"We have a problem," he said as his eyes smoldered an electric shade of dark hazel.

Chapter XVI

IT WAS THREE in the morning. The streets were empty except for the delicate patting of the drizzle finishing up before the rising of the sun. Street lights reflected off the wet road as a vehicle crept over a small pothole towards the neighborhood firehouse. It was a luxury, brand spanking new, SUV type. Loud music was reverberating in waves off the vehicle. The windows were vibrating so violently they looked as if they would shatter.

The owners, who were now focused hard on the twinkling pavement, were none other than the Farcheuses, one of the wealthiest moonshine families in the south. Tonight they were nicely dressed, sitting stiffly in their seats as a concerto played on the radio. Both were beautiful, everything pathetically contrived.

But God is fair.

Past their forced expressions and into the backseat was their nine-year-old son, Adyn. His mouth, wrists, and eyes were duct-taped so tight that his struggling was useless. He was crying until he was red in the face, but all his parents could hear were the trilling strings of the violin.

As the vehicle pulled up next to the quiet fire station, the woman turned the music up some more. The man got out and went to Adyn's side of the car. He opened the door and grabbed his son's arm. Adyn began to struggle, but his father jerked him out of the backseat. The boy's screams fought against the tape as his face turned lollipop red and he started clawing at his father's expensive cashmere sleeve. He unclasped the boy's small hands from his arms, little digit by little digit, and shoved him before hurrying back to his side of the vehicle. He got inside and quickly drove away.

Adyn heard the muffled orchestra grow fainter as it got farther and farther away. Now, it was only him with the silence. It was deafening. Adyn's senses all the more intensified since his sight had been taken away from him. His father made it impossible to take off the tape, using two or three rolls to secure nearly his whole face. He took a few steps toward the street but stopped when he felt the slope of the driveway. He stepped back and fell over, scraping his hands. He laid there on his back, quietly whimpering and curling up into a trembling ball.

Zwish!

His cries were interrupted with a knife slice through the atmosphere. It was so sharp, the air could be heard separating into two parts.

Then, footsteps.

Adyn's sniffles stifled and he stiffened, but he didn't hear anything else.

A pair of small dress shoes walked up next to Adyn and stopped. A small hand reached out, clutched the front of the boy's shirt, and pulled him to his feet as easily as if he was lifting a pencil.

Both pairs of shoes dematerialized with another slash through the air, and the streets were empty again.

***

Caiden was lying in bed in her pajamas, staring off into the small light that her desk lamp threw on the wall behind it. It had been the closest thing to the sun when she was growing up in this house. She didn't feel the need to long for the real thing because she hadn't felt it on her skin until she was seven. When she finally got the chance, it was somewhat marred by the fact that she had to share it with her mother. Self-defense was useful, but when you're seven and you've never played in your front yard with the neighborhood strays like the rest of the kids, the heel palm strike is the last thing on your mind.

"Are you asleep?" The Voice asked.

Caiden closed her eyes and turned over. She'd gotten lost in the light and now she was watching tiny glitch-colored bulbs on the other side of her eyelids.

"I can't sleep."

She opened her eyes as her lamp pretended to dim, but at the last millisecond decided not to. Lately, she'd been having to change them more often, so she went to her closet to check if the last one she had was still there before she bothered Roxa to get her some new ones.

"Do you ask me that when I'm actually asleep or do you already know the answer?"

"If you're actually asleep then why would I do a silly thing like that?"

She didn't say anything. The Voice always asked her questions that It already knew the answer to.

"You don't want to dream, do you?"

"I don't know," she said, crashing back into bed. "I know I have to or it didn't really count, but it's strange. You know, that's the only dream I've ever had?"

"Maybe that's the only one you remember."

Suddenly, the light went out, and not in a flicker. It was like someone turned it off. Then, Caiden heard something and sprang up. Her hand found Mary under one of her pillows and she was guided by her heart's glow to her door to listen closer.

"What's going on?" The Voice asked.

"I heard something."

She twisted the knob and opened her door a sliver. It was pitch dark in the halls on down. At least in the living and dining area. That was the only light she could see downstairs from her room when they were on.

"Roxa," she called out.

There was no answer.

Downstairs, Iela was in her study, dozing over those letters at her desk when her doorknob began to twist ever so slightly. She carefully and silently got on her guard as she pulled out her Glock. She went to the door and snatched it open, but there wasn't anyone there.

As soon as she stepped out of the room, someone grabbed her from behind. Iela grunted at the person's strength but managed to headbutt them with the back of her head. She spun around and kicked them in their knees until they dropped to them. Now, she had them at gunpoint.

"Who the hell are you?" she seethed.

The person slowly sat up and she saw it was a man with a gaping scar on his neck, like someone had taken a knife to it. She didn't recognize him and he didn't answer her. He just stared up at her with a pissed expression on his face.

"Iel—" Roxa attempted to call her from the other room, but all she heard after was a loud thump.

"Roxa!"

Nothing.

The intruder looked up at her, wondering what she was going to do next. His composure was irritating, so she knocked him out with the butt of her gun.

Back upstairs, Caiden had locked herself in her room with Mary's grip getting moist in her palms. She heard the knob being tinkered with and her breath caught in her throat.

"The closet," The Voice said.

"I called for Roxa. They already know I'm here," she said in the most inaudible voice she'd ever made.

The tinkering quickly turned into bangs. Her heart had never beat this fast in her life, even with Mary by her side.

The bangs got louder as the person on the other side seemed to be throwing their body against the wood.

But then, there was a sharp gust of wind and sounds of a struggle. Everything had stopped. Only silence. There were no footsteps heard running away or anything. Caiden continued to listen, but heard nothing. She inched toward the door, Mary at the ready, and started to unlock the locks.

"Caiden," The Voice warned.

"Caiden..."

She heard a muffled voice call her.

"Roxa."

Caiden cautiously came out of her room and saw Roxa bleeding out of the side of her mouth. Her eyes went straight to Caiden's heart.

"Child. You okay?"

"I am." She couldn't take her eyes off the blood. "Roxa."

Roxa saw the worry reflected in the girl's eyes and licked the wound clean with one swipe of her tongue.

"Don't worry. If he wanted it to hurt, he shoulda killed me."

Caiden watched Roxa reach out towards her shaky hand, but it wasn't for the one holding Mary.

"It's fine now," she said, grabbing both her hands. "You alright and that's all that matters."

Footsteps were heard downstairs as Iela ran out the front door. Her gun was down at her side as she looked around their house and up the street. The men seemed to have gone. Except for the one that had been banging on Caiden's door, he'd found himself stumbling out the back of the house. Bewildered and wide-eyed, he began to run in no particular direction. That is until that sharp wind was heard again and his feet were nearly ripped out from under him.

He flipped on his back and looked around horrified, but there was no one there. He got up and tried to run into the thicket of trees.

Zwish!

Again, like he was being toyed with. Another razor-sharp slice tore right through his back and wisps of smoke shot out of his chest.

And where he stood, the man literally dropped dead.

Chapter XVII

MIL'S PLACE WAS quiet this evening. Not that a peep was heard daily, but everything was more still as the house realized that this was finally happening.

For most of their lives, they'd been waiting for a particular sign that the agreement they'd made all those years ago was not in vain. They didn't know exactly what they would come across, but now that Jais was here, that meant Pneuma was as well, and they felt the closest they ever had to that elusive answer to that never-ending question, why.

Dontae was sitting on Aza's floor with his back against the other bed. They were in the middle of a round of Monopoly, but the game seemed to be at a standstill. Dontae fingered his top hat between his thumb and index as he watched his brother's hands fly across the keyboard. He stared at him a moment and wondered when he'd developed this essay-writing coping mechanism. Before, he'd just fall into this YouTube abyss of strangers' daily routines or play salon with his plethora of string. Aza was a student, so it didn't seem too out of character, but he was quite sentimental and there was always something driving even his most subtle of actions.

"I would buy the blues, but that would be too transparent." Dontae rolled the die and moved his piece.

"I'm not gonna let you..." Aza said, not paying attention in the slightest.

"Okay." Dontae took his laptop, which just slid out of Aza's hands. He looked at the screen and only saw his crashing wave wallpaper. "Ah, you were just getting your kicks."

"I finished." He began nipping at the loose skin on the back of his knuckles, lost in thought. He glanced at Dontae and flinched when he saw he was already looking at him. "What?"

"Yeah, what. You're sitting here writing blank-v-blanks for a class you've taken over a hundred times."

"Three times."

"Okay, three times."

Aza looked at Dontae and saw he wasn't angry, just concerned. He didn't know how much he wanted to share with him though. Aza never defined the line between human and Void because it was simply too stupid, but sometimes he had to remind himself that Dontae was more than a human to him.

"Where's Jais?" He began putting away the game. "He just left us at that bar without a word."

"Where do you think?"

"I know both of them can look after themselves, but shouldn't we all be together right now? I mean, Caiden's coming over and it would be better if everyone was here."

Aza got up and put the game in his closet. He looked down at Dontae who was waiting for him to explain what he just said.

"She said she would," he said, slumping on his bed.

"Did she?" Dontae got up on the other bed. "I think it'd be better to meet somewhere neutral."

"Why not here? It's where she's gonna end up anyway."

Dontae leaned in closer. "All the more reason not to."

"Oh, right," Aza sighed and went to the door. "It's not kidnapping if she's willing."

"Look who's throwing around incriminating jargon. The things blind loyalty will make you do."

"I'm going to the kitchen. You want something?"

Aza went out the door and Dontae was right behind him.

"Yeah, I wanna know what you won't do for that man." Dontae reeled himself in a bit, catching a glimpse of Aza's profile. "The list just seems to be getting shorter every time I come back here and it's pissing me off."

Aza didn't respond right away. He could tell Dontae was holding back. He turned to him, but couldn't look him in the eye for what he was about to say.

"...I actually thought about lying to her. She can't read us— I mean she can, but not when we're Hiding."

"Congratulations to all of you."

"Trust me," Aza said, now catching his baby blues. "I'd rather be human in this sense. You can't lie to her at all...Every time I Hide, I'm making a conscious effort to do just that."

Dontae leaned on the counter next to him and smiled a little to himself. "Of course you're doing unnecessary extra credit for this. If she's like you said she was, then she'll come on her own. Without you committing a felony."

"I wasn't gonna do that," he said, grabbing his favorite mug. He noticed another bowl and spoon were out to dry and put them away. "I would never do that to her."

Dontae bumped his arm with his elbow. "TMI."

Thump. Thump.

Aza nearly dropped his mug as his head lurched to the kitchen door and exchanged looks with Dontae.

"I got it." Aza set down his cup and Dontae followed him to the front door. He peeked out of the window but saw no extra vehicles. He opened the door.

"Jais."

Dontae noticed that he didn't look at them long before he guided their eyes down to his feet. There wasn't a porch light, so what they could see from the light in their living room was a small bundle.

There, balled up and unconscious on their welcome mat, was Adyn, still bound with duct tape.

***

Iela was sitting at the table, nursing her favorite red-eye. While she was going over all the possible ways she could've taken out the intruders, Roxa and Caiden were sitting on the couch in the living room. A bruise on Roxa's temple and lip had darkened to the shade of eggplant. Caiden was trying to hold an ice pack on the bruise on her head.

"If you put that freezin' thing on me again..."

"I'm sorry."

She immediately backed off but continued to eye the purple mark.

"No, I am," she said, heaving herself up with all the strength she had left. They were all up way later than usual, but Roxa was too riled up to sleep. "That was supposed to be directed at the cause of this whole mess."

"You haven't touched your bag in the closet?"

Caiden finally looked up at her mother and sensed some quiet determination.

Yes, she and her mother always had a getaway bag packed and ready just in case they needed to get out of town at a moment's notice, but Iela mainly only skipped town when she got restless or she'd sworn some stranger had made her in a store or on the street.

"Yes, ma'am."

Iela put the glass to her lips and let the brown, viscous liquid lap over her tongue. She'd been at a loss since those men broke in. She didn't want to set her mind to think that William could do something like this. Not after how she left him the last time. This was a deliberate and desperate scare tactic, but it didn't reek of William.

At least, not at first. Iela had always been confident in her hold over him, but remembering his face after their last meeting, she wondered if he'd mistaken boldness for stupidity.

"You not goin' anywhere," Roxa said, shuffling around in the kitchen.

"I have a place we can lay low just south of Monterrey—"

"You better stop talkin' if you know what's good for you."

"Monterrey," Iela repeated. She put her glass down and turned on Roxa. "We can be out of here in under thirty minutes with or without you."

"Listen to ya self. You gon' pull her outta school, outta this town, cuz yo' past caught up with you. Not while I'm still breathin'."

"What do you want me to do, then? Wait for them to keep coming back here until they get it right?"

Caiden watched them go back and forth as she sunk deeper into the couch. She knew that her going to school was too good to be true. The ice pack resting in her hands had turned warm. She wouldn't have thought it strange if they'd only took the ice out of the fridge an hour ago, but it had only been five minutes. Caiden felt her wrist for a pulse and it was beating at a ridiculous pace. She looked down at her chest out the top of her neckline and saw that her heart was brighter than usual.

"Caiden. What's the matter?" The Voice asked.

"I can't breathe," she said in what she thought was a whisper, but Roxa heard her and stopped mid-sentence.

"Put your head between your legs— Stop bringin' up Mexico!" she spat at Iela who was so dead-set on getting her point across that she'd completely tuned out any other voice in the room.

"She's fine." Iela threw back a considerable amount of drink left in her glass and went to the kitchen to get a cup of ice water.

Caiden had obeyed and had her head between her knees though she didn't feel any different.

"How's your breathin'? Okay?" Roxa had sat back down next to her on the couch and was rubbing her back.

"I feel the same."

"See." Iela brought the glass to Caiden and she started drinking it. "That's not an attack."

"You don't know a damn thing."

"I've had a few before, and that wasn't it."

"Then, what was it?"

Caiden could see that Iela had no idea, but she also hadn't seen her mother look at her like that since their first and last trip to church.

***

Dontae, Aza, and Jais had been stopped in their tracks. They were standing around Adyn, who was still knocked out on the couch, but they were interrupted. Well, Aza and

Jais were. Dontae was left to his imagination as to what Aza, who'd already witnessed Caiden's influence, called the loss of his self-control. They'd been quietly discussing who or what this child could be that Pneuma gifted to them when they suddenly felt something. It pulled on their insides right near the heart and they all exchanged looks.

"What?"

Dontae had no idea what was going on, but it didn't last long as Jais and Aza's expressions went back to normal.

"What the hell was that?" Jais asked as if he got injected with a shot of adrenaline.

Dontae glanced at Aza before watching Jais' eyes stop simmering. "What'd it feel like?"

"Like a wave or something...I don't know."

"I think that was him..."

Jais looked at Aza and he mirrored his expression. Dontae, on the other hand, naturally looked toward Adyn, but the boy hadn't seemed to have done anything since they brought him in the house. He had the urge to check for a pulse, but Jais would say something about not trusting Pneuma to do his job, and he didn't want to start anything this far after midnight.

"Not him. The Soul." Aza looked at Dontae. "You didn't feel that?"

"Obviously not," he said, crouching by Adyn, but keeping an eye on Jais.

"You can't feel him." He didn't intend for it to sound like a statement, but he could tell Dontae understood him. He and Aza were the only ones that didn't treat him like a human. "That doesn't make any sense."

"None of this does..." he said, trailing off. Dontae was closely examining the boy's clothes and what little of his facial features he could see outside the tape. It wasn't much, but his clothing was saying something to him. "I think he's brethren. That's about a hundred thousand from head to toe."

Dontae paused and glanced at the boy's shoes again.

"My mistake. This kid wears Beppoti's on his field trips." He looked up, satisfied, at his puzzled audience.

"Just say he's filthy rich." Jais got up and kneeled next to the boy. He gently tried to remove the tape, but there was no way it was coming off without the boy jolting awake from the pain. His jaw locked as he stood to think some more.

"I've never heard of Beppoti's," Aza admitted.

"He's not exactly famous in the modern sense. Just some Italian schizophrenic who makes incredibly nice shoes. If he has a pair," Dontae said, examining the craftsmanship, "then it's the only pair of its kind."

"How do you know all of this?" Aza asked, quietly impressed.

"The house of Cahill," he said more to himself. Then, childhood memories began to muddle his mind as he crouched back down by the boy's side. "...You think his parents did this to him?"

"You got that from his clothing, too?" Jais watched as Dontae went away for a while and had to bring him back. "We can ask him when he wakes up."

"Jais."

They all looked up and saw Mil standing in the doorway. None of them knew how long he'd been there.

"You have something to tell us," Mil stated.

Dontae and Aza looked at him, but he never took his eyes off Mil.

"Looks like you already know."

"Did something happen?" Aza asked, waiting for Jais to answer.

"She's fine. They all are. That's why I came here tonight, but I thought this kid would take priority."

"Why would you think that?"

The few seconds of silence that Jais held in his eyes as he looked at Mil made Aza want to jump out of his skin.

"He took care of it, right?"

Jais finally tore his eyes away from Mil. "He always does...They're fine."

"Weapons," Volx said from the other doorway to the hall. He came into the room when Mil did, but they always seemed to notice him when it's too late.

"I'm not sure from what genus, but they were small enough to be comfortably concealed."

"Thank you, Jais." Mil gave his last look to the boy on the couch before he started to go into the kitchen.

"Wait, what about the kid? The other one?" Jais asked, his head going from Mil to Volx. "We let him go for what? How do we know he didn't have anything to do with the attack tonight?"

"Volx?" Mil said.

"There were three people behind the bar. The mother, unidentified, and bait."

"Thank you, Volx."

And like Mil's departure was an order, Jais begrudgingly scooped the child up in his arms.

"What are you doing? You're not even sure if he's a blue blood or not." Dontae felt he was already getting attached.

"I'll be careful."

Jais turned to leave towards the hall, but Volx wasn't done yet. He was still posted up in the doorway, staring off at something across the room. They waited for him.

"I need a body."

As if those were the magic words, an unconscious man fell onto the coffee table out of nowhere with the sound of a knife slashing through the air.

Dontae nearly fell back into Jais as it just missed him by a hair. It was mangled, due to the fall, and didn't have a single mark on him. It would look like he was sleeping if it weren't for the fact that he hit the table head first.

"...Jesus, Pneuma." Dontae had to grab his heart as he and Aza watched Volx, who wasn't a tinge unnerved, pick up the body and leave the living room for the backyard.

Chapter XVIII

IT HAD BEEN a few days since David saw Caiden in the halls. He never noticed how much time he'd spent stealing glances at her detached earlobe and the faint hairs that curled just beneath the ending of her sideburns. When he'd watch her head dip slightly down, gazing about at the students whose auras drew her attention while walking to her next class, and she, attempting to smile but never fully getting there. At first, he thought she was avoiding him after their meeting at the deli, but realized if anyone was to do any avoiding, it was him. He did admit that Caiden made him curious and creeped him out at times when she did that little reading people thing, but he saw some of that outsider in her that he thought went well with his outcast label.

David felt a wave of nausea as he opened his locker. He was so distracted he forgot what he was going in there for.

"David, right?"

His stomach dropped to the deepest pits when he saw Aza peeking out from the other side of the locker door.

"Y-Yeah?"

"I was wondering if you'd seen Caiden around. It's been days." Aza noticed his fidgety hands.

"Um, did you text her? Maybe texting—"

"She doesn't have a phone," he lamented as he gripped his own. "I mean, I could drop by her house, but her mom's strict."

"You've been to her house." David tried to frame it as a question, but his mind and his heart didn't want to work on the same team at the moment.

"Can't do that again...Thanks, anyway." He was about to finish and give the guy a breather, but something about him made Aza want to keep talking. "Are you a new transfer?"

"No, why?"

"I was trying to place your face."

"What do you mean, like you've seen me before or something?"

"No, I've only seen you at school. I'm sorry," he said, quickly.

"It's fine..." David closed his locker as his hands steadied around one of the straps of his backpack.

"If you see Caiden, let her know I was looking for her."

David gave him a silent nod as he watched him turn the corner. He exhaled a deep breath and headed out the nearest exit.

***

Dontae knocked on Volx's bedroom door and went in. He was ready to give Adyn the cheese crackers and apple juice he had swaying in a grocery store bag off his wrist, but the child was still in the same spot where he left him. Dontae looked over at Jais who was lounging on Pneuma's bed with one of his books.

"He should be up by now." He was taking in the barren room, wondering if it always looked this way. Plain, empty, and lifeless. "Where's the other one? I know you know."

"He's around," Jais said, turning a page.

Dontae watched him for a moment, studying his rugged appearance. For the others, it'd been nearly a year since he last saw them, but he hadn't seen Jais in almost eighteen months. His hair had grown and he was wearing sneakers now. Before, it was some casual chukka or work boot. He didn't know if that meant he was becoming more relaxed or if he'd come across some more bad news.

"I got 'em on sale." Jais moved one of his shoes a little in Dontae's direction, but never took his eyes off the page.

"In town?" Dontae asked as he crouched next to Adyn's bed.

"Which is it?" Jais closed the book and gave Dontae his undivided attention. "You wanna know when I got here or when I'm leaving?"

"Neither. I was gonna ask where you're sleeping."

Jais smiled and slid the book under the mattress next to a few of the others that were hidden there.

"In my car—"

"As in on the streets—"

"As in you know I don't sleep."

Dontae looked up at him.

"You look good. Dashing," he observed, scanning his prim and proper clothing. "I thought after you turned legal, you'd grow out of all of this."

"Just because I can drink now doesn't mean I'm supposed to stop worrying about you."

"Your concern is misplaced." Jais lingered on Dontae before going to the boy.

"We have to take this tape off." He checked to see if there was a loose opening anywhere and slid a small antique dagger out of his pocket.

"That would be easier if he was awake."

Jais watched Dontae carefully saw away at the layers of tape around the boy's wrists with one of the sides of the blade and his leg twitched.

Dontae moved his knife out of the way as the boy moved again. He exchanged looks with Jais and they backed up to give the boy space. Like he suddenly remembered what happened, he sprung up and got on his knees. He then began feeling around to get a sense of where he was.

"Hey, you're okay," Dontae said gently.

Adyn stiffened at the sound his voice and began backing away from it.

"It's okay," Jais jumped in. "We just wanna get you loose."

The boy's head swiveled in Jais' direction and he lifted his hands to him. Dontae quickly gave Jais his dagger.

"I gotta knife, so don't move or you'll cut yourself." Jais took his small wrists into his hands. "I'm gonna cut it now."

Jais began sawing where Dontae left off away from the boy and towards himself. It was quiet except for the boy's breathing in and out of his nose. Once the tape was cut, he gently peeled it off and handed it to Dontae, who then left the room.

"How about your mouth now?"

The boy inched closer to Jais, closer to the edge of the bed.

"That's good. Okay, I'm gonna get close to your skin now, because this is pretty tight on here. Try to be extra still. Like a statue. Okay?"

The boy froze on the spot, even holding his breath.

"You can breathe," Jais said with a faint grin. He leaned in closer to see if there was another opening and he found one behind the boy's ear. "I'm about to start."

Jais began just below the ear and worked his way up, making sure to keep the tip of the knife away from the boy's neck and head. He got up a significant piece of tape on the back of his head and slowly started pulling it off the hair on the nape of his neck. The boy's breathing slowed for the duration of the cutting. He flinched a little once Jais started peeling the tape away from around his mouth. His skin was red and quite raw. Jais got the apple juice and handed it to him. The boy emptied it at once.

"The one on your eyes might hurt the worst," he said, picking up the knife again. The boy turned away and Jais backed off. "Okay. It's okay...Can you speak?"

He nodded and slowly turned back around.

"What's your name?"

The boy lifted his head to Jais' voice. "...Adyn," he said hoarsely.

"I'm Jais, Adyn." He set the knife on the dresser. "What happened to you?"

"Are you the police?" he asked, following Jais' voice whenever he moved.

"Far from it."

"Then, you're the others...The ones that are supposed to kill me."

"No one's gonna kill you here," he said, kneeling in front of him. He could tell the boy was crying when his nose started to run. He grabbed one of Pneuma's handkerchiefs and put it in Adyn's hand. "Who wants to kill you, Adyn?"

He wiped his nose and tried to calm down to answer, but it seemed like every time he thought about it, that brought on more tears.

"It's okay. You don't have to tell me now." Jais got up and grabbed some of Pneuma's clothes out of the dresser.

"Let me get the rest of the tape off, so you'll be more comfortable."

Jais calmly went over to Adyn again and reached out for the piece he'd separated from the bottom half of the tape that wrapped around his mouth.

"Don't!"

Adyn's cries stopped mid-sniffle as he threw himself as far away from Jais as possible. If Jais wasn't sure he was a blue blood at first, he was starting to think he was now.

"Adyn. What is it?"

Trembling, the boy lifted his head to Jais in an almost pleading manner.

"He'll die."

***

Mary was hanging tight in Caiden's hand. She'd been waiting for Iela for almost an hour now and the sun was close to setting. They rarely sparred in the evenings unless she cut their earlier sessions short to go do an errand. After the attack, Iela was more on edge than ever. It had been a while since Caiden saw her mother finish one of her whiskey bottles in one sitting. Coupled with that break-in, she wasn't sure what side of Iela she was going to see tonight.

"She's taking her sweet time," The Voice said.

"She's done this before, so I'm used to it."

"Yes, and that's the problem," The Voice countered.

Caiden stood on the side of the house and looked toward the clump of trees, wondering why that hit her so hard. She never questioned Iela because she was her mother and she always seemed to know what to do when things got bad. Her own feelings about how a certain situation should be handled never crossed her mind, even when it dealt specifically with her. She feared that her emotions about simple things that should've naturally occurred to her had been drowned out by those around her, and she didn't know how she truly felt about that. But The Voice was right, she just couldn't help the way she felt.

The quiet had gotten to be too much and she knew something was wrong. Just as she turned back to the house a bullet shot right past her; grazed her arm. She spun and shot back.

"Caiden!" The Voice screamed.

"I'm good," she said, checking herself. It almost missed compared to Iela's nick. Whoever they were, was seriously trying to get her.

Someone quickly grabbed her from behind and she jerked her head back. She heard the crack as she shoved the person off of her to aim her gun, but before she could get Mary up, another guy ripped it from her hand.

Caiden's head darted between the two men as her eyes changed color.

"The prince bleeds."

The man now holding Mary crouched down in front of Caiden, his eyes drawn to her wounded arm.

They both stared at her in silence for a while. Caiden couldn't keep her attention on both of them at the same time, so she watched the one with her gun instead.

"No," he said, inching closer. "You're more than a prince."

The other man mimicked him and took a step toward the girl. "The other night, one of our buddies came by for a friendly chat, but didn't make it back."

"I didn't do anything," she said, just barely.

Caiden had never felt fear before to this extent, which was a good thing because now she'd made them out as Voids. But that also meant that the heat on her back and the weakness in her knees were all her. This was a one-eighty from fighting with Iela or even what happened to her with Roxa's church. There was no immediate sense of danger, not like now. The way the man's eyes caressed her face made her want to claw her way out of her skin.

"We know you didn't, beautiful. One of your shadows."

Schwep.

Caiden jumped back as blood splattered her face. A bullet had lodged itself right in the middle of the guy's forehead. She watched the man's life fade out of his eyes as he seemed to take forever to hit the ground. Zinc's barking was getting crazed as it got closer and closer to them. She was so horrified that she hadn't noticed Zinc's presence the second the men attacked her.

The dog dashed out of the wood and was about to rip the head off the survivor. He tried to run but Iela caught him in the throat with her gun and he dropped to his knees. She kicked him in the face and planted her boot on the side of his temple. He was pinned to the ground.

"Who sent you?"

"...I can't...I can't," the man began to sob.

Caiden came back to her senses as Zinc whimpered and nuzzled his nose into her side. He began licking her wounds as she saw her mother trying to stomp a name out of the man. He was sputtering and spitting. Caiden felt sorry for him and tried to get a sense of if he knew anything of value. She suddenly felt his energy mingling in with her mother's. All she could tell was that he was scared of what Iela was going to do to him, but not more than the person who sent him.

Iela put pressure on his face and pointed her gun closer to the back of his head. She minded her trigger finger, but it was shaking impatiently.

"When I pull it, you're gone."

"Wait," Caiden begged.

"Shut up," Iela barked. "He's damned either way—"

"Please" The man's face was a drippy, dirty mess. His mouth was twisted to one side of his face just enough to breathe out of his free nostril. He was keeping his eyes steady on Caiden, who was delaying his execution.

"...Please, don't." Caiden's voice cracked as she fixed on her mother.

Iela looked her dead in the eye and took one solid breath.

Then, she pulled the trigger.

Everything slowed down to a near halt.

The bullet left the chamber, but before it penetrated the man's skin and Caiden could attempt to do anything to help him, there was a sword slicing vibration that severed the air in half, more powerful than before.

Within the next second, the man's body was gone.

Chapter XIX

IELA WAS CALM. She looked at Caiden, but then became focused on the bare ground where the body had disappeared. Now, there nestled in the dirt was the home of her mother's bullet and nothing else.

Iela ran to Caiden and snatched her up by the wrist. She allowed herself to be dragged into the house where Roxa was just now coming downstairs. She took in the state of things and wrested Caiden loose from her mother.

"Take care of her," she breathed, rushing back out the front door.

Her tone had darkened and even her eyes had changed. Roxa hadn't seen Iela so panicked in a while. She led Caiden to the restroom and began cleanup and first aid, while Iela grabbed a tarp out of her car. She laid it out next to the remaining dead body and rolled him over. Then dragged him to the trunk where she gathered all her strength to heave him into the back of her car, one end of him at a time.

When she got back in the house, no one said a word. Iela had strapped herself with an extra handgun she had hidden in her study. She set Mary down on the table in front of Caiden as she eyed Roxa's handiwork.

"Get Mary and get in the car."

"You not takin' her anywhere."

Roxa's rage hit Caiden like a brick. She looked up at her and naturally reached for her hand, but that didn't stop her from going after Iela.

"I didn't say anything before because I ain't got a lot of say in any of this Blackheart business. But this girl here is my business."

"That girl is my child." Iela's pulse hadn't settled as her eyes glanced at the time. She fixed on Caiden again. "Get in the car."

Caiden didn't waste any time getting out of her seat, but Roxa had gripped her hand so tight her knuckles were rubbing together.

"I remember you told me that you was lettin' her out there into the world so that you could clear your conscience."

"Caiden, let's go," Iela persisted, but Roxa was holding fast. She was going to say what she needed to say whether Iela wanted to hear it or not.

"Yo' arrogance is gonna get her killed, and that's somethin' that'll never come off." Roxa loosened her grip around Caiden's hand. "I won't forgive you."

Caiden watched her mother, who she could sense was heeding Roxa's words this time. She had an expression on her face that indicated she understood, but that understanding was going to be on her terms.

"If she stays here, then you'll be another body I'd have to take care of."

"Roxa," Caiden said, gently placing her hand on the old woman's. Roxa gave her a rough hug and kiss before heading down the hall to her room.

Iela shut off all the lights in the house and locked the door behind them. Caiden gave one last look at Zinc before she got in the car and Iela drove off. She didn't want to make a big thing out of it; she had to know that she would see him and Roxa again or it wouldn't come to be.

The silence was stark as they drove out of the neighborhood and into the dark streets. The Voice began to hum, softly this time, but Caiden couldn't relax for the life of her. After a night like this, she didn't know when she'd be able to do something like that ever again.

***

Mil was dining alone tonight. His smoked salmon nestled in a bed of rainbow vegetables and his staple Riesling was being slightly neglected in favor of his notebook of which he was scribbling in again. Details were what they mostly were, but they were whatever Mil deemed as such.

Dontae came into the kitchen but stopped at the door when he saw it wasn't empty. He noticed the tape that Jais had cut off of Adyn was on the counter and he put it in the trash.

"Hungry?" Mil asked, but he didn't lift his head. He slid his untouched plate across the table as Dontae sat down. "If you're waiting for me to hand over my glass, you'll starve."

Dontae wasn't going to pretend that he didn't want to sink his teeth into the crispy metallic skin. He couldn't remember the last time he ate an actual meal, just asking for domestics left and right since he got there. Next to seeing Piccolo and the Soul, of course, Mil's cooking was one of the main reasons why he came back here. He'd have to blame his lavish upbringing for his addiction to fine foods. Even Mil's seasonings conjured up several memories of his often ten-course dinings for one.

"Did it work?" Dontae asked as he motioned to the trash bin with his head and daintily cut into the fish's plump pink flesh. "I didn't know if it'd be enough. There wasn't any blood or anything." He put the small piece in his mouth and had to compose himself from the sudden blood rush throughout his veins.

"Anything the body secretes will do, though Volx surmised that the culprits were amateurs."

"And Caiden?" he asked, taking another arousing bite.

"So it is true." Mil glanced up at Dontae while he took a small sip from his glass. "The gods are cruel. To be so close and yet so inconsequential."

Dontae stopped chewing as he watched Mil's attention linger on him a little longer than necessary.

"From where I'm sitting, it seems we're both the same distance away," he said, picking up his plate and taking it to the sink.

"We'll know soon enough," Mil said curtly.

Dontae put his plate in the microwave and glanced the drying rack to see yet another bowl and spoon, then briskly left the kitchen. He was too old to throw a tantrum, so he calmly walked to Volx's room and knocked on the door.

"Is it safe?" he asked.

He heard footsteps and waited. Jais came out and closed the door behind him. Dontae was about to mention how he looked like he needed a nap but forgot that was just his natural face.

"He took a bath and passed out again."

"He mention anything about why he kicked me out earlier?" Dontae asked, opening Aza's door. He was coming out of it and almost knocked heads with him.

"Sorry."

"He's probably a blue blood."

"The little boy?" Aza asked, patting his bun. "...I hope not."

At about the same time they all paused for a moment and their thoughts went to Volx.

"Women and children," Dontae stated firmly. "Those were his words."

"That's not gonna matter if he's a danger to the red-blooded public. That's why he told me to let that other kid go," Jais said as he picked up one of Aza's ribbons off the floor and handed it to him. "You're going to the kitchen?"

"Yeah," he said, giving Dontae a sympathetic look as he went on ahead.

"I guess I'll see you guys later." Dontae waited for Jais to make an alternative suggestion to him leaving for an unspecified amount of time. He didn't know how long Mil would keep Adyn as his houseguest. Maybe until he found out who he was, but that wasn't a guarantee, especially if he could utilize the child in some way to assist them. For Mil, the Soul was always his first and foremost.

"You'll be at Piccolo's?" Jais asked.

"I'll be at your hotel."

Jais eyed him a moment before he reluctantly pulled out a hotel keycard from his pocket. He didn't mind sharing a room with Dontae since he would most likely not be there anyway.

"Don't wait up." Jais gave him the key as they walked to the front door.

"I'll try," Dontae said and left.

Jais braced himself before walking through the kitchen door. Mil had put away his notebook and was standing cross-armed by the sink. Aza seemed to be waiting anxiously for him so they could get started with whatever this was.

"How's the boy?" Mil asked.

"He's fine. What do you plan on doing with him?" Jais didn't waste any time. It was best to be blunt when talking to Mil. Jais wasn't like Aza or Volx, taking orders without a thought. He didn't trust Mil as far as he could throw him.

"That's not clear to me yet, but what is clear is what he is."

"We're not gonna kill a kid."

"Who said anything about killing him?"

Jais glanced at Aza and realized that he and Mil had started the conversation without him.

"We need to see what he can do."

He looked at Aza's dismal expression, then at Mil, who looked like he just finished reciting his favorite quote.

"...You want him to kill someone."

"Don't worry," Mil said darkly. "They'll deserve it."

"Like that makes a difference." Jais got up and left. Aza followed behind him.

"Where are you going?"

Jais turned on him, piercing his deep violets.

"I know you have a debt to that man, but I didn't think you'd blindly go along with something like this."

Out of everyone there, Jais could count on Aza to be the most humane if not the sanest of them all.

"I need to think," he said, snatching his keys out of his pocket. "But I don't wanna leave him here."

"Mil's not that impulsive," Aza said, allowing his soft tone to act as a calming effect. "He'll wait."

"You're right, and he'll do something sadistic like make me deliver the boy to his victims."

Aza instinctively glanced over his shoulder and followed Jais out of the front door.

"Probably, but how else are we gonna find out what he's saying is true?"

Jais dropped his head, still thinking. Then, he looked up at Aza as his mind began to gradually go blank.

"...I have to get outta here."

Aza headed to the end of the driveway. "Which way?"

Jais locked the door behind them, contemplating whether or not he wanted Aza for this ride-along. He suddenly felt sorry for him, thinking of all the times when he was younger and wanted to storm out of the house to get away from Mil's calm domineering character, but could only go as far as his box of a bedroom.

"To your left," he said, catching up with him.

"You never park in front of the house."

They got into his unassuming coupe several houses down from Mil's.

Volx, who'd heard them drive off in the distance, had turned on the water hose in the backyard to begin spraying the scarlet stained wood in the storage house. It creaked as his tactical boots walked over to a bucket of soapy water he'd prepared. He got on his knees and began scrubbing with a handheld hard bristled brush.

The overhead light was on so he could see better the droplets that had made their way as far as the ceiling, but he wouldn't get to that tonight.

Volx welcomed his cleaning routines because it re-inforced his success on a mission complete. If there was no blood spilled, then he couldn't call it a victory. Though there was one exception. He had a plan for the one that he let get away. A sacrifice disguised as a potential win. Not just for himself, but the Soul as well.

Suddenly, something incredibly heavy hit the door of the shed as multiple gusts of sharp winds were heard in succession, one right after the other. Volx looked up into the night but didn't see anything. He knew it was Pneuma and could sense something was wrong, but he was gone as soon as he arrived.

Volx got up and dropped the brush into the bucket before going to the door. He leaned out and his nostrils flared briefly at the stench of Voided blood. He reached out into the darkness until he felt an ankle, then dragged the body into the outhouse and flipped it over.

It was a man. His nose was bloodied and bent to one side of his face. He was alive and well, but Volx's hands were itching. They needed to be scratched. So he closed the door to begin his next mission.

Chapter XX

IELA TURNED DOWN a street that quickly became familiar to Caiden. She had walked that very cracked sidewalk with David on their way to Faber's, which is where Iela parked the car. Caiden remained calm as she glanced over at her mother. The skin between her eyes was creased and her brow was furrowed. She wasn't getting a feeling of anger. Well, no more anger after what just happened, so Caiden figured that was a good sign.

She looked up at the dead neon "open" as Iela got out of the car and headed towards the back of the building. Caiden wasn't about to question anything until that dark aura around her mother had resided to its normal shade.

"Caiden," The Voice called.

"I'm good."

"That's fine, but I was going to inquire about your mother's state of mind."

Caiden's head fell as the look in Iela's eyes as she pulled that trigger replayed over and over in her head. There was no mercy and she knew her pleading for the man's life was in vain, yet she did it anyway. She began to feel stupid thinking of how she thought she could help him in the first place. That made her head a little lighter and she looked up.

Something did save him, she just didn't know what.

"...I can't read her mind. Only how she feels," Caiden said as she saw a light come on in the back of the deli.

"Just be careful," The Voice cautioned.

Caiden became alert when Iela appeared from the side of the building. She headed straight to her side of the car and opened the door.

"Come on."

Caiden got out and followed her mother to the trunk. Iela opened it up and Caiden saw the bulky tarp. She balked as Iela motioned to the corpse's feet.

"Get that end."

She hesitated a second more as Iela lifted the man's shoulders and tugged his heavier half out of the back. Caiden heaved with all her might the rest of the body out of the trunk and followed her mother's lead to the back of the deli. The hefty butcher was in an undershirt and khaki's when they came down a short hall into the kitchen. He'd just taken out the headless body of a chilled pig and was sharpening a cleaver. He didn't turn around until he heard Iela drop her end of the body on the floor.

"What's that?" Faber tossed over his shoulder. He was too focused on the swine to see that the tarp was leaking on his gray tiled floor.

Caiden was careful with her end as she set it down gently. She looked at the stiff and couldn't believe that moments before he was accusing her of murder. Her attention then went to her hands and she sprawled them open and close. Open and close.

"Don't call me—" Iela said, turning to leave.

"I don't have your number. What's that?" he repeated as he turned around. His face was pudgy and his hair short and curled only on the ends. He hadn't cut anything and yet Caiden saw blood already on his shirt.

"I don't have time for this. Just take care of it," Iela said and headed out the way she came. Caiden kept on her heels.

Faber finally looked at the bloody heap and went after them. He slammed open the back door and caught them before they turned the corner.

"And what the fuck do you want me to do with that?" he asked in a borderline incredulous tone.

"I want you to do your job."

Iela left him pissed and fighting back the urge to heave that cleaver through her skull. Caiden watched him slam the door back shut as she made her way to the car. They both got in and drove away.

They rode in silence for nearly the entire ride. Besides The Voice humming to her softly, the only sound was coming from the car. Caiden looked around at her surroundings and saw that they were parked outside a hotel. It was a smaller one, a garden, or an inn. She couldn't see the full sign from where they were parked, but they'd stayed in only one of these before while they moved around as she grew up and she knew the name was too much for their wallets.

"How long are we staying here?" The question didn't want to be asked. Iela had taken on a permanent glare and Caiden felt like she did something wrong every time their eyes met.

"Come on," she said, getting out.

Caiden followed her mother through the glass doors and to the front desk. A casually alert clerk gave them a tired smile.

"Morning."

"Waters," Iela said.

The clerk was expecting a cordial reply but got on the computer to begin searching for their reservation.

"Two queens, non-smoking?"

"Yeah."

Caiden glanced at her mother and their eyes locked for a second. The clerk handed over a pair of keycards and they headed up to their room on the third floor. It was spacious with two welcoming beds, a flatscreen, a wardrobe, a microwave, and a fridge.

"You got Mary. Don't leave this room until I get back." And she was gone as soon as they entered.

Caiden went to the peephole, then hurried to the window to see if she could see the car. In less than a minute, Caiden saw it pull out of the lot and away from the building. She ran back to the door and locked it.

She stood there a moment just listening to her breathing.

It was very quiet and she realized the AC wasn't on. She was hot but didn't want to take off her clothes and shoes because then she would be comfortable. Caiden didn't want to be comfortable, even if she believed she wouldn't ever feel that feeling again.

Tonight she touched a dead body.

She began to feel lightheaded and sat on the foot of the bed near the window. Her breathing started to get shallow and her pulse was racing this time. This was different from before. She dropped her head between her legs as her mind went to Roxa. Tears wanted to come out, but her body was still in shock from the situation that they remained trapped inside; safe inside. If she started to physically feel anything, then people would know. Her mother would know. Even after the tears had dried and the redness faded away and the puffiness went down, people would still know. Iela would know.

The Voice began humming again more firmly.

"Please stop," she managed to say.

"Forgive me."

"I'm sorry. I just need some quiet right now," she said as her stomach growled.

Caiden sat up and froze at the sound. It grumbled again and she wrapped her arm around her belly. She couldn't remember the last time she ate. Any of Roxa's hearty spreads sounded good right about now. Hell, even a cheeseburger, but she quickly shook those thoughts from her head. She felt she was truly going to start crying if she kept riding on that train of thought.

She decided on taking a shower in hopes that would relax her so she could sleep what was left of the night away. When she placed Mary safely under her pillow and went inside the bathroom, she realized she didn't have any extra clothes. She decided she would have to wrap herself in one of the extra-large towels.

As soon as she cut on the water, two knocks were heard at the door. Caiden's heart leaped and she twisted the knob back until the water shut off. She got up and rushed to get Mary. She was about to check through the peephole, but images of a bullet shooting right through her eye and out the back of her head made her stop.

She grabbed Mary with both hands just to steady it. Iela had left and it was just her. No one was going to pick up her slack this time, so she had to prepare to do any and everything she could. Her mind began to play reels of her sparring sessions with her mother and with each step she took towards the door, she felt more and more ready to face whatever was on the other side.

Caiden's hand reached out for the door handle and her breath caught in her throat. In that second, a thought of remembrance flickered across her face.

It couldn't be.

She swung open the door, but the only thing she saw was a lonely takeout bag from a burger joint.

***

Dontae had been trying to get Piccolo's attention since he walked through the door. It was the start of the weekend and the crowd had been growing exponentially with each hour. White collars schmoozed with bus drivers and nearly every definition of section eight had someone's drink in their hand. After Timothy's death, a slew of other Void incidents had taken place throughout their town. Burglaries and vandalism of the small handful of Void-ran businesses had put the owners either out of business for a few days or a few weeks. Some of them were knocking back drinks tonight with their old customers, while the others had taken to moving out of the city completely.

Piccolos was a very much needed catharsis for the slow-burning tension that was thickening the air. Dontae could feel it in his bones.

"Hey, are you gonna take my order now?" he shot at the Adonis from several people away.

Dontae couldn't take his eyes off of him.

Why did he look so different and yet the same?

He continued to watch him squeeze between Rane and the other guy helping them tend the bar. His dark golden rods catching in his eyelashes and his skin taught around the soft curvature of his cheekbones.

Dontae stopped himself for a moment, wondering what the hell he was doing.

"Sweetie, he do the same thing to me."

He turned around and saw Nova giving him a pearly white smile. She had on a lengthier wig this time, tones lighter, like singed honey and her dress was a sequined royal blue.

"You're Nova, aren't you?" he effused, taking her hand.

"Yes, sir and you are?"

"Dontae. Picco's friend."

Dontae kissed the back of her hand. He couldn't help himself.

"Picco. That's cute."

She smiled and took his hand into hers as she led him to the bar. The crowd parted like the Red Sea when they saw who was coming through.

"The power," Dontae said, amazed. "Thank you."

"Any time, baby."

She flashed her teeth at him again and they kept their eyes locked until she got back on stage to start her next set. Dontae turned back to the bar and instead of seeing Piccolo, Rane was there, giving him a sheepish grin.

"He just disappeared."

"I'll check the back."

"Dontae," she called. He leaned back over the bar. "I thought you weren't coming back."

"What did I tell you about getting attached?" He gave her a charming smile and she slid him a beer.

Dontae's smile faded as he made his way to the back. He stopped when he heard voices on the other side of Piccolo's door. He couldn't understand anything but heard the other door in his office bang open. He carefully checked to see if it was unlocked as he twisted the knob and pushed it open a sliver. He peeked in and saw the room was empty, but the back door hadn't closed all the way. He went into the room and locked the office door behind him. The voices were clearer, so he got closer to the other door.

"...that last time shit. I need you right now."

That was Iela.

Dontae opened the door a little more. He felt slightly foolish for eavesdropping, but being the only human in a group full of blue bloods had caused him to do some things that may make him seem spineless, but have never failed him in the long run.

"You know where you need to go. Why are you avoiding the inevitable?"

There was either a long pause or she lowered her voice to answer him, so Dontae couldn't hear anything. He opened the door a little bit more.

"Where's she now?"

"She's safe. I just need some time."

"Where are you going— Iela!"

Dontae quickly closed the door.

When Piccolo came back into his office, Dontae was leaning on the front of his desk, scrolling through his phone.

"She's the most stubborn creature I've ever met," he said, going to his desk drawer. "You shouldn't be here."

"I've got a human killing child at Mil's, a talented, but long-winded songstress on my next best thing, and an empty, depressing hotel room." Dontae turned to Piccolo, who'd just pulled another cellphone out of the drawer. "I like to sleep in familiarity."

"Go back to Mil's."

"Did you hear what I said?" Dontae had never seen Piccolo look at him so sternly before. "What's the matter with you?"

"The Soul. He was attacked."

"That was already taken care of."

"Again," Piccolo said, texting dexterously. "Her mother's not gonna ask for it, but she needs help."

"What are you doing?" Dontae asked, alert.

"I'm reaching out to our mutual friend." Piccolo quickly finished up and pressed send before putting the phone back in his drawer. "And no, you can't spend the night."

Chapter XXI

WAY UP NORTH in South Dakota at Bethesda Cancer Center, Nania Mendola's head was buried in the emaciated chest of her nine-year-old son.

His name was Carmo.

He was pasty and his dark hair had been pushed back away from his gaunt face. He'd only had one round of chemo before his brain cancer had a spontaneous remission, so his mother was thankful for that. She didn't want her son to lose any sort of normalcy like his appetite and hereditary thick hair.

But the tumor had come back more vicious than before. Nania knew he wasn't going to win this round. She sat awkwardly on her knees in that unergonomic hospital chair, cupping Carmo's tiny, cold hand in her own. She touched her forehead to his skin to pray. The doctors and nurses had cleared out and she was left in the freezing, sterile room to mourn in peace.

At first, it was just a slew of gibberish rushed under her breath. She couldn't find her mind after she mercifully pulled the plug, her eyes wandering around at the blur of faces as they gave her sorry for your losses. Nania collapsed over her son's body and sang to him for hours. Until it was time.

"Ms. Mendola..." Carmo's doctor called to her somberly at the door.

Nania trembled at the onset of more tears, but got up and kissed the boy on the cheek before she sprinted out of the room.

Days later, Carmo was buried in a nice cemetery with a comfy casket to match, made possible by the donations through a website his mother had made for him after they got the diagnosis. The site was her saving grace, providing her with hope for her child's future no matter if he recovered or not.

It was a few hours before dawn in the humble boneyard and the grounds were chillingly peaceful. Carmo's grave with its freshly patted down dirt was the only thing causing a disturbance. The dirt began caving in and out at the same time as something was forcing its way through the cool pit towards the surface.

In a flash, an ashen, boney hand shot up out of the ground followed by the rest of the body it was attached to. It was Carmo's body.

But it wasn't Carmo.

The boy quickly tidied up the plot and dusted the dirt out of his hair and off his clothes before he wisped into thick gray smoke, dissipating into thin air.

***

When Iela got back to the hotel, she'd found Caiden wrapped up in a towel asleep in bed. She had an emergency overnight bag in the backseat with essentials and extra clothing that she brought up to put in the wardrobe. The sun hadn't risen yet and though she was exhausted herself, she couldn't risk dozing off. She went to the bathroom and tried calling William again, but he didn't pick up. Ever since she gave him that warning shot, getting a hold of him was becoming more difficult, the opposite effect of what usually happened when she threatened anyone that she found herself begrudgingly working with. She never conditioned herself to trust people and William's behavior was the main reason why.

She dialed again and got his voicemail.

Iela came back out into the room as Caiden's eyes slid open. She saw her mother and tightened the towel around her body as she sat up.

"There's a change of clothes and a toothbrush in my bag in there."

Caiden could only give her a heavy nod as she went to get the clothes and dress in the bathroom.

Iela noticed the look in Caiden's eye hadn't changed. It was something she hoped she would've grown out of already. She thought training her for immediate threats in an environment that she had complete control over would've toughened her skin, but she hadn't counted on that empathic nature to become her only nature.

When Caiden was a child, it started with animals, particularly dogs, like Zinc, that had taken to her even without her feeding him her table scraps. She would cry and laugh seemingly for no reason, and go quiet when she felt anger. Iela could only watch from afar, only teaching her how to defend herself and never believing a word anyone said. That didn't matter though. If Caiden could sense who wanted to harm her and whether or not someone was a liar, what had Iela truly taught her?

Caiden came back out dressed in Iela's leggings and thermal top. Iela felt like she was looking in a trick mirror. Caiden was a fuller spitting image of her teenage self.

"Go back to sleep if you can. I don't know what's gonna happen tomorrow," Iela said, taking off her boots and sliding into the other bed.

She didn't say anything but watched her mother lean back on the headboard and close her eyes. Iela could feel them; the questions telepathically bombarding her. She didn't know what was going to happen next or where they were going to go if they needed to move again. Monterrey was just to throw off Roxa, but Iela had burned so many bridges, she'd left her and Caiden stranded on a deserted island.

"Remember when we spent the night parked downtown in Houston? Out of the thousands of loans I applied for, one was stupid enough to approve me and I was waiting for it to show up in my account?"

Caiden remembered, but didn't know what kind of answer Iela wanted to that question.

"I parked somewhere dark near some other empty cars until it came while you slept in the backseat."

Iela opened her eyes as she remembered herself. She didn't want to look at Caiden, knowing what she'd find if she did. She wasn't in the mood to be understood.

"You were always scared, even though you didn't say anything. You never did." Iela turned to face Caiden. "It didn't matter that I already knew. You didn't tell me...Until tonight."

Caiden looked away and dropped her head. She heard her mother move and felt movement from the other side of her bed. She turned around and was startled to see Iela sitting cross-legged in her socks. Caiden tried to mimic the forced familiarity in her posture, but couldn't pull it off, so she let one leg dangle off the side of the bed while her hands rested on top of her ankle and inner thigh.

"Just like you pleaded for that man's life, that's the same reason why I shot the other one."

Caiden finally fixed on her mother and this time she didn't look away. She couldn't. She wanted to feel what emotion would elicit such muddled reasoning.

"...I didn't want him to die."

"I didn't want *you* to die."

Out of the blue, an emotion came into Iela's aura, like colored dye dispersing through a glass of water. It slowly danced, solid and independent, before becoming one with its surroundings. Caiden didn't recognize it at first because she so rarely felt it associated with her mother, but even now she couldn't fully put her finger on it through the confusion.

"Then the other one..."

"I know," she said going back to her bed. "You don't have to worry about that."

"He's okay?" Caiden was sensing that Iela knew something, though it was murky.

"We're okay, so go to sleep."

"Are you gonna sleep?" Caiden's words were being forced out. She was still treading lightly even though she felt her mother had calmed down a bit. The only reason she was able to sleep, even a little, was because Iela had left the room.

"Worry about yourself," she said, leaning her back against the headboard. "You're the one they want."

"Why?" she asked more to herself.

Iela had closed her eyes again to rest them, but she took her time to answer. She knew William was doing this, she just hadn't noticed before how much sway he had over anyone, let alone the freshly Voided. Iela didn't know how long William had been sharpening his knife to stab her in the back. Already, they'd been attacked three times in less than two weeks, and judging from how often he'd been taking on new personas, she knew this was just the beginning.

"You're different," she said after a moment. "People will do crazy things to get even a little bit of that."

"But I didn't tell anyone," Caiden said, immediately turning around.

"I know." Iela didn't have to look at her to know she was telling the truth. Caiden was good at not getting into trouble on purpose. "Go back to sleep."

Iela cut off her light and Caiden, hers. She tried closing her eyes, but every time she did, she saw that surprised look on that man's face when Iela put a bullet in it.

At precisely the same time Caiden's head hit her pillow, just downstairs in the lobby, Dontae walked through the front doors and headed toward the elevators. He got off on the second floor and found Jais' room at the end of the hall. When he opened the door, Jais was sitting at the desk and Aza was lounging in what looked like his assigned bed.

"Aza," he greeted, confused.

"What happened?" Jais asked standing to his feet. Dontae hadn't closed the door yet.

"Caiden."

Aza jumped out of the bed. "When?"

"You guys didn't feel anything?" he asked oddly, going back out into the hall. "I just left Picco's and heard a very rousing conversation between him and Iela—"

Swoosh!

A blade of wind sliced past the three down the hall in the opposite way they were walking, nearly knocking Dontae and Aza off their feet. Jais turned behind them, already knowing.

"Someone's here."

They followed the wind toward the direction of the other elevators and got inside. Dontae felt something on his sleeve and saw that where the wind had clipped him, that piece of fabric was now frozen under a very thin layer of ice. He rubbed his palm over it until it melted, his eyes in awe.

"Then, that means she's here, too," Aza said as he followed Jais and Dontae out of the elevator. They saw an exit sign and went out of the door.

"Whoever it is, must be tracking her mother. She hasn't really been keeping a low profile," Dontae said as he spun around, but he didn't see anyone in the back parking lot. He exchanged looks with Jais and saw his eyes smoldering. He followed them to a shadowed area under a broken light.

"Does that mean you're doing your thing?" he asked, making sure they had as much protection as possible.

"I wasn't flirting with you," Jais said, his focus never faltering.

"You're Voids, too..."

A gruff voice had shaken up the stillness. A man soon came out of the darkness until he was in the lights of the hotel building. He looked around Jais' age and had on regular street clothes. He seemed to have been waiting for a long time by the looks of his bloodshot eyes and dark circles.

"We're nothing like you," Jais said, eyeing his every move.

"You're not here for the prince?" the man asked as he took another step forward. "I followed him here. I know he's in one of those rooms."

"What exactly do you want with him?" Dontae played along. This was his first time hearing the Soul being referred to by such a name.

"We were told to find him and that he would have the cure," the man said, taking another step.

"A cure for what?" Jais asked, gruffly. Every time the man moved, he tightened his fists.

A look of pure despair had fallen over his face like a shadow. He stared at the Argenta in an almost pleading way and his eyes changed to a molten orange.

"For everything," he said. "My life, my job, my kids...I don't feel any different from the person I was before, so why am I being made out to believe that I am?"

Dontae, a little taken aback by the man's freakish eyes, took a step toward him, having heard many a story just like his. He thought he would try to resolve this without it getting any more out of hand than it already had.

"You're right. We're all Voids here, and we've all lost some precious things because of it."

Jais and Aza's jaw locked, patiently waiting.

"But what's in there isn't gonna save you." Dontae took another step towards the man, keeping eye contact to make sure his words were reaching him. "I've seen a lot of people like you and they've gotten through this. They still are getting through this...I know because I'm the one that helped them...I can do the same for you if you'll let me." He took one more step towards the man and was now about arm's length apart.

The man could tell that Dontae was sincere. He wasn't getting a stench from from him, but the one thing he learned about people since turning into a Void was that they meant well only to benefit themselves. He pulled out a gun and aimed it right at Dontae's chest.

"You seem like a good person," he said softly. "But I'm not going anywhere until I get what I came for."

"Don't do it," Jais yelled.

"I got this," Dontae calmly called back.

Aza had to stop himself from running ahead. He looked at Jais, silently telling him he was going to try and do something.

"Don't," he said under his breath.

Dontae had fixed on the man, not letting his attention stray no matter how shaky the man's finger was on the trigger.

"I don't want to."

"I can see that."

Dontae moved a little closer until he felt the barrel brush against his chest, but before he could continue his negotiating, two things happened:

Zwish!

Bang!

The gun went off and cemented the Argenta where they stood. Dontae couldn't tear his eyes away from the man as his life seeped out of his eyes like someone turning down the fire on a gas stove. His own gun was pointed underneath his chin and the bullet had blown straight out the top of his skull. Dontae was waiting for him to hit the pavement but saw that something was holding him up.

A rainfall of blood, small particles of bone, gray and white matter showered Dontae. When he looked down and saw a child in front of him, he jumped back in surprise. The boy had taken his hand off the man's trigger finger and let him go. What was left of the man's head slapped against the shattered pieces of his skull on the pavement as blood oozed out of the hole in his crown.

The spectacled boy quickly turned away from the body, closing his eyes for a moment as he took a deep breath into his mouth and exhaled. Then, he looked towards the hotel like someone called his name and up at Caiden's room a moment before his eyes landed on his comrades in front of him.

It was Carmo. But not Carmo.

"Pneuma."

The boy glanced at Jais before dematerializing into the night.

Hours later as the sun's rays poked through the sheer curtains in Iela and Caiden's hotel room, something was slid beneath their door. Iela, who was too alert to get any REM sleep, heard the footsteps come and go. She grabbed her gun and walked to the door. When she looked down, there was a business card with one of its corners still trapped. She picked it up and almost threw it back down.

Her heart nearly stopped at the glistening silver lettering of the Argenta engraved in the pricey card stock. It only had their name and a number to call on the front. Iela flipped it over and saw a small note on the back that read: "*It's time*" and it was signed by Mil.

Chapter XXII

IELA AND CAIDEN had gotten back to an immaculate home. Now that the Argenta knew where they were and made it clear that no matter where Iela went they could and would find them, there was no use in trying to get away. She wasn't sure how that guy disappeared until she got that card. The Argenta was the only possible way anyone was getting away from her.

Ever since they'd left, Roxa didn't know what to do with herself. Cleaning always calmed her nerves, so that's exactly what she did. All the nooks and crannies, she got in there with a broom, a mop, a toothbrush. Caiden had never seen the house look that clean and that's all she's ever seen Roxa do since she'd been alive. And cook.

When she walked through the door, her nose began searching for flavored aromas, but Caiden's face waxed dismal upon entering the dining room and seeing an empty table.

"Get whatever you need upstairs and I'll take you to school."

Caiden's pace stuttered as she looked at her mother, but Iela never met her gaze. She seemed to have been in deep thought ever since they left the hotel.

"Yes, ma'am."

She went upstairs to her room, put Mary away, changed clothes, and grabbed her briefcase. When she got back into the hall, she had the urge to check the library. Caiden touched the knob and felt a rush of serenity flow up her arm and throughout her chest. She opened the door and peeked inside just to look around and get a good sniff. Then, she closed it back and went downstairs.

Neither one of them saw Roxa before they left the house. Iela didn't look like she was even thinking about their argument. As they got in the car and drove off, a question had wanted to fall off the tip of Caiden's tongue, but she kept pulling it back off the edge. It wasn't a few minutes before she was in front of Myerworth. She watched the students casually walk through the front doors and was eager to follow them.

"I'll pick you up."

"Okay."

She didn't move, feeling that question still banging on the back of her lips.

"What is it?"

"...Is it okay?"

Iela had been looking straight ahead and her hand on the steering wheel momentarily tightened around the wrapped leather; the other had been resting on her thigh near the door where her mini pistol was concealed.

"I wouldn't let you go if it wasn't."

What was that?

Caiden got out but watched her mother drive away. She wanted to stay in those words so that she could find out the feelings behind them, but she would definitely be late if she did that.

She walked into the school and some of her emotions from the first day snuck up on her. For a second she forgot where her first class was. She peeked through the classroom door before opening it and was met again with stares, but there was something different. A majority of the students had changed their seats. Alise and a couple of other students were on the other side of the room, away from where she, Aza, and one other girl sat.

She made her way to her seat behind Aza, who she could feel was staring at her. She didn't make eye contact, but Mil did.

This caught her off guard. Since Caiden's first day, she noticed that Mil was one of those teachers that gave each student the same amount of friendly attention; their only objective each day was what they were initially getting underpaid to do. But not today. It was brief but lasting.

Caiden took out some things to take notes with when she saw Aza sliding a folded piece of notebook paper behind his back and to the top of her desk. She didn't open it right away, staring at his back and waiting for an explanation. She glanced at Mil before she unfolded it.

It read: "*ZZZ >o<*"

It took her a laughable amount of time to figure out what the little doodle meant, but when it smacked her in the face, she was now at a loss for how to respond to it. Her pen hovered below his message before something came.

"*Late night?*"

She folded the paper and slid it to the top of her desk until one of the corners gently poked Aza in the back. He secretly took it and wrote something, then sent it back.

"*Yeah. But I made it.*

I'm glad you did, too."

She read that last part over again before she looked up at the back of his head. She thought he'd sneak a glance or pretend to stretch just so he could turn around, but he just sat there and took notes.

Caiden touched her pen to the notebook paper but didn't know how to respond to that, or even if she should respond. Aza had been transparent about his knowing more about her than she knew about herself as soon as she got to Myerworth. She just thought he was being nice, Voids sticking together and all of that, but him knowing about her and Iela being attacked and that electricity that she felt when he came to her house, that was something more, and her heart could feel it.

She wrote something down quickly just so she could get back to her studies and folded it. She pushed it to the top of her desk, and like he was anticipating her sending it back at that exact second, Aza pretended to scratch his back and hid it in his hand. When he opened it up, a faint smile appeared on his face.

"*I don't eat mushrooms.*"

***

Pneuma was casually lounging on Mil's couch reading a book. His small legs resting, one dangling over the other, with his black loafers and knee socks. He had to change immediately out of Carmo's clothes and get into something more familiar to him and his liking. They were easier to maneuver in and reminded him of his home. His first one in his first childhood. Though he never got to live it, whenever he adorned the garments of his father's time, he felt like he had. He adjusted his glasses before turning the page of Camus' L'Étranger.

"Americans always seem to have the dullest fascinations."

Jais and Dontae had been sitting in the two big chairs on the other side of the coffee table. They couldn't seem to take their eyes off the little boy since they got back to the house. He'd been in the same place with his book when Jais and Dontae walked through the front door. The first thing Jais did was check on Adyn to see if he was there, then to see if he was okay. Dontae hadn't been to sleep yet and after last night he didn't know when the next time he would.

He found himself studying this new body of Pneuma's. The boy's pallid skin and dark circles made him curious and a little sad.

"What happened to him?" Dontae asked.

It'd been so quiet, hearing any sound, including his voice was unpleasant.

"Tumor."

Pneuma's accent forced the simple things he said into something condescending in Dontae's opinion and that feeling was more amplified with his lack of sleep. He became slightly annoyed at Pneuma and himself for asking the question.

"Thanks for last night. I was sure it was all over for me."

"It's my job."

Dontae got up and went into the kitchen to make some coffee. He was too worn out to take any more of Pneuma's non-insulting insults.

He glimpsed Jais with a bored expression and turned another page in his book. He was waiting for him to say his usual. It was something that couldn't be helped.

Jais and Pneuma sat without a word between them until Dontae came back into the room. He was holding two cups of coffee.

"It's black."

"That's fine," Jais said, taking out a pack of cigarettes. He lit one and saw that Pneuma was almost done with his book. "Pneuma."

He didn't react to his name, but Jais could tell that he was listening. It only took seconds for Pneuma to finish a page and he was already on the last one. Plus, he'd already read that book numerous times.

No, he was waiting on Jais to tell him something he'd heard before and hoped for any hint of variation.

A long moment passed before Dontae noticed that Jais wasn't going to say anything else. He just smoked and sipped his coffee, his head back, thinking at the ceiling. Pneuma didn't bite. He never did.

Dontae watched the two from behind his mug as he moved to the edge of his seat.

"Volx found Adyn's parents." He directed this piece of information at Pneuma since he found the boy.

He closed his book and wisped out of the room. At nearly the same time Jais put down his cup and left the living room. Dontae followed, not knowing what the rush was about. When he got to the hall, he saw Jais standing in front of Volx's room with the door open, the cigarette hanging out of the side of his mouth. Dontae went to the door and saw Pneuma standing next to Adyn's bed.

"What are you doing?"

Dontae didn't like that Pneuma was even in the same state as Adyn, let alone the same room.

"Taking him home. We'll be in the car."

Jais' eyes never strayed from Pneuma as his gears began turning. He put out his cigarette between the tips of his index finger and thumb.

"Pneuma."

The boy finally granted Jais eye contact, already knowing what he was going to say.

"Dontae's driving," he said, scooping the boy easily into his arms as he started to wake up.

"Where are we going?" Dontae didn't understand what was happening yet.

"...Who are you?" Adyn asked Pneuma, sleepily.

Pneuma looked at Jais when he answered. "I saved you, remember?"

"Don't." But Jais' words fell on deaf ears as Pneuma wisped away.

Only a second passed before he came back. He put Adyn back on the bed.

"What'd you do to him?" Dontae said, checking Adyn's limp wrist for a pulse.

Pneuma didn't look at either of them as he shoved his fists into his pockets. "Quickly get him to the car. I'll be with you shortly."

He disappeared again and Dontae looked up at Jais. "I guess he forgot he wasn't a corpse."

"Go start up the car."

"Jais, we are not gonna do this." Dontae's tone was almost incredulous. "Is this who we are now?"

Jais found himself fingering the cigarette he'd just put out and giving Dontae a disheartened look. "That's why Mil will never take you seriously. You're too human for your own good."

He attempted to go for the boy, but Dontae got in his way.

"I can get him somewhere safe."

"I'm sure you can," Jais said, gazing into that despairing cloudless blue sky. "Away from Mil."

His soul left him after that truth seemed to echo once it hit the air. He moved out of the way and watched as Jais cradled the boy in his arms.

"Tell me you got a plan."

"We'll see when we get there."

They all left the house and got in the car. Dontae was quiet the whole ride, only reading the directions that Volx texted to him, which was written as civilian as he could get it.

A little over an hour passed before they got to an excessively gaudy mansion on the edge of town, about an acre of land between the homes in the neighborhood. Dontae got a look on his face that Jais could feel out of his peripheral. He then checked in the back seat to see Adyn had already come out of his sleep. The tape was still over his eyes, but the boy's head had been turning up to the new smells in the air.

"What happened?"

"You fainted," Dontae said as they turned off the path a considerable distance from the front of the house.

Pneuma appeared in the backseat next to Adyn, who shivered upon his arrival. The boy had naturally cowered away from Pneuma's presence even though he couldn't see him.

"We'll go through the front," Pneuma said as he opened the door.

"Where are we?" Adyn asked, shaken. He felt Pneuma's hand carefully grab his wrist and instinctively pulled it away. "What's that?"

"We have to hurry."

"What's the rush?" Dontae asked.

Pneuma ignored him and took the boy by the hem of his shirt this time as he guided him out of the car.

"Pneuma."

Jais got out, not sure what he could physically do.

"Adyn, you don't have to do this if you don't want to," Dontae said, glaring holes into Pneuma's unbothered face. He knew nothing he said mattered, but he couldn't keep his mouth shut.

"Adyn," Pneuma said, speaking to the boy, but looking at Jais and Dontae. "Do you want to be with your parents again?"

"Yes..." the boy sputtered through his sudden tears.

Pneuma gently took Adyn's wrist and began leading him down the dirt path toward his abode. Dontae reluctantly followed Jais as he had a look of wariness resting on his face. Countless contingencies were flying through his mind of how to get the boy away from Pneuma, but none would end without a casualty.

They got up to the door and Pneuma rang the doorbell. He then started to take the tape off of Adyn's eyes.

"It hurts," he complained.

"What the hell are you doing?" Dontae had taken shelter behind Jais as Pneuma tossed the tape to the side.

"Just in case they answer their own doors."

"And what if they don't?" Jais asked.

He didn't say anything and they all waited for the door to open.

As soon as it did, a maid in an actual black maid's uniform clutched her throat when she saw who it was.

"Mrs. Farecheu—!"

Her body hit the floor before anyone realized what happened to her. Adyn, still trying to adjust to seeing again after nearly two days, was taken aback when he saw Pneuma disperse through the woman and come out through her back in a cloud of light gray smoke.

Dontae tended to her immediately.

"She's still breathing."

He was touching his two fingers to her pudgy neck, making sure to stay out of Adyn's line of view. He could tell the boy was trying not to look at him also.

"Come on."

"...No."

"Why not?" Pneuma asked, stone-faced.

"...I don't want to," Adyn said, his eyes and skin red and wet. He squeezed them tight in defiance. "I wanna leave."

Pneuma shoved his hands in his pockets and got in the boy's face, alarming Jais and Dontae, who stood helpless on the sidelines. Pneuma felt a small pinch at the corners of his mouth but didn't allow himself to be swayed.

Adyn's tears; his fear, didn't make sense.

"You have two choices," he said in his most grisly tone. "You go upstairs or you turn around."

When he said that, Adyn had to hold himself in place.

Dontae was too stunned to say anything.

"Pneuma—" Jais started to say as he had his fears realized in just those handful of words.

"We need to see how you work. I know you've killed before," Pneuma enticed as he got closer to Adyn's face. His eyes had opened at Pneuma's accusation and now he couldn't blink if he wanted to. "I know you thought about doing it again."

"This can't be the only way." Jais was only praying. He thought about mentioning the only person that had some hold over the miniature weapon in the hopes that would make him reconsider what he was going to do. But the longer he stared into those steely muted eyes, the more fruitless his actions were turning out to be.

"...I don't wanna do that anymore," Adyn managed to say.

"You will."

Adyn's expression dropped with the rest of the only energy he had left in his tiny body. Jais' attention never left Pneuma as he was trying to stay one step ahead of him. He knew he'd already planned how this was all going to play out.

Suddenly, Pneuma wisped away.

"Adyn!" Jais shouted, but as soon as the name left his lips, his choice was already made for him.

Before the boy could react, Pneuma reappeared in front of him holding the throats of both Mr. and Mrs. Farecheuse, who, by their kneeling position, had already submitted to their fate.

Chapter XXIII

"GUESS WHAT TODAY is."

David spotted Caiden's puffy ponytail before her withered briefcase in the throng of shuffling bodies. She wasn't adorned with her usual blissfully pensive expression and assumed that had something to do with her absence.

"It's Tuesday," she said, slightly distracted.

"Yeah and early dismissal." That didn't register to her so David decided to be straightforward. "...Your friend was looking for you."

"I don't have any friends." Caiden had fallen into the steps of a group of students who were heading toward the back of the school. She wasn't paying that much attention to anything.

"Aza?" David regretted saying the name as soon as it was uttered. It was what finally got her to snap out of it. "He was just wondering why you hadn't been to school. Same as me."

"I just didn't feel good, so I stayed home."

She paused to look around the halls again. They'd gotten emptier as the two of them were talking.

David watched her eyes as she glanced down at her watch. "Are you...successfully lying to me?"

A small laugh popped out her mouth as she finally looked up at him. "No. Where is everybody going?"

"Home."

"Now?"

"Yes, now," he said, grinning. "This is a good thing. So let's get the heck outta here."

He spun on his heel in place toward the other exit and cleared his throat, trying to get his next words in order before he lost them completely.

"Um...Is it okay if I walk you home?"

Caiden felt his nerves in a bind just from the "Um." She studied his expression. He wasn't making much eye contact, so she continued to watch him until he stopped drilling holes in everything but her face.

"David?" she asked with much curiosity.

"Yeah?" Now, he was trapped in that comforting umber.

"Yeah."

"Yeah like yes?"

"Yeah," she said, finally releasing him from her invisible hold.

They began walking out the door and down the steps. Her peers didn't waste time and most of them had cleared the grounds already. Any left lingering behind were either waiting for a ride or making plans to go waste away the rest of the day. Caiden glanced at David and caught him looking at her again. Naturally, he pretended that he wasn't and her curiosity had gotten the better of her.

"Why do you like me?"

David's head snapped front and center like he'd been caught doing something naughty.

"What?"

"It's only been a month, right?"

"I don't know. I think almost."

"But you do, right?" she asked, stopping at a crosswalk. "I'm feeling something that I can't put into words."

David's first reaction was near horror looking down at her prodding expression. He didn't know if her business-like line of questioning was softening the blow of a potential turn down or just making him examine his initial feelings about her.

"It's okay," she said after a considerable amount of time had passed in silence. She could see he was seriously lost in thought.

"No, it's not." His face was still stuck in denial, but it relaxed a bit when he saw that Caiden was genuinely all right with his confession. He didn't know if that was a good thing or not. "What are you thinking? No, I don't wanna know."

"I don't know what to think. That's why I asked you...This is the first time somebody's ever told me that before."

"I didn't say a word, you mindfucked it right outta me," he said half-amazed, half-amused. He glanced down at her soft brown eyes through the flutter of her eyelashes as they crossed the street. She was looking ahead, seeming to daydream with a smile on her face.

"I'm sorry," he said abruptly. "You look super uncomfortable."

"Smiling means I'm uncomfortable?"

"Could be. Are you?"

"I don't think I am."

He laughed a little. "You can read how other people feel, but you can't read yourself. How does that work?"

"It doesn't," she said, letting his words sink in. "...Sometimes I've wondered if my feelings were my own or just the feelings of the person I'm with."

David felt bad immediately and didn't know how to respond to that.

"It's not your fault. It's mine," Caiden said.

"No, it's not."

"It really is mine."

"No," he said, waylaying her. David fixed on her and already could see she could feel what he was about to say. "I do like you...I don't know you, but there's something there and I don't know what it is, so I just call it like. I don't know how I'll feel in the next hour or the next year. Maybe it'll turn into something else or stay the same. But right now it's this...whatever this is."

Now she was at a loss of what to say.

"That should clear things up for you," he said, turning on his heel.

A quiet smile crept onto her lips and she began walking again.

The energy that David was giving off was new to her. It seemed to have taken a lot to say what he said, especially since he felt he didn't have a choice in the matter. But he was right. Everything had taken on a clarity that it didn't have before and the burden of this "gift" had lost some of its weight.

"You know you smile a lot for no reason," he observed, wondering what thought brought her back to her usual self.

"There's always a reason," she said, glimpsing her house from the entrance of the street. "She's not there."

"You worry too much about your mom," he said, relieved that the subject had changed.

"You don't live with her."

"Did you attempt a funny?" he said, wanting to steal a peek at the apples of her cheeks. It was still too soon to look at her again.

She smiled as they got to her front door.

"You live really close to school."

Caiden suppressed a grin at the disappointment in his voice. The lines in David's forehead always smoothed out whenever he'd talk to her and he'd developed a habit of eating his lunch at the table where they first met even though only Voids ate in the courtyard. She started to think that that's why none of the humans bothered with him.

"You missed your bus," she said, spinning around just as she was about to stick the key in the door.

"Eh, buses are everywhere." He started to back away, making his departure.

"Thank you for walking me home." She naturally glanced down the street for a black blur and stuck her key in the lock.

"No one's ever walked you home before, right?"

"No."

"And no one's ever told you that they liked you before, which you're a liar, but okay."

"...No," she said, not following him at all.

"So, I'm your first," he said, allowing himself to get caught in her gaze. "You'll remember me."

Caiden had to smile at that and David couldn't take it anymore. He happily sprinted off her porch and down the street.

"And I was worried I'd have some competition."

The Voice had taken her by slight surprise as it seemed like she hadn't heard another voice in her head besides her own nearly the whole day. Then she remembered that the day was still happening.

"You've been quiet." She massaged her cheeks, pulled her book out of her briefcase, and slumped on the couch. Roxa had the record player on when she came in. Humming cello strings. She didn't know what that meant but assumed it was a good sign, or a better one.

"And you haven't. I've never seen you so talkative."

"I'm trying to make friends." She closed her book and sat up not having read a single word.

"With a human and a specious Void."

Caiden's brow furrowed at It's choice of words. She got up to cut off the record player as there were too many sounds coming from too many places.

"We're restless," The Voice said.

"I think I'm bored," she said to herself. It was almost like she couldn't believe such a thing could happen to her as she didn't have any memory of having free time before.

"Bored?"

Caiden spun around and Roxa was standing there with a broom. They were both suspended in an awkward eye lock that was usually made so after an argument, but Roxa's face indicated that she didn't mean to shut out Caiden, she just couldn't ignore one without ignoring the other.

"Apologies," The Voice said a moment too late.

Caiden was sure that she was caught talking to herself again.

"Couldn't take it anymore, huh?" she said, trying to lighten the mood. "I'd a done the same."

"I didn't know it was a half-day."

"Those shelves in the library are callin' ya name. Since you bored." Roxa suppressed a grin seeing Caiden become attentive after being given something to do. "And after that, you can fold those towels when they come out the dryer."

She dropped the basket of sheets on the coffee table and Caiden picked it up to go put them away. The corner of Roxa's eyes wrinkled watching the girl, like someone she missed finally came by for a visit after a long time.

"Jesus, you frustratin'."

Caiden hesitated, stuck in a limbo of what to do. Seconds passed and she saw Roxa was playing with her.

"Child, you have a whole half a day without Iela to do whatever the hell you want and you inside doin' laundry. Get outta here."

"...I can't." She said that more in asking as she looked hopefully at Roxa. Caiden knew the woman had no say in whether or not she could go outside alone, but The Voice was right. She was incredibly restless.

"But you can."

Caiden stood there a moment as Roxa's eyes playfully widened. She put her book back in her briefcase and set it up right next to the couch before she headed out the front door. She wandered around squashing weeds with her boots and kicking up loose sediment from the cracked driveway. She found a stick and began swinging it around.

"The youth are quite resilient."

"I don't feel anything." She looked around at the houses and the street when she said that. It was still early in the day.

"Is it nice out?" The Voice asked.

Zinc's barking pulled her toward the clump of trees and she kneeled in welcoming as he came galloping out toward her. A beam warmed her face as he smothered her with kisses.

"Hey. Where you been? Where you been, baby boy?"

"I've upset you."

"No..."

Zinc barked and ran toward the trees, wanting her to follow him. They walked and threw the stick around, getting farther and farther into the thicket.

"I'm waiting."

"I need to find out about this thing. Why I got it," she said, now noticing the unfamiliar territory they had ended up in.

"And you think that Void will know."

"He knows a lot of things he shouldn't know already."

"Which should make you more wary."

Caiden's boots came to a halt as she looked up at a semi-shading oak. The cluster of trees had gotten farther apart as they went deeper into the small thicket. There were houses on the other side and it seemed like she was near the back-yard of an empty one. The grass hadn't been cut for months and the wooden gate was missing a considerable amount of slats.

"I'm gonna head back," she said softly as she raked her fingers through the wispy hairs on the top of Zinc's head. "Zinc looks hungry."

"Caiden," The Voice called.

As soon as It finished saying her name, Zinc's head snapped and his canines made a grand entrance. Caiden froze in place as his growl sent chills up and down her spine. She didn't need to turn around to know that the presence of another had joined in on their afternoon stroll.

She turned with caution as she felt a tumult of anger emanating from the space behind her. There was an old man pushing seventy holding a shotgun aimed at an imaginary target on Caiden's back. He flashed his yellowed teeth as he quickly licked his cracked lips.

"What you doin' back here?" His tone was laced with a pleasant malice.

Caiden wanted to answer but that gun was a natural silencer. She swallowed what was left of the spit in her mouth until she was able to speak.

"... I—"

"This my property, you know. And I don't like people on it." He set his jaw on his molars and eyed Caiden more properly. "You one of them thangs aren't you? With the crazy switchin' eyes."

Caiden watched the gun slacken in the old man's hand, but that put her more on her guard. The man's energy had changed as well and Zinc began to bark again more incessantly than before.

"I got no qualms shootin' him too."

"Zinc..." she choked, trailing off.

The truth was she knew why Zinc had seemingly lost it. She could tell he felt that change in the atmosphere as she did. The old man had his mind made up to do one thing when he came upon them, but had a change of heart for some reason.

Suddenly, they heard something move in the trees to their left. The man shot in that direction so fast that the speed seemed superhuman taking his age into account. Caiden dropped to the ground covering her ears. Zinc was the only one not bothered by the sound, but he did cease his snarls.

"I thought you was alone," he said, reloading his weapon.

Caiden's face got hot and tremors raced throughout her chest. It was more galvanic than how she'd felt at school; more alive. Not just on the inside, but on the outside of her body.

Zinc's head was darting from her to the old man, who was watching her and saying something about if she was all right, but Caiden could only focus on her heart at the moment to make sure it wasn't going to explode.

Zinc couldn't take it anymore. The dog lunged at the man.

"Get it off me, please!"

The man tried to hit Zinc with the barrel, but the whole gun went flying out of his hands. Zinc was relentless at the man's arms, and even made several attempts at his neck but the man kept protecting it with his now chewed-up hands.

Caiden snapped back to the present and saw the two wrestling. She didn't know what to do.

"Zinc, stop!"

The beast remained focused as the old man began edging closer to what she now recognized as his shotgun. She started to run to it before he did, but he got there first. He beat Zinc over the head with it, victorious this time, and pulled the trigger. The target was on the dog this time and he didn't miss.

Zinc's yelp pierced through Caiden's chest like a flaming sword. She was grounded in place and couldn't recall where she was or how she'd gotten there.

Her eyes fell to the animal as his body went down for good. Caiden's dark russet gaze turned a pale shade and she couldn't bring herself to breathe. Her legs gave out from under her and she dropped in the dirt next to his body, praying that none of this was real.

"I didn't wanna. I'm sorry," the old man threw up. "I didn't mean to."

Caiden never left the animal. She gazed at him through the blur of tears as she let out a staggered breath.

"...Zinc."

His name had become hard to speak—

In a flash, Caiden's back stiffened like it'd been hit with a thunderbolt.

Peace.

An overwhelming amount of it had overtaken her grievous state. She didn't want to turn away from Zinc, but there was a familiarity in this feeling of unbridled stillness.

When Caiden turned around, she saw the old man on his knees staring up into the face of a tall radiant figure.

"Jesus, Mother Mary," the old man sputtered as he was totally and utterly beside himself.

"Fear not."

The figure placed its hand on the old man's head and executed him.

Chapter XXIV

CAIDEN WAS SO transfixed by the figure's presence that she hadn't fully taken in what just happened. All she could feel was the warmth and images began popping up in her mind until it morphed into a flip book of her life starting from her first day of school.

Her eyes strayed to the elderly man on the ground, silent and emotionless. His face contorted in a finite look of bliss. The eyes were still open, seemingly wanting to close as a shallow trail of tears soaked his weathered, wrinkled cheek.

There was nothing left to feel coming from him. He was dead.

Caiden held her breath as her attention snapped back to the thing she had a difficult time accepting as real. His clothing was loud, giving the impression of a lustrous glow, though he was clad in a simple henley and jeans. The lack of complexity in wardrobe adorned by a thing that couldn't be fathomed by anything of this world made Caiden question whether or not the last few minutes had even happened.

He captured her gaze and she recognized those eyes instantly, for that was the only feature she could see. The lower half of his face was covered in a thick black mask that seemed to meld to his skin. She only saw those eyes for a second before the dazzling azure subsided into a calm brown, not unlike her own. He then got on bended knee and bowed his head as if he was about to say a prayer.

"I'm called Lision." His voice was thin and fragile like he hadn't spoken for a long period of time. "Caiden."

She reacted to her name by reaching for a weapon that was all the way upstairs under her pillow. She got to her feet when she felt her back and grabbed air. Lision got up as well and lifted his head to look at her carefully, but not at her face. Caiden noticed that his eyes had gone to her chest for a moment before he locked eyes with her again.

"...Are you..." She couldn't finish because the word she was searching for hadn't come to her. Caiden had no idea what he was, but she knew he couldn't possibly be a Void.

Lision remained stoic as he walked toward the direction of Caiden's home and waited for her to follow him, but she panicked at the thought of leaving Zinc's body alone without a burial.

"You need to go back," he said, in a monotonous tone that made Caiden's trigger finger hungry.

"Who are you?"

She felt her insides recoil when she heard her voice, tinged with a vomit-inducing venom. It didn't sound like someone she knew at all. Caiden looked back at Zinc and the hot tears welled up again.

"He won't be alone," Lision said. "We never are."

His words gave her little comfort as she stood staring at him in wonder. Her mind went to a place that she thought was surely impossible and for the first time, she saw Lision's expression change for a second as he watched her begin her leaded strides toward her house.

The entire time he didn't say anything but led her back the exact same way she had come before. She'd occasionally glance at him and realized if her eyes never left his own he'd still focus on getting back to Roxa's house.

Caiden went to the door and wasn't going to say anything else, but his silence irked her. It was a sensation that made it like he never showed up in the first place. She paused to fix her face in case Roxa was cooking or, god help her, still cleaning.

"You may ask."

Caiden turned around and saw that look again. It was just slightly changed from what seemed to be his default of showing no signs of emotion at all.

"Ask what?" The words fought hard to stay in her mouth so they had little volume when they came out.

"I'm not one of you."

Caiden figured that but wasn't sure. However, that didn't explain how he answered a question that she never asked.

She turned back around and went inside the house without another word. She concentrated on breathing deeply, in and out, putting all that happened in a safe corner of her mind for later when she was more ready to deal with it.

"I know that's not you comin' in here now," Roxa yelled from the kitchen over some golden oldie's track. "That wasn't five minutes if it was twenty."

Caiden hesitated before going into the kitchen to get a bottle of water. She just needed Roxa to see that she was okay before she disappeared to her room to cry until she drifted off to sleep.

***

Piccolo lugged a case full of vodka from the back room and saw Dontae lying on the stage staring intensely at his phone. Everyone had gone home, including security, who were usually still calling chariots for the mini entourages that forgot they needed a designated driver for the night. It was the end of the week so Piccolo was used to shutting down an hour or two after closing. These days, Piccolo was finding it harder to kick out his patrons when they asked for another round.

He glanced over at Dontae again as he put away each bottle in its place on the top shelf, patiently waiting to lend another ear to what was troubling the young master so early in the morning.

"I can't sleep," Dontae said with his eyes still glued to his screen. "I know I should, but I can't."

"I got something in the back that'll put you out for days," Piccolo said with a faint smile.

"I'm serious." Dontae sat up and their eyes met briefly before he went back to his phone. "Answer me this. With the truth." He had to add on that last part because Piccolo always gave him vague answers that seemed so much like the truth that he wouldn't ask any more questions.

"Don't I always?" he asked, more businesslike.

"I'm not in the mood, Picco. Just listen."

Piccolo sensed his reluctance and could guess what the subject of this query might be about. It was quiet, still, as Dontae finally put his phone away and got up off the stage.

"Never mind," he said, dejectedly.

Piccolo watched him contemplate whether or not he wanted to leave the bar or not. He lingered where he stood, no longer having his phone to occupy his idle hands.

"Come on."

Dontae looked over at Piccolo as he headed to his office and a rush of heat filled him from within, welting the skin on his back and neck as his eyes followed the able-bodied bartender toward the back of the house. He didn't know what that meant, but his feet began to move in baby steps as he disappeared down the hall. He found himself pressing his tired forehead onto the office door. It was cracked so he caught glimpses of Piccolo going to and fro across the room.

"...Picco," he said in a small voice, but when he walked into the room he saw Piccolo with a huge teacup and small jars of herbs and oils.

"Milk doesn't keep here, but I do have peppermint."

Dontae was only half-relieved to see the desk speckled with loose leaves and he eagerly took the warm cup between his palms.

"My father loves tea."

"I know," he said, putting the electric kettle back on its port.

Piccolo leaned back in his chair and watched Dontae put the cup up to his face just so the steam could get into his nose. He hated tea but would drink it for the maker's sake. He sipped, but couldn't get comfortable in his seat, so he leaned his elbows on his thighs and stared off in a daze a bit as the silence settled in the room.

"I told you how I got this place, right?" Piccolo asked.

"Yeah, but it's a lie." He wasn't expecting such a segue into their past, especially now when he was functioning on scraps of sleep.

"I don't lie."

His tone made Dontae straighten up some.

"You also don't hurt people on purpose," Dontae said, a little more exhausted than how he was acting. It wasn't from the tea though. Piccolo had only mentioned that anecdote twice since he'd met him, and no matter how much it attached itself to his amygdala, he wished he never knew this piece of information about one of the only good things that had ever happened to him.

"Saying that makes you feel better," he said, coming to his point. "Then feel better, Dontae. Feel better and do whatever you need to do."

"Just tell me straight up. As you well know I'm running on fumes," he said and began gulping his tea.

"What did you do when your father told you that you weren't obligated to follow in his footsteps, though you were his only heir?"

"Tch. Heir." He massaged his eyes and set his empty cup on the desk. "Till this day that was one of the most selfless things he's ever done for me. I was happy as hell."

"Were you?"

"Yes? Was I not allowed to be?"

Dontae watched him lean back in his chair for a moment before he did the same.

"Is it possible to feel two emotions at the same time?"

"Sure."

"Okay, so yeah, I wanted him to want me to take over the reins. Even though I didn't want to. Even though I would've gladly ruined his name..."

"You want some more tea?"

"No, I don't want any more of your poison."

Piccolo got up and leaned on the desk in front of him. "He's grown on you."

"...I can't find out anything about him," Dontae said in almost a whisper. "Nobody knows anything."

"I'm sure that's on purpose." He watched the unease bunch up around Dontae's eyes. "You can't unknow something once you find it out. I don't think you wanna do that so early on anyway."

"You haven't met this kid." Frames of the Farecheuse bloodless massacre flashed behind his eyes when he looked up at Piccolo. "He's lived so long that life is meaningless to him. Especially mine."

Piccolo studied Dontae for a moment and pushed back his hair from his face.

"Picco, stop." Dontae got up and went to the couch. He was so tired he couldn't think straight.

"You can't help anyone like this." Piccolo got up and pulled a small throw out of the closet. There was already a pillow on the small sofa across from his desk, but he was already prepared to make his desk chair a bed whenever Dontae paid him a visit.

Dontae laid down but didn't want to close his eyes. He'd only couchsurfed at Piccolo's a handful of times, preferring the open stage, but he was suddenly filled with anxiety.

"Relax," Piccolo said, hiding his slight amusement.

"I can't..." His head finally sunk into the pillow and his eyes formed into slits.

Piccolo gently touched the back of his head and waited for his eyes to close completely.

"You'll be alright as long as she is." His voice was calming as he stroked his dark golden locks one last time before going to his desk to put away the tea.

"...I'm still awake."

"I know," he said, smiling to himself.

Dontae let go and wafted away to an overdo REM cycle he wouldn't remember, but not without a struggle. Piccolo's words echoed long after, shackling him with more chains of trepidation than any murder he witnessed the day before.

***

Iela parked outside Roxa's a little more in front of the house than she normally did and sat there a moment. She stared absentmindedly at the dark windows on the second floor before reaching over to open the glovebox. What she saw gave her pause.

Another letter.

Same white envelope and seal. Resting on top of it was Mil's invitation. The card taunted her; the silver letters attached with an annoying megaphone. Iela took the letter and closed the glovebox before getting out of the car. She walked briskly to the door and got inside.

At first, she wanted to grab something quick out of the kitchen, but she headed straight upstairs to check on Caiden instead. Seeing Mil's note set a fire under her that made her skip stairs to get to her daughter's room as soon as she could.

The dim light peeking from underneath the door stopped her in her tracks. She made her way soundlessly to the door and carefully turned the knob. Caiden was knocked out near the edge of her bed, the glow from her heart mesmerizing Iela for a second.

No matter how often she saw the strange glow, she never got used to it pulsing beneath Caiden's skin. Iela never thought in a million years that something like that could come from her. Nothing much or good ever did.

But this child. This blessing. It was hers. A gift she didn't deserve.

Iela went to Caiden's side to watch her sleep without a care in the world. Her child was great indeed and everyone who was in her presence long enough saw that without a doubt, even when she didn't see it herself. Even when she didn't want to.

The older Caiden got, the more of a liability she became to Iela. Everything that happened wouldn't have happened if it weren't for her. And Iela knew that was her fault. Letting her go to school was a mistake, but she was in far too deep to do anything about it. Now that William and the Argenta had her in their sights, there was nowhere for them to turn.

She gazed at the glow for a moment, getting lost in the magnificence of it in such an ordinary setting. Iela wanted to reach out to her to make sure she was real but instead found her hands tightening around the letter in her lap.

Chapter XXV

CAIDEN WOKE UP to a damp pillow. It was almost forty minutes past six. A staggered sigh toppled out of her mouth as the thought of moving and thinking made her body heavy. She was going to be late for school.

She'd been ensconced by her duvet for most of the weekend, locked in her room trying to force-feed herself Aeschylus until she memorized every comma and period. Roxa could tell something was wrong but didn't want to make it worse by forcing small talk. She was used to Caiden dealing with her own problems, knowing that if it came to it she would ask for help. What Roxa didn't know was that it pained Caiden even more to do that. If she were wounded and confided in another, then they both would be injured.

The Voice started to hum to her softly as she gazed vacantly at the soft light the lamp threw on the wall across the room. She didn't want to move but crawled out of the comfort of her bed to the closet. She grabbed some clothes, which were almost all the same, never bothering to mindfully pick anything out whenever she got ready to go out, and headed to the bathroom to get dressed. On her way back, she stopped at the library doors.

"You're late already," The Voice said.

Caiden took a step toward the door and let the warmth soak into her skin. She twisted the handle and went inside. The sun hadn't fully risen yet so she cut on the light. It was still and the books peered at her from the shelves and floor as she stood there and waited. She knew he was there.

"You're late," she heard a voice say.

Lision walked out from behind a bookshelf in the back of the room and Caiden eyed him warily. He was in the same attire and his eyes were still that chasmic brown. She realized that she couldn't feel anything from him. No emotions, no energy. The sense of whether he was a body that took up a small space in time diminished more and more as they stood there facing each other.

"You've been here a long time," she said in quiet realization.

"I have."

"Caiden," The Voice called.

She already knew about the time, but there were too many questions that she didn't want to leave without getting an answer to first. She just couldn't find the one to fit right now. Lision was already looking at her when their eyes met again. She could see he was waiting for her.

"I forgot your name."

"Lision," he said. "You may call me Zai."

"...Okay."

Her mind catapulted to the thicket and the locker room. "At school..."

He didn't respond, patient.

Caiden stood there fixed on him. He saved what she thought at the time was in peril, her life. She had no idea why or how, but that warmth is the only thing she recognized. There was so much happening with her mind and her heart and her body that all she could do was stand there, frozen.

"Caiden," The Voice called.

"Thank you."

She managed to get that out and left to head downstairs.

"Mornin'." Roxa was removing food from the table, a first for Caiden. "Finally."

"Sorry," she said, reflexively glancing behind her like Lision was coming down to join them.

"I'll be in the car."

Iela came in, grabbed her keys, and went out of the front door without a second glance at her or Roxa. Caiden felt that she'd shifted back to neutral; the feeling of simmering anger had returned bearing a slight difference. Iela seemed relaxed some, but it felt incomplete.

"Here." Roxa handed Caiden her lunch and a breakfast sandwich. "You betta eat it all, too."

"Yes, ma'am," she said, only now getting a few jutting hunger pangs.

She picked up her briefcase and left the house. The car was already humming, so she jogged to the passenger side and got in.

"Keep that in your lap."

Caiden greedily chewed through the sausage and eggs while keeping her hands cupped beneath her mouth. Iela kept her eyes ahead and Caiden was expecting to get a talking to about being late, but she thought Iela might've been going easy on her because of everything that happened and was still happening. That wasn't in her personality, so it must've been something else.

They pulled up to the empty front steps of Myerworth. She felt a little nauseous and thought it was a mixture of inhaling that sandwich coupled with her being late to school for the first time. She didn't know what the punishment was going to be but it was biting at her, nonetheless.

"We gotta stop somewhere after I pick you up," Iela said as Caiden opened her door.

"Another hotel?"

"No," she said. "I'll be right here as soon as the bell rings."

Caiden got out and Iela drove away. She went inside and didn't see any teachers or staff, just two or three students going to the restroom and getting a forgotten item out of their locker. Caiden found Mil's class and was reluctant to go inside. She wondered how many days she was going to have that felt like her first.

She opened the door, making no eye contact, and headed to her seat.

"Ms. Waters, do you have a note?"

Caiden looked up at her teacher and felt her face get hot as a few of her peers glanced her way.

"No, sir," she said.

"Would you like to go get one?"

"No, sir," she said, without thinking.

If no one was paying attention before, they were now. Those glances quickly turned to stares. In one of the most boring classes, any interruption was welcome.

Caiden only answered with the first thing that came to her mind which was the truth. Anything other than that might've set off her eyes, and considering how sparse her classes have been looking lately, she didn't want to make any of the humans more uncomfortable than they had become since the semester started.

She saw Aza turn a little in his chair, but didn't want to take her eyes off of Mil.

"I think you would," Mil said rather pointedly.

Caiden glanced at Aza who's expression remained soft.

"...Yes, sir."

She got up and left the room like a child being put in a corner. It felt strange walking half hurriedly down the empty halls on the way to the office, which she only visited a couple of times. Her pace stuttered when she saw the door open. It was David and he had a bluish hue sitting just north of his cheekbone.

"What'd they get you for?" he asked with a crooked smile.

"Your face."

"Yours," he jabbed back after noticing the tiny cloud she had hovering over her head. "You really in trouble?"

"I'm getting a late note." She couldn't take her eyes off his bruise.

"So we've both been naughty," he said, wincing after poking his face. "Let's get outta here."

David walked past her towards the front of the school and Caiden noticed that he rarely had any books or a backpack with him. He turned around when he didn't hear another set of footsteps matching his own.

"Let's go," he said, casually. "We'll do the same thing we did last time."

Caiden stood there, torn. School was the last place she wanted to be right now. It was so much easier to mourn when she didn't have to go through the constant cycle of an angst-ridden breakup or untimely manic-depressive shifts over the course of two classes. This place was unpredictable and she needed a break.

"Mr. Gunde sent me here. He saw me already."

"Gunde. Gov?"

"Yeah."

"Say you got lost."

"For forty minutes?"

"Right." He walked back to her with a little less pep in his step and could see she was worried. "Let's go anyway. I can tell you don't wanna be here."

Caiden looked towards the office then turned around to head back out the entrance. David picked up his pace again, keeping his strides shorter than normal. She began to slow down a bit and David sprinted out down the sidewalk in front of her.

"Where are we going?" she asked, trying to keep as cool as possible. She could still head back into the school if she wanted to.

"You got any change?" He threw his hand up to wave the bus down.

"No."

She saw a city bus pull up in front of a bus stop sign she only saw now. She watched David hop on and throw the change in the little slot next to the driver.

"Get on or I'm a leave ya," the woman said half-jokingly.

Caiden stepped on the bus and followed David, taking care of her briefcase so it wouldn't hit anyone on the way to her seat. She sat down and he took up the two seats in front of her.

David watched her eye the other passengers.

"Oh, she's at work."

Her response was a fixed somber fascination at a bag lady at the next stop. David leaned his back on the window, taking note of her shrunken shoulders. His mouth opened a bit to let something out, but he thought better of it and directed his attention to his phone.

"What happened to your face?" she asked, staring at the smear of people and buildings they zoomed past.

"You, is what happened."

Caiden wasn't in the mood.

"Fight," he said, playing the brawl out in his head as he flipped his phone from one palm to the other. "I'm over here thinking you guys could take care of yourselves. Or at the very least people would shit themselves than take a swing at you. I guess after expulsion I'll head to the circus."

"You're getting expelled?"

The joy that pricked his skin when concern for his permanent absence from school showed on her face. David turned around to rest his chin on the back of his hand clamped on the seat, watching her eyes.

"Would that make you sad?"

"Yes," she said in earnest.

"More sad than you are now?" he pressed, hoping for a less confusing response.

Caiden looked back out the window again.

"Of course not..."

She thought about whether or not it was okay for her to divulge something so real and a part of her to David. What gave her pause wasn't the fact that he was a stranger to her, but letting him know that a piece of her had departed from this life was more important than any light in her chest.

"My friend died."

David sat up and that spritely expression slid off his face.

"Oh. Sorry...But you said you didn't have any friends."

"At school."

"Oh."

He didn't know what else to say. Nothing ever felt right in those situations. He suddenly spasmed and grabbed his phone to show it to her. Caiden looked at it. On his lock screen was him taking a selfie with a golden retriever.

"Toothpick," he said.

Caiden gazed at the photo for a moment. It looked like they were at a restaurant on a beach. He and the dog were grinning ear to ear. David had to tap the screen again and that's when she looked back out of the window.

"Thank you," she said, finally making steady eye contact.

"...Yeah, anytime."

David cradled his phone to his chest, grateful to Toothpick who was a blessing to him even in the next life. He pulled his knees in and leaned back on the window to share in Caiden's pensive silence. They were like that for the remainder of the trip, David explaining some of the surroundings to Caiden now and then. They got off at a strip mall and David's pep had returned.

"You been here before?" he asked, knowing she hadn't.

"I've been to malls," she said, reading all the blocked lettering that made up the store signs.

"This ain't a mall, first thing. Second," he explained, opening the door for her to one of the stores that was built specifically to not look like the others. "action or comedy?"

Caiden walked into the bright lights from a movie theater sign and the pungent smell of popcorn.

"You choose."

David turned around and Caiden had an expression on her face he couldn't place.

"Action, it is...What'd I do now?" He was playing but this longed-for trip had not resulted in any good responses so far.

"Nothing."

David eyed her as he bought the tickets. They both walked to their theater and got inside. There were maybe three people in the cramped room already. Caiden followed

David all the way to the back and they sat in the center. The perfect spot.

He leaned back and pulled out a bag of sour candies from his jacket pocket. The movie's beginning credits were already showing on the screen so Caiden wasn't paying attention to him. He tapped the side of her arm with the bag. Caiden glanced at it then up at David who was lifting his eyebrows. She gave him a forced faint smile and shook her head no before going back to the film. David smiled too as he counted the four seconds it took for her smile to disappear.

"They're good," he said, popping a few into his mouth. "I know you haven't tried them."

He wasn't loud, but he wasn't whispering either and the few people in there wanted to turn around just to gesture him to shut up. She could feel it.

"I'm trying to watch," she whispered.

"You should. It's acclaimed."

"Then let me."

David threw up his hands in mock surrender flashing his off-white incisors. He spoke in the same volume as before and Caiden noticed he'd turned in his seat so that he was able to keep an eye on her and the screen. She thought he was about to do that piney thing that he sometimes did when they ate lunch together, but felt something entirely opposite emanating from him this morning.

"What was their name?"

Caiden didn't answer right away. She wanted to let the question sink in to see how okay she was.

"His name was Zinc," she said after a very long moment. She focused very hard on the film's protagonist as she snapped the neck of one of her enemies. "I didn't even know what kind he was..."

"I thought you could tell us apart?"

"Not dogs."

David covered his mouth and fell dramatically back onto the other armrest. It was so over the top that Caiden had to look at him.

"What happened to him?" David asked, pulling himself together. He went back to watching her profile and could tell she wasn't fully invested in the story.

"Shotgun." Like the word had made the sound itself, it replayed in her mind before the blood splattered the dog's white fur.

For an instant ice shot up David's spine. In that split second, he believed that Caiden had taken her dog's life. He had no idea why this thought came to him or how, but an unease reached inside him and tugged at his intestines. Caiden naturally looked at him, unable to dismiss such a feeling.

"I'm sorry." He sat up in his seat. "I didn't mean to— I mean it was an accident."

Caiden's hands went to her mouth as she smothered a laugh. It was slightly louder than David's speaking had been and people turned around to see what was so funny. She quickly quieted down and sunk in her seat as a second wave hit her, this time with a little sparkle in her eyes. She covered them in order to stop them, but a few made it out.

"Thank you," she whispered.

"You're a lunatic." David sunk down, too, confused again but glad she wasn't falling into hysterics and offered her more candy.

"I want some red meat," she said, turning away to wipe her face and glancing at her watch.

"And a cannibal, too," he said, standing up. He motioned the way out. "After you."

They left the theater with Caiden's mind a little lighter than it was that morning. She didn't want to think about how long it was going to last. Just that it was there and she was in the midst of it was more than enough.

She followed David to the bus stop as his arms flailed just as the bus was about to leave them. Caiden found herself laughing again and it felt genuinely good. Too good.

The bus pulled off, headed back towards their neighborhood. And following closely behind them was a dark gray tinted-window coupe.

Chapter XXVI

CAIDEN AND DAVID made it back to Myerworth by a mere hair. They'd dropped by Faber's to wolf down his signature corned beef like it was their last meal and decided to run back to school after they missed the bus. Caiden was relieved to note that Faber was not present for this visit and instinctively thought about that dead man that they left there. Her mood dropped like that despite trying to keep her expressions natural.

She thought the run would be so exhilarating that it would've dissolved the gruesome images that Faber's conjured, but her reveling in the wind beating against her face as she pushed herself harder to keep up with David didn't last long. Her eyes immediately searched for any and all black cars, but she didn't see any.

"Five minutes..." he said, catching his breath. "You're pretty slow."

"We can't do that anymore," she gasped, still keeping a lookout for her mother. She then turned to David who was still steadying his breathing. "This was too close."

The bell had cut her off and her head swiveled down the street as Iela's black car showed up right on time.

"That's me," she said with relief.

David watched her walk to the curb and opened his mouth so the words he wanted to say knew that they were safe to come out.

"Caiden."

She turned around and he'd taken a few steps toward her.

"I like hanging out with you..." he said, glancing at Iela's car that unmercifully got stuck behind a school bus.

"Me, too."

"Conceited," he joked, then quickly regretted. "Um, I'd like to do it again. Maybe when we're not skipping school...If you want."

"Yeah." She didn't understand the anxious air. "I wouldn't mind that."

"Alright." A smile just slapped his lips as he began backing toward the bus stop. "That's really alright."

"You're happy."

"Hell yeah."

"You're welcome," she teased.

David continued to watch her, elated and on cloud nine as Iela cut out from behind the bus and pulled up in front of Caiden.

She got in and made sure not to look David's way as they drove away from the building.

"I have to meet someone," Iela said about five minutes in. "It's not a place for people like you, so when we get in there, don't talk to anyone and never leave my side. Same as before."

"Yes, ma'am."

Before, as in before this semester started. Before she was allowed to go out alone without someone holding her hand. Caiden felt the energy coming from her mother was something she hadn't experienced yet. It was a similar feeling she'd only just recently felt for the first time just minutes ago. Admittedly, this emotion made Iela seem like even more of a stranger to Caiden than she already had.

Iela's phone buzzed and Caiden saw it was a text.

"We got a route change..." She eyed the phone with furrowed brows. "What is he doing?" she questioned under her breath.

With that change, Iela's feelings shifted as well. It made Caiden look at her for a long while until she got caught.

They made a u-turn and picked up the speed a little. In less than half an hour, they were in a very quiet neighborhood. The houses were mostly one-story, all brick with state and country flags proudly out front.

Iela was about to pull up to a quaintly indistinguishable house with a couple of cars out front, but stepped on the gas and whipped out her weapon instead.

"Grab Mary in the glovebox."

Caiden obeyed like it was her own intent, not about to question why her gun was already in the car. She searched around with no luck for this enemy that only Iela saw.

"What's wrong?"

Iela sped up and was almost at the end of the street when the radio suddenly spazzed on in a scramble and the car slowed as the life got zapped out of it. She kept jamming her foot on the gas, but nothing happened. Then they came to a complete stop.

Caiden instinctively cocked her weapon, but not out of fear. There was no threatening force she could feel coming from anyone. Her mother on the other hand was silently simmering. She swapped her gun to the other hand and grasped Caiden so tight on the wrist that she was sure her circulation was cutting off.

"Come on."

Iela got out on her side and Caiden had no choice but to cross over to follow her. Her grip was firm as they stood in front of the car; Iela's eyes darting all around her. At the windows, the trees, and the empty vehicles lining the street, parked eerily still in their driveways.

It was motionless. Not a breeze or a chirp. It was as if all sound had been vacuumed out of the atmosphere, except for their breathing. The pounding of her heart was heard with a crispness that was even more startling than the silence.

"Ms. Waters."

Iela and Caiden reacted to that familiar voice for two completely different reasons. Iela jerked Caiden behind her to safety as she aimed her weapon toward the house they were supposed to pull up to.

At that moment, Mil stepped out from beside his SUV and Iela stiffened. Caiden had never seen her mother illicit such a violent response of distaste to another person that she was ready to take down without a thought.

"Ms. Waters," Mil said, looking at Caiden. "It was wise to accept my invitation. Please, come inside."

"She's not going anywhere." Iela's voice was steady and calm. Caiden had never seen her explode so softly before. Everything about her screamed control, but her eyes were the bloodiest Caiden had ever seen them.

"I was being courteous with my card," he said, composed. "But I must insist that you come inside."

Iela fixed on him as something crept into her peripheral. Volx had appeared coming from the backyard of the house; his boots and a better part of the bottom of his pants stained with sanguine traces of his most recent guest.

Iela put her gun down and continued to squeeze Caiden's arm as they followed Mil inside.

A distant scent of cleanser welcomed them as they stepped into the living room. Caiden took in the place like any other that she'd never been before, but felt a little intrusive as this was her teacher's home. Her eyes scanned the furniture, tables, and walls and she was reminded of her own home for a moment. Like her barren room, Mil's house also didn't have a sense of its inhabitants.

"You're welcome to sit," Mil said, while sitting in one of the grandfather chairs. "We may be here a while."

"What do you want?"

Iela adjusted her grip on both Caiden and her weapon, but Caiden watched Mil as he pulled out his phone. She didn't know if it was his nonchalance or his silence that sent Iela's arm shaking for a brief second, but she didn't have to be empathic to know that her mother was beyond angry. Caiden attempted to touch her mother's hand that was clamped around her wrist, but her hand fell after she remembered who her mother was, and she was also holding Mary.

"After dinner, so we won't ruin the appetite." Mil got up and headed to the kitchen. "This was a little abrupt. I sent my son out for some wine and an extra something for the girl."

His speaking had gotten fainter towards the end as he was in the kitchen. Iela was standing her ground firm, but when Mil mentioned Caiden, her heart slightly leapt. She had no idea what kind of person Mil was, but she never got a snitching vibe from him so she was praying that her field trip with David was kept under wraps.

"We have our meals in the kitchen," he said, poking his head outside the door.

"What do you want?"

"The kitchen," he said and went back inside.

Iela stood there a good stubborn moment before she turned to Caiden.

"Don't eat or drink anything."

Caiden was about to reply with her staple response but remembered that she wasn't supposed to talk. She nodded once and Iela dragged her gun first into the kitchen.

Mil was already seated at a table set for four. Iela snatched one of the chairs away from the table and sat down. Caiden had no other choice but to sit in the chair on the right. Their backs were to the door which was done on purpose, but Iela knew the most dangerous person there was seated right across from them.

It seemed like a lot of time passed by of Iela watching Mil pour water into their glasses and him glancing at the clock on the wall once or twice. He never looked at Caiden again once they got inside the house. Caiden thought it was because that would tick her mother off more, but she noticed that Mil wasn't trying to ease her fears either.

She had never felt Mil's energy before. Since they met on the first day he had been to her what Aza had been to her at first, unreadable. Caiden snuck a peek at him from across the table as he left the kitchen. Maybe if Aza was the type of Void that could cut it off at will, Mill was, too.

Iela sat motionless, glaring at the empty seat Mil got up from as she listened to the conversation that was happening in the living room.

"...They were out of the kind you liked."

At the sound of Aza's voice, Caiden's eyes dropped to her lap. She knew Iela would look her way after she did that, but she couldn't stop herself. Something was going wrong, and it was her fault. This wasn't like with Alise and having some innocent meal with a group of humans, Caiden had managed to attract the attention of someone that was closely associated with a regretful piece of her mother's past. She didn't know that, but to Iela it didn't matter.

Mil came back into the kitchen with Aza holding two bottles of wine and a plastic bag. It didn't take long for him to read the room and his ice cream smile melted off his face.

"We have guests," Mil said, sitting. "You know Caiden."

Aza could only stare at her hunched over in what looked like a mixture of shame and prayer. He sat down in the empty seat near her and couldn't even attempt to get her attention after he saw the look on the face of her mother.

"This is Iela. The original Ms. Waters."

"Nice to meet you." This wasn't the time to be cordial, yet it slid out of his mouth almost on its own.

Iela didn't say anything, focused only on her gun and Mil.

"Right, then. What do we want." Mil held both of the wine bottles in his hand and gave one to Aza, who went to the cabinet to get a glass and opened a drawer to get the corkscrew. "Our children are our life, so I understand why you were so hesitant to meet with me...Why you still are."

Aza opened the bottle at the table and filled Mil's glass up halfway before sitting down in his chair. He looked at Caiden, whose head was still slightly down and he wondered what monstrous things she was thinking about them.

"If you already know that, then what are we doing here?"

Caiden lifted her head a little, but she still couldn't look at her mother. She didn't need to when she heard the quiet burning in her tone.

"I think you know. No, I'm quite positive that you've known for a long time. Years," Mil said, sipping from his glass. "Iela, let us help you."

"I don't need your help—"

"Then, let us help Caiden." Mil looked at Caiden and she had no choice but to look back. "Don't you want to know everything?"

Caiden felt her eyes start to change, but like a switch, Iela's grip clamped down on her arm tighter than before and it stopped. Iela slid the hand holding her gun to rest on her lap. She didn't know how long she could sit there and not shoot something.

"You can't tempt her with lies," Iela spat. "There is no everything, only one thing."

"Really? And what is that?"

Iela answered with a glare.

"Since we're on the subject of lies, here's one of my favorite of yours: 'You don't exist, so act like it.'"

At nearly the same time as Caiden's head shot up at Mil, Iela jumped up from the table with her gun cocked and ready aimed at his emotionless face. Aza had gotten up as well just in case, but hoping not in case. He was definitely trying not to reveal one of his deepest kept secrets with Caiden in the vicinity.

"Aza, relax," Mil said, his heart rate not accelerating in the slightest. Mil finally looked at Caiden again. "...Our precious soul. Do you know who your mother is?"

She turned to him and he was smiling warmly at her, like a parent avidly awaiting the first steps of their child.

But soon the smile faded into oblivion as he slowly stood to his feet. Her eyes went to Aza and he looked like he wanted to tear out of his skin.

Caiden hadn't realized why the atmosphere in the room had shifted until she felt that hard, warm steel against her temple.

***

William's eyes shot open as he inhaled all the air he could. He struggled in this foreign skin as he sprung up off the cold thicket ground. He didn't know how long he'd been out or what the hell even happened to him, but he was certain he was alive.

Drenched in an unholy amount of sweat, he ran to the old man's house and barged into the bathroom. He was shaking so profusely he had to bite down on a towel so his teeth wouldn't slice through his tongue. He turned and the dead body in the tub startled him. He grabbed a knife that was sitting in the sink and kneeled by it. He balked a moment at what he was about to do.

What he had to do.

William began cutting off as much skin and hair as he possibly could from the body's forearm and head and shoved it all in his mouth. It was thick as it brushed against his tongue and the roof of his mouth. The hair was even worse, making it difficult for him to swallow. The skin was too thick to chew, so everything was forced down whole. He ran to the sink and began gulping handfuls of water to make swallowing easier and looked in the mirror.

He didn't feel anything. There was no change.

He went back to the body and held each side of its face. William made like he was going to headbutt the corpse but instead dove into its skin with his teeth, ripping and tearing off as much of it as he could. After some time, the tears welling up in his sockets had blurred his vision. He could no longer see what part of the face he was biting, but after a few moments, it didn't matter. He was nearly full. He was nauseous, but his appetite was satiated.

There was a gnawing sensation shooting throughout his insides as he felt them expanding. He gripped himself as tight as he could, keeling over until his forehead was roughly rubbing against the bath mat. He locked his jaw so that the screams wouldn't escape from his bloody lips.

It was no use.

William had collapsed and was writhing on the floor; the skin he was in began to take the form of the remains of the body that was in the bathtub.

After several moments had passed, when he felt he could stand to his feet again, he stumbled to his mirror and saw that his transformation was complete. He was now gazing into the face of his next identity.

He looked behind him at the tub. The body had already blackened some. He touched a little of what used to be the face and it crumbled beneath his fingertips. William took a deep breath and slowly lifted his arms above his head. His hands tightened into fists as he began beating and breaking the remains in a frenzy until it resembled the dirt where he was lying dead just nearly an hour before.

Chapter XXVII

A MINUTE HAD never felt so long. So full. Each second embodying what it was made to think it was. It had to have been more. Those sixty-seconds and only those had aspirations of being bigger; hours and days. That minute that Iela's gun was pressed against Caiden's skull was the most filling minute that she'd ever felt in her life. She was full to the brim; gorged to her bursting point. She didn't crave any more time if these kinds of seconds were the only ones left. Caiden would beg for death instead.

Iela's breathing had slowed as her palms moistened under the scorching tension. She didn't know how she wound up at this point, but this was the only thing that ever brought her any satisfaction. Though the look on Mil's face gave her a certain pleasure that he never could purposely give her in the little time that they knew each other.

College felt like a short dream where she only attended when she was asleep. The first day she walked into his philosophy lecture, she could tell he wasn't a full-blooded instructor. It was something in the way he carried himself like he knew more than he should for any teacher at a local college. That air of entitlement was what drew her in, but not in a seducing manner. Iela fed off those types of people that had possession of something that they didn't deserve and used it as a guillotine over the necks of others that would surely benefit from it. Even save their life. During a very bleak period of her own, she was one of those people, and to Mil, knowing what they shared that term and witnessing the blasphemed act of which his late star pupil was the author of in this moment, he thanked his Maker that he saved her life all that time ago.

"...You make it so incredibly easy," Mil's rumbling low tone was like a scream after the stark silence. "being what you are."

Caiden's body was perfectly stiff, so she felt that "what" knife Iela straight through her chest.

"That's a joke coming from you in this den," she snarled as she took a step back to the door. "You're not taking anything else from me."

Caiden watched Mil at that moment to see what kind of response he would give from such a suggestive statement. Nothing on his face was telling. Mil didn't seem totally surprised by Iela's actions. The polar opposite of Aza, who'd been frozen in a stance of near pouncing. He met Caiden's eyes and he looked like he relaxed a bit, but that could've been her wishing this standoff would end as soon as possible.

"She's not mine to take," Mil said, picking up his glass. "Nor yours."

"We're leaving right now."

Iela backed up more until she felt the kitchen door. Caiden allowed herself to be dragged, getting a tremor whenever the gun brushed against the thin layer of skin covering her bone.

They got to the living room, then left out of the front door. Iela dashed to her car. Caiden nearly tripped after not having the speed nor the will to keep up. She was leaving what might've been a Void information goldmine all because her mother had history with her soon-to-be ex-teacher.

Iela started up the car after a few tries and hauled ass off that street and out of the entire gravy-tinged neighborhood. Caiden buckled her seatbelt and fought off a laughing fit. The evening took a peculiar turn, and not because her mother pulled a gun out on her or she found out her teacher may have had a relationship with her mother in the past, but Caiden's thoughts about why Mil never emitted any energy eluded her even more.

She still couldn't feel anything coming from him, but after this meeting, she began to think that even if she could read him, it would feel exactly the same as not being able to read him at all.

***

Dontae had been staring at his lock screen hoping to get a notification from one of his ears to the ground. Though he'd linked back up with the Argenta, he was still in business on the side. No one had contacted him. He guessed because word had got around that his plate was full, but even so, not everyone he talked to knew that. These were people from all walks of life hitting him up to inform him about a potential Void in dire need. But it's been quiet, much to his detriment.

He'd wanted to distract himself from any and everything involving the Argenta. And by Argenta he meant Pneuma. There was a little bit of Mil in there, for he and the English plague shared a transparent dislike for him being a part of their club. He knew what he was getting himself into, knowing that neither side had a say in what was to transpire. This was beyond human or Void and Dontae was feeling the burden of witnessing that truth more than ever.

He sat up, dabbing the light drool that almost escaped the corner of his mouth, and blankly looked around Piccolo's office. He saw his chair pushed up to the desk, but didn't see his pillow. As Dontae got up he saw that Piccolo had propped his pillow under his head while he was sleeping. He stood there a moment staring at it before he picked it up and put it to his nose. It had a faint trace of his scent, a mixture of light rain and peony. Dontae had to stop himself before he and his body became strangers.

He left the room, heading to the front, and saw Rane and Nova talking in hushed voices. It was noon so the bar was closed. He liked it that way sometimes, especially after just waking up. It was nostalgia for this place during its first year when things weren't looking too hot. He didn't know how Piccolo did it with the vandalism and death threats, but that was New York. Piccolos was home, both the man and the bar.

He took down the bamboo chair from his reserved table and sat down while he flashed the two women his knee quivering smile. He could definitely devour some home cooking right about now.

"Which one of you divine creatures is gonna make me some breakfast?"

"I don't mind," Rane said as she seemed to want to end her conversation with Nova.

"Girl, sit down."

"I was kidding, Rane," he said, getting up and walking to the bar. He caught both of them becoming oddly preoccupied with organizing bottles and untangling their hair. "I just realized my ears were burning. What's up?"

"Nothin' darlin', just the same shit."

"Piccolo has to leave again," Rane clarified softly. "Well, you know."

"No. I don't."

That was another oddity about their relationship, that Piccolo seemed to know a lot about him and Dontae only knew basic stuff about him. And by basic, he meant his physical appearance. Anything beyond that, like his passions and his childhood, was unknown.

"Now my ears are burning."

They all were a little startled by his entrance, but because of his natural soothing tone, it wasn't so dramatic. They weren't even made to feel bad for talking about him behind his back.

"You're leaving." The heartache in his voice was cutting.

"Yeah, for a little while," Piccolo said, walking up to him. "Only for a little while."

Dontae felt his muscles lock in anticipation as Piccolo closed the distance between them. A faint grin glided across his lips and Dontae saw, wondering if he gave himself away this time.

"So, you're closing down or leaving us to fend for ourselves?

"What do you want me to do?" Piccolo asked this while placing one of his hands on Dontae's head.

"You know what I want." Dontae pretended to be annoyed and shook it off. "But I guess you have business, so what anyone says doesn't matter."

"Everyone matters," he said, touching Dontae's cheek. "which is why I need you."

Dontae felt his face getting rosy and went behind the bar to get something cold.

"That better mean you leavin' baby boy the keys, cuz I can't afford to go off to a zen cabin for a month to meditate or wherever the hell rich people go for 'business'."

Dontae was waiting on Piccolo's reply as he took a sip of his ginger ale, but it didn't come and he turned around to a sunbeam.

"I can't." He studied every vein in the man's eyeball. "You know I can't."

"Why not?"

Dontae nearly gave him a puppy head tilt to signify his continued confusion. He couldn't see anything beyond what he was asking him on his face and thought it'd be better if they talk in private.

"Can we talk about this later? I have to get back..." He trailed off thinking of going back to Mil's and finding Pneuma haunting every room he decided to go into.

"Nova doesn't have faith in my return, so please ease her mind."

Nova was looking at her phone and Dontae, waiting on a yes.

"You want me to run this place for a month?"

"Not alone," Rane piped in, sure of herself.

"Where are you going?" Dontae asked, not understanding Piccolo's line of thinking.

"Away on business like she said."

They watched him head back to his office and continued thinking of what the next four weeks could possibly turn into.

"It'll be okay," Rane assured him, cleaning a beer glass.

"If you say so."

"Mr. Cahill."

Dontae, clearly triggered, spun around and saw a pair of keys flying right at him. He barely caught them as they hit him in the lower part of his abdomen.

"Those are just a copy," Piccolo said, before vanishing to the back of the bar.

Nova had been closely watching Dontae ever since Piccolo came into the room.

"Hey," she lowered her voice, "what the hell was all that?"

"I don't know," Dontae said, still looking at Piccolo's face behind his eyes. "He's becoming more human than I'll ever be."

"He trusts you," Rane said. She got a hefty bottle off the top shelf. "They all do, mostly."

"He asked me because he knows it kills me to say no to him."

"And that brings me back to my first question," Nova said, tapping her nails on one of the three shot glasses that Rane set out on the bar. "What the hell was that?"

"What?" Dontae eyed Nova, who enjoyed not giving him much of a hint and then to Rane, who dropped her head a little in embarrassment as she filled up the glasses with the motor oil.

"You and Picco."

"No." Dontae sat down on a stool, now realizing what she was getting at. "He's the definition of the father I never had." He grabbed one of the glasses as he needed something to occupy his hands. "So, no..."

"You ever fuck your father?" Nova asked, raising her glass to him in premature cheers and holding in her laugh at the two warring emotions that flitted across Dontae's face.

"Are you projecting or is this a vicarious fantasy—"

"All of the above, sweetie."

"This isn't polite conversation—"

"Not a ear, a eye, a mouth, a nose—"

"My g—"

"I'm talkin' about all the orifices—"

"All the what?" Dontae snorted.

"You heard me. All of 'em," she repeated finally, letting the audible smiles out, one after the other.

"All right," Rane cut in before her face got any redder. "To the night?"

"Yes, please."

Dontae gave Rane a gracious look while Nova continued to laugh quietly to herself. They all lifted their glasses and knocked them back. Dontae immediately poured himself another. He would keep drinking until his mind decayed the pictures that grappled him through Nova's not-so-subtle use of imagery.

***

When Caiden got home, she went straight to her room. Iela didn't have to talk to her and explain what she did wrong, she just knew and went upstairs. Iela was left to fend off the questions from Roxa, who would never fully get over being pissed at such a hard-headed daughter.

"What you do to her?"

Iela stopped herself from saying the usual and decided to tell her the truth.

"This man wants her and he's not gonna stop until he has her."

"You wanna have children now so I guess you scared out yo' mind." Roxa tried to hide her disappointment, but couldn't.

"Yeah, I'm scared for her...He always gets what he wants." Iela ached for her bottle, but she needed her mind right to figure out how she was going to survive this. The problem was, no one survived the Argenta.

"That don't explain why Caiden walked past me without a word." Roxa knew she'd try and go to her room or the study so she reached for her arm. "Talk to me."

"I don't want to—" she said, attempting to take her arm back, but Roxa jerked her around so she could see her face.

"It's not about you. Don't you see that?"

Iela felt that familiar fire begin to rise in her as she looked into the old woman's eyes. It was frustrating that she would never understand.

This human would never understand.

"It is about me because I gave birth to her. I did it and it all falls on me." Her voice went up in volume as she got toward the end, feeling every sharp word that she'd not been saying after all this time, beginning to slice through. "I have to live with the choices that I didn't make and should've made. This is about me and they're going to pit her against me because of who I've been."

"Because of who you are," Roxa corrected in an almost incredulous way. "The only thing you ever done right was protect that child and that might be the same reason why you gon' lose her."

Iela didn't say anything. She stared off into the kitchen in the small corner where her cabinet was. She wanted it so bad but knew that drinking it would prove Roxa's point. She suddenly longed for her letters. That would be the perfect end to a day like this.

"What happened today?"

"...I was about to test myself," Iela said, still staring off, but her mind had left the whiskey. "See how far I can rely on her."

"You her mother," Roxa said, with near pity. Iela rarely discussed what was weighing her down so Roxa took advantage because she would go back to her usual self in the morning. "She put her worries on you. You want somebody to rely on, what I been here for?"

"Not Caiden..." Iela said to herself.

Roxa watched her massage her head and run her fingers through her curls. This was a personal stress habit, not a Caiden one.

Knock. Knock.

Iela went for her gun, but it wasn't there. Even her subconscious was telling her she went too far.

"Who is that?"

"I ain't expectin' anybody," Roxa said as Iela went to the door.

She peeked through the curtain and threw the door open immediately, but before the guy could say anything, Iela slung him in the house by the throat and slammed the door.

"Who the hell is this?" Roxa asked, alarmed.

"The prick who killed me."

"Pl-Please..." he heaved as Iela's knee was dug into his back.

"How the fuck did you get here? Answer me!"

He wanted to give her everything he had, but he was too busy sputtering incoherently through his tears.

"Get off the boy and let him speak," Roxa yelled, still trying to take in that this little kid tried to murder her daughter.

She did after putting all her weight on his bones to get to her feet. Iela dragged him off the floor and he finally lifted his head.

"...It's you."

The boy was shaking at his discovery. His eyes were red and his face drawn down like shades. He was crying and his clothes wrought with stench and stains. He dropped to his knees and lifted his hands in welcoming and surrender when he saw Caiden staring at him from the bottom of the stairs.

Chapter XXVIII

"IT'S BARRY..."

It had taken Barry about an hour to calm down from when he first got inside Roxa's home and saw Caiden up until after Iela hurried her back up to her room and out of his sight.

He was now still in the kneeling position in front of the couch that he refused vehemently from Roxa. Iela was standing all the way in the kitchen, keeping her eyes locked on the backs of her unwanted guests.

Mil and Aza were standing at a comfortable distance over the young man having a very familiar conversation. When Iela saw that silver SUV pull up to rest in the curve of their driveway, there wasn't enough time for any of her exit plans. She just forced Caiden upstairs to her room and invited the Argenta inside without a word.

"There, there, Barry." Mil gently patted the young man's greasy head. "Do you know who we are?"

"No, and I don't care...He's gotta help me."

Aza wanted to pity the man, but he suddenly showing up at Caiden's home, her last safeguard, had thinned his sympathy. He glanced back at Iela who's attention never left the two of them.

"Aza, take him to the car."

"No," Barry's head snapped up and his tears seemed to come out as if on cue. He was still and he looked hard at

Mil, a feat so rare that some of the Argenta have yet to master it. "I can't leave here without seeing him."

"Why would you think that was possible for someone like you, Barry?"

Aza stared at Mil a moment. He'd never seen the man mock someone that they were meant to help. He got Barry to his feet, who couldn't recognize a hypothetical to save his life.

"It was promised to me," he said as his face became wetter. He jerked suddenly and started trembling again, violently this time.

"What's with you?" Aza asked, annoyed as he nearly knocked heads with him. It was obvious he wasn't special so Aza couldn't understand why he was being adamant, especially about something that he'd yet to show he deserved.

"Why didn't you stay dead?"

Barry hadn't looked Iela's way as he was taking his phone out of his pocket to cancel a call that had physically irritated him further, but she was obviously the only one to whom he could be referring.

"No, Barry," Mil said. "Why did you kill her?"

Iela shifted on her feet as she watched the kid. He just looked at the man as his face turned red with bitterness. Barry wasn't going to tell the Argenta anything. He was warned if he ever crossed paths with them to surrender name, date, and serial number. Nothing more.

"You have to protect me."

"No the hell we don't." Iela couldn't silently fume in the kitchen any longer. She came into the living room as Roxa hugged herself in anticipation of a showdown.

"Why Barry?" Mil asked, not paying Iela any mind.

Barry dropped his head as his face tinged to a tomato paste color. He was crying again and Iela was getting impatient.

"What did William tell you?" she demanded, fearing the answer she already knew.

The boy's body just went limp in Aza's grip as he collapsed to his knees, crying more than he ever had since entering the house. They all watched him for a moment without another word. Iela was the only one getting more agitated the longer he didn't open his mouth. Mil simply waited until he calmed down like he had all the time in the world.

"Do you need your memory jogged?" Iela asked, pulling out her weapon. She made sure to have it on her from now on.

If Barry's face got any redder, he would surely pass out, but the sudden sound of creaking wood severed his cries completely. He barely lifted his eyes and only glimpsed Caiden's shoes past Mil's legs and his head dropped to the floor.

"...Please. The prince has to save me."

They all turned to look at Caiden stepping off the bottom step, but all she cared about was Barry.

"Get back to your room," Iela said, glancing at Mil. Her gun was still holding steady, but she couldn't trust herself after earlier.

"Impossible..." she said under her breath as she took another step towards the tortured body. Caiden felt the glow in her chest brighten as she got closer.

"Baby, maybe you shouldn't be in here." Roxa knew she shouldn't have said anything, but the look on Caiden's face was something she couldn't bear.

"It's okay," she said, kneeling in front of Barry, who had crawled to her feet.

"No, it's not," Iela said at a loss at what was going on. Her first thought was that Caiden had become emboldened with the company in the house, but remembered that didn't fit her personality at all. So the only other explanation was that damned thing in her chest.

Caiden looked up at her mother, her expression attempting to convey what her heart was pumping through her veins. "...It hurts."

Iela just pierced her in disbelief. Gradually, her gun floated to her side as Caiden went back to the soul at her mercy.

"Ms. Waters," Mil said after a moment. "We shall relieve you."

Aza picked Barry back up off the floor, but Caiden couldn't leave him alone.

"What are you gonna do with him?" She stood up, looking to Aza this time. He was the only person she felt had been honest with her since day one. "Are you gonna save him?"

Before Aza could answer, Mil responded instead.

"No, Ms. Waters. He's going to save you."

***

Jais got back to his hotel, rubbing his eyes and picturing that six-pack tucked behind yesterday's leftover Mexican in the mini-fridge. He looked down at his watch and forgot the thing had been broken since the eighties. He let out an exhausted laugh; exactly two ha's, not three, and dug in his back pocket for his room key.

"Damn it."

He pulled out his phone as the door opened up. Dontae was in his monogrammed pajamas and house slippers drinking one of Jais' beers. He was never without minuscule remnants of that old silver spoon.

"You forgot your key."

"I didn't," he said, taking the key card that Dontae was holding out to him. "...and I was going to ask what you were doing here, but it's obvious I'm the lesser of the two evils."

"You are...But then I realized that it didn't matter where I went."

Jais got a beer out of the fridge and collapsed on his bed. He cut on the TV and got pulled into a cop drama.

"Stay as long as you want," Jais sighed, sipping his beer. "Just don't get lost in my six-packs."

"Don't worry. I'll be out of your way soon enough."

Jais looked over at Dontae who was staring past his phone and noted the distance in his tone.

"C'mon, man. None of that. What do I always keep telling you? We don't rest until we can breathe..."

"...Or we'll die in our sleep." Dontae sat up but only to watch TV. He could feel those hunter greens on his cheek and didn't want to say anything else. Too much was already going on. "Did Aza sleep in my bed? There're still hints of him in the room."

"It's sad, but that leash is still short." He finished his can and set it on the side table between their beds. "Aza's not the reason you're drinking my *un*domesticated beer."

Dontae didn't say anything and slid under the duvet. He even put his phone down on the side table before closing his eyes.

"So, you've chosen death."

"No," he countered, muffled beneath the duvet. "I'm just not in the mood right now."

"You don't look like you ate." Jais got up to cut off the TV and undressed before getting back into bed.

"How's eating supposed to make me look?"

"Less anal. More sensible."

"Please, don't say anal," Dontae sighed to himself and turned on his side to face Jais.

"I don't wanna know."

He placed one of his arms behind his head and closed his eyes. Dontae, sure that his interrogation was over, reached to turn off the light when—

Whoosh!

A sharp, quick gust clipped his sideburns and Pneuma materialized right next to him. He was asleep.

"The hell—"

"Shh, shh."

Dontae threw him an astonished look, shushing him like he was in the wrong. They both looked down at the boy swimming in a worn but clean powder-white nightgown. He was balled up and unbothered in the middle of a catatonic slumber.

"You two should talk in the morning," Jais whispered, eyeing the boy to make sure he was really asleep.

When Dontae didn't say anything, he figured he was picking up where he left off, but when Jais caught his eye, it went back to his abdomen where he'd lost his words.

Jais grabbed a shirt out of his bag and put it on. "You can sleep in my bed."

"I'm fine over here," Dontae said. His gaze fixed on Jais in a particular way that only he could understand.

"...I am, too. For real."

Jais got back in bed and cut off the light because that was the only way Dontae was going to stop giving him that look.

He was never to be pitied. Out of all of them, it should never be him.

He laid on his back, his eyes adjusting to the near darkness. The shallow light seeping through the edges of the curtains barely allowed him to see any of Pneuma's facial features. Dontae had turned his back to both of them.

Something was bothering him, besides Dontae's recent rift with Pneuma. Before, he would've just said it like a five-year-old incapable of lying, but now the timing felt off. His hand slid to the half-foot scar near his pelvic bone and the memory from that fateful morning was absorbed through the nerve endings on his fingertips.

He got out of bed, grabbed a couple more beers out of the mini-fridge, and leaned back on the headboard to watch the gradual heaving backs of his roommates; his brothers. Both of which happened to wake up briefly a couple of hours later when he popped open that final can.

***

Bzzz.

David slumped into Faber's back door with his trusty illegally copied key and made sure the big guy wasn't working overtime before going into his office and closing the door.

Bzzz.

He threw his phone on the small cot and slid his backpack from under it. He pulled out some clothes and rushed to the restroom to change. A simple tee and sweats. Then, he went back to the office and closed the door—

Bzzz.

He forced his body to sink into the rough fabric. David didn't know how long he'd have to endure any more of this, but he didn't want to think about it. He was told the last guy staying here had skipped town, no longer having the patience to see this out till the end. David felt for the guy. Not just because he'd run out of options and had to take shelter in the back of a deli, but because he was like Caiden and so many others that he'd come across in his life. He was thankful for people like Faber who didn't give up on them. But that never lasted long because they eventually gave up on themselves.

Bzzz.

David twisted his arm around his body, then over his back once he remembered he wasn't double-jointed and snatched his phone out from under himself. He had been ignoring text messages all day. He didn't want anything to ruin quite possibly the best day of his pathetic life. Caiden was unexpected kindling to his dying fire and wanted to prolong the time they had together as long as—

Bzzz.

David unlocked his phone to a slew of texts, all from the same person. When he saw the last one, he nearly shit his stomach.

It read: *"Plan A"* from William.

Chapter XXIX

BAM!

Caiden jumped a little when a fancy-looking flyer was slammed on a locker just inches from her face. It had to be David because Aza was less inclined to bring attention to himself.

"What's that?"

"A dance. We're going."

Caiden laughed like that was the funniest thing she ever heard as her steps fell in stride with his. They were on their way to lunch, the only time they got to hang out during school hours.

"What happened to pretending to bump into me and secretly shoving notes in my hand?"

David's face soured and he sucked in air. "Let's pretend like that never happened."

"A dance? We're not going," she mocked with a smile.

"I would be hurt, but you're always so happy it's disgusting."

"Now, you're an empath."

"No, I just know that look now."

Her smile faded some as they headed out to the courtyard. David jogged to their table like they were in a race and sat down in her seat until she shooed him out of it.

"Isn't a dance just a huge party? You don't seem like you're into social gatherings," she said, taking her chicken

Alfredo out of her brown bag. "This is just another excuse to spend time with me."

"Yeah, I like you."

"Well, that's what you're calling it," Caiden reminded him.

He watched her respond in her usual way when he said or did anything that indicated something beyond friendship. David preferred her honesty over anything else. He wondered if he'd be able to distance himself from her if she'd suddenly decided to string him along. He stopped and straightened up in his seat.

"That looks good." He took out a colorless sandwich that he made hastily with the stolen ingredients from Faber's kitchen.

"You want some of this?" she asked, holding her fork out to him with a juicy piece of chicken jabbed on the end.

"Stop changing the subject." He lunged forward to take a bite and surprised her at almost clenching the meat between his teeth.

"You know I can't go."

"Ah, your mom. Don't worry, I'll get rid of her," he said casually, biting down on the thick baguette bread.

"I would love to see that." She was a little shocked at how her half-kidding was also half-serious.

She picked up the flyer and looked at it again. The formality of the wording and baroque-themed background was very enticing. If she did get that never-in-a-million-years permission from Iela, she could truly see herself getting excited about something like this. It would be another first in her series of firsts.

"What if I snuck out?"

"Okay...That's a little more dangerous than my plan, but we could figure something out."

"David, it's not happening." She slid a piece of broccoli into her mouth.

"That's a shame."

Caiden and David looked up and saw a girl coming over to them. She was digging in her distressed blue jean bag when she got to their table. Neither one of them knew her, but she had an expression on her face that indicated that she spoke to strangers all the time.

"Just a quick trust exercise."

The girl pulled out a precision knife and proceeded to make a small cut on her index finger. Caiden and David could only stare at her in silence as the act of drawing blood in front of people you've never met before was not something that was done so casually.

"Like I was saying," she said, shaking her black bloodied finger from side to side. "It would be a shame if you didn't come. The deeper the void, the better."

"Uh, yeah, it's tragic. I was just telling her." David was sizing her up immediately. Just because she was out there with them and a Void didn't mean she was pro-Void.

"Well, I'm going," she said matter-of-factly as if someone argued with her.

Caiden handed her a napkin, still having nothing to say.

"Thanks." The girl took it, her brown eyes shrinking in a smile. "Maybe I'll run into y'all. And you can save me a dance."

Caiden glanced at David as the girl caught up to a group heading into the cafeteria. She jumped into their conversation as she did theirs, in media res, somehow knowing exactly what they were talking about.

Something didn't feel right. She didn't feel right.

"I think she was hitting on us," David guessed, picking up Caiden's fork with some Alfredo on it.

"I think...I have to go." Caiden got up and grabbed her briefcase in a rush, even leaving behind her lunch. "It's yours. I'll see you later, okay?"

But she was halfway across the courtyard before he could answer.

"What's got your heart racing?" The Voice asked.

That's exactly what Caiden reached for when she heard that voice. She dipped into the first girls' restroom she saw and made certain that it was empty before she started her soliloquy.

"Where have you been?" she asked, locking herself in the stall. She placed her briefcase over the toilet and sat down on it, focusing on coming down from that feeling that knocked her off balance. "Where do you go when you go silent?" Her head naturally went to the heavens as she asked this, having no idea how this seemingly imaginary friend worked It's magic.

"I'm always here," The Voice said. "Always listening, always worrying, like now."

Caiden sat glued to the dark brown leather, breathing as quietly as possible just so she could feel the pumping of her heart.

"You mean that girl..."

"Yes, mentioning a dance."

"Yeah..." she trailed off and picked up her briefcase.

"I pray your next destination is a classroom."

"I'm leaving now," she said, coming out of the stall. "Don't ask me anything."

"I know."

She exited and found herself following her feet. Caiden didn't know where to search, but somehow her feet did. Not a few seconds later she found her boots halting in front of Mil's classroom door. She glimpsed his back and a flyaway from Aza's bun before she jumped out of view. Then, she paused and wondered why she was hiding.

Tap. Tap.

She turned and saw Aza smiling at her from the window before opening the door.

"Hello," he said, looking down at her expectantly.

"Uh, hey."

They gazed at each other a moment too long until Mil's voice snapped Caiden out of it.

"Ms. Waters."

Aza stepped aside and Caiden inched into the room. Mil was sitting on the edge of his desk with an expression on his face that indicated he knew things would turn out in his favor. Caiden could sense that they were both acting as if they weren't interrupted. Aza closed the door and they waited for her to speak, but she was taking too long for Mil.

"Something's got you scared I see," he said, eyeing her taught knuckles clasped around the handle of her briefcase. "If my guess is correct, I assure you, the enemy lies without, not within."

"You came looking for us, so you've got some questions?"

Her eyes followed Aza as he glided to an empty desk in front of her. He was way too blasé considering all that went on the last couple of times they were together.

"I have a lot of questions, but I don't think I should ask them here."

"Thanks to our companion, not only can you ask them here, but you can ask as many as you want and it'll seem like time has stopped completely."

She didn't understand and turned to Aza for a better explanation, but he'd just finished giving Mil a worried look before meeting her gaze.

"But ironically, there's no time for that." Mil grabbed his notebook off the desk and opened the door for her. "I can only give you answers."

Caiden hesitated as Aza swooped past her like they were about to go to an amusement park. The small crease at the corners of his mouth had returned and his eyes had nearly sunk behind the apples of his cheeks.

"I can't leave," she said, noting the faint anguish in her tone.

"It isn't that you can't leave," Mil said, wringing the door handle until his skin turned white. "If we wanted to harm you, Ms. Waters, we'd have chosen a more opportune moment than this one."

Aza had to be certain that he was joking before he looked back at Caiden to make sure that that didn't have her scurrying away, but the expression that he found embedded onto her face was the polar opposite.

"I'm not afraid of death, Mr. Gunde," Caiden said in the clearest voice she'd ever mustered. "I'm afraid of bringing it."

Mil stepped back into the classroom; he and Aza were slightly shocked at her answer. There was something that changed in her eyes. Not just the color, for it seeped back to its natural brown as he observed this newness in the young girl that was absent her first day. He could sense some authority in the way she stood and spoke those words as he'd just witnessed a hushed awakening right before his eyes. Mil couldn't help but wonder if that was Caiden or the Soul.

"Well, death is similar to our God, Ms. Waters. It cannot be brought, it just is," Mil said darkly. "I know you've seen it. Felt it...The end is here, Caiden, and fortunately for us, it lies with you."

Mil walked out of the classroom with the confidence that she was surely behind him. It took a moment, but not longer than when she first entered the room before she was right behind him and Aza, closing the door behind them.

Less than an hour later, Caiden was standing face to face with one of her self-proclaimed subjects.

***

Dontae jerked awake before he remembered where he was. He was freezing and was about to get up to turn off the air conditioner when he saw that Pneuma was still sound asleep on the other side of his bed. His breathing was drawn out to where it seemed as if he wasn't performing the natural reflex at all. The boy's face was about as peaceful as a gargoyle's.

Jais' bed was empty.

Dontae got dressed and was about to go into the bathroom—

Swish.

"Damn it, Pneuma."

A moment passed in silence before Pneuma came back out, by opening the door, dressed in his staple clothing. Dontae looked him up and down to make sure he'd at least had them washed.

"We leave when you're finished."

"Sorry," Dontae said, nowhere near in the mood. "I just got a promotion and I'm not gonna be late."

Pneuma silently watched him put on his shoes and go into the bathroom. He waited until he was done, grabbed his wrist as soon as it passed the door jamb, and hit his line of view.

Dontae didn't have the ability to understand what took place after because they both now stood in a living room of a tiny apartment.

He dropped to a knee, cradling his aching wrist and fighting down vomit. It wasn't a long battle, for last night's takeout had come up fresh all on the shiny hardwood floors. He'd never experienced a feeling of wanting and willing to be in two different places at once. His entire being felt like it would split in half if he'd only surrendered to it.

"Pneuma?"

Dontae spun around and found himself locking eyes with Adyn of all people.

"You're still alive," Pneuma said, utterly bored. "This concludes our 'talk'."

Dontae felt ready to explode until he saw how relieved Adyn was. He was almost in tears.

"...I can see you," he said.

"Yeah." Dontae staggered to his feet only now realizing that he'd looked at the boy and hadn't turned into a pillar of salt. "You're here alone?" he asked, scanning the small and comfy one-bedroom.

Adyn didn't respond and looked at Pneuma. Dontae followed him.

"I'm gonna clean this up, okay," he said, going into the kitchen to look for cleaning supplies. He glared at the ghost and hissed under his breath. "I didn't realize how much you hated me until now."

Pneuma eyed Adyn until he went back into his room.

"I don't hate or love anyone. This was simply to ease your human heart."

"Yeah, I'm human." Dontae grabbed some paper towels off the kitchen bar. "It's better than being whatever the hell you are."

Pneuma watched Dontae go clean up the mess he made in silence. It wasn't that he was hurt, rather he was trying to find a way to end this spat that he still to this very second didn't know how it grew to be what it was. He and Dontae were never buddy-buddy to anyone with sense, but he didn't think he'd have to go through all these trivialities just to explain to this pampered layman that his decisions have always been prudent and that even a simpleton wouldn't disagree to the extent that Dontae had. Pneuma found this Blackheart sympathizer very intriguing.

"I don't know what I am."

Dontae looked at him and couldn't tell if he was being serious or just British.

"But I know that it's more than what you'll ever be."

"What are you gonna do with Adyn?" Dontae had heard stuff from him like that so often that it didn't faze him. "How long has he been your prisoner?"

"That's funny," Pneuma said, dryly. "What makes you think he's here against his will?"

"I have to be here."

Dontae turned around and saw Adyn standing a little behind the doorway like he still shouldn't get too close even though he was proven harmless.

"Adyn, all this stuff that happened...Your parents...It's not your fault."

"I don't wanna hurt anybody else," he said, his eyes watering again.

"You won't," Dontae said, getting on his level. He looked around the room and saw a takeout menu. He scribbled his number on it. "Here. I'll always be on the other end."

Suddenly, Pneuma felt a distant wave and wisped to Adyn just to push him in the room and close the door.

"Grab my hand."

"What's going on?" Dontae was confused, looking around the room again, this time for a threat, but there was nothing. "Adyn, you all right?"

"Yeah—"

Trumpets.

Loud and wailing came down over the room like it was being consumed all in one bite. Dontae began to tremble as the sound got closer and his head was jutting all around, searching in vain for the invisible musician.

"Grab it!" Pneuma spat.

Dontae reached out and had barely wrapped his hand over the tiny boy's before they dematerialized out of there and back into the hotel room.

"You left him," Dontae said, hitting the floor and clutching his stomach. He'd thrown up everything he had from the first trip.

"He's fine."

He was still in the kneeling position as he crawled to the side of his bed, so he had to look up at Pneuma to see his face. He'd look like he'd seen a ghost.

"Answer your phone."

It took a moment for Dontae to hear anything with that brass still ringing in his ears. He slid his phone out of his pocket and saw a couple of texts from Volx.

"'*The prince is home*'," Dontae read. He then looked up at Pneuma, whose expression went a little back to its normal brooding.

"I'll meet you in the car," he said, before wisping away.

Dontae looked down at the second message that he didn't want to read aloud. He figured Pneuma would just appear at Mil's as he did everywhere else instead of enduring a thirty-minute ride in Dontae's backseat. He scooped up his keys with the Soul being the only bright spot at the end of this long journey home.

Chapter XXX

FIFTY-SEVEN, FIFTY-EIGHT, FIFTY-NINE...an hour.

Barry had been staring at Caiden for an entire sixty minutes. Sometimes gaping, occasionally gawking like she was the only person in existence. She just sat there massaging her fingers.

When Caiden left school in the middle of the day and reluctantly got in the back of Mil's SUV, she did think that she was being stupid and irresponsible. When she followed Mil inside his house, she thought not only will Iela kill her for dinner, but she'll torture her as an appetizer. And finally, when Mil offered her a seat across from this shell of a person and she took it with the most gracious of silences, she knew that it wouldn't be an easy task getting out of there without someone's feelings getting hurt.

She'd plugged herself into one of the corners of Mil's sofa as far away from Barry as she could get. Before, at Roxa's, she'd only looked at Barry's tortured aura. It had called out to her as Timothy and Alise's had. Barry was pitiable and incredibly sad at what lengths he had to go through to feel and be human again. Caiden wasn't looking at his lustful teeth and despairing eyes at the time because his will to live had overpowered all of his physical deformities.

She glanced up at him to see if he'd moved but looked away when she locked eyes with his leer. After so many years of being in the shadows, Barry's twisted idea of imprinting made her want to lock herself in her room again.

"You're a little girl," Barry observed.

"I'm not that little," she replied calmly.

Barry wanted so badly to lean closer in his chair but kept his waning composure.

"You were nice to me before," he said as one of his heels perched on the wooden leg of the chair. He had to sit on his hands so they wouldn't abandon his limbs. "I think you're gonna do it again."

A creaky floorboard forced him to inhale any words that wanted to come out after. Barry's foot relaxed flat on the rug as he sat back in his chair. Caiden could only look for an instant at the corner of the room to see Volx standing at ease. Both of them had forgotten he was there.

"You killed my mother," Caiden said, almost question-like. She didn't understand how her mother died and was still alive, knowing full well she avoided any form of assistance, medical or otherwise.

"I knew she would come back," he said, the words flooding out of his mouth. "I'm not a killer."

Caiden fixed on him and for the first time since they met, he avoided her eyes.

"Caiden," The Voice said. "What have you done?"

It knew she couldn't answer, but the question was asked just as a reminder of her impulsive actions. Caiden had no idea what being there would accomplish, all she knew was that she had gotten more answers from them than from her own mother. Considering how much Iela wanted to keep her away from them, they might be the only people that could help her.

"Sorry to keep you waiting."

Caiden stood up as Mil and Aza entered the room. He didn't look sorry at all with an outfit change and a wine glass in his hand.

"For an hour," Aza added.

"I do have to get back soon," she said, looking at her watch.

"Oh, Ms. Waters, you can forget about all of that." Mil had sat in the other chair next to Barry, who was hungrily waiting to be acknowledged by anyone who would grant it to him. "You've come here willingly alone and that could only mean you accepted what fate has bestowed upon you."

Caiden stood there dumbfounded and had to backtrack everything that happened from when she found Mil in the classroom to him sitting languidly in front of her with his weekday partial white.

"I just wanna know why I'm different," she said. She didn't want to contradict her present words with her past actions. "You and Aza obviously know more about me than my own family...I wanna know why."

"Barry," Mil said, lacking any sort of mercy. "You said she can save you, correct?"

"Yes," he said, getting excited as much as Volx's presence would allow him.

"Tell us how."

Barry gazed up at Caiden as she and the others listened for his reply, but it never came. He sunk back in his chair and continued to keep his focus on his savior who felt his mood shift like it was her own. He'd stumbled onto this emotional staircase and hit every step on the way down. She slowly sat and watched as darkness clouded his head.

"Read the message, Barry," Mil said and then sipped his wine.

Barry didn't want to and was in no rush to pull his phone out of his pocket. Naturally, Aza assisted him.

"'*We'll all be cured Friday, seven-thirty*,'" Aza read. "'*Myerworth.*'"

"The dance," Caiden said, remembering the flier. "But I'm not going."

"You're not?" Aza didn't intend to sound so torn up about it, but after losing his temper with Barry, he was still in the process of reeling his emotions back to their proper places.

"You're funny, too," she said, standing up again. The bell was getting closer and closer to ringing. "I'm not even supposed to be here and you want me to go to a dance."

"You can't go," Barry urged.

Volx took a small step closer to Barry's chair and he quieted down.

"I'm afraid you're going to have to make an appearance, Ms. Waters." Mil's subtle pull at Volx's puppet strings gave him a small pleasure as he emptied his glass. He now put on his business face. "This is no ordinary Void. He's an outlier. Something far more daunting than Barry. And from the beginning, he's had no qualms about doing and using whatever and whoever he needs to get what he wants, including your mother."

Suddenly it dawned on her what Mil was suggesting and she felt her hand grip a gun that hadn't been by her side in a while. Her eyes began to shift as she felt the weight of where she was and what she might have to do press down on her shoulders.

"Caiden, calm down." Aza went into the kitchen and came back with a bottle of water.

"I'm sorry." She took it, but only to hold and accidentally caught sight of Barry gnawing at his bottom lip. He looked like he was feeding off just being near her. She almost willed Mary was in her possession so she could skip the dance in its entirety and let her steel get all the information they needed and more.

What?

Caiden caught herself as her eyes went back to normal.

The Voice was right. What was she thinking?

"May I use the bathroom?"

"Of course," Mil obliged. "Our home is your home now."

That snaked a chill evenly throughout her body. Aza led her to the door and she locked herself inside. She looked around, noticing the frilly motif throughout the house was continued in the bathroom. Thick teal rugs were in front of the tub, toilet, and sink while towels of the same shade were on the back of the door and wall hooks.

She went to the sink and turned on the water, but didn't wash her face.

"God, help me," she whispered to herself.

"If you heeded any of my words, you wouldn't need to call for anyone," The Voice said.

"I always listen to you," she said, looking for an escape though she knew that wouldn't matter.

"Except when it comes to these particular Voids."

"I don't know..." she paused, watching the water spin down the drain. "I don't know what's wrong with me."

"Nothing, Caiden...Nothing."

She found it strange that The Voice went from scolding to comforting in less than a second. Roxa came to mind and she got a surge of motivation to try and finesse her way out of this situation.

Then a lightbulb exploded.

"Zai."

"Yes."

Caiden whipped around so fast she fell back and hit the tub. Lision caught her forearm before she toppled over and cracked something.

That's when she felt it. The warmth.

She fixed on him as he released her arm and dropped to a knee. Caiden watched him bow his head and she felt more questions coming on.

"You may ask."

"...Not here," she said, sitting on the edge of the tub.

Caiden watched the back of his head for a moment waiting for him to disappear, but he remained in that position without another word.

She felt her neck get warm and it rose to her face as the memories of Zinc, Timothy, Alise, and even her mother all shot through her at once. It seemed like all of their energies struck her like a lightning bolt and were zipping through her nerves until they found a way out. The problem was that there wasn't one. When she took on the emotions of others, they stayed and made her their home without her permission. That wouldn't be so bad if everyone were good.

Iela's was the most potent of them all. That feeling of putting a gun to her daughter's head, the grueling training sessions before the sun had time to rise, and the obligation to protect something that she felt she was owed was unbearable on levels that Caiden had been suppressing since she could remember.

The tears began to claw up from that deep part of herself where she'd locked them away, but she couldn't lose it now.

"Zai..." She called him with a cracked voice.

He lifted his head, but his expression was something that Caiden didn't expect to see. Lision had a look that was similar to what she imagined she looked like to Bryan when she found him behind the school after Timothy's death. There was a consciousness shown in his eyes that she didn't think she'd ever see from a human or Void. Or whatever Lision was.

"...Just thank you," she said quickly, dropping her head and dabbing what little stray tears managed to escape.

"Please," he said, finally. "Never lower yourself before me."

Her expression softened at his words and she got to her feet.

"I won't if you don't do the same thing to me."

He didn't move at first, expecting her to elaborate, but he lifted his head some more and saw she was no longer looking at him. Lision rose to his feet and only then did Caiden's head turn up to him.

"Okay. We can get outta here."

He didn't feel his actions were appropriate considering who he did them in front of, but because of who allowed them, he needn't question the decision made.

Caiden glanced in the mirror at Lision who turned into a statue again. She continued throwing water on her face until the whites of her eyes were no longer red. She dried her face with a tissue and opened the door.

"I was standing by in case you fell in."

Aza was waiting for her and Caiden couldn't tell if he'd just gotten there or if he heard her entire conversation with herself. Both of them.

"My bad. I said that to prove that I wasn't funny," he said, taking note of the pinkish tint in her eyes. "Also, we have a guest."

Caiden self-consciously patted her eyes again with her sleeve before she followed Aza back to the living room. There was another person there and after speed reading him like a book, she wondered why he was among such common folk as them.

"This is my brother, Dontae."

Dontae was stuck briefly before he reached out for her hand and kissed it.

"Pleasure."

He gently let her go and went back to where he was, but not without a side-eye from Aza.

"This is excellent," Mil said, standing to his feet. "Shall we get going?"

"Where?"

Mil eyed her and could tell she'd been bawling in the bathroom or was on the verge. He looked over at Barry, who'd picked up where he'd left off, staring her down and felt his heart change at the moment.

"...Actually, we're staying right here."

The Argenta collectively turned to him to see if they could get a sense of his state of mind from his ever casual countenance.

"Mr. Gunde, please," she said, purposely not looking Barry's way. He was the only one in the room content with the new plan. "What about Iela?"

"She's precisely why you're staying," he said, fingering the stem of his naked wine glass. "This has gone on too long, don't you think? This entire 'mother' thing."

Dontae and Aza quickly looked at Caiden who had forgotten how to breathe.

"What?..."

"Aza, take out the ground lamb. It feels like that kind of night." Mil gave Caiden a gentle smile. "Do you like lamb, Caiden?"

Aza hadn't witnessed cruel Mil in some time and he felt a little how Caiden looked. He didn't want to leave her side at all but went into the kitchen.

Low and behold, an opening.

Barry jammed back his armchair with every ounce of strength he'd been charging up all those hours, Caiden, his prince, being the primary energy catalyst. He slid a pocket knife out the front of his jeans and lunged straight for her.

Zwish!

Just as soon as he left his chair, Barry's corpse hit the Egyptian rug with a finalizing thud.

Chapter XXXI

CAIDEN COULDN'T TAKE her eyes off the dead body.

Barry. His name was Barry.

After what they'd both been put through in the last few days; for him, months, from what she could feel, it didn't seem right for him to end up in a stiff cold sprawl in front of her like this. His prince looking down over him in relief that he could no longer harm her. Caiden wasn't sure if that was his real intent. The room felt emptier now, his wired energy no longer zipping through her in a frenzy. The only consolation was that Barry's soul was finally at peace.

She watched Volx pick up his body and head toward the kitchen door.

"What are you doing with him?" she asked, slightly delayed as her voice lost all its punch when the pillar made eye contact with her.

"He will be properly disposed of," Mil answered, picking up Barry's pocket knife with his handkerchief.

"Are you okay?" Aza asked, offering her help, but she declined it and got up on her own.

"No. Not for a while now," she said to herself. "What was that?"

"Pneuma," Aza said, softly. "He's one of us."

"Did he have to kill him?"

None of them responded.

"I have to go home."

"I must say your tone offends me." He walked up to her and saw that she wanted to retreat, but stood firm. "We're here solely for you and this relationship will only work if we're all on the same page."

"After what just happened, only my tone offends you?"

Aza and Dontae watched Mil as a faint smile appeared on his lips. Caiden's heart was racing as she looked up at his relaxed face, but she never averted her eyes, even when they changed.

"I suppose you think we're evil, now; you've seen what's behind the curtain. But he was going to kill you, so we simply did our duty and stopped that from happening."

"Were you sure that's what he was gonna do?"

"Ms. Waters, were you?"

Caiden let her head drop as she pondered this.

"This is one of those answers that I told you about," he said, picking up his empty wine glass. "The question: Will we, the Argenta, do anything to protect you?"

She couldn't lift her head, waiting for her eyes to go back to normal, but she had a feeling they never would. When she finally fixed on him, she still couldn't find any hint of his rationalizing the taking of a life. She then turned to Aza, who was giving her an understanding and helpless look. When she looked at Dontae, he was sitting on the arm of the couch, hunched over, with a numbed expression on his face like he heard this countless of times.

"Take me home," she managed to say as she felt her eyes seep back to normal. "Please."

Aza would usually look back at Mil to gauge how much patience he had left, but the aching in Caiden's voice wouldn't allow him to turn away from her.

"As you wish," Mil said, finally. "Aza."

"Can he take me instead?"

Caiden fixed on Aza to show him that it wasn't personal, then faced Dontae, who was as surprised as the others. It was the first time that she elicited any form of authority over them and all she did was simply ask a favor. She wondered if anyone could get a taste for the minuscule drop of power that she accidentally swallowed and not become addicted.

"Do you mind?" she asked.

"Course not."

Dontae stood and motioned to her to lead the way. She waited for him to open the door and left with her head down. She could tell Aza was still boring holes in her cheeks, but the only thing she wanted to do was get to someplace familiar. Mil, on the other hand, was what Caiden imagined The Voice would look like if she disobeyed It. She didn't know how to explain to them that even a little bit of a good thing was sometimes too much.

They got outside the door and Caiden saw another car pull up.

"Party's over already?"

Caiden saw a scruffy guy get out of the car, cheesing at Dontae at the end of the driveway, but his demeanor changed when he saw Caiden standing behind him.

"You're the Soul," he said, in greeting.

Caiden couldn't read his expression, but she also wasn't trying to. She felt all used up and just wanted to slip into a few good hours of unconsciousness.

"It's Caiden," Dontae corrected, signaling to Jais that now wasn't the time.

"I'm sorry, I just got here and you're already leaving." He didn't want to sound too pushy, but the Argenta's entire new life was about to be driven away.

Caiden looked up at him and was reminded of Aza. That same longing in their eyes for things to finally make sense was a look she'd never thought she'd see beyond her mirror.

"I'll be back," she said, taking a small step toward him, just so he could understand. "I promise."

All Jais could do was nod. At that moment, whatever she said was law and he had to believe her. Dontae stared at Jais as he led her to his car.

The ride back to Roxa's was quiet. Dontae would occasionally glance over at Caiden to see if she at least looked alright until she fell asleep, and then at that point watching her made him feel uncomfortable. So he turned on some soothing alternative music and tried to avoid every pothole and bump in the road until they turned on her street. That black car was like an alarm clock as Caiden woke up as soon as he parked in front of her house.

"Thank you, Damien."

"You never have to thank me."

He didn't want to correct her, not with the day she's had.

They both waited for her to get out, but she feared what she would walk into once she got into the house.

"You want me to go with you?" Dontae asked. He could pick out that look from any of his childhood photos with his eyes closed.

"Goodness no. That would only make it worse." She opened the door and it took another moment for her foot to touch the pavement.

"One more thing," he said, not wanting to hold her up any more than she was already doing. "Why was I the lucky one?"

"There's no such thing as luck."

She granted him a tired, but kind look as she got out of the car and walked to the door. He didn't drive off until she got inside.

The house was calm and she smelled lingering aromas from Roxa's afternoon snacks. Caiden wanted to sneak up to her room, but it made more sense to meet her punishment head-on.

"Child, where you been?" Roxa had come from upstairs with a few books and a look of relief.

"Where is she?" Caiden asked in the tiniest voice.

"Oh, I don't know what she gon' do, but she gon' do it."

Caiden's insides started churning as Roxa went into the kitchen to fix some tea. Instead of waiting, she decided to go find Iela.

"Caiden," Roxa called to her hushed-like.

She gave her an almost confident look that she knew what she was doing before the dark hall to Iela's study ate her up.

She stood outside the door and didn't have to knock. It was cracked which meant Iela probably heard her talking to Roxa.

"Now you want my permission?"

Her voice stopped Caiden's heart for a second. She inhaled and opened the door, and that's when she saw white.

Iela slapped her so hard it knocked her clean off her feet.

For an instant, Caiden forgot where she was and touched her inflamed cheek to bring her back. She was too shocked to move or cry so she just remained on the floor until Iela made up her mind of what to do with her.

"I hope you enjoyed school so far," she said, after a striking minute of silence. "Because today was your last day."

Caiden hadn't exhaled and after what she just heard, she couldn't. She sat there staring off at the small scuffs and scrapes in the hardwood. Then, the screws and the various shades of brown and burnt yellow. Any and everything to draw her away from the reality that she was living in.

"Oh my God," Roxa cried, rushing to help her off the floor.

"She's fine," Iela said, leaving the study.

"Do it look like— That girl ain't got no kind of sense and out here punishin' you for it."

"I...I got it, Roxa," she said, as they both noticed how she slurred Roxa's name. "...I just need my room."

Roxa was her unnecessary crutch as they left the study and got to the bottom of the stairs.

"I'm okay."

"No, you not. None of y'all are."

Roxa stood there fired up with nowhere to spread the flames. She waited until she heard Caiden's door close before she got busy in the kitchen with dinner.

Caiden cut on her lamp just to see if there was blood on her hand after she touched the inside of her cheek. There was, but she didn't know how bad it was as it mixed with her saliva.

She grabbed the least fuzzy of her nightclothes and went to the bathroom to take a shower. There was not enough time to let the steam get into her skin or the hot water to scorch away the toll that the events of the day had taken on her body. Caiden just bathed and got dressed. She avoided the mirrors and didn't think twice about not brushing her teeth. She got to her room and drowned beneath the waves of her sheets, pillows, and duvet. Then, The Voice started to hum her a lullaby.

"...There you are," she said to herself.

"Shall I try something new?"

"Something silent."

"As you wish."

She watched the light on the wall in the hopes that she would be hypnotized and go out when it did, but no matter how exhausted she was, the influx of information she received and the people she met today was so overwhelming that she couldn't relax.

"...Zai," she whispered, reluctantly.

It was right before she finished saying his name that his shadow appeared in the light on the wall she was facing. She turned over and he was kneeling next to her bed, his head bowed like all the other times before.

"I didn't wanna call you," she said, lying on her side. "But I couldn't stop myself."

"I can take the pain away." He was still staring at the floor.

"How did you know I was in pain?" she asked, forgetting that Lision knew things that he shouldn't know.

"Because you are alive." With that, he looked at her briefly, but it was only to look at her cheek.

She studied him as he studied her and was bursting with curiosity.

"...Zai, who are you?" she asked, unable to restrain herself anymore. "I feel nothing from you except warmth...And in that, I feel everything."

"I'm your Archangel, Caiden," he said after a moment. "I was sent here by our God."

Caiden was expecting him to say anything other than what he actually said. That he was a super deluxe Blackheart and possibly born one like herself was the only rational explanation for the abilities that he'd displayed. Not that he was a full-blooded, high-ranking angel from the Heavens.

"...God sent you to Texas," she stated just to hear it out loud and hope to make it more believable outside her head. "For what?"

"For you."

Caiden just gazed at him in more wonder than before. Today had to be a dream for it was too much. The day wasn't near finished and already it was too much for her.

"Will you talk to me until I fall asleep?" she asked as her head slid off her arm and sunk into her pillow. "About you, angels...anything."

"The Soul," he added, already knowing that was something she'd wanted to ask about.

Caiden's drooping lids sprung open. "That's what they called me." She didn't know why she suddenly felt sleepy.

"It's not you," Lision said, his head fully lifted now. "It's Him."

She locked eyes with him as her mind went blank instead of where it was supposed to go. A deep, buried, dormant part of her knew what he was talking about, but that was a Caiden she hadn't met yet. Or a Caiden that was still slumbering.

"You may ask." Lision interrupted her train wreck of thoughts.

"...Ask what?" But it was clear by the color of her eyes and the glow from her heart that she had an inkling of the answer before she felt safe to ask the question. "Ask what?" she repeated in a voice just below a breath.

Lision never averted his eyes from hers, trying to understand this human fear that was weaved throughout her dying voice. Caiden had been put through a lifetime of ordeals that some humans pray to avoid, and now she was looking to him, her sired whole armor of the Savior Themselves to take away her worry.

"Caiden."

He reached out and gently hovered his hand over her cheek as her eyes closed. That addicting warmth in its purest form spread into her blood and up through her skin.

"Fear not..."

Chapter XXXII

THE ARGENTA WERE gathered in the living room. After Barry's departure by a very deft, but much too thorough Pneuma, they were pondering another way to lure out the elusive Void who had managed to assemble a small army just to capture their supposed prince.

"She has to go," Jais said, taking a drag from his cigarette. "That's the only way we're gonna see what this guy looks like."

"You're correct," Mil said, knowing Jais never took his pats on the back in kind. "Her emotional prowess should be more than enough to end all of this on the night in question."

"But not if he's Hiding," Jais countered as he watched Mil sip from his glass.

"If she can't sense the attack coming, then she's just an easy target."

Aza was sitting on the floor, but he shifted to sit on the back of one of his heels and rested his chin on his knee.

"This man has convinced at least seven people that the Soul can fix them." Dontae was staring off in thought at the now naked floor as he pondered to himself. "But he waited until Caiden started school..."

"She wasn't a hostage before," Jais added. He took another puff from his cigarette. "He figured it was go time when she finally left the house."

"Did Pneuma say anything?" Aza asked, hopeful, as he inched closer to the couch. "I know he can't be everywhere at once..."

"He hasn't said boo to me." Jais lifted up his lighter to relight his cigarette when a subtle breeze blew it out.

They all waited a moment for him to appear, but he didn't. Mil adjusted himself in his chair and fingered the end of his fountain pen.

"How do you get a man to do your bidding when you have no power to keep him under your thumb?"

They were all silent a moment, thinking.

"Proof," Dontae said. "That's the only currency the desperate use to get what they want."

"But it must be real, right?" Aza asked, suddenly intrigued. "If they believed him."

Aza's attention slowly swiveled to Mil, who had turned pensive.

"We will go to this dance and see for ourselves."

"That's fine. But I can only shield with certainty or not at all," Jais explained, feeling Dontae's eyes on him. "We'll be there unofficially, but you and Aza are her only defense, and no offense, but Caiden might as well be dancing the night away by herself."

"And yet I'm still offended," Aza said, steadily.

"Don't be," Jais continued, trying to smooth it over quickly, and glanced at Mil. "It's not your fault."

"You're forgetting that there are forces beyond our little band of brothers here that have an agenda of their own." Dontae eagerly moved to the edge of his seat, casually looking to Mil. "The Archs."

"Arch." Mil kept cool and took another swig from his glass. "His Arch."

"I thought we all wanted the same thing," Aza said, fidgeting with his sleeves. "To protect the Soul."

"We do, but it's our ends that may differ."

Dontae's phone vibrated and he went off to a corner of the room to check it.

"What do you think they'd want with him?" Jais asked, truly curious. He didn't know if his abilities would stand up to the hierarchies of heaven.

"I'm sure you're familiar with the ways in which our Creator works," Mil said, swirling the last sip of his wine in his glass, then said to himself, "...Or even if he's involved."

Dontae saw Jais light another cigarette and thought it a good time to jump back into the conversation.

"I suppose I'll answer my own question and assume I won't be there."

"Why make assumptions?" Mil said lightly. "Every plan needs a contingency, and if you're as invaluable as you think I think you aren't, then I'm sure when or if the moment comes, you'll prove me wrong."

Dontae felt like he'd fallen into a trap of some kind, but could see that his time holding the floor had ended.

"Aza, you'll continue to message in Barry's place if there happens to be a follow-up text between now and the night of the dance."

"And if there's a call?"

"Don't answer it," he said. "You'll be mimicking Barry's actions to reflect his state of mind. We have to proceed as if no one knows he's a traitor and as if he's already been deemed useless. We've already caught this man once in our crosshairs. He seems far too paranoid to let it happen again."

"You're welcome."

"Thank you," Mil said as Jais leaned forward to tap his ash in a mug on the coffee table. "Dinner will be a little late tonight as I have to drop by the market."

They all got up to leave and Dontae headed out of the front door. Those small meetings never lasted that long, but he always felt an urge to skip them just to avoid all the negative back and forth.

"You know he belittles you because you do it to yourself."

Jais had followed him outside, putting out the cigarette he just lit between his two fingers.

"He does that because he and my father attended the same prick academy," Dontae said, checking the time.

"Off to the dollar theater?" Jais asked, smiling to himself.

"I'm gonna tell him you said that."

"Tell him what you like. You want company?"

Dontae suspiciously eyed Jais' brighter-than-usual demeanor.

"Jais," he said, walking up to him. "Have you seen Pneuma?"

"No, not physically. Not since Adyn. Why?" he asked as his energy fell.

"Adyn's fine. I think. I mean, he looked alright the last time I saw him." Dontae tried to assure him. Then he looked deep into his eyes. "Did you find them?"

"No," he said as his spirits dropped another peg. He didn't need him to specify. Dontae had been asking Jais this question every time he seemed like he was happier than normal. "I wouldn't be here if I had."

"You'd leave?"

Jais could see the heartbreak all over his face. There was never another place that Dontae didn't wear his emotions and nothing even happened yet. "Only for a little while. Don't cry."

"Shut up," he said, checking his phone again. "I was wondering what got you so high when I left here yesterday."

"Caiden," he said without a thought. "I feel like I can rest now. Sort of speak. After all this time, dead-end after dead-end, we find her in cow state Texas...I don't know. I just don't know how to act."

Dontae watched him talk with fervor but felt a pang of something raw bite him from the inside when he heard the way Jais said Caiden's name.

"Yeah, it's crazy," he said, backing up to his car. "I gotta go."

"Piccolo?" Jais guessed.

"Iela," he said, jumping in his car and speeding away.

***

Caiden awakened with wet eyes and a damp pillow. She'd never woken up this way this much until she started school. She sat up and dabbed her face with the sleeve of her shirt. Her cheek felt different, softer. She could barely remember last night. Lision was there telling her about something for she didn't know how long, but that was it. Caiden looked down at her chest and saw it was glowing more than usual. She was pulled in by the light and her hand hovered over it. Maybe He remembered.

Her hand dropped and she sat there for a moment. All of her life she wanted to know why she was the way she was, then suddenly an angel explains that her soul, the Soul, might not even be hers. The light grew a little more and she felt a wave of sorrow, like her heart was mourning the slow death of her old life all on its own.

She crept out of bed and went to her drawer to get a flashlight and Mary. She held onto it tight, gripping its handle just in case they parted ways for too long, slipped on her boots, and tiptoed as quietly as she could downstairs.

It was after two so the house was as still as the night. Caiden walked closer towards the front door and a dim light down the hall made her freeze on the spot.

Iela's light was on.

She slowed down her pace, cautious, thinking that her mother might've fallen asleep at her desk. She knew after what happened yesterday, sneaking out would probably make her move Caiden out of the state, but she was longing for something from before. She'd already taken her out of school, one of the things she asked for the most throughout her childhood. She didn't think Iela could do anything worse to her.

As soon as she made it safely on the other side of that door, relief rained down on her. Iela's car wasn't there. Even without that piece of fortune, Iela's punishments seemed minuscule next to what she had to do at that moment. With her legs wobbly walking through the crisp dark, she was chilled to the bone but wasn't going to risk going back inside to get a jacket. She turned on the flashlight and vanished into the trees.

The time it took to get to the gravesite wasn't long, even though she thought she was taking her time. A part of her didn't really want to go. Remembering the sound of that gunshot blast and Zinc taking his last breaths were images she'd rather lock away. Yet she needed to be near him and not even the thought of his decaying body was enough to make her turn away.

Caiden stepped past that last tree and stood there awhile. The silence was needle-sharp as she turned to the area where Zinc's body was supposed to be.

But he wasn't there.

The closer she got to it, the more sadness she felt. It had gotten so strong that she no longer needed her flashlight. She cut it off and the glow from her heart was more than enough.

She sat for a while next to the grave, her hand pressing firmly on the dirt, mentally flipping through each memory that she had with the dog since they met. That first encounter was sort of murky, she just knew that whenever they moved to a different city, he'd be there with his tongue out, waiting to play or be fed. She didn't deserve him.

While she sat, the silence of the night began to feel less trusting. It felt like everything had become too still, and that feeling was made worse in the darkness. Her instincts kicked in at that moment. She slid Mary out and stood up waiting for the intruders to come at her. It was futile to hide for she became a moving target as soon as she'd left the house.

She readied herself, but not before being nearly clipped by a short—

Swoosh.

The flashlight flew out of her hand and she swayed on her feet. Her head swiveled in all directions, but she couldn't see anything. Or get a sense of anything.

What the hell was that?

Her light wasn't bright enough to see, so she paused to listen and that's when her unwanted visitors revealed themselves.

Caiden cocked Mary, reminding herself again that this wasn't some mere sparring lesson with her mother. If it came down to it, she prayed that she'd choose herself over them.

Caiden sensed something to her left, getting one of them in her crosshairs, but she heard that sharp gust again and a dark figure hit the ground before she could pull the trigger. She carefully went up to it. It was the body of a woman who looked a little younger than her mother. Caiden bent down and was about to check if she was still breathing when another body slammed into the dirt beside her. Mary flew up ready to fire, but couldn't sense a target.

Then, as if it was hurricane season, bodies began to pour down all around her, one by one, and always after she heard that slice of wind.

A stray had managed to survive the fall and she sensed them jump out from behind her. Caiden shot without taking a breath, but this one cried out in agony first before he hit the ground.

She heard that wind again from behind and spun around to shoot. Instead of hearing a hard thumping sound, she heard a very soft one. Assuming she missed them, she tried to listen for their footsteps and pinpoint where they were.

"Don't worry, Goddess," the accented voice said, reassuring her. "That was the last one."

Caiden stood wide-eyed looking into the void.

That was a child.

She immediately used the light emanating through her skin to find the flashlight. She turned it on and pointed it in the direction the voice came from.

Of all the things she thought she'd be surprised to see, casting her shifting eyes to a breathless little boy in the wee hours of the morning surrounded by dead bodies was not one of them. He was on his hand and knee with his triumphant gray eyes penetrating every inch of her being.

"Ugh, fuck!" The man that Caiden shot had gained consciousness and was scrambling in the dirt. "You got my fucking shin! Fuck!"

Neither she nor the boy could break the other's gaze. After he was sure she didn't have a scratch on her, he found his attention gravitating towards her face, which thanks to her light, he could see a small portion of. Caiden didn't realize that she still had the flashlight directly in his face because he didn't seem bothered by it at all. He was too busy boring holes in her to be distracted.

He wisped abruptly through the man just to shut him up.

Caiden whipped her flashlight over to the body until she got it on the boy again.

"...What did you do to him?" she asked, not able to contain her awe.

"He tried to take you," he said, checking the man's wound and turning away from the body. "He's unconscious."

Caiden gradually moved the light over the other bodies that were now lying motionless on the ground until it landed back on the boy. He'd shoved his fists in his pocket and momentarily turned away from her.

"It didn't hurt."

So they were dead, too.

With barely the start of the second day and already the body count surrounding her had accumulated to six. Whether she was at school, or Mil's, or even at her own home, fate wasn't going to deter her from finding out whatever truth that she had a sole right to know. She gripped Mary tight in her hand as she managed to get to her feet.

"...You killed Barry."

The boy turned and fixed on her.

"Before he killed you, yes."

"You're Pneuma."

"Yes," he said, trying to interpret the expression on her face. "Of the Argenta."

"...Argenta."

"What were you doing out here alone?" he asked, carefully pushing the unconscious body onto its stomach. "Didn't Mil inform you that you were not to go off by yourself?"

"Mil didn't tell me a lot," she said, quietly marveling at the strength his tiny foot had over the hefty man. "But he said you all were here because of my soul..."

"The Soul, yes." He still wasn't grasping what she was getting at.

Caiden watched him for a moment and he unclenched his fists, gradually pulling them out of his pocket. He was anticipating what she was going to say as she was summoning up her strength to speak. Maybe it was a request or to assign him a duty of sorts. He wanted to be annoyed that he felt hopeful but remained silent until she was ready to say what was on her mind.

"Then, you can help me," she said, slightly more forceful than she meant, thanks to Mary.

"Yes." Pneuma responded as if he had no restraint.

"How do I wake Him up?"

Chapter XXXIII

IELA HAD FALLEN asleep in her car parked across the street from Piccolos. Her head was nestled between the headrest and the seatbelt. It was just a quarter before seven when she woke up and saw Piccolo through the windshield cupping a coffee mug. He was giving her one of those all-knowing looks. He knew why she was there. He knew she wasn't going to leave without getting it. He knew because this was their regular song and dance, but Iela was not about to be a broken record today.

She sat up straight and checked that all her weapons were still in their emergency locations before she got out of the car.

"I would've made up the couch in the back for you if I knew you wanted to talk so bad."

"No, thanks to your couch and your coffee," she said, hoarsely as she closed the door.

"It's tea and it's mine."

She caught sight of her reflection in the window of her car and casually tucked back any stray hairs that were out of place.

"I was looking for you," she said, following him back to the bar.

"I know." He let her inside with a faint smile. "The last time you were here got me worried."

She headed straight behind the bar to his top shelf and poured herself a drink. Piccolo let her do as she pleased and sat on a stool opposite her. She reflexively tensed up and took a sip of her chosen vice. Iela purposely avoided eye contact just in case he was looking at her.

"...We're leaving," she said, glancing at him from behind her glass. "I just wanted to let you know."

"Really? So am I," he said, putting the mug up to his lips.

"Where are you going?" This news caught her off guard and she had to look him in the eye to see if he was messing with her.

Piccolo smiled and emptied his cup. "Are you really going to leave things like this?"

"You're talking about that bullet I owe you." She tried not to allow her feelings to overpower her anger. "It's a good thing I was born with low expectations."

He watched her pick up her drink and turn her back to him.

"That's not true," he said, his voice tinged with melancholy.

Iela turned back to face him, her drink considerably lower in her glass before she turned away from him. Piccolo did indeed seem sad, but only for her, at that moment.

"You wanna feel sorry for somebody, feel sorry for my daughter."

"Why? Did you hurt her again?

Iela's hand tightened around her empty glass as she stopped herself from reacting. It was that same hand that struck Caiden just last night.

Her letters. She needed her letters.

"I'm not a threat to her."

"They aren't your enemy, Iela." His demeanor had changed. "You are."

She slid her glass across the bar, wishing she'd at least brought one of her weapons with her.

"You have to put your trust in someone or you'll find yourself alone at the end of all of this," he said, continuing to hold her gaze. "You can start with your daughter."

"I didn't come here to hear you preach at me." She was unsuccessfully holding in her anger. "I taught her not to trust people because people are shit and I don't want her to be taken in just to be disappointed. You've proven that already."

All of that had come out in a rush and touched on slight rage. She felt her past weave between her words and mid-sentence had to remember that she wasn't talking about herself. She was about to grab an entire bottle but decided she was tired of looking at Piccolo's beautiful face. He watched her head to the door and try to open it, but it wouldn't budge.

"Iela."

She turned around and saw that look again.

Never in her life did she think she could hate him, but this was damn near close. Her blood began to boil as his second betrayal became more apparent. The front door of the bar opened and she got her fist clenched, ready for a brawl.

***

Caiden got up a little after six and jumped out of bed. She got ready in a hurry and rushed downstairs before Roxa set the table.

"Girl, if you don't slow down..."

She did, almost immediately and calmly sat down in her chair. She'd already made up her mind of what she was going to eat. The eggs were a must, then whatever meat she had fried up, and the orange juice. That should satisfy Roxa enough to where she won't be worrying about her. For some reason she already thought she didn't eat her lunch at school, which she had with only one exception where she gave it to David. She left so fast and without seeing him off after school. Guilt had tinged her excited aura as she dug into her eggs.

"Ya mama's not here," Roxa said, eying her as she inhaled a piece of sausage. "So you can slow down before you choke and piss me off."

"Yes, ma'am." She chewed down a couple of big pieces before she could swallow without hurting herself to answer.

"Let me see it." Roxa got up out of her chair and Caiden stiffened as she took her by the chin. "The way you was on that floor, I thought she sure smacked ya jaw outta place. I see she ain't bark or bite."

Caiden watched Roxa as she sat back down and gently touched her cheek. Thanks to Lision, that pain didn't last.

Roxa was right, though. She didn't want to see her mother, afraid she might hit her again or worse, actually take her out of school like she said she would.

She was taking a big risk today. She didn't know Iela wouldn't be home this morning and thought she would try and sneak out. Caiden didn't think that David was a bad influence on her, but cutting school and skipping class had been something she wanted to try on her own just to see if she would have the nerve. The only place to test was at home, and she thought last night was a success. When she went to Zinc's grave, she only felt afraid of getting caught when she got back safe in her room. Even though she knew Iela wasn't home yet.

That's the sort of fear she wanted to kill.

With all the fighting and shooting Iela had taught her, that fear of anything beyond her four walls and front yard haunted her like those shrill echoes from the emotions of some of her fellow peers at Myerworth. She needed them to die or she didn't think she'd be able to find out about her soul; her reason for being.

"Roxa," Caiden said, standing up and fixing on her. "I'm going to school. But if Iela..." She found it difficult to speak the rest as she'd never done something like this before.

"Child," Roxa set down her tea. "I was listenin' at the door. I ain't seen you today."

Caiden let out a breath as she put up her leftovers and headed to the front door.

"Caiden."

She turned around and Roxa took on a somber expression. Caiden had to go to her then.

"I'm so sorry," she said, sinking into her embrace. Roxa's energy hit her like a brick wall. "I'm sorry for everything. For the way that I am—"

"Now shut that up," she snapped, nearly shaking her by the arms. "I ain't ya mama. Don't you ever apologize to me for no stupid shit like that ever again."

Roxa hugged her more, tighter and longer, almost trying to squeeze the tears out of her until they were all gone, but she couldn't do that now.

She said goodbye to Roxa and left the house.

"You're making us all quite sad," The Voice said.

"I don't mean to."

"Caiden, are you sure you want to do this? I've recently become afraid for you in the midst of all this Argenta business."

"I know it's way too early, but I feel I can trust them," she said, picking up her pace.

"But can you even trust that?" The Voice asked. "Or is it just your wanting to rebel against your mother?"

She slowed some. She didn't think her choosing the Argenta over her mother was an act of defiance, but now that she heard it, she wondered if this going off alone had a little to do with going against her mother's wishes.

She finally saw Myerworth and a bus was pulling up at the same time. David got off and they greeted each other with a smile, though hers was a little breathless from speed walking.

"Fate is what this is," he said. "Let's ditch and go shop for some dance threads."

"Sorry, I can't ditch with you today." She closed the distance between them as her shoulders slackened a bit. "You don't know how much I want to. I'm more excited about the dance than you are."

"...I didn't know you had a built-in gauge," he said to himself, knowing that would make her smile. "It's in two days. What are you gonna wear? That?"

Caiden looked down at her boots, jeans, and sweatshirt then back up at David. He had his eyebrows lifted pretending to wait for an answer.

"That's why you're ditching by yourself today," she said, playing along.

"You're cold-blooded."

"And you like it."

They both laughed awkwardly at her last statement. Caiden always acknowledged David's feelings for her, but she didn't realize until this moment that her honesty might be hurting him. He continued talking about what kind of clothes he was going to buy and even made suggestions for Caiden, but she could feel he was still stuck on what she said.

"I hope, I pray, I beg, I bleed your mom says yes."

"She's not," she said, grinning at his enthusiasm. He looked like he was going to pop a blood vessel. "Well, maybe if you bleed."

"Then I shall bleed."

"You better leave now if you're skipping." She was watching the time for the both of them. Iela could show up at any moment with both of their lives in the trunk of her car, ready to drive out of this city like they never existed there. Caiden had to act like everything was going to be okay or it wouldn't be. She wouldn't act as if this was her and David's last conversation or it would be.

"Caiden."

They both turned and saw Aza coming down the sidewalk. Caiden recognized Mil's vehicle, but he didn't seem to be parking. She noticed that David stood a little closer to her when Aza called her name.

"Hey, you both trying to skip again?"

David looked at her.

"I didn't," she said.

"I was kidding."

Aza exchanged looks with Caiden and smiled to himself.

"I'm the lone delinquent today."

Caiden felt his energy drop and naturally looked up at his faux relaxed face.

"I hope I see you at the dance," he said, backing away.

"Me, too," she said, her eyes never leaving his.

"Conceited."

They both watched him jog down the sidewalk and cross the street until he disappeared around a corner at an intersection.

"He seems like a cool guy," Aza observed while reading her expression.

"He doesn't seem. He is." His kind aura lingered around her body. "You seem like you don't like him."

For a second Aza thought he'd accidentally come out of Hiding. "I can't trust anyone around you," he said. "'I', the Argenta," he added quickly.

"I know what you meant," she said, unsure of her words. She realized she just followed him back to Mil's ride. "You're not going to school?"

"No," he said, giving her a bright smile. "And neither are you. Get in."

"Tell me where we're going first," she stated as she fixed on him. He'd opened the passenger door instead of the back. Mil wasn't in the car.

"You'll find out when we get there." He got in the driver's seat and waited for her to get in.

Caiden reluctantly got inside and closed the door. It wasn't because of Aza, but because of Iela and Mil. One was trying to keep her away from the truth and the other was trying to shove it down her throat. The problem was, it was simply too big to digest in one sitting.

"Two things," he started as he revved up the SUV and drove out of the school zone. "Good and bad."

"What happened?" she asked, a little anxious.

"You'll see."

She watched him turn a corner and kept his eyes straight ahead. He seemed to be intentionally not looking her way to avoid any more prying.

About ten minutes had passed during their somewhat quiet ride. Aza spoke briefly on the phone to who Caiden guessed was one of his brothers and asked if she was hungry, to which she replied in the affirmative, knowing she ate before she left the house. She didn't want to be rude.

"We can eat here." Aza got out and went around to Caiden's side to open the door. It took her a second to get out as she was too busy scanning the place.

"This looks like a bar." He gave her a warm smile, assuring her as she followed him.

They had to cross the street and knock a certain amount of times on the door before it opened. Caiden was waiting to be greeted by someone, but she just kept on Aza's heels as he let himself inside.

"Ah. Now, we can begin."

Caiden was so stunned that she could only stand there at the door. She'd walked into a scenario that hadn't crossed her mind before, for it was too impossible to even imagine. And yet it was happening.

Her mother and Mil were sitting down together, eating and drinking like she didn't want to snatch his heart out of his chest a few days ago.

The smaller tables were stacked against the wall with the chairs and a few were pushed together in the middle of the room with a large oblong tablecloth placed over them to create one big table.

"Aza, please get her a chair." Mil motioned Aza with his wine bottle as Caiden watched him bewildered. "Where are the boys?"

Caiden's first instinct when she watched Aza pull out her chair for her and sat down across from Iela was that this was a part of her plan. There was no way Caiden would believe that her mother gave into Mil so easily. They made eye contact and she watched for the hint of a fight that was always just resting in the colors of her eyes. There was nothing there from what she could see, but she also didn't get a sense of any surrender either.

The boys, all of them, came from the back with the same expression. Caiden couldn't tell if they'd just gotten there or not, but from the looks on their faces, they didn't expect to see her or her mother dining with daddy dearest.

"Please get comfortable," Mil said to the Argenta, who were wondering what the hell was going on. "For we all have much to answer for...Don't we, Iela?"

Chapter XXXIV

CAIDEN WAS STARING at a ribeye steak. The thinning, reddish juice from the mixture of grease and myoglobin had settled beneath the four stalks of seared asparagus. Her hands were wrung together in her lap as she listened to the delicate scraping of silverware against china. She could feel two energies and only one of them was preventing her from lifting her head.

"Ms. Waters, at least taste the food," Mil insisted. He swirled the wine around in his glass. It was red this time, she noted as she looked up at him.

"...No, thank you."

"She's wondering what the hell we're all doing here so early in the morning," Jais said, tapping his ash onto his untouched steak. "Besides, I'm sure you're the only one here that eats red meat for breakfast."

Caiden peeked up at Jais as he leaned back in his chair and took a drag from his cigarette. He caught her eye and shook his head slowly from side to side before she went back to her plate again.

The food had been delivered from one of Mil's favorite restaurants that hadn't opened yet. It was for Caiden and Iela, but Caiden's appetite had vanished when she got inside the place. She didn't have to assume that Iela's rules of speaking to her and no one else still applied, but she didn't seem to mind. She had her eyes locked on the Argenta only. Particularly Mil, who seemed to be the only one at ease.

"Even your mother is drinking," Mil said, wiping his mouth with a cloth napkin.

Caiden looked up at Iela, her chair angled to the table so that everyone was easily visible in front of her. Mil was seated directly across from her, then she next to him, Aza on the other side of her, Dontae, Jais across from him, Pneuma, and Iela. She'd seen Volx briefly when she got inside the building, but he'd left soon after.

"You know I never turn down a free drink," she sung, putting the whisky glass to her lips. "I'm just a little sad that I wasn't given enough time to doll up first."

"In due time," Mil simpered, leaning back in his chair.

Caiden could tell Iela was thinking of every possible way that they'd be able to get out without anyone getting hurt, but that made her even more nervous. Iela hadn't seen what the others were capable of.

She found her eyes straying to Pneuma, who was directly across from her. He hadn't touched his plate either, fixing on her with calm curiosity. To Caiden, it almost seemed like the boy was so bored that all he could do was stare off into space, and the only reason why he was staring at her was that she just happened to be in front of him.

"You never struck me as an eccentric," Iela said, crossing her legs and folding her arms. "Toting around a human. An expensive one, at that."

"Resourcefulness does not a rich man make?" Mil countered. "William for example."

Iela and Caiden locked eyes briefly. She could feel Iela's patience getting thinner by the second, but she felt something coming from the end of the table and glanced down there. She couldn't see Dontae, just his plate, which was empty but had a to-go container sitting on top of it with an opened domestic beer. Aza got caught in her line of view. He'd been in the process of breaking up his asparagus with the side of his fork, consciously making an effort not to look at her at all.

"We knew that Barry was working with someone named William. You informed us of that piece of information during our first meeting with the newborn Blackheart in your own home."

Mil stood and looked at Iela, who just calmly sipped her drink.

"There's no use in Hiding now," Mil said, touching the back of Caiden's chair. "How else did they know about our little prince here?"

The Argenta's attention went to Iela, whose face was about as telling as a brick wall.

"I've never Hid from Caiden before. Unlike you, I have nothing to hide." Iela gazed right through Caiden when she said that. "If you were as thorough as your reputation boasts, then you'd know that William was a gifted locator, which means he could've found out about Caiden way before he even met me."

Caiden looked up at her mother taking a sip from her whiskey glass, her false bravado was shooting through Caiden across the table. She was playing the part like she was getting paid, but didn't know if Mil would believe it.

"Well, I'm sure that'd be convenient for you."

Iela glared at Mil and gradually stood up from the table. Caiden felt the tension solidify on a dime as the Argenta became poised in their seats. All but Pneuma, who seemed to be dozing off.

"What are we doing here?" Iela asked as if she was unsheathing a sword.

Mil's expression had shifted and his eyes rested within Iela's. Caiden and the other's felt the air in the room become thinner at the exact same moment.

"It's not like you to ask for help. You don't burn bridges, Iela, you wait for an audience to watch you pretend to set it on fire and utilize it later when no one's watching."

Iela's hand tightened around her glass, but she didn't break eye contact. Mil's determination was proving to be much more formidable from what she remembered.

She slowly put down the glass before it shattered in her palm. "He's a blue blood. I didn't know that when I found him."

"Common knowledge."

"He thinks Caiden can save them."

"How?"

"Lay hands on 'em. I don't know."

Caiden felt Iela's energy shift some as she picked up her drink to finish it. She then looked at Mil, who's gears seemed to be working.

"I suppose we'll have to ask him in person."

"You wanna use her," Iela surmised under her breath.

"We want to help her." Mil matched her tone. "What's been puzzling me is why you don't."

Iela felt her facade slide to the floor and shatter. She went around the table and took hold of Caiden's hand. She almost tripped out of her seat as everyone got to their feet.

"She'll be there," Iela said, squeezing Caiden as she did before, but Caiden was so stunned to hear what she'd said she couldn't feel the pain. "And so will I."

Mil and the rest of the Argenta were waiting to hear the conditions under which she'd allow her daughter to be led directly to the person that's been trying to kidnap her this entire time, but it didn't come.

"Let us outta here."

"Caiden," Mil said, purposely giving her his full attention. "Is that all right with you?"

Caiden naturally turned to her mother.

"I'm talking to you, Caiden." Mil was almost annoyed. "This isn't your mother's life—"

"And it's not yours either. None of you," she spat. "She's gonna do this thing for you and you're never gonna see her again. I think that's more than fair."

Caiden's head shot up to her mother's face. Her emotions were so strong that she knew she was telling the truth. She found her eyes being pulled toward the Argenta posted up behind Mil and they caught Aza. The thought of not seeing him again, and even the others that she'd just met and would never get to know. She didn't think she would feel this way for strangers that didn't feel like strangers.

"You misunderstand." Mil had walked closer to them. Iela stood her ground, gripping Caiden tighter still. "Wherever Caiden is, we are, for not even you and all of your weapons will be able to separate us from our divine fate."

"Open the door," Iela said icily.

Swoosh.

And the door opened like that. She sent Caiden out first and then slammed the door behind her.

She didn't let Caiden go until she got to her car and that's when she got a text.

It read: "*Looks like I'll see you Friday.*"

Iela's head swiveled around the street but didn't see anything suspicious. They hurried and got in and she sped off.

"Don't believe anything they tell you." Her mind was spinning as she continued keeping an eye out of her mirrors and windows.

"I can read only one of them," she said, struggling to put on her seatbelt due to all the sharp swerves.

"And?"

"I don't feel anything wrong."

Caiden watched as her mother pondered this information, but her face didn't change. They got to Roxa's and hurried inside.

"What you doin' back here?" Roxa was sitting in the living room with a book when Iela came in and slammed the door. She saw Caiden slowly come in behind her. "I don't care what happened, you ain't takin' that girl anywhere."

"No," Iela said, going to the fridge for a drink. She grabbed a water bottle and tossed it to Caiden. "We have to go to some fucking dance..."

" A dance?" Roxa got up and took the water out of Caiden's puzzled hands. "At ya school?"

"Yes, ma'am."

Caiden watched as Roxa's face lit up.

"Somebody's trying to take her." Iela's mind was racing as she sat down at the table. "They're with the same person that cold-cocked you the last time. So this isn't some night out on the town."

Caiden glanced at her mother as she felt a shift at the word "somebody." If she'd already explained her relationship with William, then why was she feeling ill at ease?

"Well, I would love to see 'em try," Roxa said with a confidence that echoed an absolute truth. "You ain't got nothin' to be scared about with a mama like her, ya hear?"

She felt that change again, but didn't turn to her mother, who she could feel was already looking at her.

"Caiden," Iela said in a more subdued tone than before. "Get upstairs. We need to talk."

***

It was nearing four in the afternoon when Piccolo came back to his bar to find some of the Argenta still there. Their takeout had been discarded and their used and unused glasses had been put away. His tables were even back to their normal places, ready just in time for opening, so he was wondering what they were still doing there.

"Master Cahill, you can't run a business this way."

Dontae's PTSD hit him like lightning at the sound of his childhood misnomer. When he saw Piccolo's smile, that rush of anxiety subsided a little.

"We're opening up later due to unforeseen circumstances."

Piccolo caught Jais and Aza's eye.

"You're Dontae's...clients?" Piccolo asked, going behind the bar. "I remember you two from last time. Is that kid all right?"

Dontae cut in before either one of them could come up with a convincing lie. "You know bloody well who they are," he said, unamused.

"We're his brothers," Aza said, enjoying himself. "His big brothers."

"What are you doing?"

Aza and Piccolo shared a grin at Dontae's expense before Jais broke it up.

"Hey. You must get a lot of types coming in and out of here," he said, sliding a fifty across the bar. "Have you heard any of them mention a Lesly Steele? Or anything close to that?"

Jais felt Dontae quietly simmering out of his peripheral and had to look his way. And just like he thought, he was giving him one of the most disapproving and mortified looks he'd ever seen.

"...If you were my actual blood you would know that gauche displays like this are beyond inappropriate." Dontae's social etiquette sometimes came sprawling about, especially when he had to call out his close friends. "And why are you bringing this up years after I put you onto their scent?"

He was waiting for Jais to answer him and put his money away, but Piccolo took it.

"You know that bottle is a little more expensive," he said, tucking the bill in his pocket.

"How..." Jais started, a little confused.

"Did I miss something?" Dontae asked.

"I swiped a bottle of 80-proof about an hour ago," Jais explained. Then, he turned to Piccolo. "But how did you know that?"

"You. Did. What?"

Dontae had to stop himself from exploding, for that would be inappropriate as well. Instead, his eyes fell back on Piccolo. He stared at him, wondering what it meant that his super knowledge was seeping over into the lives of his friends. He quietly waited for an explanation.

"Lesly Steele. The lawyers," Piccolo said. He was giving the place another inspection before he came out from behind the bar. "Ask Dontae."

"I don't know anything," he said, unable to read his expression.

"Yes you do," Piccolo said simply. "I'll see you in a month."

"Wait," he said, jumping out of his seat. "You're leaving right now? I thought your flight was in the morning?"

Piccolo gently patted the back of Dontae's head. "I have some things to take care of. Outside of the bar. We'll see each other again. Here or somewhere else."

"...Okay."

"Take care of things or you're fired."

Dontae's eyes followed him until he disappeared to the back. He turned to Jais who'd spun on his stool to face him.

"I really don't know much about them," Dontae said in earnest. "Only that they had a reputation for representing anyone for the right price. You could've figured out they were demons all on your own."

"I believe you," he said, getting up. "I thought I'd try here because of the traffic. When I find them, I'll let you know."

"You'd better." He watched Jais smack Aza on the back as he headed toward the door.

"I'm gonna stay here a little while," he said, slowly twisting idly on his stool.

"Alright," he said, walking out the door. "Later."

"You've been quiet," Dontae observed as he took up his place behind the bar. Mira and Rane had come in with another employee so he thought he'd start bracing himself for the after-work crowd. He looked back at Aza, who'd fallen into a daydream. "Hey, what's up with you?"

"Something bad is gonna happen." He stopped his twisting.

"Always," he agreed. "But you guys will be there so she'll be fine."

Aza nodded, but that didn't convince Dontae. He didn't have time to settle his nerves though as Piccolos' doors were about to open to a very restless line outside.

"Rane, could you?"

"Sure, boss," she teased, taking the keys from him.

"Please. Not tonight." He was already sweating as it is and he hadn't done an ounce of work yet.

"Bossman."

"Not you, too, Nova. I thought you liked me," he said, turning around.

She was staring at him like she wanted him to come over. Dontae admittedly was too stunned by her sparkling sunflower-colored gown to notice that she needed to tell him something.

"I'll be right back," he said to Aza, whose attention had been briefly captured by Nova as well.

As Dontae got to her, the people started flooding in, heading straight to the bar.

"There are more subtle ways of getting my attention," he said, not sure of himself if he was kidding.

"I didn't mean to be listenin' to y'all, but I was," she said, slightly agitated. "I know exactly who them Lesly Steele muthafuckas are."

***

Caiden had been waiting in her room for Iela for a while now. She knew their talk was probably going to be about the rules of going to this dance so that she wouldn't get hurt. Iela had a track record of setting these rules for

Caiden's benefit, but in the end, they mostly only bene-fited Iela. Caiden prayed that wasn't going to be the case this time. Going to this dance would be one of the most normal things she ever got to do outside of her house; one of those first of firsts. She wanted to try to enjoy it as much as she could without Iela, this elusive enemy, and even the Argenta ruining it. She just wanted one thing untouched by the presence of her unnatural heart.

"So, you're going to a ball," The Voice said.

"It's a high school gym," she corrected, smiling to herself.

"Pardon me."

"I shouldn't be talking—"

"Especially to yourself."

Caiden spun around as Iela came into her room with a small black clutch bag. They both stared at each other for a moment before Iela closed the door and set the clutch on her bed. She pulled out Caiden's desk chair and sat down.

"Open it."

This didn't feel like a trick, but Caiden felt reluctant to go anywhere near that bag.

"What's in it?" she asked, brushing her fingers across the black panther suede. She lifted the latch and poured the contents onto her bed.

"Since you can't take Mary to school." She caught her daughter's eye. "You're welcome."

She got up to leave, but something else was nagging at her so she didn't walk out immediately. Iela turned back around and saw Caiden examining the disguised weapons a moment before she looked up at her again.

"Um, you're gonna wear those black jeans and top? What you wore on your first day?"

"Okay."

"No, I'm asking you."

"Oh, I don't know." Caiden was sensing some nervousness as her mother stood in front of her not able to hold much eye contact.

"I got some stuff in my closet if you wanna look at it. I mean so you can wear something different."

"Okay...thank you."

Iela left after that and The Voice erupted with laughter.

"What's funny?" she asked, grinning a little herself.

"Your mother's face," It said, getting a hold of Itself.

"Yeah, that was new."

She put the stuff back in her clutch and set it on her desk before she got some clothes to go take a shower.

"Does your mother believe that a bag full of toys is going to do anything?" The Voice asked. "Your admirer has already proven that even their so-called allies are disposable."

"I don't think those toys are for them," Caiden said, heading down the hall for the bathroom.

Chapter XXXV

CARAVAGGIO. BERNINI. RUBENS.

Myerworth's gymnasium had been transformed into an amalgam of gaudy opulence from the familiar classics and the minimalist modern luxury of the present. Tastefully distorted regards of anguish, rippling biceps, and arched angel wings were projected on every wall and ceiling. Impressive duplicated sculptures of Olympian gods greeted the mesmerized students as they entered the room to a trap-style rendition of one of Vivaldi's Four Seasons. With the tragic death of one of their own and the constant breaking news of human on Voided crimes, the students of Myerworth High were long overdue for any form of catharsis. Tonight was going to be a night they wouldn't forget.

David, out of character, had arrived early. As soon as he parted ways with Caiden and Aza that day, he wandered around the mall until he saw something that screamed eighteenth-century bourgeoisie without the ridiculous price tag. He found a pair of black dress pants on a sale's rack and borrowed a silver-printed button-down from a different store. He went back home after that. He didn't have a need to go back to Faber's, not after—

Bzzz.

David ignored his vibrating pocket and got comfortable at the snack table which consisted of an incredible amount of meat. He grabbed a drumstick, keeping an eye on the entrance.

Bzzz.

He was about to check the text when he remembered that he didn't want to. Of course William would pick this night. After everything he'd done for him, he chose to ruin the brightest thing that going to school ever allowed him to have. It was something different and new, and it didn't hurt. Doing trivial things like skipping class for a movie and getting overly dressed for a few hours on a Friday night was something David never thought he'd be able to do, especially with someone like Caiden. It was unfair.

But so was becoming a Void.

David's hand shot up in the air when he glimpsed a black poof of hair coming into the gym. He immediately dropped it when he saw it wasn't her.

"Looking for me?"

All David had to do was look down to see that it was that girl that he and Caiden had talked to in the courtyard. She was wearing a ravishing oxblood tulle dress walking right toward him and he couldn't even see her.

"My date, actually," he said, throwing away a chicken bone.

"I hope she knows that," the girl jabbed, scanning the table for anything not made of meat.

"Don't you have someone else's business you have to go get into?" David nudged back.

"I didn't think being friendly was a character flaw." She watched him fill two cups with a champagne-colored beverage. "You're so sweet," the girl said, taking one of David's drinks out of his hand.

"It is if you don't mind boundaries," he said, glancing at the door again.

The girl followed his eyes then looked back at him.

"...You're right." She picked up a carrot stick, but didn't eat it. "I'll see you around."

David wouldn't have paid her any mind as she retreated from their lopsided conversation, but the way she looked at him when she left made him watch her until she was fully out of his sight. She was smiling like he'd given her some top-tier sage advice. His mind went to his initial vibes he got from her when they met and thought maybe she was a little touched. He felt bad for some reason.

He sipped his drink as Caiden walked into the gym. David didn't waste any time, but his steps began to slow when he saw Iela linking arms with her as they stood at the entrance. When she saw him, her face lit up. It was mostly at his attire as he always looked like he shopped in a derelict's closet during school hours. Iela noticed him giving Caiden the up and down. She recognized the look on David's face and then she looked at Caiden, who was so excited to be doing something so mundane that she didn't care.

"Don't get lost," she warned, after scanning the room.

Caiden knew she meant in the delusion. She stared at her mother and still couldn't believe where she was. She'd thought Iela agreed to this because it felt like they didn't have a choice. All Caiden had to do was show up, William would reveal himself, then people would stop trying to come after her. But having been watching Iela since the school year started, she'd witnessed a change in her energy, mostly towards Caiden. The feeling that she felt before was covetous in a sense. Because of what Caiden was, Iela felt obligated to protect her and teach her how to protect herself. Even if she wasn't supposed to be there. She couldn't put her finger on what it was now and she didn't think Iela could either.

Iela's arm fell away from Caiden's and down at her side. Their eyes met a moment before Iela went back to watching the crowd.

"Thank you."

She didn't wait for Iela to look at her, knowing she wouldn't. Caiden walked toward David, who was dancing with his cup until she was done talking to her mother.

"Wow." He wanted to stop dancing, but he couldn't if he wanted to.

"Yeah, you, too."

Caiden smiled, checking herself out again. She was in a pair of black tapered dress pants with a matching blazer. She walked with care as she made her way to David who couldn't hide anything to save his life.

Roxa had bought everything secondhand after taking into account Caiden's tastes, but the heels were Iela's. She'd even let her wear her red lipstick. Caiden slicked her hair back into a ponytail herself. When she saw the finished result in the mirror for the first time, she figured she looked exactly how David was ogling her now.

"I like your shirt." Caiden pinched his sleeve and turned him around. "Oh. We're matching. A little."

The silver pattern on David's shirt vaguely matched the muted black velvet design on Caiden's suit. She didn't know why, but that made her a little happy, like they'd gotten ready for the night together without knowing it.

"You're killing me," he said, taking his drink to the head.

"Before you die, tell me where I can get one of those." She was looking around the room when she said that. "And a chair."

Bzzz.

"I'll show you," he said, mildly flinching. "There's no way in hell I'm leaving you alone tonight unless it's an emergency."

She eyed him as they got to the snack table, not wanting the change in his aura to be on the front of her mind tonight. With this faceless enemy, Iela, and the Argenta pulling her from all sides, Caiden wanted to enjoy as much of the right now as she could before this floaty feeling evaporated.

"What are you looking at?" he asked, filling up her cup. "You wanna dance?"

"I really am looking for a chair."

Her feet weren't hurting yet, but remembering the times Iela came back home with her shoes in hand, she wanted to be prepared.

She spotted an incredibly small group of students of maybe nine congregating near a fierce King of Israel in one of the corners of the gym.

"Are those the only Voids here?"

"Maybe," he said, handing her a drink. "But you know some can Hide."

"Like Aza. I know." She watched as his face turned to stone. "Something happen?"

He shook his head no and looked toward the entrance. Then his face got even more rigid.

"What kind of sorcery is this?" he sighed under his breath.

Caiden's eyes followed David's to the door and indeed saw Aza standing with a lavishly dressed Mil. Aza found her in a few seconds and made his way through the thickening crowd.

"I gotta piss," David said, still gripping his phone. "I got dibs on the last dance."

"You mean the only dance."

He had to smile a little as the crowd ate him up. "Oh, we're dancing more than once."

"No, we're not."

When Caiden couldn't see him anymore, she turned back around.

"Yes, we are!"

She grinned, shaking her head, and sipped her drink.

Her eyes followed Aza as he was making his way to her in what seemed like slow motion. His jet black hair bouncing in a long braid draped across his shoulder and his gaze only fixing on her as if she was his only and final destination. She wanted to avert her eyes, but couldn't.

What is this?

"Evening, beautiful."

"I was gonna say that to you," she managed to say, utterly shocked as he was now closer to her and was fully taking him all in.

He was adorned in a flowy sheer midnight blue dress shirt, black tailored trousers, and black suede loafers. His waist-length braid had a silver ribbon interwoven throughout until it tied into a lazy bow at the end of his plait. He was unnecessarily stunning.

"Stop it," he said, pleased at what he saw in her eyes. "Speaking of beauty, your mother cleans up pretty nice."

They looked at Iela in her simple side-split maxi near the DJ with a resting bitch face that could stop anyone in their tracks. Mil was standing by her, just as cool, admiring the decorations. He was dressed in full-blown 18th-century attire, jabot and cape included. Some of the students were even complimenting him, which Caiden and Aza noticed, he enjoyed at a level they'd never seen before.

"For a moment I forgot why I was here," she said as she got trapped in her mother's occasional scans of the room.

"Hey." Aza made sure she was looking at him. "We're here, too. Even when you think you're alone, Pneuma or Jais will be there."

"Or Lision," she added, forgetting that she'd never mentioned him to the Argenta before.

"Oh, so you've met your Arch." He held out his hand to her and she took it not knowing what he was going to do with it. "You know what he is, right?"

"I have an idea." They were now standing in the middle of the dance floor with the other students who were letting loose. "How do you know him?"

"I don't," he said, letting her go. "We just knew he'd show up."

She eyed a rowdy bunch on their right and started laughing. "You brought me out here for nothing because I'm not about to dance."

"That's fine. I'll dance enough for the both of us." His eyes disappeared as he began to move to the beat of the song. "So, what's he like? Your Arch." Aza started dancing circles around her.

"He's quiet, so I don't know much about him," she said, turning left and right every time he glided out on the other side of her. "Do you?"

"Not much. Just that he's supposed to guard you..." then he hesitantly added, "hasn't been doing a very good job of that."

Caiden naturally thought of him, and with her next breath, she caught sight of him in a dark corner of the gym.

He gave her a slight bow of his head before walking around to observe.

"So, all of you are here to protect my soul...souls?" she asked, confused. "Seems like a lot for this one small thing."

He stopped mid-orbit and backtracked to face her.

"Believe me, it's necessary," he said in a more serious tone. "That *small* thing and you and us are a part of something that is far beyond anything human or Void-related. It has been for a while now."

"Is that why people are after it? What are they gonna do if they get it?" Caiden fixed on him in the hopes he would stop Hiding from her at that moment so she'll feel his real feelings, but he didn't. He couldn't. Not when she was already surrounded by so many fluctuating stimuli.

"We'll die before we let that happen."

She gazed up at him, wondering if he had now let down his guard, but again she could feel he hadn't. There was a small part of her that knew he stood by every word that he spoke, and the bigger part wished he hadn't made such an unkeepable promise. The last thing she wanted was their deaths decomposing in her conscience.

"And you have one soul," he said as an afterthought and began swaying again.

"But it's not mine—."

"No, it's yours," Aza said, firmly. "It doesn't matter what Mil says or what those fanatics who call you their prince say. If you were born with it, then it's yours."

Caiden nodded slowly in agreement. Fired-up Aza was a soft force to be reckoned with.

"May I cut in?"

The girl in the red tulle dress popped up before them, staring at Caiden with bedroom eyes. And right then is when she felt that nothingness that she experienced from her at lunch that day. It was an unforgettable chasm.

"Uh, Caiden, do you mind?" Aza asked.

"Yes, Caiden. Do you mind?" she echoed, borderline mocking him.

"Sure..." she said as she gave Aza a small smile and turned to go back to her search for an empty seat. All she did was stand there and yet her feet felt like they had a million tiny needles sticking in them. She took a few steps before the girl grabbed her hand and took her by the waist.

"I was talking to him," she said breathily. She was so close to Caiden's lips, she felt the heat emanating off them.

Caiden glanced over at Aza, who didn't look at all surprised, and put up both of his hands, mouthing the word "minutes." She nodded once and went back to the girl holding her like she was hers.

Aza found Mil still mercilessly chatting up Iela as they'd moved away from the DJ table and to a sparse corner of the gym.

"Was that wise, Aza? Leaving her to the wolves?" He was referring to the bustling crowd of pent-up adolescent stress.

"She's fine," he said, waiting for his request because he felt it coming. "Nothing so far."

"Good." Mil passed Iela on his way to the exit.

"Where are you going?"

"Surely, you don't expect me to endure another hour of this without a Riesling intermission?" he said in a hardened voice. "Aza will keep you company."

Iela was about to say something but held back. She didn't know what she could possibly say to a person like Mil who believed that he was always right. She kept her eyes ahead as Aza stood a comfortable distance next to her, watching

Caiden stiffly dance with that girl, and making sure not to bump into her fellow peers. He felt eyes on him and looked over to find Iela giving him an emotionless glare. He quickly turned away, wiping the palms of his hands on the insides of his pockets. Iela went back to people-watching, having her suspicions realized.

Back across the room, Caiden had been trying not to step on the girl's feet as she was wearing open-toe heels as well. They weren't really talking much, just swaying side to side. The girl kept looking Caiden in the eye, so she was focusing a lot on the other people and checking to see if David had come back yet. He'd been gone a long time.

"This is your first year. I would've remembered seeing you in the halls."

"Yeah." Caiden happened to get caught in her eyes and saw she was piercing her with intent. "I suddenly forgot you're a Void."

"Yeah, I am," she said, grinning and pushing a couple of brunette strands out of her face. "And you're this prince I've been hearing so much about."

Caiden stopped swaying and one of her hands resting in the girl's palm went limp, but she gripped it tight so it wouldn't fall.

"Keep moving your feet so nobody will be able to tell," she demanded, taking the lead more forcibly than before.

"Or what?" she asked, fighting her every time she took a step to each side. "Where's David?"

"I don't know where your boyfriend ran off to," she said, annoyed. "I came here for you, darling."

Caiden felt her eyes about to change as the girl's emptiness intensified that inexplicable adrenaline-like substance in her veins. It was burning her up from the inside out in a way that some kinds of darkness should never meet the light.

"If your eyes change, your people will know something's up, so stop it."

The girl's tone turned on a dime, but her expression continued as they were when she interrupted Caiden moments ago.

"Caiden," The Voice, called. "Your Arch."

"Come on," the girl said, linking arms with Caiden. "I need to reapply."

The girl tugged on Caiden's arm as they headed toward the exit, but before they got there, Lision seemed cocked and ready, posted at the door.

God, please not here.

That was her first thought as she looked him right in his striking royal blue eyes. The next thing she knew, he was gone and the girl had pulled her into the hall where they saw David.

"Where are you taking my date?" he said, not reading the situation.

"Ladies' room." The girl passed him by and—

Bzzz.

Bzzz.

They all stopped.

David turned around and so did the girl. He fixed on her, wide-eyed, and noticed her grip on Caiden's arm and the silent message she was trying to convey to him with only a look.

"...You're Helena." It came out breathless.

Caiden stared at him as he was flying through so many emotions.

Shock, confusion, betrayal.

She watched the gears turning in his head, trying to figure out a way to get the girl away from Caiden.

"I have the prince. I don't need you or William," she spat.

Caiden's head spun to the girl. Then, to David, whose aura was growing more fragile the longer she looked at him.

"...David." She needed him to defend himself, but he was frozen to the spot with his phone vibrating limply at his side.

"Helena."

Caiden turned on the girl and there, crawling out of her pores was what she had been waiting to see. That black hole of nothingness was consuming her right where she stood. There weren't any aural echoes from her past beating against her eardrums, but it was plain that Helena had fallen victim to her own desires. Caiden hadn't a clue what the thing was that sent her over the edge and Helena could only guess herself, but she could imagine it had something to do with filling a part of herself that she believed she was missing. Her remains had become desolate and barren. Caiden wondered if there was any hope at all left for her.

"I'll go with you alone."

"Shut up," David spat, cutting her off. "You're not going anywhere."

The girl yanked her toward an exit door and pushed it but it was locked.

Swish.

"Pneuma, don't!"

The words had flown out of her mouth almost before she recognized the sound. She looked all around the hall but didn't see the little boy, but she knew that didn't mean anything. Helena and David were so focused on each other that they didn't hear a thing.

Helena began dragging Caiden down the halls around the gym when David reached out and grabbed Caiden's hand. They all halted their rushed steps.

"Let me go," Caiden pleaded to him.

Helena's aura was getting bleaker the longer she was around her. She had no idea what she would do to anyone standing in her way, especially someone as vulnerable as David. There was no talking sense into her. She'd long ago lost the ability to comprehend it.

"What is she gonna do?" David was glaring down into her calmly crazed eyes, realizing that Helena was absolutely powerless. "William associates himself with only one type of person. Why else would you leech off of someone else's dirty work?"

Caiden could see he was grouping himself with those people and she didn't want to believe it. She didn't want to see the David that was standing in front of her right now. It couldn't've been the same person. It wasn't.

"You're just like the rest of us."

Helena's eyes nearly bulged out of her head and she began to shake as her grip around Caiden's arm turned into a vise.

"Shut up!"

In one quick motion, Helena ripped a gun from around her outer thigh and didn't blink once when she pulled the trigger.

Chapter XXXVI

WAIT.

Caiden was being dragged by her ponytail. Again. Except for this time, there was a gun stopping her from grabbing ahold of Helena's wrist, twisting it behind her back, and pushing her facedown to the floor. Mary was in the top of her closet and she'd dropped her clutch sometime during their struggle when they got into the hall. She only held onto Helena's hand wrapped around her ponytail. Her heels were an unfortunate hindrance as she kept falling and her arms were flailing after trying to steady herself on something, anything. Helena had aimed her weapon at her, but her mortality was the furthest thing from her mind.

"Helena!"

David was crawling after them, trying to hold in his blood. Caiden had never left him and he never left her, but once she hit the corner, only then did she focus on the person holding her life in her hands.

Helena had made it out a side exit after testing every door that she came across. They were outside in the back of the school and not a soul was in sight.

"Caiden..."

"David."

It was clear he'd used up all he had in him to keep up. Caiden gaped at his shirt in horror as the entire front had nearly been dyed crimson.

"Caiden!"

Jais had skidded around the building but balked when Helena shoved Caiden to the ground and proceeded to crush the gun barrel into the back of her head. Her eyes wide, she stared up at Jais who didn't need her words to know what to do.

"Help me, please."

And that was all it took.

His eyes simmered a striking green and soon he, Caiden, and Helena had all disappeared, enveloped within his shield.

"Caiden!" David yelled hoarsely as the last thing he saw was her face before it vanished into thin air.

He could feel his body shutting down and he collapsed face forward onto the concrete. His focus never veered from that spot where he last saw Caiden, hoping that fate wouldn't be so cruel as to not let him see her one last time.

Swish.

Pneuma materialized in David's line of view. He felt the darkness coming down over him and didn't want to waste time disturbed by the boy's supernatural arrival. His lids were becoming too heavy to hold up on his own and he felt an intense urge to fall asleep.

Pneuma walked up to his body, watching with steely intrigue.

Just then, the door burst open. Iela, Mil, and Aza stopped dead when they saw Pneuma hovering over David's body. Aza rushed to him immediately to make certain he was alive. He prayed, but as soon as he turned him over, a gush of blood poured out of the wound. He immediately placed both hands over his abdomen and pressed down.

"Mil, he needs a hospital," Aza called frantically.

He glanced at Pneuma focused on the empty space in front of him and Volx blocked his view. The soldier looked past him and Aza followed his eyes down to David's stomach where his hands were soaked in his blood. He removed them and fell back onto his heels.

If there was any hope at all, Volx would've reacted before he even called Mil's name.

"Where are they?" Iela ran past Pneuma.

"There."

They all looked out at the empty lot. Only the gate and street lights were seen in front of them.

"What kind of shit is this?" Iela said, haunted. "Where's Caiden?"

"She's perfectly fine," Mil said. "Pneuma?"

He didn't answer at first and just stood there, internally flaying his backside. He could've ended all of this in one second before it got to this point. But when Caiden called his name, it was like her will and his collided. Now, he was feeling like how his comrades always must've felt as he consistently took matters into his own hands.

"Jais is with her." That was all he said and he didn't turn around.

"What about him?" Aza asked.

"That girl you left her with shot him."

That knocked the air right out of him. Aza sunk further into the ground in a daze as he stared at Pneuma's tiny back.

"Now, now, Pneuma," Mil said as he draped his cape over his arm. "We should get going. There's nothing else we can do tonight."

"You aren't going anywhere," Iela seethed. "You guilt my daughter into doing your job for you just so you can leave her here? What about the fucker that's still after her?"

"That's your problem," he said, invading her personal space, his skin prickling at her heaving chest. "You lack that mustard seed faith that everyone's always talking about."

He was really close. So close that Iela could see the flecks in his eyes.

"I'm not leaving her here."

Mil dropped the end of his cape and it hit just where his ankles were. He only took one step closer to Iela, knowing her volatile disposition, going any further would conjure up memories that needed to stay buried.

"Despite whatever's happening on the other side of time at this very moment, your daughter is the safest person in existence."

***

Wait.

Caiden knew that she should've been paying attention to Helena, who was freaking out that she was talking to people that couldn't hear or see her on the other side of this invisible wall, but another emptiness had taken up another spot next to Helena's.

It was different. Cold.

David's energy had diminished. It was now an open space ready to be filled by whomever she came across next.

"Caiden," she heard The Voice say. "Come back. You can't do this now."

She didn't know what she was doing, but she was finding it hard to come back to wherever she was.

"Caiden."

Jais had been staring at her the whole time. As soon as she realized that they were all protected under his shield, she forgot about him and Helena.

"Hey," Helena snapped, taking Caiden's face in her sweaty hands.

"Don't do it," Jais grunted and took a step toward them, but Helena cocked her gun.

"Who are you people?" Her eyes were darting between Jais and the rest of the Argenta on the other side of the shield. "You can't have her until I get what I want."

"What do you want?" Jais asked as composed as he could.

Helena's eyes had gotten bigger as she ignored him and crouched down in front of Caiden, blocking her view of David's dead body.

"You know what I want?" she asked not expecting an answer. "You have to take it away...He said you could take it away."

Caiden was pulled back to her surroundings and became trapped in the sea of pain that Helena was slowly drowning in. She felt her eyes changing and simply couldn't help leaning in, trying to get closer to what it was that had afflicted her. She couldn't find anything in the darkness of her aura to grasp on to.

"...What happened to you?"

Helena stared at Caiden for a moment and saw that she could only trust her. There was no one else in the world that she could place all her beliefs in without paying for it in the end. At this moment, it was only her.

Helena reached behind her back and began unbuttoning her dress. Caiden didn't know what she was doing at first, but when she took off her heels and the dress began to slide down her shoulders, she braced herself for what was coming next.

Scars.

Thin and pink. Fresh and old. They were all over her belly and the upper part of her inner thighs. The ones that healed were now whispers on her skin. Helena was looking avidly at Caiden, wondering if she was worth the blessing of being cured. Her tears stopped to await the verdict.

"Is this enough?...How much will it take for it to ever be enough?"

She was in her underwear and Caiden didn't want to look at her. Being vulnerable was something that she'd always done in private, but here this stranger was bearing all her secrets because she knew without a doubt that she could save her.

"You did this to yourself," Caiden guessed.

"I had to hurt myself to protect myself," she said as she took Caiden's hands in her own. "You understand."

At Helena's touch, she began to hear those screams that she couldn't hear before. They were Helena's screams. Caiden's eyes began to shift as the energy that she'd been trying to read in vain was finally spilling over all around and through her. And it seemed like Helena could feel it too as she fixed on Caiden, tears flowing down her burning cheeks.

Jais was poised on the sidelines. Though he felt sorry for Helena, she did just murder someone to get what she wanted, and she was now holding her prize in her hands.

"I can't save you," Caiden said helplessly. "I don't know how."

"Caiden," The Voice called.

"That's okay," she said, edging closer to her. "You don't have to do anything. I will."

"Helena." Caiden felt Helena's grip tighten around her wrists.

Before she knew it, her nails clawed out and broke Caiden's skin. She drew blood instantly.

"Wait!"

Caiden had to say something as she saw Jais move in her peripheral. She wasn't going to leave Helena. With her nails digging and scraping against her flesh and bone, she wasn't going to break her gaze.

"You're asking too much of me right now." Jais didn't know how to reel himself in, wanting to grab both Caiden and Helena for two different reasons.

Caiden could tell that he was internally struggling, but she wouldn't let him interfere.

Suddenly, she flinched as Helena's nails sunk deeper into her skin.

"Helena..." Caiden managed to say between clenched teeth.

It was at the sound of her name when she let go and time, already being tampered with, seemed to stop in place. Caiden watched as Helena's hands went to her lips, the tips of her bloody fingers touching the thickest part of her tongue. And like that, Caiden's left hand shot out and grabbed her throat.

"Caiden!" The Voice called.

Her whole body was trembling and her eyes were shifting like crazy. Helena's eyes were wide as well as she was scratching the concrete to get ahold of her gun, but Caiden's grip was so tight that Helena was starting to get light-headed. The hand squeezed tighter and tighter.

Caiden didn't know how to stop; she didn't think she had that much strength in her non-dominant hand and yet the power that was shooting throughout her palms and fingertips was something extraordinary.

"She's dying," Jais said, not sure if he should stop her or not. Her expression mirrored his thoughts and that made him even more confused.

"I can't," she said in the calmest tone.

"...It's too late," Helena strained, her teeth tinged a translucent red by Caiden's blood and her saliva.

Caiden's grip was becoming ironclad and she could hear the ticking of her heart counting down the clock.

What the hell is this?

That something was back with a vengeance. The trembling that she had before from fear was now overtaken by this thing.

Her heart. It was on fire. She could feel the light beaming through her skin. If it weren't for her opaque blazer and undershirt, she would be blinding Helena and herself.

This feeling had coursed through her bloodstream and now it was heading to a place it'd not been before. Like Helena had gotten ahold of her gun and pulled the trigger, a needle of unfathomable pain shot straight from her carotid through her trachea and into her brain. She lifted her chin like she was trying to keep her head above a nonexistent ocean.

Then, it went dark.

Caiden collapsed and Helena clutched her throat, gasping for air. She crawled away from the unconscious body like she could get back up at any moment, the thin layer of skin on her knees coming off like wet parmesan.

"Caiden!"

As soon as Jais ran towards her—

Boom!

A roaring sound of thunder sent a crack through Jais' shield and shattered Helena's eardrums. The next thing they felt was a growing warmth.

"Oh my fucking god!" the girl cried.

Jais turned around and saw that Aza and Pneuma were standing vigil with David's body. All eyes were on Lision who was towering over the half-naked Helena. She was dabbing her bloody ears and screaming hysterically, but as soon as she looked up at his face, she'd ceased her sniveling.

"...Oh my god," she barely managed as she seemed to believe that her Maker had actually arrived.

Lision gently touched the side of her head and she smiled through her smeared makeup. Helena had never felt more loved in all her life than in those few seconds and her head naturally fell into the Arch's merciful hand.

"Fear not."

Helena hit the ground and all was silent.

***

Mira's ample bosom had a front-row seat to Dontae's first night bartending. It was busy as hell and Piccolos was packed to the seams. Nova was tearing up the stage, having added a few dance numbers, which drew in a handful of potential new regulars. Rane was sweating off what little makeup she wore running back and forth from the bar to the tables.

"Two Hi-Hybrids and a Midnight Stroll."

"Sure, but can you wait till I get off?" Dontae teased and gave a tired grin.

"No," Rane said, not even attempting to return his smile, not when Mira's chest was distracting her. "Are you gonna order something else?"

"Nah, I'm still working on this one." She seductively caressed Dontae's frame with her big brown eyes.

Rane had might as well not been there at all as she ground her teeth watching Mira finish up the last few drops in her glass.

"Two Hi-Hys and a Midnight," Dontae said, passing her the cocktails. "I need to hit the stash in the back. Mira's glass is finally dry."

"Don't keep me waiting," she said, playfully.

"Rane, do you mind?" he asked, heading out from behind the bar.

She glared at him holding her tray of drinks like she wanted to fling it across the bar at his face.

"Or do." He smiled sheepishly. "Four seconds."

Dontae quickly jogged to the back and went into Piccolo's office. He closed the door and reveled in the peace for a moment. He didn't think he'd sweat this much making drinks. Rane had blasted the AC and yet his shirt was nearly damp.

He took a few more deep breaths as he went to the reserve in the corner. The room still smelled like him. Delicate, but still a tad intoxicating.

"Bad Dontae," he said to himself and grabbed a couple bottles of vodka.

When he turned around to leave, he felt something wet trickle down into his mouth. He dabbed the wet area under his nose with the heel of his hand but saw that he wasn't sweating. He touched his nose and his fingers came back bloody.

Dontae felt himself getting hotter and his knees buckling. He soon fainted where he stood, and he and the bottle hit the floor at nearly the same time.

Chapter XXXVII

VOICES WERE SPEAKING softly through some sort of barrier. Either a door or Caiden's sanity. They were very muffled and she couldn't sense anything, so she knew she wasn't back at Roxa's. Caiden moved her head and felt the softest fabric on her face. She opened her eyes and her chest tightened.

David.

She sat up, careful not to disturb that peaceful image of him. He was in the other bed, still in his dance attire. She got up and her ankles twisted as she stood. Her heels were still on, scuffed and dirty. Carefully, she slid them off and placed them neatly by the bed David was in. There, she kneeled, studying his resting face. Caiden hadn't noticed how quiet it was without him. His energy, both from his aura and from his being.

Tears began to gather on her bottom lid when she heard a knock on the door.

"Caiden," Aza called to her softly.

She didn't respond and hid her face in her arms on the bed. After a moment, when she was sure he wasn't there anymore, she looked back at David until she felt herself doze off again. Into a dream. The only one she could remember the most. And she stayed there for a couple of hours, her heart racing with each new landscape she encountered, completely not knowing how or why. But she had a sense

of familiarity so her heart skipped beats because it remembered even when she couldn't.

"Caiden."

"Yeah..." she answered in a cracked voice.

"May I come in?"

Her eyes flew open. She was already on her feet.

"Caiden?"

"Yeah, I'm sorry," she said, finding David again and sitting
down on the opposite bed.

The door opened and Aza flinched at the dead body.

"Pneuma," he fumed under his breath.

"...It's fine."

He looked at her to make sure that it was, but her face
was showing no emotion. He walked all the way in and
closed the door.

"I can cover him," he said, pulling the sheets up from
underneath David's shoes.

Caiden didn't say anything but watched him take care as
he placed the sheet over his face.

"How did I get here?" She didn't recognize her voice as it
sounded so subdued. "Where's Helena?"

"Your Arch," he said. "To both questions."

"And William?"

Aza hesitated, uncertain of how to answer. He walked up
to her, waiting to see those doe eyes, but it was like she was
still so far away.

It was a few seconds longer until she finally looked up at
him. They were like that for a while and Aza could tell she
still couldn't see him.

"Aza?"

Without thinking, he dropped down on his knee and continued to gaze into her eyes. That brought on some reaction.

"What are you doing?"

"Pledging his fealty."

They both looked toward the door and saw Pneuma had appeared in the corner of the room. A stray curl had flopped onto the other side of his part from his short travel as he shoved his tiny fists in his pockets.

"Not to you, but to Him. *The* Him. That peculiar, and what's now becoming insufferable, soul in that frigid body of yours."

"Shut it," Aza hissed at the unperturbed child.

"I'd rather not," he said blankly. "I'll be even more damned if you think some gnostic second coming of the Son will transform me into a bloody-hearted disciple of your illusory Christ."

"You only talk like this when Mil's not around." Aza turned back to Caiden, deciding that indifference was best, though his presence alone was testing him.

It was taking awhile for Caiden to catch up to where she was; her present. A part of her was still in the school parking lot. And another part was in her dreams. So she hadn't fully registered what the little boy had said at first. It took her a moment to respond.

"...You think I have God in me?"

Hearing it sounded as ludicrous as them believing it was the actual Creator.

Caiden couldn't imagine what her face looked like to them, but as those words left her mouth, she knew she'd get a reaction similar to theirs.

Aza seemed almost sorry that he gestured so grandly and was caught, but he didn't regret it at all. Pneuma, on the other hand, looked as if he was explaining pound conversions to a banker.

"God is said to reside in everyone." He fixed on her, his gray eyes darkening. "Unfortunately, He lies dormant in most."

Aza knew he was talking about himself. He looked back at him over his shoulder and he was drilling holes in Caiden's face.

"Hence, the Voids," he said, leaning on Aza's desk. "Although, once that thing wakes up...no more."

Caiden regarded Pneuma, haunted. "What do you mean?"

"What I said." There was a smirk in his voice.

"You never told me how to wake Him," she said, fixing on the boy. "Is it because none of you know?"

Aza and Pneuma exchanged subtle looks.

"...Or you're afraid how I'll respond if you tell me?"

They remained silent, but Caiden knew they wouldn't say anything.

Suddenly, they heard raised voices coming from the living room.

Pneuma wisped away while Aza went to the door and cracked it.

"It's Iela."

Caiden quickly grabbed her heels from the side of the bed. Then, she stopped and looked over at the sheet again.

"We'll take care of him," he said, wanting to comfort her. "Or your Arch will."

"That's not it." Caiden looked up at him, hoping she wouldn't have to say what she felt, but that only worked on other people.

"You don't wanna go," Aza guessed.

"How did you know?" she asked, slightly surprised at his deduction.

"I met your mother."

Caiden had to stop herself. "Please don't make me laugh."

"Sorry."

He watched her for a moment.

"What?"

"Nothing. It's just she's been waiting outside this whole time."

She didn't say anything and followed him out.

"...the fact that you're a liar, Mil, that's why I'm angry."

Caiden had stopped in the hall, readying herself. She'd never heard Iela say a person's name like that before. It was full of disappointment; the kind that was only reserved for people you cared about. She wasn't raising her voice either, which was another sign that she was actually beyond pissed despite what she said.

"Iela," Mil responded as steady as his nerves would allow him. "We brought her here because it's still not prudent to go anywhere else. And what baffles me is you know that better than anyone."

Caiden thought it was the perfect time to walk in, but Aza gently grabbed the cuff of her blazer.

She could feel her mother was grasping at all the possible answers she could give Mil. Caiden knew Aza wanted to hear her explanation, as did she, but control was something her mother would rather die than relinquish up to any man.

"...You don't know what you think you know," Iela said carefully. "Everything I do is to protect Caiden and myself."

"If what you say is true, then let her make the choice herself."

There was a long, bothersome silence and Caiden had to see her mother's face. She braced herself before stepping into the doorway of the living room and her heart knocked a little against its cage.

The remaining Argenta were all present and the room had never looked so ominous. Volx was at ease, but alert at the front door; Pneuma still had his fists balled up in his pockets leaning against one of the grandfather chairs where Jais was seated on the edge smoking a cigarette; Mil was in the other one in front of a breathing bottle of Riesling, and Dontae was sitting in the corner of the couch near her with a nosebleed plug in one of his nostrils.

When Caiden got to her mother, she was already looking at her.

How much relief could be mistaken for concern? That's what she saw on her mother's face, but her energy was touching Caiden in a different way. An artificial way.

What was happening?

Iela calmly walked up to her and took her arm. She led her to the door and waited for Volx to get his ok to let them out. Caiden took notice of his hesitation before they got outside as far from the house as they could.

Iela let her go and Caiden waited. Her mother took her time before she turned around to face her.

"Are you okay?"

She seemed to ask about her welfare in earnest, but Caiden was getting a sense that she wanted to know where her mind was.

"Physically, yes."

"What about your heart?"

Iela fixed on her daughter hoping to see a little less of her signature naïveté, and she saw that it had diminished.

But there was something new there that she couldn't pinpoint. It was something she'd never seen before in Caiden and that made her slightly nervous.

"...I don't know."

Caiden's head would usually drop around this time to focus on the grass between her toes or the piece of string on the side of her pant leg that was too short to pull, but instead, she looked her mother dead in the eye.

"I don't know anything."

"I can't tell you something I don't know myself," Iela said, trying to be sincere. She didn't want to say the wrong thing right now.

"Then I need to find out."

"I can't let you go back in there," she said, her voice rising.

"Why don't you trust them?"

"Why do you?" she countered. "You can't trust those people no more than you can trust me."

Caiden felt a pang of Iela's energy hit her at the same time those haunted, muffled screams swooped down and hovered over their conversation. She instinctively took a step toward her mother and her eyes began to change.

"Stop it," Iela spat.

"Iela—"

Smack!

Iela's hand had reacted before she could stop herself. The last of her power was being stripped away in what had been a few months and by the one person who she believed could never hurt a soul. Like Mary, Iela had given a loaded gun to the world and the wrong hands were about to pick it up.

"Still...You still don't call me mama. After all the shit we been through."

Caiden stood there, rooted to the spot. Her hand was on her cheek, yet the only pain she could feel was the little that Iela had a hard time keeping in.

"Let's go." She grabbed Caiden's wrist and she snatched it back.

They both looked at each other in surprise. The pain from when Helena gouged her had sprung up just now. Caiden rolled up her sleeves but didn't see anything.

"I'm sorry."

"Get in the car."

Caiden didn't move.

"Don't make me say it again."

"I can't."

Iela got in her face and Caiden expected to get hit again, but she didn't. She didn't do anything, but stood there and glared into her eyes. To Caiden it looked like she was thinking of what to do next. She'd never seen her mother look so lost. The next thing Iela did was something she'd never thought her mother was capable of doing.

She gave up.

Caiden watched her mother turn around and walk right to her car. She didn't hurry or look back, she just got in her car and drove away.

Caiden stood there and felt like her mother slapped her again.

She was now alone. The night became darker than it actually was despite the street lights. Caiden didn't know whether to cry or to finally breathe out as she felt like she was always holding her breath whenever she was with her mother.

"Caiden," The Voice called.

"She left..." she said to herself.

"Isn't that what you wanted?" The Voice replied.

Caiden was standing barefoot in the front yard of a house of special Blackhearts that seemed to want to cater to her soul's every whim and her overprotective mother just left her there.

Alone.

Her body was struggling to go to its default whenever it was left in Iela's aftermath. The thing is, she was fine and her heart was beating regularly, nowhere near the fast pace of her previous panic attacks. Caiden felt fine and that was a problem.

"Ms. Waters?"

She turned around and Mil was looking down at her feet.

"You can get cleaned up if you'd like," he said, trying to gauge her expression from the porch light. "I'm sure someone in there will give you the shirt right off their back."

"Mr. Gunde..." Caiden started.

"Mil."

Caiden had lost her train of thought. Even after being out for nearly six hours, she was incredibly tired.

Master.

"I still have to go home," she said, reluctantly heading back towards the house.

"That can be arranged, of course."

When Caiden got to the door, Thiere appeared at Mil's feet and Lision appeared at the entrance to the living room where a lone Dontae was checking his nose.

"Does it hurt?" she asked, going to him fully aware of Lision just existing in her peripheral.

"Bar fight. I'm alive," he said, eyeing her. "They left the least threatening person here. Walking into a room full of 'roided Voids would make even Zeus piss himself."

That didn't seem to ease anything as Caiden didn't respond.

"How was the dance— I'm sorry," he quickly interrupted himself. "You want me to go get Aza or Jais? I promise I'm much more polished than this...It's just not my night."

"I'd never done anything like that before," she said, thinking back to what little part of the dance she did enjoy. "I had a good time."

"I'm glad," he said, making sure she meant that before standing. "We're all in the kitchen if you need anything."

"Damien."

He smiled as he stopped at the kitchen door.

"Thank you."

There were simply no other words she could think of to say.

"I didn't do anything."

"For before. I forgot to tell you..."

"Oh. Well, you never have to say that here," he said, seriously. "But the pleasure is always mine."

Dontae went into the kitchen and Caiden turned to Lision still standing at the door. He let her by and she went to the bathroom where Aza had laid out clothes for her. A t-shirt and pajama bottoms that looked like Volx's military hand-me-downs. She hurried and took a shower and got dressed. She wanted to take her time but she wasn't at home. Despite what Mil said, she wondered if she would ever go back.

Caiden looked at herself in the mirror. Her hair had puffed out from drying it and she scanned the sink and opened up cabinets, but couldn't find anything to tame it. She needed to go back home.

Her face looked like a stranger's as she studied the thin hairs and the small bumps on her left cheek. Even her eyes. They were still hers, but more.

"I'm fine."

Lision was behind her doing his stoic routine, but Caiden couldn't think of another reason why he'd let himself be seen if he wasn't wondering if she was feeling okay or not.

"Are you really?" The Voice asked.

"I'm gonna have to be," she said, leaning back on the sink. "What about David?...His body, I mean."

He didn't answer and Caiden looked up and saw him holding out his hand to her. Resting in his palm was David's phone. She looked up at him for a moment, not wanting to touch it. It wasn't hers, but she reached out and cradled it in both of her hands.

"Zai..." she felt herself about to cry, so she shoved the phone in her pocket and left the bathroom.

She headed to the kitchen door and slowed down to gently tap on the chipped wood.

"It's safe," she heard Aza say.

Caiden pushed open the door and saw Aza, Jais, and Dontae about to sit down to a full course meal of leftovers. The table was covered in glass food containers and china.

"They fit alright?" Aza asked, referring to the clothes that he looked too pleased to see her in.

"Yeah, thank— Yes, they're fine," she said, catching herself. "...Um, do you have any olive oil?"

"That's all you're gonna eat?" Jais asked, fixing everyone's plates.

He caught her eye and they looked at each other a moment too long. Caiden didn't know how to feel after what happened. He was the only one in the world that had seen her in such rare form. So rare that she'd never been that way ever in her life.

"No, it's for your hair, right?" Aza asked, going to the pantry and getting a bottle.

"Yeah."

She took it and stood there as they all began to eat.

"Your plate's gonna get cold," Aza said, waiting for her to sit down.

Caiden was starving and she internally cringed at the disgusting sounds her stomach must've made while she was passed out. She sat down while Dontae went to the fridge to get some water and juice. Jais picked back up on an anecdote that he apparently started before she came in the room and Aza and Dontae strolled down memory lane with him, filling in the blanks where Jais was taking too long to remember.

She truly appreciated the stories from their glory days, letting her imagination of how they met and the times they spent together, take up as much space in her mind as possible. Anything to take her away from her own shambled life at the moment.

Though she was hungry, she couldn't eat that much. Whenever they would glance at her plate and glass, she would take a small bite of food and a short sip. Caiden even felt her smile struggling to push through her lips at times, but it was never freed. Even so, she was grateful to them for—

Bzzz.

Chapter XXXVIII

ROXA WAS ALLOWING the smooth jazz sounds from her lightly scratched record to soothe her nerves. Sister Lucy was sitting next to her on the couch with an untouched cup of tea. It was cold, but she wasn't leaving until Roxa gave her an answer.

"I woulda fixed you a pallet if I knew you was gon' spend the night."

Sister Lucy watched her simper into her tea cup.

"I won't leave until I know they're safe, no matter how much you make fun of me."

"Well, I'm goin' to bed." Roxa heaved herself to her feet and cut off the record player. "You can wait for Iela if you wanna, but that won't be a funeral I'll be fallin' all over myself to make."

"You scare me with how little concern you have for your so-called family," Sister Lucy said, pulling out her phone.

"What you doin'? We don't do that here."

"None of this would even be happening if you'd come to church like you said you would." The woman felt her blood pressure rising and took a deep breath. "I don't wanna leave until they get back. If that's okay with you."

"They fine," Roxa said, not sure herself. "I'm sorry that you wasted your time. I'll see you out."

She waited for Sister Lucy to get up and led her to the door. Roxa let her out and that's when Iela pulled up to the driveway.

"Praise Him."

Sister Lucy turned to Roxa but could see her heart was still troubled.

"I'll be back tomorrow," Sister Lucy said, walking out the door. "I won't give up on you."

"What's she doing here?" Iela asked, not looking the woman's way at all.

"Iela."

She stopped and gave Roxa a look before she turned around. Sister Lucy never addressed a Void directly, so Iela couldn't wait to hear what she was about to spew.

"Where's the child?"

"None of your business," Iela said, somberly and turned around.

Roxa was glaring at her, wondering the same thing.

"You lost her, didn't you?" Sister Lucy's tone indicated that outcome was to be expected. "We deal with situations like this all the time. She would've never strayed if you'd all come back to Him. To your home."

Iela couldn't take it anymore. She spun on her heel and had a gun pointed in the middle of the old woman's forehead.

"Iela!" Roxa nearly tripped out the front door.

Sister Lucy was too secure in her faith to fear anything, but when she fixed on Iela, her pulse suddenly increased. There was nothing there.

"...Like I told Roxa, I'll be back tomorrow," Sister Lucy said in a shaky tone. "Y'all have a blessed night."

Iela didn't put her gun away until the woman had driven off their street.

"What the hell is wrong with you?!" Roxa yelled as they got back inside the house. "What did you mean about Caiden?"

"She's where she wants to be..." She had already retreated into her head. "I'm going to sleep."

"The hell you are!"

Roxa took Iela by the arm and whipped her around, but she saw Iela's face wet with tears. Once she started she couldn't stop and she was trying to catch her breath. She couldn't even do that.

"It's okay, baby," Roxa said, vigorously rubbing her back. "It's gon' be okay."

Iela didn't know what had come over her, but she stayed in Roxa's arms like that for a long while. She didn't plan on avoiding a conversation with Roxa in this way, but she had to endure it until she stopped. Towards the end, she could feel some of her stress had disappeared from her body and she told Roxa that she needed to rest. They would discuss what they were going to do about Caiden tomorrow.

Iela took a shower and checked on Roxa to make sure she was in her room before she locked herself in her study. She went to her desk and opened it up to where her letters were. She'd never longed to be wrapped up in another's words. She needed a constant right about now; something that she knew would never let her down or abandon her.

She pulled out the white envelopes but didn't open them. She just put them to her chest and the words just floated through her mind. Iela sat for about an hour reliving every ink stain on those sheets of paper, realizing that they were never going to be enough. No one was ever going to be enough.

Only him. Only the author of those words could do that.

Iela's eyes glided open and she slowly went into her drawer to pull out a lighter. She wasn't sure what she was doing at first, which was why her mind was struggling to keep up with her body. She gathered her letters, still clenching them to her chest, and went into the kitchen.

She felt herself about to have another crying fit, but she clenched her jaw and let the letters fall from her hands and into the sink. Every last one of them. Iela flicked on the lighter and moved the flame toward the corner of one of them, her mind and actions now on the same page. It burned achingly slow and for a second Iela's hand was about to shoot out and grab them all before they'd been inflamed, but she didn't. The old Iela would've; the Iela that had put a gun to her daughter's head. But not this one.

This Iela let her child go.

The flames sparkled in her eyes as the last of the paper was nearly burnt; the final spark dying out with a whisper of smoke. She turned on the water and watched the ash and the small burnt pieces swirl down the drain. When she cut it off, she stood there to let what she'd just done settle within her. The words were still echoing through her, and his words, in his deep, sultry voice returned as if he was in her ear.

At that moment, she heard a car door close outside and paused to listen. Before she could grab one of her guns from the utensil drawer, she felt something incredibly blunt hit her in the back of the head. Before she lost consciousness, she felt someone take her body in their arms and drag her toward the front door.

Down the hall in Roxa's room, she'd been dozing, but fighting sleep and heard that same car door. She quickly got out of bed and cracked her bedroom door, but all the lights were out and she couldn't see anything. Not even the lamps in the study were on.

Before she could call out her daughter's name, a hand clasped her mouth, muffling her cries for help.

***

The word had spread throughout the halls of the death of David Manes. He was now the third student at Myerworth to die in the last three months. There wouldn't have been such an uproar from the parents and even some of the school staff if David had been a Void. No one was saying the name Helena Talbert, and she, being the killer, wasn't the only reason why. Caiden was the only student that knew that Helena was a victim, too.

She walked down the halls, trudging through the expected overload of grief and anxiety. Attending class was the last thing on their minds. The teachers were sympathetic, but who knew how long that would last. There was about a little over a month left in the semester and surviving was the only thing on everyone's plates.

Caiden felt eyes and heard whispers as she made her way down the hall. For a person that no one seemed to like, David had a considerable amount of love surrounding his locker. Flowers, cards, and even bad candid pictures of him in the school halls from his elementary and middle school years were placed among the mourning debris. Caiden didn't know how to feel as she stood there soaking in all of the emotions of her peers. They were genuine for the most part, but at the same time contrived.

This was what people were supposed to do when someone died.

David didn't have a lock on his locker because he didn't think he had anything of value. When Caiden opened it up, she saw how true that was. There were only three textbooks and a binder in there. She grabbed the binder and put it in Aza's backpack since she didn't have her briefcase with her and closed the locker. He and Dontae were waiting for her out front.

Caiden stopped and looked around. This was her last day of school.

She wasn't sure how she felt because she was surrounded by so many people and they weren't giving her a moment's peace. She'd have to wait until she got home. Her new home.

Bzzz.

Caiden's hand flew to her pocket. It had to be David's mother again. She dreaded reading the messages asking where he was and how much she was worried about him. It seemed she wasn't in the country at the moment, so she hadn't gotten the news yet. It was not her place to answer. She didn't know to whom that place was now, but it didn't even feel right reading the texts.

Caiden took out the phone and did see a message from David's mother, but the new message didn't have a name.

It just read: "*Don't go to school today.*"

She naturally looked up at her surroundings, like she expected something bad to happen in that instant, but of course, nothing did. Danger was all she seemed programmed to look for nowadays. Her first thought was that it was from a friend wanting him to see a movie. She didn't know much about David's personal life, so she had no idea if he even had other friends besides her.

She stopped herself, remembering how she told David that she didn't have any friends. Maybe he knew they would be. Suddenly, all of their conversations began flooding her mind, remembering how she treated him. It wasn't bad, just honest. The more she thought about it, the more the two words started to sound the same.

Bzzz.

Caiden looked at the phone again and saw it was a text from Aza asking if she was done. She felt awful using David's phone, but she didn't have one. Aza had unlocked it and Mil insisted that she use it until he bought her one, which made her feel even worse.

She messaged him she was on her way out and headed toward the front of the school.

"Open it up! Open up that bitch!"

Caiden froze.

The screams.

Not just inside her head, but outside as well. The halls seemed to darken as Caiden slowly turned around. Students had rushed past her to see what the commotion was and she followed them. When she got to the growing crowd, she couldn't believe what she was seeing.

A group of human students had a Void pinned against the wall and one of them had a pair of scissors opened and ready to slice up his arm. Teachers were trying to pull the boys away from one another, but the leader of the mob had gotten in a good slice before he was torn away.

Black blood had splattered the faces of the students and their phones that were nearby. That's when the crowd went wild.

"It's on me!"

"I got some in my eye!"

"Get it off!"

The students were yelling, horrified at what their curiosity had gotten them. Caiden had never left the Void who one of the teachers let go of to get to the other humans that had him pinned. She fought through the crowd and grabbed his hand, but he didn't follow her until he saw her eyes change.

The students were trying to get away from the group that had started the whole mess because they'd become violent in their attempts to get away from the teachers. One of them managed to disperse with the students that thought watching a student-teacher fight wasn't worth the social media post and he had his eye on the Void trying to get away. He'd watched Caiden lead him out of the brawl and followed them.

She thought they'd made it far enough until she felt something wet splash on her face.

Water?

No. Gasoline.

She saw empty water bottles being stomped and kicked across the floor. Before she or anyone else knew what was happening, the Void that she was holding onto for dear life had gone up in flames.

"Caiden, let go!" The Voice yelled.

"No," she said in wide-eyed disbelief.

He mirrored her expression as his hand slipped out of hers, making the choice for her. The screams at this point were beyond any human recognition as everyone watched the burning body dawdle towards the people trying to get out of the way. All she could do was stand there, wanting to believe that this was a nightmare that they all could wake up from at any moment.

"Caiden!"

Aza had run to the boy and was putting him out with his shirt. "Hold on," he said, staring at his charred face.

Sirens from the police and the fire truck could be heard in the distance and they knew it was time for them to go. Dontae had been watching him putting out the flames on the boy and couldn't look away at what was left of him. When he met Aza's eyes, he was brought back to the present and hurried to Caiden.

"Let's get outta here."

"What about Aza?" She still couldn't fathom what the hell was going on.

"He's coming," Dontae said, taking her hand.

The last thing she saw was Pneuma's smoke shooting through the burnt boy's chest right before he passed out.

When they got back to the SUV, Aza wasn't far behind. He jumped in and they got out of there a few seconds before the police and the firetruck pulled up to the school.

Bzzz.

Caiden flinched at the vibration against her leg but didn't dare look at that phone.

They got to Mil's and she went straight to Aza's room.

Bzzz.

She was pacing, but she froze when she heard and felt that fateful sound again. Caiden was more concerned about what they were going to think of David if they saw this text on his phone.

No. They wouldn't think he was connected because they knew that she knew that he wasn't that kind of person.

He wasn't that kind of human.

Caiden steadied her breath as she pulled out the phone and sat down on the bed. She'd only read what little part of the text that the lock screen allowed her to see and that by itself made the light in her chest almost go out completely.

Chapter XXXIX

CAIDEN HADN'T LEFT Aza's room since they got home from school that morning. She'd slid David's phone back in her pocket after she saw the last message and never took it out again. It'd been silent ever since. She was struggling with the decision to show Mil and at the same time trying to preserve David's character. It was to others that she had to keep who David truly was intact for she was the only one who genuinely knew his heart.

But people didn't work like that, human and non-human. They only trusted what they could see and Caiden was sitting on that evidence now.

"Goddess."

She looked toward the door and saw Pneuma in his usual stance. She'd gotten so used to the sound of his windy arrival that it blended in with other common household sounds. He tilted his head to the side like that would help him read her mind.

"You like people worrying about you," he said, taking a step toward her.

"No."

Caiden eyed the boy warily. That would be the main thing she would have to get used to. Though she told her mother she could trust the Argenta, that was only because she read Aza and he didn't seem to have a smidgen of bad in him. That should've made her more suspicious because people are always changing, but it did nothing to deter her from believing in his benevolent energy.

Just now, Caiden realized that maybe it was just who Aza was that made her decide to trust the entire Argenta, and she had no idea what that meant.

"They don't know I'm in here groveling at your feet to persuade you to eat your evening lunch."

"I'm not hungry," she said, waiting for him to wisp away. "You don't knock or anything..."

"Do I seem the type of person to knock on doors?" he asked in a patronizing droll. "And you are hungry. It's no fun when you lie." He took another step toward her. "Those imbeciles will forgive you anything, but my intelligence is much more difficult to insult."

"Sorry, I just wanted to be by myself if that's alright."

He fixed on her and she on him. Both trying to figure the other out. Both on opposite sides of the morality spectrum.

Pneuma took another step toward her and she involuntarily pulled back a bit.

"That boy's still alive. That's what you're concerned about."

"He is? You saw him? After, I mean."

Pneuma didn't respond, studying the subtle movements of her eyes, lips, and jaw.

"Yes," he answered, quietly.

"That's good."

"Does that bring you happiness?" He took another step and Caiden's back straightened some more. Pneuma's eyes had moved down to her chest. "Or is that just Him?"

"This has nothing to do with my heart. This is how I feel," she said, mildly confused at what he was getting at. "I know you don't want me here. Hopefully, I can leave after everything is over."

"Or leaving was never your intent." He was in her face now. "A damsel wielding her authority over a harem of servile men that would willingly die for her seems like an envious wet fantasy."

"Would you talk like that if we weren't alone?" Caiden was fully put off by his surprisingly vulgar tongue but wasn't letting it show on her face.

In one lightning flash swoop, Caiden was pinned to the bed by Pneuma's small but Herculean strength. His palms flat against her wrist were like tons of marble, so heavy that she couldn't even squirm. Caiden stared wide-eyed at the boy, who even in this awkward position, looked bored beyond reach.

"Where's your fear?" he asked, waiting for the color in her eyes to shift.

"What am I supposed to be scared of?" she countered, finally understanding what he was doing. Caiden looked into his eyes and felt something familiar. He was still Hiding, yet she still could feel him. It was so far away, she wasn't sure Pneuma knew that it was there. "...You're just a little boy."

Pneuma wisped away as far back into the corner behind the door as he could go. He shoved his hands in his pockets and refused to drop his head, but he couldn't look her in the eye either.

"You shouldn't pity people so much. It'll eventually become a part of your personality."

"I feel bad for anyone in my situation." Caiden became trapped his steely gaze. "We have no idea what we're doing here. Me, with this thing, and you with...you."

For the first time, Caiden saw his face morph into something different. Pneuma's hands unclenched in his pockets.

"Forever a stranger to myself."

She could see he wanted to say more and she already knew what it was.

"Goddess..."

"I'll be out in a minute," she said, not wanting to let him finish. "I will."

Pneuma wisped away as soon as he felt she was done with him.

"It'd be wise to watch him."

"He's just sad, "she replied, examining her wrists.

"And that's no boy," The Voice added. "He's not excused. He could've killed you or worse."

Caiden went to the door to listen, but she couldn't hear anything. They were probably in their rooms or the kitchen. She pulled out David's phone and opened the door. Pneuma was an unusual catalyst to make her rip off the David band-aid. The longer she waited, the worse she would feel. Maybe this information could be helpful and she'd be putting everyone in danger if she kept it to herself.

Caiden walked slowly, but with purpose into the living room and saw Jais smoking a cigarette on the couch. Her confidence diminished a little when their eyes met.

"Uh, where's Mr. Gunde?"

"Out back," he said, putting out the cigarette he just lit. "They're about to eat if you're hungry. I know you're hungry."

His quiet chuckle put her a little at ease and she inched further into the room. She sat down a comfortable distance from him on the couch and lowered her voice.

"At the dance..."

"Don't worry, it's safe," he said, fingering the menthol.

"What is?" she asked in almost a whisper.

Jais leaned in closer. "Your secret."

Caiden watched him as he got up and opened the front door.

"I need to...then I'll be back," he said, closing the door behind him.

She sunk into the side of the couch with the phone clutched in her hand, contemplating whether she should go to Mil or wait for him to come to her, thinking of what that tactic got her the last time she did that.

"Hey."

She glanced at the kitchen door and saw Aza. His hair was down and he had a fork in his hand.

"I thought I wasn't gonna see you until tomorrow." He plopped down on the other end of the couch and hugged one of his knees as he turned on the TV. "You wanna watch a movie or something?"

"No, thanks."

Caiden accidentally lit up her phone's lock screen. Aza noticed the picture of David and Toothpick. "I'm sorry."

"Why?"

"The movies..."

Caiden looked down at the phone then turned to him. She wanted to be angry that they had been following her, but it didn't seem to matter in comparison to everything that happened between her first time going to a movie and now sitting next to Aza on the couch in one of his t-shirts.

"Aza..."

"He's okay, that boy," he said.

"Pneuma told me."

He could see she was still struggling with something.

"What is it?" he asked, sucking on his fork and absent-mindedly flicking through channels. He was intentionally keeping his eyes glued to the screen, already trying to move on to something lighter.

When she didn't answer immediately, he looked at her and then down at the unlocked phone she was holding out to him. He took it and read through the messages. Then he looked up at her.

"Well, don't keep me waiting."

Caiden's stomach plummeted to the unknown when she heard Mil's voice. He was standing at the kitchen door, dressed in daywear, holding his notebook at his side. He walked over to Aza and he showed him the phone.

"That's interesting," he said to himself. "The first message was sent yesterday."

Aza cut off the TV, knowing what that calm signified. He looked at Caiden who was a fawn in the headlights.

"...I was thinking about David," she said, her voice feather-soft.

"The son of the man that wants you dead? That David?"

Caiden's blood went cold as that truth pressed knives into the skin on her cheeks and back. The amount of poison in Mil's voice was more than she could've ever imagined coming from such a steady and even tone.

"You're not yelling, but I could hear you all the way in the kitchen." Dontae came in the room, immediately reading the situation. "What's the problem?"

Caiden had been fighting back tears and her emotions so that they wouldn't see her eyes change, but she was about to lose that battle.

"I'm not sorry."

She got up and went out the front door. None of them tried to stop her because they've all been there with Mil and understood the need to get as far away from him as possible.

She felt her tears being shoved back as she walked to the end of the driveway. She found herself lost in the sunset. The sky was painted with blue, red, and purple watercolors and she got trapped. Caiden breathed in through her nose and out through her mouth, then closed her eyes because that always helped.

She couldn't see the sky so she opened them again and saw Jais was coming back up the street from his car. He just finished his much-needed nicotine break and saw her intentionally looking away from him.

"Are you crying?" he asked.

"No." She turned away some more.

"Ava's a liar," he said, shaking his head.

Caiden turned around and her eyes were going back to normal.

"And I was right." Jais regretted the playful act. "What he do?"

"He?" she asked.

"I can't think of anyone else in there besides Mil..." he trailed off. "Pneuma."

"No. None of them." She saw that his fists seemed to ball up inadvertently and she hurried to set him straight. "Well, some of it was Mil, but it was mostly my fault."

"Ava's still a liar," he said, grinding an old cigarette butt into the gravel. "It's always Mil's fault...He's the reason why we're all here."

Caiden glanced at his profile. He was focused on the sediment for a moment before looking out at the sunset.

"Who's Ava?"

"My sister," he said, giving her a sad smile. "She's been dead a long time, but I'm pretty sure she's lying to someone right now, wherever she is."

He tried to make it light, but his face gave him away. Caiden didn't ask any more questions.

"It's getting late and I need to go home." She dragged her feet back to the house.

"I'll take you," he offered, pulling his keys out of his pocket. "It's on my way back to my home, the Tindale Suites."

"Lucky you."

"No, lucky us." He was pleased that he'd gotten the corners of her mouth to move. "Come on. Poor Aza's had to deal with that bastard since the eighties. I won't make you go back in there."

Caiden's steps stuttered as she caught up to him heading back to his car. She wasn't sure what her ears heard, but it couldn't have been what he said. She didn't have time to think about it as Jais swept her up in more conversation. He talked about Ava some more to her surprise, misreading his sadness when she said her name. How she'd always visit him, his little brother, and their mother on her holiday breaks from school and how they fought all the time over the pettiest stuff. They were close it seemed and that was further emphasized in how every time he mentioned her, he spoke in the present tense.

"This is officially the end of the line," he said, pulling into the curve of Roxa's house that was the end of the street.

Caiden saw her mother's car wasn't parked out front and she felt a bit of relief, but she sat there a moment watching the sleeping house.

"You want me to go with you?" he asked, checking their surroundings.

"I won't be long, I promise," she said, unsure. "I'm just gonna grab some clothes and Mary."

"Who's Mary? A doll or something?"

"She can be," she said and got out of the car.

Caiden made her way to the front door and she was struck with a feeling of déjà vu.

The stillness, just like on the night when she went to visit Zinc's grave, was the same as the one that was getting up in her bones right now.

She walked into the darkened foyer and the first thing she heard was the absence of something that seemed to always be there.

The air conditioner wasn't on.

Roxa always had the thing blasting during the summer, and because this was Texas and summer didn't have a distinct ending, it should've been on like it always had been ever since Caiden could remember.

It wasn't and the quiet was boxing her in. She went to turn on the light on the wall and slipped.

Now illuminated, Caiden looked around the room and saw that she was knee-deep in an ocean of blood. Too much for any one person. Nailed to the spot, she didn't know what to do. She stood there in horror as something began to crawl up her throat.

The next thing she knew, she was laughing. Not just at the blood, but at everything that had happened to her ever since she started school; ever since she left the safe womb that was her bedroom. The things that happened in her life were so ridiculous because of the timing and the reason that it was just simply too funny. So she had to laugh. She laughed so that those stupid tears that kept trying to come out earlier would stay locked away. But the more she fought them, the more hysterical her laughter became, and at that moment as she covered her rising peals with her crimsoned viscid hands, an agonizing howl bellowed just outside in the distance.

Chapter XL

THE CHILLING CRY continued to rip apart Caiden's insides as she sat entranced by the call. Her laughter had ceased and was replaced by a numbness that had rendered her incapable of recognizing her surroundings. The only familiar thing was that howl. So she followed it.

Pneuma had wisped in front of her house as Jais got out of the car, but Caiden was in a trance. She was a child being led by the piper and no one was as important as the object at the end of that heart-wrenching melody.

"You felt that," Jais said breathily, touching his chest and looking at the blood on Caiden's pants and face. "Stay with her."

Jais ran into the house and Pneuma got in line behind Caiden, matching her footsteps as she walked to the side of the house. He kept a considerable distance behind her for his reanimated frame couldn't take the sanguinary smell.

Caiden had gotten to the side of the house and stopped just at the edge of the clump of trees. She felt a presence that she thought she would never feel again. It was as if she'd called his name herself. She kneeled on one of her bloody knees, looking toward the rustling dark greenery, waiting for that other ray of light to come back home.

At that moment, Zinc came galloping toward her like out of a dream. Almost floating, she embraced him like he was life itself, and didn't let go. Her heart was abounding with so much emotion, she was sure it was showing through Aza's crew knit top. The dog was doing his duty and cleaning her up well with slobbery kisses. She just kept grabbing hold of him, trying to embrace him, but his excitement couldn't be tamed.

Mil and Aza had arrived in the SUV followed by Volx in his truck and Dontae in his car. They all got out, struck by the live wire signal that Caiden had sent throughout their circle.

Had the Soul awakened?

That was their first thought, but the feeling was more of a gravitation; a spiritual SOS of sorts. They felt an overpowering need to be both her sword and shield for reasons that weren't meant to have an Earthly explanation. The Argenta were led to her because the Soul called and the choice was made for them, so they ended up in Caiden's front yard watching her ostensibly hug the ghost of her dead dog in wonder.

"What's going on?" Dontae asked, only imagining the tugging sensation toward Caiden's heart that the others were experiencing. It could be seen from down the street and he naturally looked around at the neighbors, but it didn't seem like anyone occupied the houses at all.

Jais came back out of the house and saw his comrades' attention all drawn to the light that he could see from his position at the front door. His eyes quickly flashed their simmering hazel as Caiden, Zinc, and Pneuma disappeared behind his shield.

Snapped back to the situation at hand, the remaining Argenta looked toward Jais and he turned around for them to follow him inside the house.

Volx's nostrils became animated immediately as he went into the living room and crouched down on his toes. He was careful not to touch anything, seeming to be riding a high from the aftermath. He dipped two of his fingers into the blood, then with one deliberate motion, put them in his mouth and sucked them clean.

Dontae felt queasy and turned to look around at the other rooms that weren't covered in blood. The lighter on the kitchen counter caught his eye and that led him to the sink. He saw what was left of Iela's white letters. He picked up a salvageable piece, but could only make out a few words. Together they didn't mean anything, but the word "baby" gave him pause.

"You found something." Aza peeked over his shoulder and saw the ash.

"Nothing," Dontae said, tossing the pieces of paper back in the sink. "Shouldn't we be getting out of here? We don't know how long ago the killer left."

"Good job," Mil said, turning to Volx.

"Human," Volx deduced. "And animal."

"Animal?" Mil asked.

Volx gave a silent confirmation.

"Jais," Mil said.

Jais was about to go back outside until he saw Caiden already standing at the door. Her eyes seemed to glaze over, getting lost in that crimson mirror. She felt her eyelids getting heavy and forced herself to snap out of her reverie. Zinc brushed his snout against the back of her hand, sensing that she was about to break down, but she wasn't going to cry in front of them. There was nothing to be sad about. Caiden knew the truth.

The others noticed that Jais had been staring intently at the open door and knew she was already there. Jais got a subtle okay from Caiden to drop his shield and everyone could see her again. The others that arrived late were stunned by her bloodstained appearance.

"Ms. Waters," Mil started. His voice was slightly off and the others took note of that. "Grab your essentials and hurry. We need to leave as soon as possible."

"Where?"

"Somewhere safe," he said, not able to get her attention. "The killers might come back."

"They aren't dead."

They all looked at her, watching her eyes change, and couldn't help but feel a tinge of sorrow for her.

"Caiden..." Aza said.

She turned to him. "What?"

Aza had a hard time getting his words out. He didn't know what he could say that would bring her any comfort, so Dontae stepped in instead.

"Your room's upstairs, right?" he asked. He headed to the steps and Caiden quietly followed behind with Zinc attaching himself permanently to her side.

Volx stood up and continued reporting his findings. "There's more animal blood here than human."

"What does that mean?" Aza asked.

"I think we should hold off on the questions for now." Mil began opening doors and cut on what little of the lights Iela had bulbs in. "Let's get this place cleaned up. We don't need to encourage any more bad blood between the warring public."

"I don't think anyone's checking up on the Waters'," Jais said. "Her mother seems to make enemies for sport and the human has cut contact with anyone in town from her past life."

"The church," Pneuma said from the kitchen.

"How recent?" Mil asked.

"Very," he said, shoving his fists down in his pockets. "I would have a more accurate answer if I'd not been side-tracked."

"Caiden is the only track."

The boy eyed Aza, stone-faced as he wisped away. Jais left soon after.

"You two tidy this up," Mil said, heading toward the hall. "I'm going to see if we're finally dealing with professionals."

Upstairs, Caiden was putting the last of the pieces of clothing in her bag while Dontae was looking around her room.

"I can wait outside."

"You don't have to," she said, subdued.

"It's better if I do." He eyed her clothing. "I'll be just outside the door."

Caiden watched him leave and realized he was suggesting that she change. She took off Aza's shirt and put on her own, getting a little bit of normality back. Then she went to the bathroom.

Her reflection in the mirror was startling. The smeared blood on her cheeks, lips, and chin made it look like she ravaged an antelope carcass. She stood there, fixing on her eyes and remembered the last time she was in this same place. Caiden turned on the water and watched it run for a moment before she began to rub the red off her face. She dried it and got out of there before her other self forced her to remember.

Caiden left the bathroom and vaguely saw Dontae standing outside her door. The light from downstairs barely touched his face, but his concern could easily be seen in the dim light. Her eyes naturally went to the double doors before she went back inside her room. The stack of thinly sliced trees piled next to her bed on the floor beckoned for her to get lost in their forest. She walked over and picked one up and began reading. It was something she'd read already in the not-so-distant life she had before her first day of high school. Once she sat down, her hand brushed against her pillow. She lifted it and saw there was nothing there. Caiden got up and went to her closet where she saw Mary's resting place. She opened the box and holding the gun in her second home quickly brought her back to her dismal present.

The book was replaced with the gun, which she tucked into her bag. She paused for a moment, looking at all the scattered books around her room. It was tempting, but if she couldn't take them all, she wouldn't take any.

She slung the bag over her shoulder, cut off the light, and followed Dontae back downstairs. The Argenta were waiting for her, standing now in the most spotless her house has ever been. At least Roxa would come back to an immaculate home, she thought.

"You have everything?" Mil asked, his tone indicating that they weren't coming back.

"Yes."

They cut off the lights and followed her out of the front door. She glanced down to make sure that Zinc was there and noticed that he had blood on his fur from when she hugged him. Volx stopped and pulled out a piece of cloth from his back pocket. He got down in front of the obedient animal, almost too willing to be adorned with the soldier's tattered charcoal rag. When he finished tying the knot, he walked to his truck and Caiden got in the passenger of

Dontae's car. She could feel Aza but wanted to be near something that reminded her of all that she was used to.

One after the other, each member of the Argenta reversed and drove out of the dead-end street, fully aware that they were blessed to have what their life's purpose had transformed into up to that point.

Caiden was theirs, and not a soul could separate them from what was fatefully and divinely their own.

Chapter XLI

THE VOICE HAD been trying to hum Caiden into any of the stages of sleep since they left Roxa's. She was dead on her feet, but couldn't seem to bury herself and Zinc embedded in the back of her arm didn't help.

She didn't want to close her eyes for fear that his resurrection might've been a dream. Dontae thought it was him at first after putting himself in her place. The only people that Caiden had ever known were both taken from her in one night, and she was now traveling God knows where with a group of outliers.

"Can you do me a favor?" he asked, breaking the two-hour silence they'd been driving in.

"That depends on what it is."

He smiled a little to himself. "I'm stupid for thinking you're easy."

"You want me to go to sleep."

"Yes."

"Yeah."

The Voice and Dontae answered at the same time. Caiden felt chastened as she looked out of her window.

"It would put my mind more at ease if you at least tried."

"I can't..." Caiden could feel his sincerity, but she couldn't allow herself such a comfort right now.

Dontae caught her profile and it was like her panda eyes were getting more pronounced by the second.

"Caiden," The Voice said. "Don't do this to yourself."

She felt Zinc's nose sink further into the warmth between her arm and the seat. That made her fight even harder not to close her eyes. All the good was on this side of her lids and she was going to keep putting off visiting the bad until it was impossible to go on.

"I know why you chose to ride with me," Dontae said, focusing on the road. "Even though it was for selfish reasons, thanks."

"Is it bad to be selfish?"

Dontae glanced at her to see if she was asking in earnest before answering.

"Not for you, it isn't." He instinctively looked at her again to see if she'd fallen asleep. "Was that the real Iela or was she putting on a show for us?"

"The person you saw is a person I've always known."

"...I see."

He was silent for a moment, trying to sort through all of the questions that he was suddenly curious about.

"Is it actual pain?" he asked, not looking at her. "Being around people, I mean?"

"What do you mean by pain?"

He glanced over and saw she was being serious. "Something that is physically and or emotionally unbearable."

Caiden didn't know how to answer. She'd been dealing with other people's emotions all of her life and only dealing with her own when she was alone. The thing was she was never alone. She'd never been alone. But other people's pain had always been there not giving her own a chance to be felt completely, so she didn't know whether or not pain —hers and others— was real pain. It was there all the time. She was enduring it; bearing it. It must've not been true pain.

"Can I ask you something?"

"You can ask me anything."

"Do you ever think you're next?" She needn't look at him to get his answer. "Becoming a Void."

"I used to," he started, tapping his thumbs on the steering wheel. A notification lit up on his phone and he put it on do not disturb. "But once I realized I was immune, I never thought about it again."

"Immune?"

"Being in the Argenta has its perks." His fingers stopped moving as his eyes softened. "Immune to becoming a Blackheart. Immune to human mundanity...Immune to death."

Caiden had to look at him then. He felt her silent question and relaxed a bit in his seat.

"We will die. Eventually. But not until it's time."

Caiden was intentionally looking away now, becoming momentarily hypnotized by the blurred trees catching in the headlights of the cars. She felt her head relax against the headrest as she had been leaning forward against her seatbelt since she got into the car. Something just didn't sit right with her going off to dreamland after all that's happened. Quick frames of that body burned alive had seared itself into her mind; his hand slipping out of hers. He and the others all clashed into one another until it was one bloody, fiery mess.

The Voice started humming again and Caiden took that as a much-needed cue to distract herself.

"Damien?" she asked.

"Yeah," he said, grinning and closing the distance between his car and Volx's truck.

"You always do that when I say your name. Am I saying it wrong?"

"No." He glanced at her wondering eyes. "You say it perfect."

"I was gonna ask if you can do me a favor?"

"Sure," he said without a second thought.

"Don't you wanna wait until you know what it is?"

"Okay, what is it?"

"Can you put on some music?"

"Sure," he said, plugging in his AUX cord into his phone. "And for future reference, you don't have to ask any of us for a favor. Everything is already written, if you know what I mean."

"I don't understand," she said, slightly confused.

"Maybe you've already seen it..." He smiled to himself and caught her reading him. "You can just tell us. Your will is our will."

His smile grew as he saw her attempt to ask for more clarification, but he turned up the volume on his playlist and began tapping his fingers on the steering wheel to the beat. Caiden was depleted of all her energy to retort any further.

She positioned herself in her seat to where she could gaze at the waxing gibbous until they got to their next destination, which was about a few hours later. Mil had pulled into the parking lot of a lodge-like motel. They'd been driving blind in order to put some distance between them and Caiden's home. Or so that's what Mil tried in vain to lead them to believe.

The inn was off the highway, with sparingly scattered stores within a five-mile radius of the property. They all unloaded, stretching, not able to take their eyes off the place due to its pure magnificence. Caiden was too busy keeping her eye on Zinc as he was searching for a place to relieve himself to get a good look, but when she did, she wanted to leave immediately.

"Hey."

Caiden looked at Dontae, who was waiting for a response. She then saw the others had gathered around Mil's SUV.

"Come on."

"The hell," Dontae said, spinning around.

Caiden did, too, as she was caught off guard at the sound of the boy's monotonous voice. Pneuma was standing there as if they all had gotten out of the same car.

"I thought you rode with Jais."

"Sorry to disappoint you," he said, then he looked at Caiden, who wasn't looking at him at all before he was taken away with the wind.

"What did he do?"

She didn't answer and made her way over to the others. Caiden could feel their eyes on her, especially from Aza, which seemed like such a long time since she'd spoken to him. She just knew they were thinking about where her mind was or if she'd collapse out of nowhere at the sheer amount of despair that had trampled her down in the last forty-eight hours. But she felt fine. Or maybe she'd gotten used to feeling everything that it morphed into one inexplicable emotion.

"We've just missed our check-in," Mil said. "Don't worry, I'll take care of everything."

Mil led them toward the front doors and Caiden's fingers loosened from Zinc's neck. Her hand was covered in fur and she realized that's what Mil probably meant by "take care of everything."

When they got inside, the petite woman at the front desk put on her most convincing customer service smile and tried her best to give each of the new guests the right amount of eye contact, but she kept most of her focus on Caiden because it was less straining on her neck.

"Very early mornin'. Y'all must be here for the retreat." The woman gave Zinc a double look. "Uh, is that real?"

"Yes, ma'am," Caiden said, looking at Zinc, who was standing completely still.

"Ah, the name is Cahill," Mil said. "We're running a little behind."

Mil gave Caiden a comforting smile as the woman typed away at the computer. Jais, Volx, Dontae, and Pneuma had taken to feeling out the lobby, dropping everyone's bags on the log-themed furniture. Instinctively, she checked the time as she hadn't done that in quite a while.

Three thirty-three.

"A Mr. Dontae Cahill?"

Caiden glanced up at Mil as he smiled and nodded as the woman gave him eight room keys. He gave her two.

"Who's that?" she asked, taking the black cards. It had her room number on the literature that accompanied it and the name "The Chevel Inn" written in a grayish-white.

Mil began to simper as he walked over to the others, sliding Aza their room keys.

"Mr. Cahill?" Mil called.

His spike in anxiety gave him away before Caiden met his eyes. He stood up, about to apologize, but didn't know what to say. She felt like an idiot and maybe a little angry at an irrational level considering she knew he didn't mean any harm by allowing her to call him by someone else's name. Honestly, Caiden didn't care. She hadn't felt a pure emotion of her own since she could remember and wanted to let this one flow to see where it took her.

"Let's all get some rest, shall we?" Mil said, rather pleased at what he'd just done.

Caiden knew she was still being watched as they all made their way to the elevator and she couldn't wait to get to her room.

Aza and Dontae especially weren't letting up. She knew her cheeks were rosy from the laser beams coming out of their eyes. Even Pneuma, who she noticed after a couple of side glances of her own, was watching both her and Dontae at the same time. Caiden wondered why he was even there, seeing as he was his own teleportation system.

"This is us," Aza said, following Mil, Jais, and Pneuma out the elevator.

"Rest easy," Mil said.

She only nodded, too tired to speak. Aza caught her eye before the doors closed and it quickly got warm. Not heat warm, but serene warm.

Lision.

The once empty space on the other side of her became occupied by the stone figure. Caiden looked at Dontae and Volx, who was easy to forget was present if not for his intimidating appearance. She saw his nostrils twitch as the doors opened on their floor. They all got out in silence. Dontae and Volx's room was closer to the elevator so Volx went in with his key.

Dontae remained with Caiden until they got to her room two doors down.

"Is this what your angry looks like?" he asked, clasping his hands in front of himself and leaning his back against the wall. "I was gonna tell you."

Lision was studying Dontae's face, trying to see if he could find any truth in his words.

"I know." She opened the door and Zinc dashed inside. Caiden waited for Lision, who was still counting the pores in Dontae's jaw until she remembered. She patted her pockets searching for her room key.

"Your hand."

Caiden stopped patting and opened her hands, palm up. The keys were there. A little too there. All of a sudden she had another headache.

"And the door's already open," Dontae said, coming out of his lean. "Are you okay?"

"I'm just tired." She dragged her exhausted body into the dark cylindrical box like a snail.

Dontae watched her go inside and was waiting for the lock, but the door never closed. He heard something hit the floor and Zinc's unbridled yowls filled the silent hall in a panic.

Chapter XLII

CAIDEN'S EYES ROLLED around in her sockets. She caught the dimmed indistinct features of someone hovering over her while Zinc's barking continued to bounce off the walls of the small room. They were cut off by a sharp slice through the air.

"What'd you do the dog for?"

"She's conscious. Get her on the bed."

"I don't think..."

Caiden felt cold marble brush against the back of her hand and stop. Then, the warmth came back. She felt herself being lifted off the floor and gently placed on the softest of clouds.

"Caiden," The Voice called to her.

"...I'm fine," she said with a struggle.

The next thing she saw was Lision. He was about to reach out to her and she knew what was coming next.

"Please don't."

He withdrew immediately and retreated with his head slightly bowed. Caiden managed to sit up and she turned around and saw Dontae and Pneuma staring at the creature.

"May I have some water?"

"No," Pneuma said, finally looking at her. "Your body requires nutrients."

"That wasn't demanding at all," Dontae scolded her, grabbing a water bottle out of the fridge. "What did I tell you in the car?"

"I'm sorry."

Dontae shook his head. "When's the last time you ate?"

It was like she had an epiphany as she stared at him blankly. She couldn't remember. Pneuma balled up his fists and dematerialized into the air.

"You're gonna die if you keep this up." He handed her the water and eyed Lision who was still bowing his head. Dontae sat across from her at the small table near the window, waiting for her to open the bottle.

"We're all gonna die..." she said, focusing on the coldness of the plastic in her dry hands. "That's what Mr. Gunde told me."

"Pardon my language, but fuck Mil." Dontae had to lean forward in his seat, not knowing what else to do or say. "I know you can't feel your way around the group dynamics, but you already know how I feel. Just multiply that by four."

"I think he's right."

Dontae stopped himself from arguing. His baby blues longing to connect with her baby browns.

"How do you know you think he's right? Have you read him?"

"You know I haven't," she said to herself.

"Then, it's you. Your opinion is the only one that matters."

Caiden took a sip from the water bottle in agreement and felt her stomach contract in appreciation. Her hand wanted to search for Zinc, but he'd come out of his stupor and his head found her hand resting on the bed.

"You're not sleepy?" she asked, ignoring her belly's cry for more water.

"I'm okay," he answered, slightly delayed. He wasn't sure if she was talking to him or the dog. "I won't leave you alone until you've eaten though."

"Who are you?" she asked, already reading him for his response. "Your name, I mean. To afford a place like this..."

"It isn't Damien, but that's better than Dontae." He hoped they were already past that hiccup. "It's my father's name. My father's money. That's not me."

"I see."

Caiden gave him more eye contact so that in case those few moments of meeting Iela hadn't illuminated her relationship with her mother, he would see that she truly understood where he was coming from.

It was a struggle, but Dontae broke his gaze and glanced over at the Arch. He was standing so still that Dontae only knew he was breathing by the subtle vibration of the mask covering his nose and mouth. The creature lifted his head and he looked away.

"The restaurants are closed downstairs, but I'm sure I saw a twenty-four-hour diner out there by its lonesome. I'll bring you something back."

Whoosh.

"No need."

Dontae and Caiden's head whipped toward the sound. Pneuma was in the corner on the other side of the bed holding a colossal restaurant tray of assorted pasta. He set the tray down on the bed and set his sights on Dontae, who took a noticeable gulp from all the excess saliva.

"Where are you going?"

"Nowhere now," he said, inching toward the tray.

Pneuma watched Caiden look at the food, but could tell she wasn't as interested as he would've hoped.

"You will eat," he said, eyeing Zinc from his peripheral, edging closer to the mushroom penne. "You don't want to be any more useless than you already are."

"My God," Dontae snapped. "Get out."

"With pleasure."

Pneuma wisped in front of Dontae to grab him and disappeared them both into a cloud of gray smoke.

Caiden jumped to her feet thinking more was going to happen, but it didn't. She became lightheaded at her sudden movement and was about to fall over, but caught hold of the warmth. She looked up and saw Lision, eyes still averted, but being her temporary crutch.

"I told you to stop bowing to me," she said as he helped her back to the bed. "Thank you..."

He didn't say anything but watched her pick up a fork and dig into the carbonara. She put the food to her lips and hesitated a long while before she put it in her mouth. The taste was so real, her eyes watered.

"Sorry," she said, taking another bite. She hadn't even begun to chew the first.

Caiden quickly wiped her face as she suddenly longed for home. She wanted Roxa's records and her mildewed books. She wanted the movies with David and even those brutal early morning spars with Iela. Caiden wanted familiarity and comfort, but couldn't see any signs of life at the end of this path that she was coerced into treading.

She was surrounded by forces beyond her control and yet she still felt a trickle of unease. She was shivering with unease. Suffocating with unease. She couldn't breathe. All this social and civil decay amongst humans and unrealized humans; swimming in it, just barely brushing the bottom of her chin, gradually dying to keep afloat above the lake of bodies both dead and alive. She couldn't breathe.

But, more warmth.

Caiden's mind was whirling so she hadn't noticed she'd dropped her fork and fell to her knees trying to hold onto whatever of herself that hadn't let go. And Lision was right there, allowing her to bury her face into his chest and just be. To let it go and surrender all that she was holding onto. And God help her, she did.

Caiden cried until her throat's cords were scraping against one another; until she couldn't see from the inflated balloons that had become her bottom lids. She couldn't stop and she didn't want to. The electricity resurfaced and she knew her heart was getting brighter, but she continued to grieve all the lives lost, including her own, while The Voice hummed her into slumbering submission.

***

Aza's side of the room was dark compared to Mil's. Every single light was on, including the TV. He only did this when they were on the road. The lights were used at a normal amount at his house, so he couldn't understand. When they all got out of the elevator and went their separate ways, Mil insisted that Aza take a shower first and that's where he just came from now.

His hair was still damp. It was too humid to use a blow dryer and he wasn't trying to go to sleep just yet, though he was exhausted. He'd felt Caiden's call and turned over with his hands near his chest. It wasn't a distress call, but he still wanted to know if she was okay.

Ever since they found out who Caiden was he'd felt a need to do his part. It wasn't much at first, just to observe from a distance and help her with the tiniest things like directions around school or class notes. When he graduated to the big stuff like telling her about who and what they are, he became even more determined. Aza wanted to do that slowly, but fate didn't allow it. Now, Caiden wasn't speaking to him.

"You know what I always liked about your type of face?" Mil asked, coming out of the bathroom fully dressed in fresh day clothes. "You can't hide anything. Less skin."

Aza sat up. This was the part where he'd attempt a decent conversation, but fail and go to his room.

"Where are you going?" he asked.

"For a walk." Mil took his notebook out of his bag and opened the door, but he lingered. "Aza, I know what you're thinking...I noticed almost immediately when you first met Caiden. But she's not Amiel. Don't forget that."

That name hit him like a ton of bricks.

Why was he bringing her up?

"What..." he started to say but didn't know how to finish.

"We have to come up with a game plan, so get as much sleep as you can."

Then, he left.

Aza grabbed a shirt out of his weekender and threw it on. He waited at the door to listen for the elevator, but he couldn't hear anything. He opened the door and peeked out to see if Mil had gone. The halls were empty so he began walking all the way towards the end until he got to the second to last room and knocked. Jais opened the door but didn't greet him.

"You wanna beer?" He crashed across his bed. He had on nothing but a towel, but he didn't seem like he'd just got out of the shower.

"No, thanks," Aza said, scanning the room. "Are we alone?"

"Look, the bed is free. It always is," he said, flicking through the channels. "You know Pneuma doesn't keep mortal hours."

"Yeah." Aza got in bed next to Jais and rested his head on the small of his back.

"What happened now?" he asked, his cheek pressed on his folded arms, the reflection of the TV in his tired eyes.

"...Mil just brought her up again."

"Okay, can I put on some pants first?" He let Aza's head slide off his back and plop onto the duvet. "Who's her? Caiden?" he asked from the bathroom.

"The other her," Aza said, staring off at the ugly indentations on the ceiling.

"Ah, your ex," he said, reappearing and getting another beer out of the mini-fridge. "Because of Caiden."

Aza looked at him getting settled into the other bed as he muted the TV. "What does that mean?"

"Nothing. I'm sorry." He took a long swig and rested on his elbow.

"Maybe I should've went to Dontae..." he said, trailing off.

"He's the last person you wanna take this to."

Aza sat up and looked at him. "You're right. But I thought you'd be bored of hearing the same thing over and over."

"I am," he said, getting a kick out of Aza's expression. "So how about you try not to bore me this time."

Aza's head dropped to his lap where he began playing with the ends of his hair.

"What? You like her?"

"Yeah. Don't you?" Aza looked at Jais expectantly.

"She's not bad company," he said, turning the sweating can in his hands. "I like her like I like beer. I gotta have it with me at all times even when I don't like what it could do to me."

"To compare her to beer of all things..." Aza said under his breath.

"Look, it obviously hurts. Why do you think he brought it up? Besides him just being an asshole."

"Probably just for that reason. And to teach me another lesson I didn't ask for." After a moment, he got up to get a beer from the fridge. "We're not supposed to be drinking," he said, wrinkling his nose from the fizz.

"I don't sleep and my entire family was murdered," Jais said, skimming through the muted channels again. "What's your excuse?"

"I've got three now. Pick one."

***

The elevator dinged and Mil stepped out as a middle-aged couple stepped on. They were Voids and they were in love, from the looks of it. He could tell as they refused to let the other go. Mil thought it strange that they acknowledged him at all.

He came into the spacious lobby and saw that the front desk was prepping for the next shift. Breakfast was about to open up, so he thought he would rest on the lobby sofa until it was time.

"*Master.*"

Mil flipped open his notebook to begin his scribblings and Thiere appeared before him. But he wasn't at his feet where he usually greeted him. He was standing in front of Mil, looking down at him. Though his eyes were still averted, Mil felt a sort of insubordination in his stance, but of course, that couldn't be seen on his face.

"*You seemed to have enjoyed some time to yourself,*" Mil thought as his pen glided across the page. "*Announcing the arrival of your brother and then falling into frequent bouts of blissful oblivion. Tell me, where do the Fallen go when they need a break from the world's allure?*"

Thiere didn't say a word. That wasn't a question meant to be answered but to caution. He felt his knees weaken under Mil's disregard and finally fell to the level at which he was made.

"*...Master,*" he started over.

"*I understand, Thiere. I always understand.*"

"*I fear you don't,*" he thought. "*My heart is faint and not made to withstand such a presence as my brother's.*"

Mil eyed the being. If he wasn't so magnificent, he'd be a little more perturbed. Instead, he was intrigued beyond thought.

"*Thiere, what do you long for in this second life? A lot has happened over these past few months and I've been thinking about our relationship...About where we'll both be after this has ended.*"

Caught off guard by such a thoughtful question, he attempted to meet the gaze that Mil had granted him, but his eyes searched the sand-colored tiles for a response. And then it found him.

"*Purpose,*" Thiere thought. "*It's the only trait my brother and I lack.*"

Mil chuckled quite loud and he casually covered his lips with two of his fingers.

"*Your brother, my word, Thiere.*"

"*You laugh.*" Thiere wanted to see Mil's expression. "*You're the only one with that right, but I cannot lie to you.*"

"*You amuse me,*" Mil thought, pulling out his vibrating phone. He glanced at it and flipped it over between the pages of his notebook. "*I can give you that, for you and your brother. Like I did for the others.*"

"*Forgive me.*"

"*Don't apologize,*" Mil thought, capping his pen. "*Prove to me that you deserve a purpose and I will give it to you.*"

"*And what of my brother?*" Thiere lifted his head at last. He felt himself being absorbed by Mil's intensity. "*He is Arch to your sire.*"

"*Exactly,*" he thought, darkly.

Thiere locked eyes with Mil for a moment before he felt the finality in his piercing glare.

He dismissed himself and Mil went back to his notebook. He turned the phone back over and saw that the call he got was from an unknown number. He cleared his screen and happened to glance up at the lobby to see that the Voids checking in for the retreat were already arriving. Before he uncapped his pen, he could've sworn he saw a puff of smoke.

Chapter XLIII

THE CHEVEL INN was now flooded with Voids from nearly all walks of life. The place was a nice size and the staff could see they were pushing their capacity limits, but the retreat wasn't something that happened often. The majority of the staff were Voids, but the ones that weren't, though antsy, were still excited that the inn was getting so much business.

Dontae came out of the elevator massaging his forearm. A bluish hue, a departing gift from Pneuma, peeked from beneath his rolled-up sleeves. He walked up to the front desk, catching the eye of a tattooed clerk, and made sure the mark was covered up.

"Morning—uh afternoon," Dontae greeted, flashing a charming smile.

"Been there before. Late night?" the clerk asked, kind of amused.

"Long morning," he replied, glancing at the sign welcoming the guests. "What's that about? I saw it when I checked in."

"Yeah, the retreat. It's supposed to be a getaway type thing, you know from all the shit that's been going on. Well, I'm sure you've seen the news."

"Read, mostly," Dontae said, touching his bruise. "Just the headlines. Nothing varying from the norm lately."

"The norm is killing us," the clerk said, quickly plastering a fake smile on his face at a guest that passed by. "So they figure a retreat will make everything a little better."

"You sound passionate."

At that moment, the clerk's eyes changed briefly before going back to normal.

"I think the only thing that it's doing is bringing together a mob of tired and angry people...And what nearly always happens when you mix those two together?"

"You coming down with a cough?" Dontae asked, looking out at all the new guests.

"I still got bills."

Most of them were showing typical signs of fatigue so far, but nothing tripped any alarms. He looked down at his phone and forgot it was still on "do not disturb." He quickly turned it off and was flooded with messages. Nearly all of them were from Rane, but the two notifications from Adyn are the ones he replied to first. He redialed and the boy picked up on the first ring.

"Adyn?" He gestured a goodbye to the clerk and left the counter.

"I called you," he said, rather small on the other end.

"I know, I'm sorry. I only saw it just now." Dontae went into the lobby and continued to study the guests. "How's everything?"

"...Okay."

Dontae heard his featherlight breathing on the other end and waited patiently.

"...I'm not going home anymore, am I?"

Dontae massaged his neck and leaned forward in his seat, searching for the right words.

"...You can go home, but it won't be the same." That's as delicate as he could put it. "I'll try to drop by later on tonight, okay?"

"Okay."

"I gotta go," he said, noticing Jais, who seemed to appear out of thin air by the coffee counter. "Tonight, Adyn."

He hung up and waited for Jais to spot him. It was hard to tell if he'd been out all night or if he just left early in the morning, but it'd been clear to Dontae that he'd been snooping with the aid of his shield. Though fighting the urge, he calmly cut the red wire.

"What the hell happened to you?"

Dontae was confused at first and wondered why Jais was the angry one until he followed his eyes to the dark spot on his arm. He shoved the sleeve down and stood up. Dontae was not to be distracted. He closed the space between them and stared right into Jais' soul.

"Jackhammer or anaphylactic shock?"

Jais just looked at him. His tense shoulders and furrowed brow were trapped on the same note. He gingerly took Dontae's arm which was met with some resistance and examined the mark that Pneuma left behind.

"I'll talk to him," Jais said in a small voice.

"And who's gonna talk to you?" Dontae took his arm back and breathed. "I thought you were gonna hold off until we settled this thing with Caiden. I've been making a lot of headway since I got back to Piccolos."

A few guys had sat on the couch they were standing in front of and Dontae moved the conversation to the elevator.

"You gave me Lesly Steele. I know you didn't think I was gonna slow down just because we found the Soul." Jais jabbed his finger into the button of his floor number. "I appreciate the help, but there's only so much your daddy's money can do."

"I'm trying to help you," he said, clutching his phone tight, his knuckles whitening. He was watching Jais glare at the climbing numbers, just begging for it. He always seemed so friendly with the edge, and Dontae knew that was dangerous for someone that knew what was at the bottom of the fall.

"Thank you," Jais said after a moment, finally getting out on his floor. "But I don't want anybody else's blood on my hands. I don't know if you noticed, that shit doesn't come off."

"It's not supposed to come off," Dontae countered, on his heels. "You get used to living with it."

"I don't wanna get used to it!"

Jais' voice echoed with finality down the corridor. The solemnity in his eyes of being exhausted and not having the ability to rest tugged at Dontae's heart.

"...Why would I want to get used to living with something like this?"

Dontae had never regretted saying something so much in his life. He calmly closed the gap between them, his head dropping to that hard gray speckled carpet in apology.

"...Which one is it?" he asked again, going back to his initial question. He needed an answer knowing full well he couldn't do anything about it; the sin of being human.

"Neither," Jais assured him. "I won't do that to you. I'll never tell you how I die."

The movie was playing.

The same one.

The action one that didn't really have a plot interspersed with a lot of blood and explosions. It was the exact same one in the exact same theater. That's where Caiden was sitting now. The only difference was it was empty. Everything was the same, including the smooshed pieces of popcorn that were under her seat.

Everything, except one other person.

"You're hella late."

Caiden's tears were summoned to the brim of her lids at the sound of his voice. They wouldn't fall though for some reason. Maybe they knew something she didn't and were refusing to come out as a hint of some kind.

"You're not gonna talk to me?"

She didn't want to turn her head, but David was more persuasive than the living.

"There she is."

He was leaning on the armrest furthest from her, turned slightly in his seat like he was the last time, in the same clothes from that day with not a care in the world about what was on the big screen. His eyes were fixed on her as if he was still alive.

"...I'm sorry."

"Ah, don't do that," he said, propping his scuffed-up sneakers on her lap. "Especially if you don't mean it."

"What?"

Caiden was trying to read him but couldn't because he wasn't really there. But the weight was and she didn't understand.

"You don't feel sorry, you feel guilty," he clarified, resting his head on the back of the chair. "And you don't have to do that either. Things happened the way they were supposed to."

His sad smile was faint and yet still strong enough to put an elephant on her chest.

"You're still gone," she said, not wanting to blink at all for fear she'd wake up. This had to be a dream.

"How? I'm right here," he said, rubbing his shoes together like a puppy does its paws.

Caiden was sure the tears would come out then, but she laughed a little instead, startling David and herself.

"Shhh," he said. He leaned forward and hunched down in a huddle.

Her laughter died out and she couldn't take it anymore. She lunged at him in an embrace that knocked the wind right out of him. Caiden had hugged only one other like this before and her mind wouldn't be stopped racing to the thought that David had indeed been resurrected.

"It's okay," she heard a voice say.

It seemed like it was, but something didn't feel right.

"Caiden?"

That wasn't David's voice.

Caiden quickly let go and Aza was standing before her. He was looking more concerned than usual in his pajamas.

"Aza," she said, taking several steps back. Her heart was exploding in her chest. "I'm sorry."

Caiden heard whimpers. Zinc was lying on the floor next to her boots. She realized she was in the hall, sleepwalking again. She looked at Aza, who was still watching her with that same expression. She hoped he thought this was a one-time thing under the circumstances. She didn't need to add anything else on the list of things that the Argenta needed to be worried about.

"Sorry for what?" he asked, softly.

They both gazed at each other. He watched as the color shifted and took a step toward her. She stiffened as his eyes smoldered that comforting violet before settling back to normal.

"Sorry for what?" he repeated and took another step closer.

"Stop," she said, without thinking.

And he did, almost immediately.

He was merciless, not allowing her to look away.

"Caiden," he said, breathless.

Why did my name only sound that way when he said it?

"I already know...even if you didn't Hide from me."

He had no choice but to close the space between them. She looked up at him, sure that she was right. Even if others doubted him; even if he doubted himself, Caiden knew she was right.

"Let's go."

It was a few seconds before she followed him to the elevator with her hand over her heart. He got in next to her, the back of his hand faintly brushing the back of hers. She patted her cheeks and followed him out.

It was quiet in the lobby. The only people there were the desk clerk and a few late guests trying to see about an empty room for the retreat. She watched Aza walk toward the front door and stop. He was already outside before he noticed he was alone. He turned around and was grinning through the glass. Caiden took her time, but she went out there after him.

"Nothing's gonna get you." He made monster claws, flashing his fangs. "I'm right here."

Her steps slowed as he echoed David's same promise to her, but picked back up when she saw him run smack dab into Jais.

"The hell?"

It wasn't that he didn't see Jais, it's just that he appeared out of nowhere. As she got closer, she noticed he was holding a gun and a six-pack.

"You ran into me," Jais laughed. He offered to help Aza up, but he smacked his hand away and got up by himself. He was holding his head. "Aw, you're fine," he said, putting his beer to Aza's temple.

"What are you doing?" Aza asked, now noticing the gun.

"What does it look like?" Jais' voice changed and his eyes smoldered. "Doing a little self-care."

Bang!

He began shooting at the vehicles in the parking lot and took a swig of his beer when he ran out of ammo. He turned around and saw Caiden. He damn near spat out his drink.

"Your face," he said, wiping his chin. "Don't worry, I'm not drunk."

"You look drunk," she said, not believing anything he said while he was reloading.

"He's not," Aza assured her. "He can't."

"Caiden."

When she looked back at Jais, his weapon was coming right at her. She caught it, wishing she had her own. The gun seemed old and rarely used. Caiden looked up at him, and caught his shining eyes.

"Go ahead," he said, hopping up on the hood of a car.

"Are you sure?"

"Yeah, tell her Aza," Jais said, cracking open another can. "You want one?"

"No, we don't."

Caiden felt the nerves at the corner of her mouth twitch some. She found Aza's straight-laced side a little endearing.

She turned to a car near her and aimed the gun.

Bang!

"Again," Jais called from behind her.

She pulled the trigger again.

And again.

And again.

Jais closed his eyes as Caiden pulled the trigger once more. He was being soothed by the sound of the bullets leaving the barrel and shattering the glass windows; experiencing a secondhand ecstasy.

Caiden was enjoying herself more than she thought she would. That warm steel in her hand wasn't Mary, but right now that didn't matter. As soon as she heard the click she felt a little better. About everything.

Everything was going to be alright.

Up next was Aza, who was just excited to hit anything in the vicinity of where he aimed. They continued reloading and passing the gun around, relieving whatever stress they had.

And all with an invisible audience.

Several feet away, watching with much intent and need, stood Lision, who'd appeared between the Chevel Inn next to a lone tree as soon as Caiden stepped foot outside.

There was no immediate threat, yet he felt obliged to keep a close watch. It was something a little more than obligation and curiosity. So much so that even a divine creature of his caliber couldn't find the perfect words to match what he was feeling.

He continued to stand guard from that distance for the duration of the gunplay. When he saw them pack up and make their way back towards the inn, his vision was abruptly washed in flame.

Wild, ferocious, and towering over Caiden and her guard. He took a step in her direction and everything had gone back to normal in a blink of an eye.

It was a flash and lasted no longer than a couple of seconds. Caiden, Aza, and Jais were almost to the entrance when that blink happened again and they were drowning in flames once more.

But this time it continued, and all the Arch could do was watch.

Chapter XLIV

ADYN WOULDN'T LET Dontae out of his sight. Pneuma had gotten them there way later than he would've liked and seeing Adyn's face light up at an untimely hour just reinforced his belief that children were more resilient than he thought.

He figured the kid would be asleep by the time they got there, but of course, he wasn't. Pneuma stayed, which wasn't helping Adyn's nerves.

"What'd you eat for dinner?"

"Mac and cheese," the boy said with some vigor.

"I love Mac and cheese, too."

Dontae was happy to see the boy show another emotion.

They were in Adyn's bedroom, which was oddly decorated in a typical little boy manner. Robot sheets, pictures of space, toy soldiers, and tiny cars were placed strategically all around the room. It didn't make Dontae feel any better about the boy being there, but Adyn didn't seem to mind. He was already bathed and tucked into bed. Dontae noticed his gaze straying to Pneuma during their brief conversation, but Dontae would just grab his attention again with talks of his favorite tv shows. That brought him back, but Pneuma's dark aura was hard to ignore in the corner of his room in the middle of the night.

"Hey, Adyn. You're happy here, right?" Dontae asked, feeling Pneuma's eyes seer into the back of his head. "You're taken care of?"

The boy naturally glanced at Pneuma before answering. "I like it here."

"I believe that's good enough."

Pneuma took a step into whatever light the table lamp gave off.

"We just got here." Dontae kept his tone steady for Adyn's sake.

"Do you want a repeat of before?"

Adyn shivered at the thought and Dontae slowly turned around to face the demon.

"So, you do know what that was."

Pneuma was rarely unprepared when questioned about something he didn't want to give a direct answer to, so Dontae waited with bated breath for confirmation of which he was certain.

"I don't need your permission."

"Pneuma," he said with the calmness of a thousand monks. "Is Adyn safe here?"

He sprung up out from under his covers and stared intensely at Pneuma, still partly shrouded by the darkness.

"Trumpets, Adyn," he said in a hushed voice. "Did you hear trumpets?"

Dontae turned back to the boy and their eyes met. He shook his head no, but it was difficult to find truth on such a frightened face.

"What is that? What does it mean?"

Pneuma fixed on Dontae for a moment. He was thinking of what to say, knowing how savvy the guy was with his tongue, his vast intellect couldn't calculate how fast word would spread of the events that had occurred here.

"You're Argenta."

"That doesn't tell me—"

Swish.

Adyn's light flicked off and Pneuma and Dontae vanished milliseconds afterward.

They were now standing in Dontae's room. Volx wasn't there, not that he left evidence of his existence in his wake.

Dontae wouldn't let it go. He was glaring at Pneuma now who had his fists clenched deep in his pockets. Dontae always thought he was revving up to disintegrate when he did that, but now watching the boy's hardened gaze, he was sure that that particular habit was to constrain that inner need to flee.

"What are you running away from?" Dontae didn't intend to sound concerned, but his damn sympathy for those that had no control of their merciless circumstances.

"I don't know."

The boy's frank tone made Dontae's muscles relax.

"Okay," he said, taking off his shoes. "Then, we'll figure it out...So you don't have to be scared anymore."

"You're projecting," Pneuma said, quietly.

"Then why are you still here?"

He didn't respond just like before. He felt his head tilt some and he walked up to Dontae who was bracing himself.

"You heard the trumpets."

"Yeah."

"I can't hear them," Pneuma said, turning slightly pensive. "Do you know why that is?"

Dontae didn't want to answer as he felt the room getting colder. He didn't know if that was from his imagination or if Pneuma was emitting some sort of emotional essence.

"Because only the living can."

***

Caiden woke up around dinner time the next day. After the late-night target practice, Aza walked her back to her room, but she couldn't fall asleep. She stayed up talking with Lision until she dozed off. He said about a handful of monotonous sentences so she mostly talked at him. Caiden could tell he was listening though. Lision had this intense stare whenever she said anything like he was trying to figure out some irritating mathematical quandary. She never looked at him long. She didn't believe anyone was supposed to.

Her hand reached out and touched a very chilling other half of the bed. She flipped over and no Zinc.

"How'd you sleep?" The Voice asked. "You didn't wander the halls, so I pray well."

"Where is he?" she said to herself.

"Are you talking to me?" The Voice replied.

It was being facetious which meant It was lashing out.

Caiden got out of bed and got dressed. She holstered Mary around her back as she opened the bathroom door.

Empty.

"Caiden."

"What?" she asked. She looked around the room as if a person was there with her.

"You worry me so..." The Voice started. "Not just your state of mind, but the state of your heart. A lot has transpired this week...Everything has."

Caiden reflexively clenched her fist.

"I'm tired of that everything," she whispered, walking to the door. She felt her stomach roar as she opened it.

"Cheeseburger?"

Lision was waiting for her too close to the door and she nearly ran into him. She was suddenly reminded of the night she cried in his arms. The only time she saw his face after she was drained out was by accident and his facial expression never changed. He was like a robot, but the way he spoke sometimes was dire and florally poetic. That made her want to know what he was thinking even more.

Caiden glanced up at him and he was already looking at her. She noticed his mask seemed thicker than what she initially thought was a thin black cloth. Naturally, she became curious about what was underneath. But then she remembered that he wasn't even of this world and became afraid of what she would find there.

They got in the elevator and headed to the first floor. The Argenta were waiting for her when the doors opened.

"Just in time," Mil said, eying her. "I trust you slept well."

"You'd better, it was the whole damn day."

She started following them and locked eyes with Jais. He looked to be back to his usual self.

They walked past a placard advertising the retreat itinerary and that's when Caiden felt that wet nose. Zinc had trotted up to her from out of nowhere.

"I'm afraid he's not welcome," Mil stated. "The other guests."

Caiden watched as people were already heading to the banquet hall and saw them looking at her and her entourage. She didn't know why, but from what she could feel from those that weren't Hiding, was a sort of ambivalence about what they were about to do. Caiden looked at the others all on the tip of their toes and wondered if they ever truly relaxed.

"Shouldn't we be checking out?" Dontae asked, locking eyes with Mil. "Doesn't make much sense to attend a dinner party full of Voids when we're trying to get away from them."

"On the contrary, it makes perfect sense."

Caiden caught Mil's eye and the corners of his mouth turned upward some.

Dontae's expression turned hard as he took a step toward Mil. "You think they're gonna show up here. Which means you knew this whole thing was going down."

"For someone who's built a reputation for their networking, your lack of intel seems troubling."

"When?"

"I found out at precisely the same time you did," Mil stated, stone-faced. "I leave it up to you to decide whether you want to believe that or not."

All Dontae could do was stare at him.

"Shall we?"

Mil turned on his heel and the Argenta cautiously followed him on their guard.

Caiden caught Jais exchange looks with Dontae as she knelt down to bid Zinc goodbye.

"I'll be back," she said, and before she could search for him, Lision appeared across the way by the wall.

She followed the Argenta into the banquet room as the last of the guests entered. It was separated from the quaint onsite gourmet barbecue restaurant that was situated near the back of the building. The tables were clothed in beige, the place setting was set up casually, and there was piping hot food being brought out to a back table where a catering staff was waiting to serve them. Everything looked too good to touch, but Caiden reached out to brush her fingertips on the thick-clothed napkin rolled neatly within a shiny silver cuff.

"Aht! Now it's yours."

Caiden had snatched her hand back and saw a guy sitting alone at the table. He startled her as she didn't notice his presence until he said something.

"I must smell," he said, smiling to himself. "You can sit here— Well, you have to, but your friends can join you if they want."

"Um..." she caught Aza's eye as the Argenta naturally scoped out the place.

"They're your friends, right?" he asked, leaning in and lowering his voice.

"Yeah, sure."

Aza found her and was about to usher her back to the others until the guy started talking to him.

"Your seats are here," he said, unfolding his napkin.

"We can sit together."

She'd gotten closer to his ear as the hall was filling up with lively chatter. Aza saw that there were empty seats, but scattered throughout. He motioned to Jais and he signaled to the others.

"Thanks," he said, pulling out Caiden's chair.

"Sure...?"

"Aza."

"Thaniel." He put out his hand to Aza and they shook.

"I think I wanna get my plate first."

"Same." Jais agreed from behind her. "Let's go."

Caiden saw that Aza wanted to do the same, but Thaniel had trapped him in an open-ended question. She and Jais slipped past the occupied chairs, collecting a few glances before they got to the table. The line went pretty quickly as everyone was too excited and wanted to get the night started.

Caiden went down the line with her plate, telling the servers what she wanted and didn't want. The food was steaming up her nostrils and into her memories. She couldn't help thinking about Roxa when she was around food that smelled this good. She got to one of the servers, who she'd caught staring at her when she walked into the room. It wasn't prolonged or unsettling, but similar to the other guests. She didn't pay it any mind, because the Argenta were hard to ignore as well.

"Thank you," she said, hoping she gave him a friendly smile, but she didn't feel the muscles in her face move.

He half-smiled in return and Caiden went to her seat.

"You're gonna eat all of that?" Dontae asked, looking at her overloaded plate. He'd taken the seat next to her as he was people-watching the room.

"You're not gonna eat anything?"

"I just need a good beer and I'm good."

"I'll go with you. I forgot the broccoli." She didn't understand why he was lying. She was starving. Caiden's eyes wandered past Pneuma and Volx's empty plates and to the catering tables in the back.

That server was gone.

"Mil's using you as bait again and you still haven't ordered him to stop Hiding."

Caiden had just scooped a spoonful of mashed potatoes onto her spoon when her fingers loosened from around the embroidered silverware. She looked up at Dontae, who was piercing her, his clenched fist on the table and white knuckles complimenting his soft glare.

The tapping of a spoon on a wine glass made her break her gaze.

"Good evening, my fellow second-lifers. I pray you all made it here without any trouble. And if you did have trouble, I hope you made the trouble regret it." A man about Mil's size and build had stood in the middle of the room with a mini mic, pausing for laughter.

Caiden looked around for the rest of the Argenta. Mil and Volx, who were the last to get their food, had just sat down. Pneuma, who was seated across from her, seemed to be asleep, and Aza and Jais continued eating.

"I'm not about to bore you with a speech, but I've always wanted to do that." He paused a moment before he continued." It's a pleasure to be here tonight, eating good food and with like-blooded people like the wonderful Chevel manager, without whom this dinner would not be possible."

There was some light applause as some looked around for the manager, but no one came forward.

"I hope everyone can relax and mingle with your fellow Voids tonight. Tomorrow's the big day, so continue to enjoy yourselves!" He downed the dark-colored liquid in his glass as soft music and chatter started up again.

Mil was never letting his attention stray too far from their table. Caiden watched him lean toward Volx, who'd only gotten his food for show, and whispered something to him.

The speech guy talked up a few tables before he casually left the banquet room through some back doors that led to the kitchen. He made it to the empty lobby through another door and headed to the front desk.

"The owner is still in his office?" he asked the lounging clerk.

"Yes, sir," she replied, jumping to her feet. "But he's with the manager."

He quickly headed to the back and stopped at a door that said "Management." He took a deep breath and knocked twice.

"Come in," a muffled voice said.

The man entered, no longer hiding his excitement, and locked the door behind him.

There was only one person in the office.

He was now staring at a heavyset man, with a noticeable gut and thick unkempt eyebrows. He looked pleased to see the other man, excited as well, but you couldn't tell by his tired demeanor.

He was noticeably gaunt.

"William," the man said at last. "The prince has entered the banquet hall."

Chapter XLV

LISION WAS NOW in the company of a few guests that had taken their conversation away from the noise from the banquet hall to the dry silence in the lobby. Impassively, he examined every one of them that crossed his path. With each person that caught his eye, he found it harder to believe that after death, some of these souls would become like his equal.

Zinc, who had sniffed him out, was trotting at his side, as he probably thought Lision was waiting for Caiden as well. The dog's pace slowed and he turned around, his eyes locked on another creature that suddenly appeared that had a similar scent to Lision's.

"...Brother."

Knowing who that voice belonged to, Lision didn't answer for it was impossible for the owner to show up before him after all this time.

"It has been an eternity."

Lision turned around and faced Thiere.

He was correct. It had been almost an eternity since they laid eyes upon one another. Looking his so-called sibling up and down, he could sense that Thiere had changed and not for the better.

"I am not your brother."

Lision likened Thiere's behavior closer to that of the humans to whom he'd clearly produced an attachment. The disgrace from past transgressions wouldn't allow the being to look too long into Lision's eyes. He would do that much for him.

"It's been full centuries. Too many to count on just my hands alone," he said, taking a tentative step closer. "How long do you think it will take for you to escape this purgatory? That muzzle doesn't compliment your arresting mien."

Lision didn't answer.

Thiere simpered in disbelief. "You've seemed to have lost sight of your true nature...You are different."

"My nature is as it always was."

Zinc couldn't sense any ill intent from this new Arch, so he remained calm where he stood, waiting.

"Your Master must be proud of this strong will you've been displaying for show." He said this with more disgust than he intended, but Lision's devotion to a faux human was too much to bear. "You aren't fooling me, of course. Though, your loyalty is something to aspire to," he said honestly.

Lision remained quiet and observed. Thiere was a creature of habit and Lision wasn't going to hold his breath waiting for him to go off-script.

"How is your Master?" he asked.

"He is how you left Him," Lision said, monotonously.

Thiere became trapped and his gaze was now fixed on Lision's to where they were having sort of a staring contest, except Thiere didn't ever want the game to end. This was the first time that his brother wasn't indifferent.

He reached out and gently cupped Lision's face between his hands. "Being here with these mortals, I couldn't explain to you their influence."

"It is evident." Lision took a step back.

Thiere dotingly reached out again to caress his brother's head this time, but pulled back after he felt himself getting lost.

"You abandoned me; forsook the only family you've ever known...And after all this time, you still cannot see what he has in store; what potential lies ahead." Thiere stopped and studied Lision's unflinching countenance. "...That potential lies within her."

With one look, Lision's glare sliced through Thiere at the mention of the Soul. He didn't have to say her name, but he might as well have.

"I have no brother," Lision repeated with an unsettling quietness. He walked past Thiere without another look.

"Time is your enemy. You must surely realize now that you are on the wrong side of His will." he said louder, speaking to Lision's back. "Your faith in that soul will end you, and that will end me. I won't bear that, Lision."

The mention of Caiden again made Lision stop mid-stride.

Then, Thiere appeared in front of him, believing that he'd gotten his attention. "I've no doubt we'll fight side by side once more."

Lision did nothing, still and Thiere scowled.

"You have sinned so far beyond redemption," he said, his anger rising with each word. "Your Maker no longer recognizes who you are anymore."

Lision couldn't tell if Thiere believed the words that were coming out of his mouth, but he hoped he didn't.

No. He prayed he didn't.

He prayed that this once fallen hadn't fallen so far to where he couldn't rise again. Forgetting their past completely, Lision didn't want that for him or the others.

Thiere had gotten lost in his brother's gaze, pondering the unknown thoughts of such an emotionless face. He was willing Lision to react in any other way than he had. His composure was irritating the hell out of him.

"Caiden is who I have been serving."

Thiere was in his face now. "It is blasphemous to serve two masters."

"I serve only one God," Lision resounded. "Her name is Caiden Waters."

In a flash, Thiere's gauntlet-sized manus sprawled out and latched around the Arch's throat. "Soldier, your light has dimmed."

Thiere lifted him off his feet, both of them in the air, and the Archs went down in a struggle.

The floor beneath them opened up and Zinc jumped back just in time. Flames were shooting out of the abyss beneath, spiraling down into the unknown like quicksand. For the first time in a long time, Lision displayed a minuscule hint of fear as he glanced down.

Thiere's smile was malicious as he watched conflicted at his brother's helpless expression.

"Let's go home."

His grip tightened more around Lision's neck as he was dragged down into the depths of Hell.

The next thing Zinc knew, he was alone with the Voids, who, despite the dog's few yelps of caution, never strayed too far from their menial chitchat.

***

The Argenta had been making small talk for nearly an hour. That was read as: Thaniel speaking to Aza and he replying with short polite responses between a few bites of his food. He was the only one still eating. Caiden, on the other hand, was full and was now watching Pneuma slip into the alpha stage of sleep for post-dinner entertainment.

It wasn't until Jais put up his screen, that everyone was somewhat alert again.

"We're grateful for this breather, Jais, but I don't think precious time should be wasted on something as trivial as this," Mil said seriously, taking a sip of his wine.

"Wasted?"

Caiden looked at Jais, remembering the few times that Mil mentioned time and Jais, but not really piecing the connection together.

"It's nothing," he said, sipping a beer he brought from his room's mini-fridge.

She didn't believe him. Dontae's expression aided that disbelief.

"It's not nothing," Dontae corrected in a motherly tone. "It's just too morbid to mention for polite dinner conversation."

Caiden was struggling to read Jais coupled with the emotions that she absorbed from Dontae, but it was impossible and she was giving herself a headache.

"It's just that every time I do this little trick of mine, I sort of get time shaved off." He looked somber as he said the last part of his sentence.

"Sort of?"

He'd said it so straightforwardly, it possibly got easier and easier to roll off his tongue with explaining it to each of the Argenta over the years.

"Don't worry, I won't die tonight," he assured her with a sad smile.

She mirrored his expression without the positivity and the smile slid off his face. The more she looked at him, the more pitiable he became, so she broke away and began to poke the mushrooms that were pushed to the side of her plate. She glanced up at the guests and caught Dontae drilling holes in her.

"What?"

"Nothing."

"It's not nothing," she said, echoing his words, trying to lighten things for him and her, but it didn't work.

"I was just thinking, that it's not good to feel everything," he said, eating the mushrooms off her plate. "It's hard to keep secrets..."

Caiden felt that he was telling her something. She looked around at the others, who had the same expression on their faces. Dontae's was the closest to how she felt.

"Thanks, Jais, but let's finish this up." Aza was looking at the boozed-up crowd.

Caiden followed the others in getting into a natural pose as Jais unveiled them.

"So, Thaniel?" Dontae shot across the table, leaning back in his chair. "When did you become a Void?"

She could see some of his residual emotions still lingering from what Jais had just said.

"You must be human." Thaniel laughed a little at his direct question. "Last Summer, August. Scared the shit out of my parents when they shook me awake one morning and they saw that my eyes were gone...My dad especially." He idly fiddled with the stem of an empty wine glass.

"Sorry," Dontae consoled.

"Speaking of, only my dad's name could come up in idle chatter in a random inn in the middle of nowhere." He chuckled, looking at Dontae and the others. "Maybe you guys heard of him. Matthew Cortell?"

"You've caught me at a disadvantage," Dontae said, sipping his water.

"I've never heard of him either." Aza copied Dontae just to do something with his hands. His wine glass was empty and so was the bottle next to it.

Thaniel was animated in disbelief.

"Really? You've never heard of the very first Void?"

"Who the hell is Matthew Cortell?"

Jais had put up a screen just to beg the question. Caiden had been so busy listening to Thaniel speak, that it took her a second to notice that he hadn't reacted to this blatant inquiry.

"I've not heard that name uttered in my presence for a long time," Mil said. He made a face as if he was trying to remember the last time he heard the name Matthew Cortell.

"Who is he?" Aza asked. That was the first time he looked relatively interested in anything besides the cuisine all night.

"He is like the Void said." The name had awakened Pneuma from his small slumber. "I've never seen him before, but the rumors are hard to refute."

"...Yes, they're quite hard to believe," Mil added, checking to see if there was more wine in the complimentary bottles on their table.

"Why?" Caiden couldn't get her eyes to naturally glance Mil's way as she was still stuck in the student position in their now broken student-teacher relationship.

"Do you know how many times I've run into a Void claiming to be the son of Matthew Cortell?"

"Yeah, this is the perfect time to ask rhetorical questions," Jais breathed behind his glass. He'd ran out of beer and finished off the bottle of red wine before Aza could get to it.

Mil was so relaxed that Caiden couldn't tell if the number was a huge one or not. She continued watching Thaniel talk, studying his face, maybe looking for a resemblance to a man no one at their table had laid eyes upon. She was about to pick up her drink, which was water, when she realized she had to use the restroom.

"Jais."

She'd now adopted the same look Dontae had when he looked at Jais, and he regretted telling her about his fate. He lifted the veil.

They all resumed where they left off, with Thaniel still looking at Aza, not buying that he never heard of his father.

"No, I've never heard of him," Aza said.

Caiden thought this a perfect time to leave. "Excuse me," she said, getting up.

Pneuma got up as well.

"I'll go with her." He was already by her side.

"Whoa, across the pond," Thaniel exclaimed, impressed. "Which part?"

"That part."

Thaniel laughed a short awkward while and sipped his drink, while Caiden noticed the Argenta on a slight edge as Pneuma had wisped by her side without causing a stir. The free drinks were a big help.

"We'll be back shortly," Pneuma said so dryly the words had dust on them.

He led Caiden out of the room and into the lobby. She spotted the restroom decals and headed that way.

"I'll be out in a minute," she said, contracting her inner thigh muscles.

"Take your time."

Behind him, one of the Chevel staff had been watching the two since they came into view like she'd been waiting. She was now casually walking over to Pneuma with a flashlight in her hand. The woman made sure no one was around and hit the boy in the back of the head. Pneuma was out, shattered like a busted lightbulb, and the woman wrapped him in her arms.

"Oh sweetie, it's past your bedtime," she cooed into the boy's ear as she walked to the elevator, patting his back.

In the restroom, Caiden came out of the stall and began washing her hands. As she was drying them, she heard the door open. She felt someone creeping up behind her and before she could turn around, a man tackled her. She jerked her head back, ramming his face in. He let go and she had Mary out on him in a flash.

It was the man that gave the speech.

"Who are you?" she demanded.

"My nose!" He glared at her as blood gathered in his philtrum and his eyes flamed a burnt orange.

Mary soon became hot in her hand and she dropped it. She stared wide-eyed at her reddened palms as they were left with first-degree burns.

The man picked up her gun immediately and had it on her. She kicked it out of his hands and her boot met his face. Caiden tried to get Mary back, but he got to it first and threw her against the wall.

"I don't wanna hurt you."

"Too late." Caiden made sure to look him directly in the eye.

"Kill him!" The Voice raged.

"...I can't," she struggled as her air was being siphoned by his forearm pinned against her throat.

The man watched her squirm beneath him. He had finally had her. And now, they all did.

"Let's go say hello to William."

Caiden couldn't feel the electricity that she'd felt all those times before, which probably meant the Argenta were in the dark.

But that wasn't what caused her the most concern.

The person that her mind always went to first in situations like this hadn't shown up either and he was never in the dark.

Chapter XLVI

AZA LOOKED TOWARDS the door a handful of times while keeping his interest in what Thaniel was talking about. The conversation had veered into the lane of relationships, naturally, as the curse of Fading had caused the demise of countless families.

Thaniel was a little overbearing, but Aza couldn't help but lend him a compassionate ear.

"...I left her as soon as she changed," Thaniel ruminated, leaning back in his chair. "It was scary, man. I didn't know what was going on at first when her eyes started changing colors. Of course I would find out for myself months later..."

"How did she take it?"

"She was more freaked out than I was and yet she was trying to calm me down." He paused, his mind going to the final straw. "...It was truly scary."

"She was special," Aza guessed.

He'd not touched another glass and relaxed his hands in his lap. He was finally seeing in the young man what he'd always seen in people like them. He found himself invested in Thaniel's story.

"No, I was the scary one," he continued. He idly ran his finger around the mouth of his glass. "I was scared of how easy it was to leave her."

"I'm sorry."

"Oh, it's fine," he said, becoming animated again. "I came back just the same. I had to."

"That's good, I mean for both of you. It doesn't usually end up that way for us."

He had Aza up until the last part. Briefly, he felt that he was conversing with a younger version of himself from high school. The first time he attended. The initial hurt and regret, then to final bliss, an ending he didn't have an option of getting.

He checked the door again and caught Jais and Dontae doing the same on his way back to Thaniel. They exchanged looks but kept cool as they scanned the banquet room again. Mil, whose posture had been languid for most of the night, was now erect and Volx had his arms on the table, hands clasped together, itching to spring out of his seat.

Something wasn't right.

Caiden and Pneuma were still not back and Matthew Cortell, a man notoriously known in the Void community as the source of their genesis, was brought up at a Void event that seemed to have been put together on a whim.

Another thing was their seating. Not right by the exit, but close enough. Volx had found it strange upon coming into the room that all of the tables had been taken except that one. There were no assigned seats and every guest that checked in was never in a group of more than three or four. It was possible that they got acquainted with others in the last twenty-four hours, but that didn't seem wise as Voids were not so trusting, especially amongst themselves.

Thaniel looked over at one of the kitchen staff that had come out the swinging doors during the Argenta's previous survey of the room. Volx had been keeping an eye on Thaniel, but he couldn't help watching the door for Caiden as well.

He and the others, instead of watching their table where they should've kept their eyes for the trigger, it was on the front door, the exit, the crowd. They ended up missing the look.

As soon as Thaniel caught the glare of that particular kitchen employee, he ripped a gun from underneath the table. One of the other employees saw the weapon and whipped out a gun of his own and shot Jais point-blank in the chest, like the bullet already had his name on it.

A ripple effect came next as weapons were pulled out cocked and ready. By the time everyone got a quick look around the room, every Void that was Argenta had a gun pointed at him.

"Don't."

Before Aza could do anything, Thaniel had moved his gun off of Aza and pointed it at Dontae. He couldn't take his eyes off of Jais' keeled-over body lying on the table, so that gun was the last thing on his mind.

"Well," Mil said, setting down his glass and piercing Thaniel with stick pins. "What do we do now?"

He was looking around the chattering people, undisturbed by what was now taking place. Then, he stared a moment at Jais' body.

"Impressive."

Mil was watching with contained intensity how easily this guy wielded his faux power over his only child.

Thaniel was backing up, not relinquishing his hold over Dontae when the doors of the banquet hall banged open. Caiden was shoved inside by the man that had overtaken her in the ladies' room. Her eyes went to Jais, then to Aza, whose helplessness spread to the others when they saw her wounded hands.

"Who are you?" the man asked Thaniel.

"None of your concern." He motioned to Aza. "You. Get up."

"Answer the question," Aza wasn't moving an inch.

Thaniel snatched him up by the shirt and they were centimeters apart.

"It's good, we're both curious."

As Caiden watched what she could through the lively people, her mind suddenly went to what happened in the restroom, when she thought that electricity she felt would come and it didn't. She hadn't been so vulnerable in all of her life. She'd called on Lision, she'd called on Mary, she'd even called on the Soul, though not purposefully, and nothing happened.

Aza fixed on her, but she seemed to be lost in the chaos of events unfolding before her. He was dead set on not surrendering so easily. Thaniel had begun pushing him towards the exit door and Aza knew that it had to be now or never.

So, he did it.

His eyes smoldered to a cosmic indigo and on a dime, the pressure in the room spiked.

"Agh!"

All the Voids in the room with weapons suddenly dropped to their knees as if they'd stepped off the top of the tallest building in the world. They were all on the floor, wailing in pain from having their bones crushed and muscles spread beyond the limit.

Aza was in awe as he'd only done this a handful of times before and the power just made him want to do it even more. He pivoted to Thaniel, now writhing in agony at his feet, and focused on increasing the gravity in the room. With that, the screams intensified and fed his ego.

"Aza, Stop!"

He spun around and he surrendered as soon as he saw her.

Caiden was on her knees as well, her face twisted as her arms and legs were trembling beneath the invisible weight.

Thaniel regained his strength immediately. He jumped to his feet and hit Aza across the jaw with his weapon. He shoved him through the door with the other Voids working with him close behind.

The last image that Aza left with was of Caiden's shifting eyes, who looked more concerned for his life than her own.

Dontae remained on the floor, only mildly affected. It was times like this where it was made poignant how human and useless he was.

The man dragged himself to his feet with his hand still tightly gripping Caiden and jabbed Mary into her side.

"Where's the boy?" Mil asked, only now standing up from the table.

"Taking a nap."

The doors to the kitchen opened and William walked in, only having eyes for one person.

Caiden stared at him as his aura became more familiar the closer he got to her.

"...You don't know how long I've waited to see you again." William walked up to Caiden and gently took her arm and Mary from his servile staff.

"I'd like to thank you all for your assistance." He sincerely looked at the conscious and present members of the Argenta. "You've saved my life."

"What should we do?" the man asked, referring to their hostages.

"Just give me some time," William said in an entirely different tone than his previous gratuitous statement. He then rushed toward the exit and left with Caiden out the banquet doors.

Before anyone could do anything, Mil and Volx noticed that the staff looked as if they hadn't heard their orders.

Mil looked his captor in the eye as he moved slightly from in front of the gun that was aimed at him.

"Dontae."

He was still feeling the effects of Aza's gravitational blow but got to Jais. He gently lifted him back in his chair and tore open his shirt. He could see his wounds already beginning to heal. Still, there was so much blood.

"Don't you dare do that to me ever again."

Dontae's teary-eyed threat elicited a half-wince, half-smile of relief from Jais as he removed the bullet from near his heart.

"The conscious crowd didn't give me away?" he managed to say, getting up from his chair with a grunt. "I said I wouldn't die tonight."

Volx quickly went to each of the Voids and snapped their necks like twigs before running out the door. He felt Caiden's scent getting fainter and fainter. He ran into the lobby, but stopped dead.

The trail had ended.

Volx scanned the lobby. The Voids that were there, behind the desk and sitting in the waiting area seemed oblivious to what was transpiring in the banquet hall. Until one of them caught his eye.

He began walking toward the clerk who was talking on the phone.

"...he just left, yes—"

Volx's black eyes shined as his hand shot out and gripped the clerk by the throat. The man's eyes bulged out of his head and he started clawing at the soldier's hand.

It didn't take long for him to realize that his actions didn't rouse the others into action. He looked around and saw that none of them had broken character.

Volx turned his attention back to the man in his grasp. He stared him down with daggers and could see he was attempting to say something.

"...I ...ate..." he spasmed.

He loosened his grip a fraction and was in the man's face now.

"...It's...too...late..."

Crack!

Volx let go of the clerk's mangled throat and hurried back into the banquet hall. He didn't waste time grabbing the man that had delivered Caiden to William. Dontae, who had him under Jais' gun, backed up to give Volx some space.

"Hold on!" the man struggled to yell as the soldier had him by the collar.

"I don't believe we will." Mil walked over to the man. "William. Where is he taking your prince?"

"That's right! He's mine! Ours! All of us!" The man threw his head toward the crowd that was still behind the veil. He was in a frenzy and spitting with anger. "The prince will save us all!"

Mil remained where he stood, studying the man's sudden but short stroke of madness.

"Is that what you were promised?"

The man had frozen like Mil hit his pause button, but that was just to steady himself from exploding from those revolting words.

"It's what we're owed."

"You do know you'll never see him again."

"...No," the man said incredulously. "Tomorrow is the day."

"It's not."

Mil turned away from the man in a dismissive manner, unaware that that was his death sentence. Volx snapped his neck in less than a second as Mil turned his attention upward.

"Thiere!"

Volx gathered up the bodies and dragged them into the kitchen to be disposed of, through the openings of the unaware guests who were still enjoying their evening out.

Dontae got back to tending to Jais, who kept insisting that he was fine.

"Make yourself useful and go look for Pneuma." He expected Dontae's somber expression. "Don't make that stupid face. You know that kid's stronger than he looks."

It took some time, but Jais stared Dontae down until he left the room which began to rumble and shudder as he got out. The entire place felt as if it was going to implode in on itself. Volx came running back into the room to see what the commotion was, bracing himself as Jais and Mil were doing. They were all looking around, searching.

Out of nowhere, two figures plunged through the ceiling by way of an opening only the celestial could create out of thin air. Lision and Thiere came falling from above, hitting the ground with the rumbling of thunder and crushing the tables and chairs that were in their path.

Jais felt his veil burst at the arrival of the divine beings, simultaneously the Voids occupying the room had disappeared. The Argenta watched in amazement at the unrelenting power of the two heavenly creatures.

Thiere had Lision by the jaw, but released him and went to his Master's feet immediately.

"Forgive me for my late arrival."

"What are you doing here?" Mil threw the question at Lision. His tone indicated that he shouldn't have had to ask the question in the first place.

The Arch turned to him. "I do not answer to you."

"Surely you've heard Caiden's thoughts calling to you," Mil said, nearing hysterical.

Thiere was calmly fuming as Mil disregarded him for his brother.

"There is only one omniscience."

"You're her Arch!"

Lision was silent, all too familiar with this human emotion that not even centuries could give patience to.

"It is not His will that I go to her."

The Argenta were flabbergasted at his response. It was like their hearts all collectively stopped beating in their chest.

Jais forced himself to move on at once, never forgetting that time was forever of the essence.

"They couldn't have gotten far. If we split up, we can probably catch up to both of them before morning."

Mil's face turned grave as he faced Jais.

He already knew what he was going to say.

***

Dontae had started searching the bottom floor. Looking into janitor's closets and maintenance rooms. He couldn't check the employee and management because of the staff, so he took to checking the guests' rooms, knocking on every door, hoping for Pneuma to wisp through onto the other side, and describing him to the few people that did answer, asking if they'd seen the little boy. One woman had and said he was being carried to one of the rooms on the floor they were on.

As Dontae thanked her, he saw a housekeeper about to go into a room.

"Excuse me?" he called to her, running. "You have a key to all of these rooms, right?"

"Yes, I do."

She suddenly pulled out a gun and pointed it in his face.

"But that won't do you any good."

He stared down her barrel, his mind racing.

The woman that had taken Pneuma was coming out of a door down the hall.

"I knew one of you would be lurking around here sooner or later," she said, walking towards them.

"What do you want me to do with him?" The woman asked.

"It doesn't matter, we've got the pr—"

Zwish!

Both of the women went down before Dontae knew what had happened. Pneuma swiped his glasses up off the floor at Dontae's feet and put them back on.

"Are you all right?" he asked.

"I can't feel her." He was full of rage as he looked at Dontae, not wanting to wait for an answer.

Dontae picked up the housekeeper's gun and tucked it into the back of his pants. He ran to the elevator, while Pneuma wisped away, completely void of patience.

In less than a second, he was back in the banquet hall with the remaining Argenta and the two Archs.

They all headed out of the emergency exit, Dontae bringing up the rear, leaving the Archs in their own rubble, deemed useless by the desperate Argenta.

They got to their vehicles all thinking the same thing. The vast night was the only hindrance between them and Caiden and Aza, wherever they were and wherever they were going.

The night, the darkness, and the silence were eating away at them. There was no pull. No gravitation. No light.

"She has to summon us," Pneuma said, finally.

They all thought about how all this time, they hadn't felt that immense, painstaking need to be at her side.

"Pneuma, you go with Mil and Volx," Jais ordered, opening his car door. "Me and Dontae will go after Aza."

"This is not the time to part ways." Mil had reverted to his business tone. "Caiden is our only priority. You'll be of more use to her than to Aza."

"It's just like you to tell me how much you need me at a time like this."

Mil fixed on Jais, and Pneuma, getting more irritated by the second, wisped into Mil's SUV where it stuttered to life.

"Volx," Mil said, and got into the driver's side of his SUV without another look in Jais' direction.

"Go east," the soldier said before jumping into his truck.

Jais hurried and got into his car, revved it up, and drove out of the parking lot. Dontae glanced at Mil before he got into his own car and followed him. Volx started up his truck and was right behind Mil, who left in the opposite direction.

Chapter XLVII

IN A VAN heading east from the Chevel Inn, Aza was hooded and hogtied in the back. Sweating and struggling against his restraints in vain, his abilities were next to nil against Voids as these coupled with the alcohol he'd been consuming all evening. He couldn't believe how irresponsible he'd been.

Now, Caiden and the others were paying for it.

It was quiet besides the humming of the engine. Thaniel had handed him off to the other two that had followed them out of the banquet hall and they tied him up and threw him in the back of the van. None of them spoke again, except Thaniel, but Aza couldn't make out what he was saying when they locked him inside. He felt the van slowing down some and it made a turn. Aza had to use his head and shoulders to prevent himself from getting wedged in between the seats. Then the van jerked to a halt and he flew back, slamming into the cushion.

He heard the engine turn off and a moment later the door open. Aza felt someone get in next to him. They caressed his chest, gliding their hands slowly over his skin. His body went into fight or flight mode and he squirmed as far away from them as possible.

It was the scent. The smell of apricots got into his nostrils and slinked all the way down into his stomach where his insides began to bubble. He wanted to vomit, but his mouth was taped and he'd probably choke on it if he did.

Aza felt the hands again. Those dainty and putridly delicate hands. They didn't give up as they then slid the hood up just below his eyes and touched his brow bone. They softly held the precious angle of his face and Aza soon felt the person's hot breath on the tip of his nose.

He jerked his head away, repulsed, and heard the person suppress a giggle. That's when his entire being shut down.

"Oh, how I've missed you."

With everything he had left in him, he hoped to God, to any god, that Caiden was safer than how he left her. He'd never wanted anything so much in his life before now than that one wish.

His dying wish.

***

"You're not Hiding from me."

William looked at Caiden in the rearview of the stolen souped-up station wagon. She was sitting in the back seat where he could see her, her hands clasped together in her lap with zip-ties. He even buckled her in. There were no other restraints for he still had Mary.

"Because I want you to understand, that's why." He hacked up phlegm amongst other things and looked at the concern in her eyes. "...Or maybe you already do."

He drove off a road, getting slightly distracted by her eyes. They reminded him of David. Ever since the dance, he'd been hoping that he would be forgiven for the sins he'd committed against him to get to where he was now.

It wasn't for naught.

Right in the palm of his hands, he had all that he ever wanted; ever needed since his first demise. He was looking it right in the eye as it wondered about him and felt sorry for him and wanted to save him.

Yes.

He could see that Caiden desperately wanted to save him, but was too simple to know much about anything, especially something as profound as saving a suicidal race.

But he had her.

He had it.

Every single thing that he did wasn't for naught.

William put the car in park and vomited all over the steering wheel. He quickly wiped it off with his suit jacket and tossed it in the passenger seat.

"What's happening to you?"

"...I have to show you."

She waited for him to open the back door, thinking of all the possible ways to get away without harming them both. Caiden was sure she could've gotten Mary back considering the diminishing health conditions that William was going through ever since they left the inn, but she did want to understand. He'd been after her all this time before she probably got to Texas and for what? If she had the power to save him, to save any of them, then she wanted to know how.

William led her to a pole with a torn white cloth tied to the top of it. Caiden looked around and all she could see was nothing. It was just them and the lights coming from the car.

"Dig."

Caiden didn't hesitate and got down in the dirt. She began scooping as much of the already loose soil towards herself. She'd glance at William with Mary pointed at her and could see his eyes watering the more she dug. His tears put a fire under her and she began to dig faster.

Until she felt it.

It was cold and rough. When she cleared away more of the dirt to get a better look, her head shot up to William. Then, back to the face beneath the dirt.

They were identical.

"...What happened to you?" she repeated, haunted.

"I'm a sinner," he said, deflated. "But that's now...I couldn't tell you what commandment I'd broken before I got like this."

"You killed him..."

"I had to!" William dropped down in the dirt and got in her face. "If I didn't keep going, if I didn't keep changing, then I would die. And I couldn't do that to them again."

Caiden stared at him wide-eyed. "How many people did it take to get to this one?" The interrogation was almost inaudible.

"You're judging me, but these were bad people. They were murderers. Fathers and mothers who'd molest and sell their own children for a profit. I won't apologize for these people! These humans!" William stood up and yanked Caiden onto her feet. "It's mad, I know. It doesn't make sense that such a thing should happen to me when it should've been them. Nothing makes sense."

Caiden couldn't believe what she was seeing or hearing. How was it possible that he committed a sin so profound that he forgot he even did it?

She fixed on William as he raked his stubby agitated fingers over his thinning hair.

"It wasn't until I found you, did everything become clear."

"You mean when you found Iela," Caiden corrected, getting some bass back in her voice.

"Your mother was just a job when I found her...I had no idea that I'd get you, too...My savior."

"...I am not your savior." Caiden could feel William's emotions becoming more pure to her. "...I'm not your prince."

William firmly latched onto her shoulders, his eyes peering into every pore on her face until it landed on her brown eyes. "You are. I saw it," he said, achingly. "You're the only one."

Caiden felt her hands lift and she placed it on top of one of William's which lost all of its might under her touch. She was fully enveloped in his aura now and she couldn't find it in herself to turn away from him.

"How?"

The joy that spread across his face at the sound of her mercy vanished as soon as it showed up.

"My God, that dog! It was that damned dog of all things!"

Caiden fell into his frenzied eyes as they went back in time to remember.

"Zinc?" she asked in a whisper.

"Yes! That mutt attacked you. I saw. It was so clear. It got you in the arm. I remembered the blood. And your demon of a mother! She shot it without a thought! Shot it right in the head!"

William shoved his face near Caiden's and her breath caught in her throat.

"You see, he was already dead when I killed him. He was already dead."

Caiden's entire body began to tremble.

"...I don't understand."

"The healing is in the blood."

In a flash, another car came speeding off the dark road straight for them.

William wasn't going to let another second pass being so close to his end. He pounced on Caiden, going right for her jugular, and began ripping at the unmarred skin on her neck, just like he'd done all those times before.

Caiden's blood splattered all over his and her face as she punched and elbowed William. Not stopping him from quenching his insatiable thirst from the fountain of life spurting from her neck, he shoved Mary under her jaw, but that only made her struggle more, and she tried to snatch the gun from out of his hands—

Bang!

The bullet shot right through her jaw and lodged itself into the underside of her brain. Caiden's hands dropped to the dirt instantly.

Time had been made a weight and was pushing Caiden's back into the dirt with each half-second. Everything had occurred so fast, with no warning, that she didn't have any time to comprehend what was happening to her. The energies that she felt, the whispers of emotions that used to flow in and out of her ears, were disintegrating as if she'd never known them her whole life, a life that she feared now was leaving her, too. She couldn't bring herself to believe that she was born to die a death like this.

Then, everything stopped.

The other car skidded to a halt right next to William's, who'd moved to the fresh hole he'd made in Caiden's jaw to continue getting his fill.

Schwep. Schwep.

Iela jumped out of her car and continued to shoot William in the head for good measure as he kept getting up, trying to reach for Caiden's body. The holes in his face soon became one, but she didn't stop until both of the guns she had on her were empty.

She hurried to Caiden's side and felt for a pulse.

"Fuck."

She rushed to William, nearly tripping over the buried dead body. Iela froze and stared at it a moment until it hit her.

She began digging at lightning speed next to the dead body until there was enough space. She then dragged Caiden's corpse into the hole. She patted her down to make sure there was nothing identifiable on her and felt the phone. The home screen lit up and David and Toothpick were laughing at her through the bright glass. She jabbed it off and shoved it in her pocket before she began throwing piles of dirt on top of Caiden's body.

Her heart was beating in her ears, she was sweating buckets, and her head was on a continuous swivel looking up and down the dark highway.

She stopped before she covered her daughter's face.

Tears began to gather in her eyes and she exhaled, only now noticing she'd been holding her breath and those stubborn tears that refused to come out fell quickly.

Through the blur, she shoved a pile of dirt over Caiden's peaceful face and ran to drag William to her trunk. She opened it, revealing a bulky tarp already neatly wrapped inside.

This body was significantly heavier than the last one and she used everything she had in her to lift his heftier top half into the trunk first before she lifted his legs in after him.

Iela didn't waste any more time and cut off William's engine. She took the keys, and hopped back into her car, driving off down the highway, the darkness swallowing her up whole.

Milton Keynes UK
Ingram Content Group UK Ltd.
UKHW020818041123
431893UK00019B/854